CW01237019

WHEN THE FIREFLIES DANCE

Aisha Hassan has a Master's degree from the University of Oxford. She lives and works in London and has previously lived in Lahore. *When the Fireflies Dance* is her first novel.

WHEN THE FIREFLIES DANCE

AISHA HASSAN

ORION

First published in Great Britain in 2025 by Orion Fiction,
an imprint of The Orion Publishing Group Ltd.
Carmelite House, 50 Victoria Embankment
London EC4Y 0DZ

The authorised representative in the EEA is Hachette Ireland,
8 Castlecourt Centre, Castleknock Road, Castleknock, Dublin 15, D15 XTP3,
Republic of Ireland (email: info@hbgi.ie)

An Hachette UK Company

1 3 5 7 9 10 8 6 4 2

Copyright © Aisha Hassan 2025

The moral right of Aisha Hassan to be identified as
the author of this work has been asserted in accordance
with the Copyright, Designs and Patents Act of 1988.

All rights reserved. No part of this publication may be
reproduced, stored in a retrieval system, or transmitted
in any form or by any means, electronic, mechanical,
photocopying, recording, or otherwise, without the
prior permission of both the copyright owner and the
above publisher of this book.

All the characters in this book are fictitious, and any resemblance
to actual persons, living or dead, is purely coincidental.

A CIP catalogue record for this book is
available from the British Library.

ISBN (Hardback) 9781398720206
ISBN (Export Trade Paperback) 9781398720213
ISBN (eBook) 9781398720237
ISBN (Audio) 9781398720244

Typeset by Input Data Services Ltd, Bridgwater, Somerset

Printed in Great Britain by Clays Ltd, Elcograf S.p.A.

For Dad

Chapter One

The soil at the bhatti was red and loamy, excellent for making bricks. With each step Lalloo took, the fine dust settled on him like a weariness – first his chappal, then his shalwar, making its way up his body. By the time he came to his parents' hut, his white shalwar kameez would be steeped in red.

This was the very outskirts of the city, distressed, ignored and tucked away. If he hadn't lived here fourteen years ago, he would never have known it existed, but he couldn't ever forget this place. The long journey meant three minibus changes from the centre of a bustling Lahore to its edges, until the people and the buildings died away and eventually even the road ended and the minibus would go no further. Like reaching the end of the world. A winding dirt path led from where the tarmacked road stopped, surrounded on either side by lush fields covered with trees and shrubs, and newly sown wheat, until, turning a corner, the bhatti came into view – a gaping wound on the landscape.

The ground had been rent of all its green. Uprooted, dug up, leaving in its wake red, barren earth, mounds of clay, piles of bricks and a giant chimney. It loomed over a hundred feet tall, dark and ominous in front of him, forever billowing thick, black smoke. As he passed the smouldering behemoth, he sensed its evil eye watching him – the one who'd got away. *You will come back*, it whispered. He bowed his head, refusing to look up. This wretched day and this wretched chimney.

In its shadow stood the mud huts, huddled together, with holes for windows and doors, and corrugated metal roofs. His parents' hut was the last in the row. As Lalloo pushed aside the curtain that hung in the doorway, he heard a dull sound. A thud. Dusk hadn't swooped over Lahore yet, but the windowless room was already dark. It took a few moments for his eyes to adjust until he saw his mother crouched down on her haunches, rocking back and forth. Every time she rocked, she hit her head on the mud wall. *Thud, thud, thud.*

He hurried to her and pulled her away, cradling her body. She was like a newborn bird, helpless and precious and liable to break. Cushioned in his arms, she continued to rock. He longed to tell her he'd take care of her, stitch up the torn fabric of her life and get her out of this place, but she wasn't in a state to listen and he knew he wouldn't be able to keep his promise. Jugnu hadn't been able to, and nor could Lalloo.

Shabnam was sitting in the shadows just a few feet away, leaning against the wall, hugging her knees. Her chadar covered her head and draped around her shoulders. He called to her and she looked up, surprised, so lost in her thoughts she hadn't seen him enter.

'She's been like this for hours.' Shabnam came over and touched their mother's hand, her voice creased with worry. 'I tried to stop her.'

'It's getting dark, Shab.'

His sister lit the gas lamp, casting more shadows than light into the recesses of the bare room. The family's few utensils and pots lay in one corner, their bedding piled neatly on the packed-earth floor.

Pinky came in from outside. Her shalwar kameez ragged and muddy, her short hair enclosed in a woollen cap and her usual quick gait replaced with a melancholy that set between her shoulders. Just a child, even she knew the burden of this night. Upon seeing him, her eyes lit up momentarily and she wrapped her arms around his neck. Lalloo hugged her back awkwardly, still holding his mother.

'Where's Abu?' Work had finished for the day and their father should have been there.

Shabnam shrugged. Pinky shook her head.

'Here, come and sit with Ami.' His voice was urgent as he transferred his mother into Shabnam's arms and went outside.

In front of the huts on the red earth lay row upon row of perfectly moulded bricks, waiting to absorb the sun. But for weeks the sun had been covered in a grey dupatta, leaving her silhouette visible but her heat veiled, casting a morbid light. Lahore was shrouded in a thick smog it couldn't shrug off. This smog that crawled into Lalloo's clothes, into his bones, and made him wrap his jacket close to ward off the bitter cold.

He turned as he heard a sound and followed it. His father held a shovel in one hand and crouched over a small object on the ground. As Lalloo approached, the loudspeaker in a distant mosque crackled to life and the muezzin started the Azaan.

Allah u Akbar, Allah u Akbar . . .

Abu stood up as if answering the call to prayer.

Allah u Akbar, Allah u Akbar . . .

But instead of raising his hands to his ears, Abu raised the shovel over his head. The muezzin continued to bear witness there was no god but Allah, and Abu brought the shovel down with all his might on the red earth, as if he were still working, preparing the clay to make bricks. Lalloo hurried over as Abu lifted his weapon, revealing the crushed body of a lifeless sparrow, its feet curled up beneath it. Abu raised the shovel above his head again as the muezzin urged the faithful on.

'Abu!' Lalloo called out, staying his father's hand.

Abu sagged, letting Lalloo take the shovel from him. Despite the cold, sweat peppered his father's forehead and ran down the sides of his face. He was wearing a thin cotton shalwar kameez and his back was sodden.

Abu's voice shook as he spoke. 'I brought us here. My son's blood is on my hands.'

La illaha ill Allah. The muezzin finished. Abu's laboured breathing amplified the silence that followed.

Lalloo led his father slowly to the charpai outside the hut, its jute matting creaking as it took Abu's weight, then fetched him a glass of water from the clay pot in the corner. Abu seemed diminished, a fraction of the man he'd once been. Lalloo found his own hands were shaking. That blood was on his hands, not Abu's.

When Shabnam came out, Lalloo pulled her aside.

'Is he OK?' she asked, nodding towards Abu.

Lalloo shook his head. 'Do you think we should not go this year?' His throat was dry. He kept his voice low, trying to keep the shock out of it.

'Not go?' She stared at Lalloo.

He had been dreading this day, but it was worse than he'd expected. Every year, his parents' reaction got worse. 'Look at them, I'm not sure they can take it.'

She turned towards the hut and her face in the dying light of day was thrown into profile. Her forehead was lined with creases, her fingers fidgeted with her chadar, but her expression was unexpectedly calm. When at last she spoke, her voice was tired, too old to belong to a sister only a few years older than him. 'They take it every day in this awful place.'

'Yes, but—'

'They need this, Lalloo. Today of all days.'

Overhearing their conversation, Abu stood up and looked at them. His expression was lucid, his intent clear.

'Let's go.' It was a command.

Shabnam and Lalloo exchanged a look. Pinky parted the doorway curtain and stepped out of the hut, holding their mother's hand, and they all set off on foot. As they walked, Lalloo took off his jacket and tried to wrap it around Abu's shoulders, but his father shrugged it away.

Jugnu had loved feeding the sparrows. A piece of naan, a half-mouthful of roti, even a spoonful of rice; whatever he could spare, he would leave out for them. After they had eaten, he would shoo them away. He loved seeing them fly off, swooping and soaring in the infinite sky. And now? Lalloo shuddered. The thump of Abu's shovel hitting the bird wouldn't leave him.

They walked past the neighbouring huts that were already plunged into darkness. Used to the mild winters and oppressive summer heat of the Punjab, the villagers were ill-equipped to deal with the smog that clung to every surface and sucked away the warmth. Through a window, he saw a young family hunkered down in their home directly under the chimney's fumes, exhausted from the day's labour; barricading themselves indoors would offer some protection from the cold, but not from the horrors of this place.

As he passed a heap of rubbish dumped behind the huts, a breeze picked up a pungent whiff and rushed at Lalloo, making him want to retch.

*

When Lalloo was six years old, he had followed Jugnu everywhere. One winter's day, long before the bhatti, the brothers had run through the maize fields surrounding their village. The corn had been ready to harvest, growing so tall that Lalloo couldn't see Jugnu up ahead, could only hear him as they'd trampled through the field. Ami's warning to keep his clothes clean had pounded in his ears. His rubber chappal had slapped against his heels and his lungs had hurt as he'd tried to catch up with Jugnu's voice, laughing and teasing, pulling him forward. 'Challo, yaar!'

He heard his brother come to a sudden stop and smelt it before he saw it. The sewer was three feet wide and full of stagnant black sludge. The cloying smell flared his nostrils and clung to him. Jugnu only hesitated a few seconds before he was off, flying up and over, shouting his encouragement behind him. Lalloo faltered before the frothing blackness as a bloated animal carcass floated by. But Jugnu was already on the other side, ready to race off.

Lalloo retraced his steps to take a huge run-up. Holding his breath against the stench, he sprinted and jumped, his legs flailing. He dropped, his feet splashed and he sank down into the mire. He pushed up and his head broke cover, spluttering. Black foulness enveloped him. It was in his mouth and throat and he retched. Jugnu shouted and Lalloo opened his eyes just enough to see his brother's hand reaching down to grab him. Lalloo propelled himself towards it and Jugnu half pulled, half dragged him onto the bank. On all fours on dry ground, he retched again. He tried to wipe his face with his hands, but it was everywhere: on his hair, inside his nose, his ears – every inch of his body was covered in viscous sludge.

They had no choice but to walk home. They made an odd pair: Jugnu, tall and lanky, and the small sticky monster that was Lalloo trailing the oozing muck behind him. He expected Jugnu's mocking laughter, or at the very least some gentle teasing, but Jugnu knew better. Lalloo's teeth ached from keeping his jaw clamped shut to stop his chin trembling, and because he dared not open his mouth in case more of the foul sludge made its way inside.

Shabnam took one look at them and shrieked, a sound halfway between a scream and a laugh. She ran off, shouting, 'Ami, look what Jugnu brought home!'

Their mother came to the door, dishcloth over one shoulder, a wooden spoon in her hand, thunder in her voice. 'Is this you keeping your clothes clean?'

She marched Lalloo to the bathroom and made him strip. He stood while she poured bucket after bucket of hot Dettol water over him until eventually the glutinous black started washing off. Then she scrubbed him hard with a brush and more disinfectant.

With the scrubbing came the scolding. 'How many times have I told you to stay away from those sewers? Could you not find any other place to play? They're filled with raw sewage, and chemical waste from the fields, and animal dung, and Khuda knows what—'

'Ami—' Jugnu tried to interrupt her.

'All the illnesses in the world in one place and you choose to jump right in! And don't even get me started on the rats and—'

'All right, Ma, you'll make him ill just thinking about it.' Jugnu did then what he always did, deflecting their mother's anger away from Lalloo and onto himself.

She rounded on him, brush in one hand. 'And you. You're supposed to look after your younger brother, not lead him jumping over sewers. He's only six. He could have broken his leg. And what will I do if he gets sick?'

Jugnu grinned at her. 'You should have seen it, Ma, our Lalloo went in and a kaala bhoot came out. I couldn't even recognise him. You know, like Superman getting changed – this is Lalloo's disguise.'

Ami tutted and shooed him out of her way, but she managed a smile.

Jugnu didn't miss a beat. He turned to Lalloo. 'You're a superhero, little brother. We'll call you Kaala Bhoot Man. But we're gonna have to do something about this disguise. It really stinks!'

And even Lalloo, whose eyes prickled with the humiliation of his fall and the pain of his skin being scrubbed until it was raw, who knew he'd never be able to get the smell out of his hair or the taste out of his mouth, even Lalloo was laughing by the end of it. From then on, Jugnu called him his Kaala Bhoot – his little black monster.

*

The family kept walking. They walked past the never-ending rows of red bricks laid out to dry, waiting to be fired in the kiln, past the donkey with its protruding ribs, tied to a wooden post by a metal chain around its neck. They left the bhatti behind.

It took them an hour to trudge down the deserted dirt road and arrive at the cemetery, by which time they were all covered in a sprinkling of red dust. Tonight, just like that night fourteen years ago, a brazen full moon cast its glow.

Lalloo led them single file past the tall sheesham tree growing out of the middle of a grave, the ditch filled with stagnant water and rubbish, and the multitudes of tombstones, until they came to a mound marked only by a solitary stick of wood. Whether due to wild animal or ill omen, the stick was tilted, fallen to the ground. As he reached out to straighten it, a couple of fireflies rose around them, glowing on and off. He looked up, startled, but they didn't linger. The very next moment, they were gone, so quickly he was left wondering if they'd even been there.

The family raised their cupped hands in silent prayer. Shabnam took out red rose petals from the plastic bag she carried and let them fall on the grave. Seeing the drops of red on the parched ground, Ami cried out and sank to her knees, as if willing the earth to take her. Lalloo was glad he couldn't see her face in the dark. It was all his fault; his selfishness had stopped Jugnu from leaving that night.

It did them no good to linger here. The memory of that night was beaten into their minds. The men, those dogs, that full moon.

He reached down to take Ami's hand. 'Challo, Ma, time to go.' Her hand was cold, her skin rough and cracked. She didn't move. He placed an arm across her shoulders. Her body was so thin, she felt brittle. He pulled her to her feet and steered her away. Shabnam and Pinky followed behind with Abu, and the children led their parents back to the bhatti. Back to their hut like prisoners to their cell. They would be at work again tomorrow, up before dawn, come hail, fog or burning sunshine.

They unrolled the bedding on the packed-mud floor without saying a word and lay down to sleep. Lalloo, with his parents beside him, forced himself to stay awake, waiting until he could hear the regular rhythm of their breathing. Numb with cold, he rose and picked his way over various limbs to reach the doorway. This late, the smog was worse. His mobile phone as a torch was no help – he couldn't even see his outstretched hands in front of his face. He shuffled forward, blind.

Behind the hut, he got down on all fours and his hands knocked against something hard and cold. The shovel he'd taken from Abu. Inching forward, he found the bird. Cradling its cold softness in his palm, he carried it over to a nearby wall and dug a shallow hole. The night was silent and still, the only sounds his ragged breathing and the smacking of the spade on the earth. He covered the creature with soil – but waited a long while before returning to the hut.

It was the same every year. His was an upside-down world, where Abu murdered the sparrows Jugnu used to love, and Lalloo had been abandoned far from home on the same night his brother had been buried in the ground. The anniversary of Jugnu's death was one of the few nights Lalloo would sleep in his parents' hut. They didn't have a choice. Every night, they lay in the same hut, yards away from where Jugnu's warm, broken body had been left fourteen years ago.

Chapter Two

Seven months later

An awful braying greeted Lalloo this time as he approached the bhatti, an animal in pain and misery. Shere Khan the donkey. Jugnu had called it that, because the wretched creature was so unlike any king of the jungle. This probably wasn't even the same donkey, that'd been fourteen years ago. The creature's stuck out, its back was covered in welts and wounds, and the flies buzzed around tormenting it.

Lalloo had spent so many nights of his childhood crying himself to sleep, so many days wanting to return here, and now, every time he did, he was filled with a silent dread. He had escaped, but they were all stuck here and there was nothing he could do about it.

The chimney stood tall and proud, on a platform with bricks baking underneath it. The mud huts stood to one side and everywhere were neat rows and stacks of bricks, drying before being baked. The sun had set, but the August heat was still unrelenting. Ami was outside, cooking dinner.

He hadn't been back to the bhatti since that cold, grim evening to visit Jugnu's grave. Usually, his parents wanted to keep him away from the bhatti as much as possible – 'What if Heera sees you?' – but a few days ago, Abu had summoned him about a rishta for Shabnam, and the very idea filled Lalloo with alarm. A rishta could lead to a wedding and they could afford neither a wedding nor a dowry at the moment.

'How are you, Ma?'

The gas lamp was lit and the light had stolen the colour from her face. She looked at him silently, wiping the sweat off her forehead with a corner of her dupatta. He wanted her to talk to him. To let him in on the private world she withdrew to so often.

Ami didn't talk much any more. The mother from his childhood had gone the night Jugnu had been taken and had never returned. She still did all the things that needed doing. She made the bricks, swept the floor of the hut, cooked dinner, washed the clothes, though, increasingly, Shabnam had taken over many tasks. But often she wouldn't speak. As if life had got too much for her and this was her way of protesting, of disengaging from the world. Lalloo yearned for the mother she had been – vibrant, loud when she needed to be, quick with an opinion and fiercely protective of all her children.

Sometimes he wanted to say or do something that would make her angry – he wanted to see her reaction, to hear her scolding him like she used to, because that would show she still cared. He didn't though – they all had enough going on in their lives. But he felt the loss doubly for Pinky. Pinky was only ten years old; she'd been born after. She'd never seen their real mother, the one he was convinced was still in there somewhere. The one who'd showered her children with her love and wrath with equal ferocity. Maybe because Jugnu wasn't here to deflect Ami's anger from his younger siblings, her anger had dissipated altogether.

Ami cupped his face between two rough palms and clung to it, as if breathing in his presence. Then she held his hands in both of hers, a little too tightly, and sat him down on the floor of the hut in front of her. She cradled his hands in her lap and stared at him from six inches away, her gaze flitting over his features, as if trying to find something, or someone else, in his face. All the while, he kept a steady monologue going, about his day, his friends, the people he worked for, anything to drive away the oppressive silence in her stare. He didn't think she was listening to what he was saying, focusing on the sound of his voice. She reminded him of a skinny blackbird. Hopping about on two spindly feet, her head tilted, constantly wary of the world.

He sat with Ami until Shabnam and Pinky came with pots of

water from the tube well. He reached into his kameez pocket and pulled out a present.

'Yeh lo, Shab, I brought this for you.' He held it out.

Shabnam stopped pouring the water and came over, wiping her hands dry on her chadar, her nosepin glinting in the dim light. Shabnam, who put such a brave face on things and worked so hard with little respite. Did she resent him for getting away and leaving her there? Pinky dropped the jharoo she used to sweep the floor and ran to take a look.

They craned forward to see the Lux soap he placed in Shabnam's hand. It was the one with pictures of Mahira Khan, the dazzling Lollywood star on billboards all over the city.

'Why do you waste your money? She can use desi soap like the rest of us,' Ami scolded him in a hoarse voice – one that wasn't used enough.

At last, a reaction from Ami. A reminder of the mother he used to have.

'Shabnam says desi soap smells horrible. I think so too.' Pinky sniffed the packet her older sister was holding. 'Bhai, can I have some Lux soap as well?' Beautiful little Pinky, who looked so much like Jugnu it made him do a double take sometimes. She'd already spent her entire life in this wretched place. How much difference would a bar of soap make? Lalloo smiled at her, vowing to bring her some next time, but not wanting to antagonise Ami further.

Abu was sitting outside on his charpai, leaning against the wall of the hut and smoking his hookah when Lalloo brought him a steaming cup of tea. Reaching out a sinewy hand to take the cup, he motioned for Lalloo to join him. Lalloo listened to the chirruping of the crickets, taking in the heady scent of the tobacco-water mix and the reassuring gurgle of his father's hookah. The moment was a calm one; the day's work had finished and they all waited for the guests to arrive, but Lalloo couldn't let the matter be. He felt guilty for disturbing Abu's peaceful cup of tea, but he had to ask.

'Abu, why do we need to do this just yet?'

Abu turned to look at him in mild surprise. 'Beta, your sister is old enough. We shouldn't be waiting any longer.'

Lalloo took a deep breath. 'I don't have enough money saved up for a wedding, for the dowry.' His wages were spent on rent and food every month, and he saved whatever he had left, but it was never much. 'If we wait awhile, I can save up some money—'

'No, we can't wait any longer.'

'But how will we pay for the wedding?'

Abu fell silent. The chirruping of the crickets grew louder. The bhatti had taken its toll on Abu. Whenever Lalloo came to visit, he sensed Abu was tired, with a weariness that set deep within his bones. Over the years, he talked less and less, never having the time to sit on his charpai and tell stories like he used to. His skin was the colour of sheesham wood, heavily tanned in the midday sun, stretched taut over his frame like leather over a drum. But his eyes were still warm and strong.

'We will arrange something; these things can't be delayed too long.'

'It costs so much, Abu, what can you arrange?' Lalloo was growing uneasy; there was something Abu wasn't telling him.

Abu opened his mouth to reply but was interrupted by a vicious bout of coughing. He recovered and collected himself. 'We will take a loan from Heera, we have done it before.'

'Heera?' Lalloo was stunned. After everything that had already happened, Abu would consider going to Heera for another loan? 'You can't do that.'

'We must. How else are we going to afford it?'

'She doesn't have to get married yet – she's still young and . . .' Shabnam was twenty-six, well past the age girls got married, but he had to try.

'And what? You want to keep her here for ever? Bury her in this bhatti?' Abu raised his voice for the first time. Lalloo saw his father's eyes fill up and stopped himself retorting. They had sent him away, far away from them, when he'd been a lost and grieving child.

Their voices must have carried. Shabnam came and knelt by the charpai. 'I'd rather stay in the bhatti with you, Abu, you know that.'

Abu shook his head. 'We have our responsibilities. What kind of parents would we be if we didn't get our daughter married?'

'But if you go to him for another loan, Heera will keep you here for ever.' Lalloo's voice was rising, his panic struggling to get out.

'He's going to do that anyway,' Abu said. 'The very least I can do is get my children out of here.'

That's what they'd done to Lalloo. They'd got him *out of here* that very night. And he'd spent his entire childhood crying himself to sleep, blaming himself for what had happened to Jugnu, thinking they blamed him too, and wanting to come back to them.

Abu continued, 'This is a good rishta; we can't turn it down.'

How could Abu remain so calm, so softly-spoken? Lalloo looked into the eyes of that heavily lined face and saw only sadness.

'I will get it for you,' he said.

'What?'

'The money. I'll get you the money.' He couldn't have Abu going to Heera. That's where all this misery had started. 'I'll borrow money from the Alams.' Lalloo carried on quickly before Abu or Shabnam could object: 'Omer Sahib is very kind. He always says—'

'No. You mustn't jeopardise your job,' Abu cut him off.

'Sahib always looks after his servants. The other day, the cook had to go to his village for his mother's funeral and he gave him an extra day's holiday and money for the journey.'

Abu coughed again and then indicated towards the chimney. 'Beta, these people haven't been good to us, I know, but they will give out another loan. Your job is very precious. It shows me every day there can be a way out for my children and that's all I want.'

'I'll ask for an advance on my wages, not a loan,' Lalloo improvised desperately. 'Let me at least ask him before you go to Heera.'

Abu took a long pull from the hookah, making it gurgle ferociously, and nodded.

Just then, Pinky ran over, slightly out of breath. 'They're here.'

The party of guests were the mother, father and sister of the potential groom. Lalloo and his family stood up to greet them.

'This is our son, Lalloo. He works in Lahore as a driver. Lalloo, this is Harris Sahib from Lalbagh.'

Lalloo shook hands with a small man with a handlebar moustache that curled upwards at the tips and covered most of his face. Lalbagh was the neighbouring village to Chakianwallah. If Shabnam married into this family, she wouldn't be going far.

A threadbare cloth was laid on the packed-earth floor and they sat around it cramped and cross-legged. Ami ladled hot daal onto metal plates, which Lalloo handed around, making sure the guests were served first. Shabnam cooked puffed-up rotis, infused with the aroma of the cowpats used as fuel for the fire.

When another hot roti came straight from the tawa, he passed it over to Pinky.

'You have it – she's had enough already.' His mother stopped him, though Pinky's face told him otherwise.

When Ami turned to the groom's mother, he slipped the roti onto Pinky's plate. Her extra-wide grin revealed a set of crooked teeth.

After their modest dinner, Lalloo was hungry. It was all he could do to ignore his grumbling stomach. Predictably, the guests had had the largest share of the meal, but even the watering-down of the daal hadn't been enough to make the food go round.

Ami and Shabnam cleared the dishes away.

After a few pleasantries, the groom's father spoke. 'Everything else is fine, it's just this . . .' He hesitated. 'This indenture. We don't want any trouble.'

It was the terms under which their family, and all the families at the bhatti, worked. They were bonded labourers, unable to leave until the bhatti owner told them their debt was paid.

'There's nothing to worry about, Harris Sahib. The indenture is under my name.' Abu was interrupted by a vicious coughing fit and it was several moments before he was able to speak again. 'It doesn't affect my children. As you can see, even my son doesn't work here.'

'The thing is . . . well, you know what these bhatti owners are like. It was a few years ago now, but we heard some young man asked too many questions and it led to some trouble.'

Lalloo felt his face go rigid. *Some trouble.*

Abu spoke faintly. 'Yes, I know what these bhatti owners are like.'

A stillness washed over the entire family. How could their guests fail to notice? The smothering air closed in on Lalloo. On his family. In their hut. Where *some trouble* had taken place.

There was a crash from the corner of the room. Ami had dropped the metal plates she was carrying, spraying the floor with flecks of daal.

'Are you OK, behan jee?' the groom's mother asked.

Ami leant against the wall. For a moment, it looked like she would faint, until Shabnam rushed forward to help her.

'She's fine.' Shabnam smiled at the guests as she gripped Ami by the elbow. 'Just some slippery plates.' Pinky got up and sat Ami on the floor next to Lalloo, while Shabnam cleaned up the mess.

Abu turned to the father of the groom and spoke firmly. 'I can't remember any trouble, Harris Sahib. It has nothing to do with us.'

Lalloo looked across at Ami and Shabnam in turn. Neither of them would meet his gaze.

A broad grin took over their guest's face and his moustache grew even bigger. 'In that case, we would like the wedding as soon as possible.'

'As the bride's family, we will need time to prepare,' said Lalloo. Things were moving too quickly for his liking.

'Lalloo, beta, parents start preparing for their daughter's wedding as soon as she's born. Isn't that right, behan jee?' The groom's mother beamed at Ami as she turned to her.

Ami smiled back, a stilted half-smile.

'Yes, we won't need long,' said Abu.

'We'll have to wait for this heat to ease off, maybe—'

'I think next month would work?' Abu spoke over him, and everyone else made approving noises. Lalloo looked across at

Shabnam and she nodded at him. He knew she wouldn't object if this kept their parents happy.

Pinky handed around jalebis to celebrate. Lalloo had bought the fresh jalebis for them himself, but the now tepid mithai tasted like cardboard in his mouth.

Next month was only three weeks away. He had to get the money somehow or else Abu would go to Heera for another loan, and he couldn't let that happen.

Chapter Three

Soon after the guests left, Lalloo headed home. At the end of the dirt track where it met the road, Lalloo waited for a minibus. This was the last stop on the route and they weren't so frequent here. It finally arrived and as he ducked inside the brightly lit interior and the bus pulled away, he turned and looked behind him. It was dark, but he knew it was there, that chimney and the foul smoke expelled by it. As if it were hiding in plain sight. When they had first moved there, he'd thought it was unique in its wretchedness, but now he knew there were many bhattis like this, dotted around the city, full of desperate workers producing the bricks that fuelled the building boom – each its own pocket of misery. Being forced to leave the bhatti fourteen years ago had changed his life for ever. Jugnu had always said he would get them out of the bhatti, but Lalloo had never dreamt it would happen without the rest of his family.

*

'Take him! We can't have him here,' Ami had screamed at Abu that night.

The men were just back from the cemetery, exhausted, some of them still carrying their shovels. Lalloo, seven years old and drained, was with them. He didn't know where his gentle mother was when she rushed at him, or who this was in her place. The woman in front of him was a churail – a banshee with her dupatta gone, her clothes torn and hair frightful about her face.

The others tried to calm her down, but Ami ran at Lalloo and pushed him towards his father. 'Take him away!'

Lalloo stumbled and fell in the dirt, skinning his ankle against a rock. He looked towards Abu. Any other night he would have expected his father to tell this churail to stop. But in that moment, after everything that had already happened, Lalloo was afraid. And he was right to be. Abu looked at her, this creature in place of his mother, as if considering her every word. Then he nodded and looked away, but not at Lalloo. Ami fell to the ground, letting the women pull her down and douse her in sorrow. She would not look at Lalloo as he left; it was the last time he would see his mother for ten years.

They travelled by bicycle at first. Lalloo sat on the handlebars with the wind in his face, but his throat ached and his palms were raw from digging his nails into them. When he asked any questions, he was ignored, as if his father couldn't hear him. Lalloo was numb and confused, and so fatigued that eventually he stopped speaking. He shoved a hand in his pocket and found Jugnu's cricket ball, from earlier that same day. The moon followed behind them. Lalloo couldn't believe it could shine so brightly, as if it hadn't borne witness to the events of that night. He clutched the ball tightly in his pocket.

They caught a minibus and, at some point, Lalloo leant in to Abu's warmth and fell asleep. Abu must have carried him the rest of the way because he woke curled up on a cold concrete step. It was still dark, but the night was faded, not far off morning. Abu stood in front of him, talking in a low voice to a large figure silhouetted in a doorway three steps above them. Lalloo sat up and listened.

'You're out of your mind, old man, you can't just turn up on my doorstep and expect—'

'My neighbour said you could do with—'

'Yes, but it's the middle of the night.' The man was bare-chested with a dhoti wrapped around his waist. He clearly wanted to get back to bed.

'He's a great worker, Babu Jee – he'll be an asset to your workshop.'

Lalloo was cold. So chilled, he'd never be able to warm up again.

'I'm a mechanic. I don't need the expense or the hassle,' said the bare-chested man.

Lalloo nodded, willing the man to refuse so Abu could take him home.

Abu climbed a step closer to the doorway. 'He's a quick learner and he'll be no trouble – you won't even have to feed him that much.'

The man shook his head and reached across to shut the door.

Abu fell to his knees and clasped his palms in front of him. 'Take him, Babu Jee – he's the only son I have left. I can't take him back.' Abu's voice broke. 'I won't ask anything in return. He'll be earning his keep in no time.'

The man in the doorway hesitated – a moment where Lalloo didn't dare breathe – but then he nodded. Lalloo leapt up and flung himself at Abu, clutching an arm, wrapping himself around it with all his strength. Abu stroked the top of Lalloo's head with his free hand, his touch heavy but tender. Then he pulled Lalloo away and picked himself up. He wiped his face with the cloth slung across his shoulder and crouched in front of his son, holding him at arm's length, while Lalloo silently fought against him. Fought to be with him.

'You listen to Rizwan Sahib, OK? Be good and do as you're told.' Abu's voice was hoarse.

And before he could do anything else, Abu was gone, leaving Lalloo behind with nothing but the clothes on his back and Jugnu's cricket ball in his pocket.

*

The following morning, Lalloo was running late for work at the Alams. He hadn't slept much the night before, worrying, and now he was tired, late and sweating already. His father's parting words still echoed in his head.

'Call me when you've arranged the money. And don't come back too soon – Heera might see you here. It would give him ideas.'

It had always been that way. His parents wanted him close, but not too close; they loved him, so they had sent him away. They didn't want Heera seeing him, so he could only visit in the dark. They had thought they were setting him free, but he was always pulled back to the bhatti.

He crossed the dusty road heading for the bus stop. Now there was this issue with Shabnam's dowry. The wedding was in three weeks' time. He had two weeks at the most to get the money so his parents could prepare. Usually, when Lalloo needed anything, he'd turn to Salman. His friend knew everyone and how to get things done, but even Salman would be stumped by this amount of money.

And getting it from his boss would never happen. The story he'd told Abu wasn't true: Omer had been on the verge of firing the cook until Asima, Omer's wife, had intervened. She was probably worried about replacing him at such short notice and baulking at the thought of having to do the cooking herself. The cook was given a few days' leave to go to his mother's funeral, but they'd docked his pay. If he asked Omer for a loan, Lalloo would probably be out of a job. But there was more than one person in the Alam family.

'Arré, bhai, look where you're going. You think your father owns this road?' A horn blared in his ear and wrenched him out of his thoughts. The motorbike was right behind him, its rider glaring. No, his father didn't even own the charpai he slept on.

Lalloo waved a hand in apology and quickened his pace, spotting the minibus at the bus stop. In the city, the buses were fast and busy, and the drivers liked to cram as many passengers inside as possible. He squeezed between a sweat-draped back and an armpit. With a melodious honking of its horn, the bus set off, challenging death in its rush across the streets. Lalloo looked out of the window to escape the press of so many people.

Rickshaws dodged in and out of the traffic. A boy pushed a wooden cart laden with apricots, jamun and guava in the middle of the road, ignoring the cars overtaking him on both sides. A motorcycle raced by with a family of five on board, the father driving with a toddler sitting on the handlebars facing forward, the mother side-saddle behind him holding a baby in her arms, with a child sandwiched between them. They looked carefree, the wind rushing through their hair. Lalloo willed the bus to go faster.

He finally made it to the cantonment half an hour late and started to run despite the heat. The Alams' house sat in acres of lush grounds and was surrounded by high walls, the estate an oasis amid the dirt and noise outside. Self-assured and untouched by tragedy, it was immune to the worries of the crowd of people who came to service it every day – to guard the gate, drive the cars, dust the shelves and wash the floors.

Baba Jee opened the side gate as he knocked.

'Have they called for me yet?' Panting, Lalloo glanced towards the house. With any luck, the family wouldn't notice his late arrival.

The elderly gatekeeper shook his head and pulled up a chair. He was probably in his sixties but looked much older. Baba Jee and Lalloo were stationed in front of the house under a concrete car porch, where they shared two plastic chairs and a rickety table. The porch roof provided some protection against the elements, but it had no walls, only pillars.

'How're the knees holding up today, Baba Jee?' Lalloo's breathing was returning to normal and he sat down for a moment to cool off.

'It's far too hot these days, beta. My joints swell up.'

Around them, the flower beds were full of roses and chambeli, gladioli and motia. A sprinkler was spraying water over the dazzling green lawn, watering it before the midday heat, sustaining the grass even in the driest summer. The precious monkey-puzzle tree had its own green awning to shade it from the worst of the summer heat. Tiny yellow fruit peeped out from under the leaves on the fledgling mango tree – Omer's pride and joy. All the green contrasted sharply with the deep-red bricks that made up the walls of the house. For Lalloo, they were a constant reminder of the bhatti. Every brick etched with his family's fingerprints. A stark red slap in the face.

There wasn't time to wash the cars this morning – Omer Sahib would be ready to leave soon. Lalloo picked up a dry cloth and started to wipe the Land Cruiser down, hoping the sahib wouldn't notice. Lalloo's duties weren't too arduous. He had to clean and maintain both cars. He loaded Omer's car with his briefcase and anything else he was taking into work in the mornings. His boss liked to drive himself mostly, so once the sahib had gone, Lalloo drove around his wife and daughter to their engagements. It wasn't difficult and he was lucky to have the job.

He'd started working for the Alams over four years ago. He had come across their broken-down car by the side of the road. Yasmin had sat in the suffocating heat with the windows rolled up against the dust and noise, while the driver had stood and stared at the open bonnet. Cars and rickshaws had rushed past, honking. Lalloo had offered a helping hand and had had the engine running in minutes. Impressed by this stranger, Yasmin had told her imposing father, who'd hired him as house help. When the driver hadn't returned from his village after the next Eid holiday, and upon Yasmin's insistence, Lalloo had got his job.

Lalloo had always felt indebted to Yasmin after that for getting him proper work with a proper salary, one that had enabled him to find a place to live. Over the years, theirs had developed into a strange sort of friendship. Lalloo always tried to help her out, keeping quiet when she lied to her parents about where she was going or who she was going with – usually one of her many new boyfriends. And Yasmin was far less imperious with him than with any of the other house staff, sharing her gossip and stories on long drives, and asking Lalloo about his family, enough at least to know he had two sisters and their names. Once, when he had told her it was Pinky's birthday, Yasmin had let Lalloo have an entire gift basket, a collection of sweet treats she had been given at an event. He had taken it to the bhatti the next Sunday, to his sister's outspoken delight.

'I hope the bibis are in a good mood today.' Lalloo nodded towards the house, referring to Yasmin and her mother.

'Now that would mean believing in miracles.' Baba Jee chuckled.

The door opened and Lalloo fell silent in case it was one of the ladies in question. It was Guddo, the housekeeper, carrying a tray with two cups of tea. She put the drinks on the table between their chairs.

'Oh, bless you, beti, just what an old man needs on a morning like this.' Baba Jee reached out to take a cup.

Guddo pointed at Lalloo. 'You were late again.'

He opened his mouth in self-defence, but she grinned.

'Don't worry, they're so self-absorbed, they didn't even notice.'

The housekeeper had taken Lalloo under her wing the minute he'd arrived at the Alams' years ago. She would often give him a heads-up of the family's plans at the beginning of the day so he would know what to expect. In exchange, he brought her whatever gossip he heard when he was driving. She liked to talk, but he knew she wouldn't tell on him.

She jerked a head towards the door. 'Time for you to come in.'

'What's new? Everything all right?' he asked as he followed Guddo into the house.

'I think he wants you to take his car to the garage.' She shook her head. 'Nothing is ever all right in this family.'

Lalloo was only ever allowed in the house when summoned. He stepped inside behind Guddo, the wooden double doors shutting behind him and muffling the outside world. Here, there was no chirruping of green parrots or honking of traffic. The entrance had a double-height ceiling with an enormous glass chandelier hanging from the roof. The floor was laid out in white marble, the walls hung with paintings.

Guddo disappeared into the kitchen and he walked into the lounge and stood by the door, waiting to be given instructions.

'You have no idea what he's like. Your father . . .' Asima walked into the room, her back to him, whispering furiously at someone behind her. She was a large, beady-eyed woman with thinning hair. Folds of skin around her neck had cannibalised her chin and her raised eyebrows gave her a perpetually surprised look.

Yasmin followed her mother in. With her long legs, she was almost as tall as her father. Her silky black hair was cut below the shoulders and she had a habit of swishing it from one side of her face to the other, reminding Lalloo of the horses at a polo match he'd once driven the family to. 'He is nothing of the sort. He works really hard all the time and . . .' Yasmin was whispering back just as ferociously.

Asima pinched Yasmin's elbow with her hand, pulling her in close, leaning into her as she spoke.

Lalloo was used to fading into the background, listening in on conversations, gleaning information that might come in handy some other time. It was a trick he had learnt from Guddo.

'And it's not just that. I'm sure—'

Yasmin pulled her elbow away and glared at her mother. 'Have you ever thought *you* might be the problem here?'

'Keep your voice down. You want to let the whole neighbourhood know?' Asima's whisper was forced, her perfect eyebrows arched.

They were standing in the middle of the lounge now and all they had to do was turn their heads to see him, but they were so engrossed in conversation, they were completely unaware of him.

'I think you're the reason he—'

Asima gripped Yasmin's upper arm to shut her up and both women straightened as Omer Alam strode into the room. One of the wealthier men in Lahore, he wore imported clothes and carried himself like a prince. He was tall, with a full head of hair and a body he took great care to maintain in the gym, Lalloo having dropped and picked him up on occasion. Asima watched her husband, clearly petrified he'd overheard them. She addressed him in a wary voice.

'Would you like breakfast before you head out?'

He barely looked at her, adjusting the cuff of his shirt as he strode past. 'No, I've got to get going. I've invited Akbar Naseem over for dinner tonight—'

'Who?'

He stopped and deigned to turn to her. 'Akbar Naseem? Don't you know anything? The new inspector general of the police. Make sure you make the arrangements. The man will be a handy contact.'

The inspector general was a very powerful man and Omer liked to have influential friends. Over the years, Lalloo had seen him dine with lots of important people, some in uniform and many others in suits who came with big cars and bigger entourages.

Omer glanced around and saw Lalloo. 'Here, put this in the car.' He held out his briefcase to Lalloo.

'Daddy, I need some money. I'm going out with Tania.'

Omer turned to his daughter and kept hold of his precious case, ignoring Lalloo's outstretched arm.

Asima spoke up. 'I thought you had a photo shoot.'

'I do. Then I'm going to lunch.'

Yasmin had lunch with her childhood friend most days. She spent more time with Tania than with her own family. Yasmin was a model. Lalloo would often drive her to locations for a shoot, wait around for hours and then see a photo of her months later in a magazine or on a billboard, advertising Glow & Lovely cream or Pond's lotion.

Yasmin turned towards her father, who placed his briefcase flat on the table, pressed the latches and opened it.

Even though Lalloo knew what to expect, it still took his breath away, the sight of all that cash, bound in neat piles straight from the bank, casually thrown on top of each other. Omer owned lots of property, land and various businesses and was always making trips to the bank. Omer took out a bundle, tore its paper seal and counted out some money for Yasmin. She must get paid for the work she did, yet she constantly asked her father for extra cash and he gave it to her unquestioningly, doting on her. Yasmin didn't have to think about money the way other people did; it was just there when she needed it. For once, Lalloo didn't begrudge her this. Out of all of the Alams, Yasmin was his best chance for his sister. He even felt slightly hopeful as she casually shoved several bills into her handbag.

Omer closed the briefcase and handed it to Lalloo. His boss strode out and Lalloo followed two paces behind, carrying the briefcase flat on its side, resting on his outstretched palms before him, as he'd been told.

He placed the case in Omer's Land Cruiser, in the footwell on the front passenger side, out of sight of passers-by, but easily reachable. It had to be exactly so or Lalloo got into trouble. Omer liked things to be precise. Lalloo held his breath, praying his boss didn't notice the car was unwashed, until Omer drove away.

'Come on, Lalloo, or I'll be late.' Yasmin marched out of the house, her pink satin shalwar kameez shimmering. On her shoulder, she carried a grey handbag, the one Guddo had told him was made by a foreign designer and cost tens of thousands of rupees. The wind caught her perfect hair and billowed it behind her.

She shoved an address at him and he started up the Range Rover, the strong air conditioning blasting cold air into his face, as Baba Jee held open the gate for them.

'Bibi, I needed to ask you something.' Lalloo made sure to keep his voice respectful. He might be friendlier with Yasmin, but he was still a servant and this was a very big thing he was going to ask of her.

'Hmm?' Yasmin was tapping away on her phone. 'What is it?' She looked up when he hesitated, flicking her hair from one side of her face to the other.

'My sister is getting married. My sister, Shabnam? You remember, she is twenty-six now. We have a rishta for her. I need money for the wedding . . . a loan.'

'How much?'

He told her and she whistled.

'Even I haven't got that much cash lying around.' She chuckled.

Lalloo couldn't bring himself to smile, but his shoulders relaxed a little at her casual tone. At least she hadn't said no.

'And by the way, I'm meeting Tariq after the shoot, not Tania.'

Tariq was Yasmin's newest boyfriend, clearly a passionate affair because in the past two weeks she had seen him five times when her parents had thought she'd been with Tania or working. Lalloo had already had to cover for the couple twice, once even driving to her favourite café to collect a takeaway dessert to back up her alibi when Asima got suspicious.

'And the loan, bibi?'

'Oh, all right, don't look so sad. I'll get you the money.'

He looked back at her in the rear-view mirror. Was this another one of her jokes? But she seemed serious.

'I was going to get that Dior handbag from the latest collection

– Daddy knows I've been eyeing it up for a while. I'll ask him for money to buy it and you can get your sister married.'

'But . . .' Lalloo couldn't help pointing out the obvious flaw in her plan. 'What happens when you don't have the handbag after you get the money?'

'Ah, but Tariq's going to buy it for me.' She tapped a finger on the side of her head. 'See, it's a genius plan.'

She saw him looking doubtfully at her in the mirror.

'Things are getting more serious between Tariq and I; I'll need you to cover for me a bit more.' She smiled like someone who'd got it all worked out. He wondered what it must be like to be born with such entitlement, such confidence, that you knew the world would always work in your favour. She was only a bit younger than his sister, and, right now, Shabnam would have been up since before dawn, working a fourteen-hour back-breaking day, like she did six days a week, crouching under the smouldering August sun, moulding clay with barely a moment to stop for water.

But even if she was privileged, at least Yasmin was willing to help him. He looked at the mirror again. 'I'll do whatever you need, bibi. You can't imagine what this will mean for my family, for Shabnam. And I'll pay you back from my wages. Every last bit.'

She wasn't looking at him, her perfectly manicured nails already tapping at her phone again. Her only reply was, 'Uh-huh.'

When they got to the building to drop her off, he could see the photographers rushing up to snap photos. Increasingly, these paparazzi followed her everywhere. He managed to dodge most of them by dropping her off at a back entrance. Omer had already spoken of getting extra security, but Yasmin had resisted. She didn't want anyone knowing of her clandestine dates with her boyfriend, so she'd tasked Lalloo with assuring Omer he could keep her safe by picking up and dropping her at precise points, avoiding the paparazzi as much as possible. So far, it had worked and Omer had given in to his daughter's wishes, but Lalloo knew she was bothered by the constant cameras. Lalloo felt protective of her too; it had been his idea to black out the windows in the back seats. Yasmin braced herself before opening the car door and walked quickly towards the entrance, dodging the intrusive photographers as she went.

Chapter Four

When Abu left him that night fourteen years ago, Lalloo was only seven years old. He didn't fully realise what was happening until the man Abu had been talking to ushered him into a large garage-like building and shut him in. The metallic clang of the doors and the bolt pulling tight afterwards echoed in his head long after he was left in complete silence. Lalloo crept into a corner of the room and hunched down in the dark.

The moonlight snuck in, following him through cracks and crevices, refusing to leave him alone, even in here. Eventually, he began to make out objects in the room. In front of him loomed a huge metal carcass. Raised up off the floor on piles of bricks, its two front tyres gone, the bonnet had exploded, exposing its insides, its guts pouring out. Its bumper was crushed completely, one headlight dangled, attached to the body by a wire. The windscreen was still miraculously intact, goading him, reflecting moonlight into his eyes. All around him were the hulking skeletons of worn-out cars, an old engine, a dented door frame. A graveyard of machines too wounded and weary to go on.

They looked like they'd had some violent encounter. Had they also been beaten to a pulp? Dragged out in the middle of the night? Tortured by the light of the moon? He curled up on the dirty concrete floor, felt for the cricket ball in his pocket and clung onto it, trying to shut out the images in his head. But he could still see them. He could still smell the fear in the air. There was silence among the skeletons of cars, but he could still hear the awful thudding and his parents' screams.

At some point, he must have dropped off because the next thing he knew, sunlight was thrown into his face, accompanied by the clanging of the workshop door opening. He opened his swollen eyes, dazed and disoriented and aching all over.

'Rizwan Bhai, what have you got here?' a loud voice called.

'He's the new apprentice,' Rizwan shouted from somewhere outside.

'Oi, chotay, what's your name?'

Lalloo tried to stand, but his legs were cramping up. He scrambled to pocket his cricket ball and squinted back at the silhouetted figure, hardly able to open his eyes, numb with confusion and sleeplessness.

'Hasn't he got a name? We'll call him chota.'

There were four loud teenage mechanics, pushing and shoving and teasing each other as they got to work.

Lalloo watched them from the corner and waited until he was sure his legs could take his weight before hobbling onto his feet. Outside the metal gates of the workshop was a dirt-floor courtyard facing the road. A straggly tree stood alone, decorated with tyres hanging from its branches, with two metal chairs underneath it. One was empty, and in the other sat Rizwan, where he could keep one eye on the boys inside and the other on the outside world. He was the biggest man Lalloo had ever seen. Filling up the entire chair, his flesh strained to escape its confines. He looked up as Lalloo approached.

'When will Abu come to get me?' Lalloo spoke barely above a whisper.

Rizwan started to laugh, but saw Lalloo's face and stopped himself. 'You're going to stay here now. Go to the house and fetch me my cup of tea.'

Lalloo looked at him blankly until Rizwan pointed to a house across the street with a green door, and Lalloo recognised the steps he'd sat on last night.

He crossed the road and knocked. A smartly dressed woman opened the door, saw him on the threshold and was about to shut it in his face before he protested.

'Rizwan Chacha sent me. For his tea.' He gesticulated wildly to where Rizwan sat in his chair.

She opened the door a fraction wider, tutted at him and eyed him suspiciously. Behind her, he could see an elderly woman on her haunches, mopping the floor with a wet cloth, the smell of disinfectant in the air. He must be talking to the memsahib, Rizwan's wife.

'Ai, suno, Jee, who is this?' But she wasn't talking to Lalloo any more. She shouted across the road, across the courtyard, to her husband in his chair under the tree.

'Haan, I've kept him as an assistant,' Rizwan shouted back, looking uncomfortable.

'And we can afford this, how?'

'Mumtaz, please, I will explain. Not in front of everyone.' Rizwan held out his palms in front of him as a defence. Clearly, he didn't have permission to make such decisions on his own.

Mumtaz turned her face, harrumphed and shut the door on Lalloo. He waited on the step, not knowing whether any tea would be forthcoming, but ten minutes later, the door opened again. When Lalloo finally brought it to him, Rizwan smiled and used his ample stomach as his cup rest.

'Good, now make yourself useful. You can help the mechanics.' He pointed vaguely in the direction of the workshop.

Lalloo kept his mouth shut and spent the rest of the day fetching things. He fetched Rizwan's lunch from the house, spanners and engine oil for the mechanics, and vegetables from the street stall for Mumtaz.

That evening when the mechanics had gone home, Mumtaz gave Lalloo a plate of daal chawal and an old razai and a sheet. He gulped down the food – the only thing he'd had to eat all day – before unrolling the quilt onto the oily floor of the workshop and covering himself with the single cotton layer. The nights were cold and he shivered under his bare sheet, watching the shadows among the remains of old cars, smelling the sickly smell of engine oil. What was he doing here? Surely Abu would come and get him soon. Maybe tomorrow? Was he being punished for what happened to Jugnu? One minute they'd been playing cricket and the next . . . He lay among the skeletons, bone-tired, too spent to cry, too numb to do anything but clutch his cricket ball to his chest and wait for morning, praying to be rescued.

But the days waiting for Abu to come and the nights crying for the comfort of his family didn't bring them back. He became an easy target for the mechanics.

'Arré, look, Rizwan's collected another piece of junk that's no good to fix up.'

'Who didn't want you any more, chota? We'll happily return you.'

'That's a socket wrench, idiot. I asked for a torque wrench. Were you born this way or did your parents do this to you?'

Lalloo would look at them blankly, feeling foolish as they laughed at his silence. The more they treated him like he was stupid, the less he had to say. Whole days would go by without him using his voice, numbly following commands. Would he fade away, stop being if no one missed his existence?

A few weeks after Lalloo had arrived at the workshop, the February weather was starting to warm up. Rizwan had begun to give him a little more freedom and when an old acquaintance showed up to get his car fixed, Lalloo was sent to fetch cold drinks from the stall in Sadar bazaar. Lalloo relished the independence, the chance to be away from the other boys, the feeling of invisibility among the crowds. But he had only been to the bazaar once before and on his return couldn't find his way back. He went down one street and up another. Had the paan wallah been on the corner of the first street or the second? Had he turned left at the yogurt stall or right? In a panic, he started to run, worried the drinks would be warm by the time he got back.

'Arré, yaar, what are you doing? You've been running up and down the same street for the last five minutes. Are you mad?'

He stopped. A boy his age sat in the doorway of the goldsmith's shop. The sun beat down upon Lalloo, squeezing the sweat out of him.

'I was . . . Rizwan's workshop. Do you know it?' He was out of breath.

'Sure.' The boy sized him up. 'But it'll cost ya.' He eyed the glass bottles Lalloo carried.

'These aren't mine . . .'

Tired, Lalloo made to move into the shade of the doorway, but two figures bumped into him as he did so and a bottle went sprawling from his hand.

A shrill female voice piped up. 'Oh, look what you've done, you silly boy! Now I have Fanta all down my shirt.'

He looked up, dismayed. A teenage girl was holding on to her soaking-wet white kameez, which was now stained a pronounced orange.

'Hey! You bumped into me and now my boss is going to be angry for not bringing these drinks back.' Lalloo felt like crying.

She was about to answer back, her face hostile, when her companion spoke. She was much younger, about his own age, and very pretty, with a warm face. 'We're very sorry. It was an accident.' She had beautiful, soft eyes. She turned to the older girl. 'Come on, baji, we'll go home and get you cleaned up.'

The older girl gave him a dirty look, stuck her chin up and walked past, grumbling loudly. 'Fatima, like I always say, stay well clear of these riff-raff. They don't know any manners.'

Fatima looked back, mouthing another apology at him while she steered her older companion away, her long, high ponytail swinging behind her.

Lalloo looked down at the bottle that had ended up in the dust, the rest of the Fanta fizzing a dark puddle in the parched ground. The other bottle remained in his hand, half spilt.

The boy had been sitting in the doorway, watching. He jumped up. 'OK, don't worry. First, we'll have the rest of this.' He reached out and took the bottle from Lalloo, gulping down half of what was left.

'Arré!' Lalloo protested, but before he could do anything, the boy thrust it back at him.

'Drink up, we've got to finish it.'

Lalloo gazed at the cool, inviting drink.

'Come on. You're lucky it's not broken.' The boy picked the empty bottle up from the ground. He marched off and a bewildered Lalloo followed, watching his new companion closely.

He was only slightly taller than Lalloo, with curly hair cut short above his ears and large bushy eyebrows. His shalwar kameez was clean and fitted him well, unlike Lalloo's own. And he talked a lot.

'You know, that's really not the way to talk to girls. You want to get them to like you – top tip, don't throw Fanta on them. What are you doing at Rizwan's workshop, anyway? Don't be shy with me. I know everything that goes on around here. Do you work there now? I'll find out soon enough.'

After days of saying so little, Lalloo found it hard to find his words.

The boy strode through the streets with the confidence of having grown up there. Past the motorbikes and cycles parked on the side of the road, dodging the rickshaws that drove right at them. Past a man with a stump in place of a leg, a crutch under each shoulder, his cupped palms a begging bowl. Through a narrow lane selling choorian and shawls that Lalloo didn't recognise at all. They turned a corner and suddenly were at the drinks stall.

He stopped and looked pointedly at Lalloo's hand. 'Are you having it, or shall I?'

Lalloo didn't need any more encouragement. His mouth was parched. The Shezan bottle was a quarter full and the mango-flavoured nectar slipped down his throat, cool and sweet.

They went to exchange the empty bottles for full ones.

'Don't worry, Bhai Sahib, this boy will pay you back – I'll guarantee it personally.'

The drinks wallah looked across at them, but then nodded. Lalloo was stunned. He didn't know the bazaar well, but even he knew how difficult it was to get credit with stall owners.

Two new bottles in hand, they ran past the yogurt stall and the kulfi wallah, dodging the rickshaws, the bicycles and a stray goat.

It felt like running with Jugnu. His brother leading and him following, trusting all would come right in the end. It wasn't long before they reached the metal gates of the workshop.

Rizwan took one look at them and bellowed at the boy. 'I should've known you'd lead him astray. You're the reason he's late, aren't you?' He turned and called to one of the mechanics inside the workshop. 'Saif, your brother's making mischief again.' But before Saif could come outside, or Lalloo explain what had happened, the boy disappeared.

That was Salman. Quick to help and even quicker to run away. He winked at Lalloo before he sprinted down the path. That night, for the first time since Lalloo had arrived, he didn't mind the hulking car skeletons around him. He fell asleep dreaming of running free with his brother in a tall field of maize, black kites whirling above them.

*

Salman at twenty-one years old was the same as he'd been that first day Lalloo had met him. Same cheeky grin, same 'I can fix it' attitude. Most problems Lalloo came across, Salman would be able to help in some way, though even he couldn't get his hands on enough money for Shabnam's wedding.

But now that Yasmin had promised to help, Lalloo had to make sure Abu didn't go to Heera. Shabnam could get married and leave the bhatti. Then he had to get Ami, Abu and Pinky out too. The dream of escape hadn't died with Jugnu, despite everything Heera had done. One day Lalloo wanted to buy his family out of their debt. He thought about his pitiful savings, hoarded up over the years he'd been working for the Alams with this dream in mind. It made him sick with hope sometimes. He didn't know if it was possible, but there would certainly be no chance if Abu took another loan from Heera.

He was dressing for work when there was a massive thump against the wall of his room and loud chattering from outside. Some kids slamming a football again. Since getting the job with the Alams four years ago, Lalloo had rented a tiny room in Moti Mohalla. It was barely furnished, with a charpai and a small metal cupboard that contained all his belongings, and opened straight out onto the street with a concrete step that crossed the open sewer. A typical mohalla, predating Partition, there were about twenty houses, all three or four storeys high, tall and thin, and crammed together with walls a foot and a half thick to shield their inhabitants from the jealous sun. They had been here for hundreds of years, clustered in a semicircle around what used to be a temple.

During Partition, the Hindus had padlocked these homes, taking their most prized possessions, and left, planning to return when things had calmed. When the Muslims had come, hungry and homeless, having left their own properties in Amritsar and Ferozepur and Ludhiana, having witnessed the stuff of nightmares, they'd realised there was no going back and had broken the padlocks in tears, taking shelter, seeking sanctuary. Over time, nobody spoke about *back home* any more and the temple had been converted into a mosque. The only person who still talked about Partition was Bulla Chacha's elderly father. In his eighties, deaf in one ear, he didn't care what anyone thought of him and nobody listened to him anyway. He'd collared Lalloo many times to tell him about his escape from the mob in the middle of the night. How he'd run and hidden but had lost hold of his sister's hand. They'd never seen her again.

Bulla Chacha and his father lived next door and insisted on keeping their buffalo tied outside Lalloo's room. Every time he left or entered, he had to dodge the muck on the floor. Today, he was so busy trying not to get his chappal dirty, he almost didn't notice the pair of children, barefooted and dressed only in their shalwars, charging towards him, chasing a rolling rubber tyre, whipping it forward with sticks in their hands. He navigated the children, the muck and the sewers. A large lorry was blocking the road and two men were manhandling furniture into the house next door but one. It had lain empty for seven years now, locked and shuttered, ever since Fatima had moved away with her family. It must have been sold at last. He wondered who would move in now. The houses in the mohalla were so close together, he was sure he'd bump into the new neighbours sooner or later. Chickens roamed freely, pecking at dirt, and the local busybodies gathered in the courtyard in front of the mosque, their chadars wrapped around their heads and shoulders, chewing paan, gesturing loudly and staring at him as he passed, as if he had no business there.

He'd chosen Moti Mohalla because it was near the cantonment where the Alams lived. He could catch a minibus, or it was a long walk. It was mid-August and the summer heat was at its peak, but the sky was a bit hazy, with a thin cloud covering, and this, combined with a slight breeze, meant the weather was bearable today. He decided to take this rare opportunity of the break in the heat to walk to work.

In between the mohalla and the cantonment was Sadar bazaar, where Lalloo had worked at Rizwan's workshop and spent most of his childhood. The workshop had closed after Rizwan died, but Lalloo could run through every alleyway, walk past every shop with his eyes closed.

'Arré, what are you doing here? Haven't you got work?'

It was Salman, appearing by his side in the flurry of noise and energy that he brought with him everywhere. Both his head of tightly curled hair and his eyebrows had only grown bushier with age. Salman ran a mobile-phone shop in the bazaar, from where he could keep his finger on the pulse of everything going on. Just like the boy he'd been, he'd grown into the man who knew everyone, and if you needed anything doing, Salman was your man. Lalloo had always thought selling mobile phones was a front for all the other things Salman liked to do on the side.

'Just decided to walk in today.'

Salman fell into step beside Lalloo.

'What about the shop?' Lalloo turned to look behind him as they passed it.

'Don't worry about that. I've hired a chota.' Salman was referring to the young boy of about twelve years old peering out from behind the counter. 'So, what's with the early-morning walk?'

Lalloo sighed. 'My parents want to get my sister married.' He paused and shrugged. 'You know I have no money.'

Salman had three sisters of his own and only one of them was married. He knew the worry well enough. His parents weren't rich, but at least they didn't work in bondage.

'I was just trying to clear my head . . .' Lalloo's voice trailed away as he caught a glimpse of someone in the bazaar that made him do a double take. He stopped still and grabbed Salman's arm. 'Is that . . .? But . . . it can't be?' He tore his gaze from her and looked towards Salman. 'Can it?'

He was met with Salman's mischievous grin. 'Yup, she's back. Living with her father and grandmother in your mohalla.'

The van he'd seen. It must've been Fatima's family moving *back* into their house in the mohalla. He looked again. It was most definitely her. Her face seemed more angular, her hair longer, but she had the same gentle, no-nonsense expression he knew so well.

He squeezed Salman's forearm. 'But . . . why didn't you tell me?'

'Only just happened. You didn't give me a chance.'

They started walking again and Lalloo was trying not to stare, but he couldn't help it. Her grandmother used to run a fruit and vegetable stall in the bazaar and there Fatima was, after all these years, helping her grandmother at the stall as if they'd never gone away. The two friends casually walked past and he could see her out of the corner of his eye, unpacking crates of tomatoes, setting up the display.

'Hey! Do you feel like drinking some Fanta?' Salman asked a little too loudly just as they walked past.

Lalloo's cheeks flamed. He jabbed Salman in the ribs with his elbow and stared rigidly ahead until they were well past the stall. Had she glanced up at him? Would she recognise him? Surely she must? Did she have a tiny smile on her lips?

Finally, after a minute of walking in silence, he looked across at his friend. Salman's eyebrows danced. 'She's back now. Maybe you should be thinking about asking her out on a date?'

Lalloo shook his head vigorously. 'Oh, I'm sure she wouldn't want to go out with me.' What would it be like to talk to her again? He remembered her lovely voice, quiet and serious without being harsh, and his own sheer joy when he'd been able to make her laugh.

'How do you know?'

'Her grandmother wouldn't even let her play with us as children – how would she feel about—'

Salman grinned and nudged him. 'Just ask her out, yaar. You can worry about marriage when you get there.'

When Lalloo didn't respond, Salman sighed.

'OK, look, you clearly need help. This is what you do when you're talking to girls . . . Always smile, always crack a joke, no matter how lame your jokes are, but remember to always stay cool. And since you need some serious assistance here, when I get a car, I might even let you borrow it to help impress her.'

Lalloo rolled his eyes, but Salman grinned and continued.

'Always ask for her number – even if she doesn't give it to you, she'll take it as a compliment. Never tell her she looks fat, even if she is deliciously plump. Never tell her the colour she's wearing doesn't suit her, *especially* if it doesn't suit her. Never brush up against her accidentally on purpose.' He looked pointedly towards Lalloo and waggled his eyebrows up and down. 'No matter how much you want to – unless, of course, she wants you to . . .'

Lalloo shook his head and tuned out Salman's voice as he walked, dreaming instead of scenarios in which he would speak to Fatima, where he wouldn't get tongue-tied as soon as he saw her; he could ask for her number – maybe even ask her out on a date. He smiled to himself. He couldn't believe she was back.

Chapter Five

One morning, a month or so after Lalloo had first arrived at Rizwan's workshop, he awoke to a strange silence. Usually, the first thing he'd hear would be his boss outside on his chair, muttering poetry aloud to himself. Lalloo got up, rolled his bedding into a corner and pulled back the workshop doors to let the light in before he realised – of course, it was Sunday. No customers, no mechanics, the workshop was closed and Rizwan was at home with his wife. The quiet was deafening. Lalloo sat outside in the courtyard. Not daring to sit in Rizwan's chair, he perched on the one next to it, pretending he was a customer come to get his car fixed.

Rizwan no longer locked him in when the workshop was closed, but the nights were still terrible, alone with only the brooding ghosts of discarded cars and motorbikes to keep him company. When the nightmares became overwhelming, he'd leave his bedding in the corner of the workshop and crawl among the wrecks, hide himself under a discarded bonnet or a car door, seek solace in the cool touch of machines incapable of duplicity or torture, until his body stopped trembling. Last night, he'd gripped Jugnu's cricket ball, pressing it to his hot eyes and cheeks, until the tears had stopped and the noises in his head had subsided.

He was soaking up the welcome morning sunlight when Salman appeared round the corner of the courtyard. 'Ready to earn some money?'

Lalloo didn't need encouragement, quickly falling into step with his friend as they set off on the now familiar route to Sadar.

'Saif said you live at the workshop. You're lucky – you get to be around all those cars and you haven't got your mum watching you all the time. And you get Sundays off to do whatever you want!'

Lalloo rubbed at an oil smear on his arm, only smudging it further, but he didn't contradict his new friend.

Salman looked at Lalloo wistfully. 'Ami doesn't even let me come to the bazaar. I have to sneak out.'

'Why not?'

'She worries about all the dust. She'd prefer me to sit at home and do my homework.' Salman pulled a face to show what he thought of that idea. 'I'm saving up so I can buy a car when I'm old enough, then I can get around without having to worry about dust.'

Lalloo frowned. 'The dust?'

'Salaam, Chacha Jee. How's the leg recovering?' Salman called out to an elderly man sat outside a shop selling yogurt. His left leg wrapped in a cast was outstretched on a plastic chair in front of him, and he looked up and waved at Salman.

Lalloo, realising his friend had ignored his question on purpose, didn't ask again, just followed him closely.

As they passed another man, this one scooping piles of thinly sliced potatoes into a deep-fat fryer balanced on a cart, Salman called out again. 'Bhai Sahib, I'm going to need some chips today!'

'If you can pay for them, you can have them.' The man swatted flies with a cloth, the air heavy with the smell of cooking oil.

'How do you know all these people?' Lalloo whispered to Salman. Everywhere they went, people nodded and smiled at his friend.

Salman shrugged. 'It's like ... my second home. I've always come here.'

Lalloo heard the buzzing before he could see where it was coming from. The boys had wound their way past the food stalls and the air hummed. They were in a whole street of shops with open fronts. Young men sat on the floor, black Singer sewing machines in front of them and bundles of cloth on the ground. Lalloo recognised the ancient machines – Ami had had one before they'd moved to the bhatti – but he'd never seen so many of them together. They made the air throb, greedily taking in cloth at one end and churning it out the other.

The friends stopped outside Sunbright Tailors and Salman spoke to its owner, Master Jee, who had deliveries to be made before Eid. He handed the boys three bulging plastic bags.

'Come on,' Salman said, breaking into a run, pulling Lalloo along with him. Clutching the bundles of newly stitched clothes, they dodged motorbikes and ran up the gallis, looking for the right address. Salman knew every winding path and they eventually skidded to a stop next to an old wooden door that looked exactly like all the others on the street. Salman yanked on the bell and a tiny old man opened it a crack, took the bags and then shut the door in their faces.

At the second house, the lady who answered the door gave them a couple of rupees each, which they quickly pocketed and darted away. All day, the boys ran back and forth from Master Jee's, delivering bag after bag, picking up tips from the friendlier customers and splitting them between them. It was the most money Lalloo had ever had.

'Keep up, Salman,' he said, eager to fit in a few more bundles before they each had to return home. It was hot and Salman's pace had slowed, dragging the latest bag in the dust behind him.

Lalloo turned and looked at him. Salman was breathing heavily, his face bright red with trickles of sweat pouring from his forehead. 'Let me carry it.'

Salman swatted him away. 'I'm fine,' he said, wheezing a little. He bent over and put his hands on his knees, his chest rising and falling. Something wasn't right and Lalloo wondered about what Salman had said earlier, and whether there was another reason his mother wanted to keep her son at home.

They dropped off the bag at a doorstep, then went to collect the final bundle from Master Jee.

A soft voice called out to them from a neighbouring vegetable stall, 'Where are you running off to now?'

Lalloo stopped and turned. The girl from the other day – Fatima. He'd spilt Fanta over her older companion. He showed her the label pinned to the plastic bag in his hand. 'Do you want to come with us?'

Salman gave him a quizzical look, but Lalloo just shrugged.

'I'm gonna sit this one out,' Salman said, slumping down on the ground next to Master Jee's. 'I'll wait for you here.'

And just like that, Fatima was running along with him. The two of them ran, for the sheer joy of it, thundering down the streets as people rushed to get out of their way. When they finally stopped and delivered the parcel of clothes, they were out of breath, laughing and doubling over.

As they ran back to Salman, the sun was setting behind the shops, the evening Azaan calling out across the streets. Most of the stalls were shutting up for the day, but the smell of freshly fried spicy chips lingered in the air. Lalloo's mouth watered, his pockets heavy with jingling coins. 'Let's get some before we go,' he said, turning to Salman and Fatima.

Salman grumbled. 'I'm not sharing any chips with her.'

Lalloo ignored him. When the man handed Lalloo the hot, steaming portion of chips, he held them out to Fatima.

Salman bought his own chips, stuffing a great handful of them into his mouth as if to make a point. He immediately started hopping from one foot to the other, fanning his mouth with his hand where the hot chips were burning his tongue, bringing tears to his eyes. Lalloo and Fatima looked at each other and laughed, and eventually Salman recovered enough to join in.

The three of them sat and ate the chips in contented silence. It was the happiest Lalloo had felt in a long time and he suddenly thought of Jugnu. His heart ached.

A woman's voice rang out from the stalls, calling Fatima's name. Fatima winced. 'That's my dado. I'd better go or I'll never be allowed out of her sight again. Thanks for the chips.'

She disappeared so quickly that Lalloo didn't have time to see where she went, twisting round to peer after her.

Lalloo looked across at Salman, who shrugged. 'Don't worry, you'll see her again. Her grandmother owns the vegetable stall down there.'

'We should go, too.' Lalloo stood up, pulling Salman up behind him. Rizwan's wife, Mumtaz gave him a plate of food on Sunday evenings and he didn't want to miss it. 'Another couple of weeks of this and I'll have enough money to pay back the drinks wallah.'

Salman grinned. 'Don't get carried away. Today was a good haul because of the Eid rush.'

Lalloo watched Salman go, listening to his friend's laboured breathing as he turned the corner out of sight.

When Lalloo arrived back at the workshop, he was surprised to see Rizwan waiting for him. His heart sank, wondering what trouble he was in now. He'd bought the vegetables yesterday just as, Mumtaz, had asked. It wasn't his fault the bhindi was more expensive this week. He was about to explain when Rizwan ushered him into their house. He'd never been allowed inside before. Heart pounding, Lalloo took a few tentative steps.

The entrance opened into a large lounge room with sofas facing each other. On one of them sat Mumtaz, staring at him. Behind the sofas were closed doors leading off to rooms he couldn't see, and a large chest freezer was pushed up against one wall. Rizwan sat next to his wife in silence. The sofas were pristine, the floor highly polished marble chips. Lalloo had to fight the urge to look behind him in case he'd left grease marks as he came in.

Without speaking, Mumtaz picked up the telephone receiver next to her and dialled a number written on a chit of paper.

'Mumtaz is calling your parents so you can speak to them,' said Rizwan.

Rizwan was mistaken. His parents didn't have a phone. They would have to walk to the shops at the market an hour away to use one. And surely they'd forgotten about him by now – it'd been weeks and he had heard nothing from them. But before Lalloo could breathe, he was handed a receiver with Abu's voice booming down it. Lalloo couldn't speak. He couldn't move. He'd used a phone before, of course, but Abu's voice was there and Abu wasn't and it was beyond bearable.

'Speak, boy, or they'll think we're mistreating you.' Mumtaz hovered at his shoulder.

But what was there to say? He nodded dumbly.

'Speak.' Mumtaz hissed the word.

Abu asked him something. Lalloo didn't know what. Rizwan glared, his arms crossed over his big stomach.

'Yes, yes.' Lalloo had no idea what he was agreeing to. He spoke just so Abu could hear his voice, but it came out as a croak.

Then Ami came on the line. 'Lalloo?' She sounded breathless, 'I . . . I was . . .' Her voice was flooded with tears and she wasn't able to say anything else. He stood for a moment, listening to his mother not speaking. Shabnam was calling out in the distance. He wanted to ask after her. How were they? They were there, but Jugnu was not. How could that be? How could they bear it? And Lalloo – did they miss him? Could he come home now? He'd do the bricks and his lessons without complaining. What if Shabnam had forgotten what he looked like? It had been so long. He wanted Jugnu. Why did the men do that? Jugnu hadn't done anything wrong. He would never hurt anyone.

Lalloo had no voice in his throat, just multitudes of haunting images in his head. He thrust the phone back at Mumtaz and ran from the room.

Chapter Six

'I asked Daddy for the money. He'll be able to get it for me by tomorrow.' Yasmin glanced up from her phone.

Lalloo looked back at her through the rear-view mirror and didn't know what to say. It was so much money, enough to set Shabnam on a new life path, enough that Abu wouldn't have to even think of going to Heera. He knew Yasmin had her own reasons for helping him, but he had never felt more grateful for that day when he had found her on the roadside. 'Bibi, thank you so much . . .'

She shrugged. 'Sure.'

He was already planning how he would break the news to his parents. They could plan a small wedding feast, a canopy to seat their guests under to shade them from the heat and proper wedding clothes for his sister. What things would they deem essential to buy for Shabnam's new life with her husband? Clothes, bedding, kitchen utensils, a trunk to put everything in, and, maybe, if the money would stretch that far, some jewellery. All for the price of a rich lady's handbag.

When they pulled up in the driveway of the house, Omer was already home, his car parked in the porch. Yasmin headed straight indoors. Lalloo got out and emptied the boot of boxes and bags, the result of Yasmin's shopping trip, and followed after her.

As soon as he stepped inside, Lalloo heard Omer's booming voice. 'Wait a minute, wait a minute. Let me get it.'

Omer seemed in a good mood.

'What is it, Daddy?'

Lalloo came into the lounge laden with shopping and as he set it down on the nearest table, he saw Omer presenting Yasmin with a white box with gold lettering. It was large and looked luxurious, wrapped in a velvet ribbon tied into a big bow on top.

Lalloo lingered discreetly in a corner of the room, wanting to see what this was about. He felt a sense of unease that he couldn't explain.

Yasmin looked starry-eyed up at Omer as she reached to untie the bow. She pulled out an object wrapped in some cloth, looked at it and then up at her father. 'Oh, you didn't!'

He nodded at her, smiling indulgently. 'Open it.'

She started opening the cloth bag. Lalloo was getting impatient. Any minute now, somebody would notice he was loitering. She finally pulled out a leather handbag, held it in her lap and gasped.

'Oh, Daddy, it's beautiful!' She set the gift down gently on the sofa beside her, as if it were a delicate thing likely to break, and flung her arms around her father's neck.

'Anything for you, darling.'

Lalloo stared at the bag. His skin prickled, realisation dawning.

'It's just the one I wanted. But you didn't have to get it. I could've bought it myself.' Yasmin's voice was high-pitched with excitement.

Omer was grinning. The only time Lalloo ever saw him smile was when he was with his daughter, but Lalloo's eyes kept being drawn to the bag. It was shiny and red, like the wedding dress he'd hoped to buy for his sister. Perfectly adorned with a huge gold buckle at the front, taunting him with the jewellery Shabnam could never afford.

'I thought I'd save you the hassle of getting it yourself. A friend of mine was coming over from Dubai and this way you get it sooner.'

'You're the best.' Yasmin linked arms with her father and they headed into the kitchen together.

As they passed, Omer turned to look at him and Lalloo thought he'd be shouted at for dawdling in the house, but instead his boss said, 'I'm going to be away tomorrow. Make sure you take my car in for a service.'

Yasmin gave Lalloo a sideways look and a barely perceptible shrug, as she and her father walked into the kitchen for some samosas to eat.

It was later that day that he managed to get Yasmin on her own again. New handbag on her arm, she was meeting Tania at yet another new coffee shop that had just opened on M.M. Alam Road, in the fashionable part of town. These coffee shops sold drinks and desserts at astronomical prices – he would never even think of going there – but from overhearing their conversations, Yasmin and Tania went to be seen with, and by, the right sort of people.

Despite the air conditioning going full blast in the car, he was sweating. She'd been on the phone to her boyfriend for most of the journey, arranging her next date. When she finally hung up, Lalloo was already at the coffee shop. As he manoeuvred the car into a parking spot, he broached the subject again, not knowing when they'd get another chance to make a plan.

'Bibi, how can we get the money now? Is there another way you could help me for my sister?'

Still engrossed in her phone, tapping at the screen, she opened the car door and set one foot outside before looking up blankly for a moment, recollecting. 'Yes, wasn't that funny, Daddy buying me the bag instead of giving me the cash. I can't ask him for anything else so soon. You'll just have to think of some other way of getting it.'

Lalloo felt like she'd slammed the car door onto his ribcage. He'd been a fool. His heart was beating too fast and he struggled to get his words out.

'But, bibi, you said—'

Her friend Tania appeared by her side, hair worn short in a bob, bright lipstick and the latest fashionably cut shalwar kameez. 'What's this?'

Yasmin got out of the car, thrusting her bag towards her friend. 'You'll never guess what Daddy did, only went and got me the new Dior from the latest collection. From Dubai! Sofia is going to be sooo jealous – this must be the only one in Lahore.'

Lalloo persisted. 'Bibi, please. This is for Shabnam. You know I would never ask anything for myself.'

The friends linked arms and strolled off into the coffee shop together, the gold buckle on Yasmin's new handbag winking at him in the sunlight. She glanced back at him and called out, 'You can go now. I'll get a lift back with Tania.'

His face burning with embarrassment, Lalloo swallowed his humiliation and drove slowly back to the house. By the time he arrived, he was furious. He'd thought she was different. He'd defended her, kept her secrets. Sitting in the parked car in the Alams' driveway, his hands still clenched on the steering wheel, the lush grass on the lawn beside him felt like a taunt. Of course they hadn't been on an equal footing, but he'd still thought it was some kind of a friendship. This money would've changed his family's life and Yasmin had barely blinked at it. Money problems had always followed him and his family. And they were always accompanied by indignities and shame. It was the reason they had moved to the bhatti in the first place and that had just made things so much worse.

*

He still remembered the day he realised money, or the lack of it, could change everything. He'd been seven years old and madly excited because he'd discovered where the stray cat had just had her kittens. Five tiny, cuddly, newborn bundles of fur. He'd wanted to show them to Jugnu before nightfall and had raced home across the fields, stopping only briefly to pat Makhan the ox lying down under the lean-to. But as soon as he'd got in the door, he'd known something had been wrong and had stopped in the doorway to listen.

'It's our only hope right now; Fareed said it's a good deal. They will give us a place to stay, work, and most importantly give us money upfront so I can pay back what I owe for last year's seeds and fertiliser.' Abu was pacing the floor as he talked.

Ami sat with her head in her hands, Jugnu beside her looking worried, tired, rubbing her arm. Shabnam sat on Ami's other side, subdued.

'We'll have to leave this place?' his brother asked.

'We barely make ends meet here. After the rent on the land and the costs, there's hardly anything left.' Ami shook her head.

'The harvest has failed two years in a row now. This will be like a fresh start. A new house, a new job. And once we've worked and paid off the debt at the bhatti, we can go elsewhere.' Abu's voice was sad, hesitant, as if he wasn't convinced himself.

Jugnu stood up. 'I'll help you. With the three of us working on the bricks, we'll repay the peshgi in no time.'

More boring talk about money; it was all the adults spoke about and his brother was becoming just like them. Lalloo knew he had to go to bed hungry sometimes, but even when they couldn't afford to eat daal, he would sit by the kitchen window, playing with Shabnam, waiting for Abu to come home from the field as Ami cooked fresh rotis to have with the tangy sweetness of mango achaar. He was happy. Lalloo didn't understand why they were talking about leaving. Everything they loved was right here.

'Will we take Makhan with us?' His voice came out small. They had to take Makhan, surely. He was part of the family. Lalloo was the one who fed the ox every day before school and in the evenings before bed.

All of them turned to look at him, unaware until that moment he was listening.

Jugnu spoke first. 'There's no land to plough where we're going. You know how much he likes to do the ploughing.' He saw Lalloo's face crumple. 'We'll give him to a family where he can still work the field. They'll look after him.' But his brother turned away as he spoke and Lalloo knew even Jugnu didn't believe that.

Ami stepped forward, held his hands against her body and whispered, 'I've heard where we're going they might have a horse or a donkey.' She hugged him to her, her body enveloped in sadness.

But he pushed her away from him and stomped out of the house, ignoring Jugnu as he shouted after him. The sun went down that day without Lalloo showing his brother the cat's hiding place or offering her new family any milk. They wanted to take him away from Makhan and their house and the stray cat with her kittens and that wasn't right. He wasn't going to let them.

But it wasn't their house. The roof over their heads, the fields, all belonged to the zamindar. They sold everything they owned: all the furniture in their sparsely furnished rooms, the charpais and almarees, Makhan and the chickens. And no amount of pleading or shouting from Lalloo made any difference. They took only their bedding and clothes, trussed up into bundles of cloth and balanced on their heads on the long train journey to their new life.

When they finally arrived at the bhatti, he knew this was all a mistake. The overwhelming chimney and the desolate landscape, a yawning red gash in a sea of green. He looked up at the adults' faces and saw only fear. The air was close here – even the sky looked smaller. Heera was there to show them to their new home, a smug look on his face. The hut they were meant to live in was a single room with bare earth for a floor, the space for a fire outside was their barren kitchen. Abu looked towards Heera as if to say this wasn't right, but he stayed silent. Lalloo was sure any minute now one of the adults would admit this was a mistake and they would go back home, where he only had to share a room with Jugnu, where they could get back the chickens and Makhan. But no one did. Lalloo felt a huge lump in his throat he couldn't swallow.

Jugnu saw his expression and squeezed his hand. 'Don't worry, we won't be here long.'

A few weeks after they moved in, his parents realised the school was too far for Lalloo and Shabnam to get to every day, so Ami said she'd teach the children at home. It would be many more weeks before they realised working off their debt wasn't even possible.

The debt was already exacted such a heavy price and still imprisoned them at the bhatti, fourteen years later.

*

Now that Yasmin was no longer helping him get the money, Lalloo needed another way and quickly. He kept telling himself that Yasmin didn't owe him anything, that he was just a servant, but he couldn't forget how casually she'd offered to help and had then so easily dismissed him. He had to get the money for the wedding and dowry in two weeks and Abu would get impatient soon. The only people he knew with the kind of money to help were the Alams and he knew his best chance of asking them now was getting Asima on her own. It was a slim chance, but she would be more likely to help him if her husband wasn't around.

The following day, Omer went off in an Uber, leaving his car for Lalloo to take for a service. Even though he didn't usually drive Omer around, his boss preferring to drive himself, Lalloo was surprised his boss hadn't asked to be dropped off. He wondered where he was going.

Lalloo drove Asima back from the beauty parlour and, on the pretext of bringing in the shopping bags, followed her into the house. He put the bags in the kitchen and couldn't see Guddo anywhere, so he went into the lounge, where he found Asima slumped on the sofa in front of the TV with her feet resting on the table. She didn't sit around like this when Omer was about; she must not be expecting him back any time soon.

Lalloo hesitated. His palms were sweaty, his feet unwilling to move. He took a deep breath and approached her, unsure if this was the right thing to do, still smarting from Yasmin's rejection, but knowing he wouldn't often be able to get Asima on her own.

'Bibi, your hair is looking lovely.' The beauticians at the parlour had worked their magic on her sparse, limp strands, puffing them up into a beehive.

'What?' Her beady eyes stared at him like he'd sprouted two horns on his head.

That had come out wrong. He didn't want to sound like he was flirting. 'Can I get you anything? A glass of water ... or anything from the bazaar?'

She turned back to the TV. 'No, you can go.'

He cleared his throat. 'Bibi Jee, I wanted to ask you a favour.'

She didn't say anything and he didn't know if she hadn't heard or had chosen to ignore him.

'My sister is getting married.'

'Congratulations.' Her response was expressionless and automatic. She pointed the remote at the TV, flicking through the channels. Lalloo shuffled from foot to foot, hating this but aware that it was too late to stop now. He might as well ask and see what happened.

'You see, weddings are very expensive.' He paused, then blurted out his request. 'I need a loan to pay for it.'

Asima put down the remote. She'd found the channel she wanted, one of those horrendous TV dramas, and she looked at him finally, rolling her eyes. 'This isn't an almshouse.'

'I'd pay you back, every paisa.'

'You know we don't do loans in this house, not for any of the servants. I'll give you some clothes for your sister.'

'I need the money for the wedding. If it were for anything else, I wouldn't ask. My parents are very poor.' She'd gone back to watching the TV, losing interest in what he was saying. 'I would always be grateful to you, bibi, I'll do anything you ask me to do. Any extra help you need, just say so. I'll be at your service.' He dropped onto his knees, his hands clasped in front of him. 'Please, bibi, this way my sister can get married and I'll always be your loyal servant.'

Reluctantly, she turned towards him. She looked like she was thinking something over. 'Omer Sahib wouldn't be pleased.'

Her tone had softened. This had to be a good sign.

'Think of it as more of an advance, bibi. You can cut my wages every month.' Asima handled all the wages for the servants. If he were lucky, Asima would give him the money and Omer wouldn't find out.

'Hmm . . . I do like it when servants are loyal to me.' She nodded slowly. 'How much do you need?'

But before Lalloo could answer, the front door slammed shut and Omer stormed in, briefcase in hand.

Lalloo leapt to his feet and froze, wishing he could disappear.

Asima sat up, quickly taking her feet off the table. 'I thought you were going away?'

'Meeting got cancelled. Bloody timewasters.' He dumped his briefcase on the sofa and slumped down beside it.

'How did you get back all the way from Gujranwala?'

'What does it matter to you? Stop prying, woman.' He kicked off his shoes and left them lying in the middle of the floor.

Omer didn't pay any attention to Lalloo. If Asima didn't tell her husband about the conversation they'd been having, and Lalloo could leave the room quietly, maybe he could try again another time. Then he would have made a good start at least.

'Where's Guddo? I need a drink.'

Asima got up to ring the call bell for the servants and Lalloo chanced a step towards the door. Omer whipped his head round and stared at him, hawklike.

'What's he doing in the house?' Omer's voice roared and Lalloo flinched, feeling the strain in his body as he tried to stand still and be anywhere but here at the same time.

Asima hurried over and sat down next to her husband. 'He says he wants a loan for his sister's wedding.'

Lalloo felt the energy seep out of him. There was no hope now.

Omer let out a snort and waved a hand in his direction. 'You know what these people are like – today his sister's getting married, tomorrow his mother's ill, day after that he'll want money for his father's funeral.'

Asima nodded, as if she hadn't been contemplating lending him the money just a few moments ago.

Lalloo could feel sweat prickling his armpits as he chanced one more desperate attempt. 'Not a loan, sahib. An advance. You can cut it from my wages.'

'That's very generous of you.' A sneer played on Omer's lips.

Asima smiled at her husband's joke.

'Aren't we lucky, Asima, to have such generous servants? They'll even let us take back the money they borrow from us.' He leant back on the sofa, stretching his arms out behind him. 'Now, call that lazy Guddo so I can get a drink.'

Asima got up without looking at Lalloo and her husband picked up the TV remote, shouting out to her, 'What's this rubbish you're watching?'

Lalloo felt like a stray dog, begging on the roadside, but he knew that if he asked again, he could lose more than just his dignity. He imagined telling his father he didn't have the money, or even a job any more. He turned to leave, arms heavy by his side. Before he shut the door behind him, he saw Omer pick a mobile phone out of his pocket and slip it into his briefcase, snapping the clasps shut before returning the case to its original spot on the sofa, all the while keeping his eyes on his wife's retreating back.

*

With any hope of getting the money destroyed and feeling a headache coming on, Lalloo decided to walk back home at the end of the day, unable to face cramming into a hot and sweaty minibus.

He'd thought a walk would ease the burning behind his eyes, but as soon as he set off, he wasn't so sure it'd been a good idea. The road was busy at this time of day, with cars and trucks overtaking and honking at each other. The footpath was narrow and sporadic, occasionally ceasing to exist altogether, forcing him to walk on the road. As he entered Sadar, he spotted Salman talking to the butcher and raised a hand in greeting.

Salman rushed over. 'Two walks in two days. What's going on?'

Lalloo shook his head. 'It's been a long day.'

'So have you come to see the fabulous Fatima again?'

'Just trying to clear my head. Some of us have proper work to do, you know – we can't all hire chotas to do it for us.'

Lalloo knew he was being unfair, but he could still feel the burn of Omer's casual put-down, the look of disgust on his boss's face. Then he realised what Salman had said.

Fatima. He'd thought she'd gone for ever. They'd spent so many precious moments as teenagers stealing away from her grandmother, meeting under the neem tree on the edge of the bazaar, discussing the best places to eat golgappay and samosas. Lalloo had felt he could talk to her about things he wasn't able to say to anyone else. But then her father's job had moved to Faisalabad and her family had moved away from the mohalla. She'd gone, leaving a hole in his heart so big that even Salman knew not to tease him about it.

And now? What did he feel about her now? His thoughts were a confused hot mess. It was easy for Salman. His friend was always talking about girls, obsessing over them. Sauntering over and striking up conversations with them. He never seemed worried that they wouldn't speak to him or that they would think him beneath them. But Salman had big dreams and a stable income to offer a potential wife. Lalloo had nothing. Just some meagre savings, in the hope that one day they would be enough to buy back his family's indenture.

There was some commotion ahead of them as they rounded a

corner and he turned to Salman. 'So her grandmother is running the fruit and vegetable stall again?'

But Salman wasn't paying any attention to him. 'It's your lucky day,' he said softly, staring pointedly ahead of them.

Lalloo turned to look. A large figure was sprawled on the ground, groaning loudly and surrounded by scattered fruit from a torn plastic bag she was holding. At first, he didn't recognise her, but then a young woman kneeling beside her raised her head and looked directly at him.

It was Fatima. The blood rushed to his face and he turned to Salman for help, but his friend had vanished. He couldn't turn away now – both women had seen him. Fatima gestured to him and he forced himself to walk calmly up to them, his heart pounding in his ears. She'd been gone from his life for so long and now he'd seen her twice in two days. Could fate be bringing them back together again? He shook his head. This wasn't Bollywood; things like that didn't happen in real life. He needed to get a grip.

Just seeing her felt like he was back where he belonged. He nodded at her, but addressed the older woman out of respect.

'Chachi Jee, can I help?'

Chachi Jeera was Fatima's grandmother. When Lalloo was younger, he'd seen her often enough outside the mosque in the courtyard in Moti Mohalla, scolding children for not doing her bidding or grabbing a child by the ear with those firm fingers and frogmarching them to their parents. She was the sort of matriarch he'd been afraid of as a child, somebody who'd catch him doing something wrong and take her complaint to Rizwan.

'*Can you help?* You think I want to sit in this dust in a heap all day? Help me up.' She grabbed his arm with her large chubby fingers and he looked behind him again, searching desperately for Salman, but his friend had truly disappeared.

'Let's get you back up on your feet.' He hardly had a choice with her gripping on to him like that. Chachi Jeera was a woman of substantial size. She usually walked with the help of a stick and Lalloo could see it fallen beside her. He put a hand under each arm and heaved, but it was no good.

'Why don't you try that side and I'll try from here,' Fatima said.

Her voice. Exactly as he remembered it. As sweet as chilled Chaunsa mangoes on a hot summer's day. He looked across at her again and felt his cheeks blaze. Was it being so close to her or the fact he hadn't eaten that was making him giddy?

'Ready?' he asked, nodding back at her. 'Together on one . . . two . . .' He grasped Chachi Jeera once more, and, somehow – he wasn't sure how – with a lot of grunting from the old lady, they managed to pull her upright.

Fatima smiled at him. 'Thank you,' she said and he found he couldn't stop looking at her, searching her face for everything that was familiar and noticing the subtle ways in which she'd changed, grown up.

'You're back,' he mumbled.

She nodded. 'Abu's job got transferred. We've moved back to the mo—'

'Hai, hai, my foot!' Chachi Jeera cried out.

Lalloo wanted to tell Fatima they were neighbours now, to fill her in on so much that had happened while she'd been away, but he reluctantly pulled his gaze from her and they both looked down to see Chachi's ankle swollen to the size of a grapefruit.

Lalloo cleared his throat. 'Do you want to get her stick?'

Fatima stepped away and Lalloo was left supporting the very heavy old lady by himself. When she fetched it, he reached out quickly and ended up placing his hand on top of hers. He pulled back immediately, his skin burning. Their eyes flew to each other and he knew she'd felt that moment as acutely as he had.

Between them, with the help of the stick, and Chachi Jeera hobbling slowly, they managed to move Chachi onto the white, plastic chair behind her vegetable stall, Chachi complaining all the way, as if blaming them for her predicament.

When she was planted on her chair, Fatima knelt to examine her ankle with confident yet gentle fingers. 'It looks like you've twisted it. Some painkillers and rest will do it good.'

She sounded so quietly assured in her manner and he wondered if she'd managed to fulfil her dream of becoming a doctor. There was so much he didn't know about her.

Chachi scowled. 'And what about the stall?' Then she looked up at Lalloo. 'And you? Who are you? You look familiar – are you from around here?'

'His name is Lalloo, Dado.'

The old lady looked from Lalloo to her granddaughter. 'You know him?' Then, in a moment of recognition, her eyes swung back to Lalloo and narrowed. 'The street urchin?'

'I . . . I live in the mohalla now, rent a room from Kaka.'

Chachi kept staring at him, clearly not impressed by this promotion in his social status, and Lalloo felt compelled to keep on talking.

'I work as a driver. For the Alams in the cantonment.'

All the while, he was aware of Fatima's intense gaze on him. This would all be news to her too. When she'd left, he'd still lived and worked at Rizwan's – he'd still been the ragged street urchin her grandmother remembered him as.

Chachi sniffed and turned her face away. 'And what about my amrood? Are they all spoilt?' She pointed with her cane and they looked towards the guava spilt all over the floor.

'Don't worry, Dado, we'll get them for you.'

Fatima looked at him and they both moved as one, away from Chachi. Crouched on the floor, under the guise of picking up the heavy yellow fruit, with their backs to her grandmother, he spoke softly.

'I wasn't sure you would remember me.'

'Of course I remember you, Lalloo,' she replied, her eyes sparkling.

Lalloo felt a familiar speechlessness come over him. *Do you remember the last time we saw each other?* he wanted to ask. But why would she? He had been fourteen years old, waiting under the neem tree, hands trembling, trying to make sense of what he'd felt about her. But when he'd tried to talk to her about it, to share his thoughts in that last anxious moment stolen from chaperones on the edge of the bazaar, his breath had caught, his tongue had locked, his cheeks had burnt. She'd moved away without him knowing if she'd felt the same huge, complicated longing in her chest when they'd been together. She'd left, and he'd thought it was for ever.

Fatima snuck a glance behind her at her grandmother. 'Thank you for helping us. She won't say it, but Dado is very grateful too.'

There was so much he wanted to say to her, so much he wanted to ask her, he didn't know where to start. What was it Salman had said he must do? Smile? Or crack a joke? Or both? But his mouth was dry and he couldn't think of anything funny to say.

'I'm glad. I mean . . . not glad that she fell, obviously.' He realised he wasn't making much sense and stopped and looked at her.

She was smiling.

'It gave me an excuse to talk to you.' Why did he say that? He was certainly not heeding Salman's advice and acting cool or aloof.

'Why did you need an excuse?'

Chachi's voice erupted behind them. 'How long does it take to pick up a few amrood? We do have the rest of the stall to pack up.'

Lalloo stood up in a rush, relieved not to answer Fatima's question. Three of the fruit he had gathered in his arms fell to the floor.

'Dur fitay moo, what are you doing to my amrood? They're all bruised. I'll never be able to sell them now!' Chachi Jeera cursed from behind them.

Fatima giggled and leant over to help him, but two fell from her own pile.

Chachi swore loudly behind them again as they stifled their laughter, more and more of the heavy fruit spilling from their arms until Lalloo finally picked up the ends of his kameez, and Fatima piled all the guava in it, enveloping them both in the peculiar musky odour unique to the fat, ripe fruit.

'Well, it certainly took you two long enough. Fatima, give Shahzad a call. He's going to have to come and fetch me on his motorbike; I can't walk back like this.'

Under Chachi's watchful glare, Fatima mouthed her thanks to him, before turning to make the call to her cousin, and Lalloo, feeling deflated at having to leave her, retraced the steps he'd taken earlier on his way to the mohalla. But as he rounded the corner, out of sight of Chachi, who he could still hear grumbling and swearing at the world in general, he couldn't resist turning to look at Fatima and waited, staring at her back. Willing her to turn around. Until finally, she turned and met his gaze, and smiled.

He felt as if he were floating, walking on air the rest of his journey home, not caring how many ditches he had to stumble through or how much diesel fumes he inhaled. She'd looked back at him. Just once.

That *did* happen in Bollywood movies.

Chapter Seven

The next day was a Sunday, Lalloo's day off work. He'd gone to bed thinking of his time with Fatima, replaying everything that had happened over again in his head, but, as he'd fallen asleep, the familiar night terrors of his childhood had soon returned and he'd woken up drenched in sweat. For the brief moments he had been with Fatima, he'd forgotten about his parents and his sisters and the money. He'd forgotten about their daily, never-ending misery, his beautiful brother and everything Jugnu had tried to do for them. But in his sleep, it all came flooding back and hit him with a vengeance. Lalloo had spent the rest of the night tossing and turning on his charpai, feeling every minute pass when he wasn't finding a solution, but unable to think of an answer, afraid of what his parents would do if they found out he didn't have the money.

As soon as the sun rose above the flat-roofed houses and the minaret of the mosque, he dressed and headed out into the fresh air, unable to stay in his room any longer. He was meeting Salman that morning, not far from where he'd first met him all those years ago. Sundays spent together in Sadar bazaar were something he and Salman had shared for years. But this didn't feel like a usual relaxing Sunday and Lalloo wasn't sure he would be good company. He'd promised his father he would get the money, but he'd failed at his two best chances. Asima had asked how much he needed just before Omer had walked in. Had she been about to give him a loan? He'd never be able to get one from the Alams now that Omer had refused. He'd hoped he'd be able to persuade Asima without her husband knowing, but he'd got even that wrong.

His stomach grumbled, reminding him he'd been so carried away by meeting Fatima that he hadn't eaten anything the night before. He marched off to the bazaar, hands rammed in his pockets. Donkey carts were already lined up on the street, piled high with lychees, deep-purple falsay and ripe, juicy watermelons, their colours almost too vibrant in the first rays of the sun. Lalloo bought some lychees, dropped them into his pocket and made his way slowly up the street.

Corrugated tin roofs stretched into the road, providing a canopy overhead. The little patches of sky left visible were criss-crossed with a mess of electricity wires and large shop signs. He could barely see any blue. Most of the walkway was taken up by open-fronted stores spilling out onto the street selling every household good imaginable. There were shops with mounds of neatly folded cloth bought by the yard; a stall hawking everything made of plastic – lotas and buckets and footstools; a MoltyFoam shop with a mattress standing upright by the doorstep; a women's stitched-clothes store, with kameezes hung on hangers all the way across the street, like ghosts of women come to haunt the bazaar. The first time he'd come here as a child, he'd been fascinated. His mother had never been to a shop like this, always sewing her own clothes or wearing second-hand cast-offs. He'd thought if he ever had enough money, he'd buy his mother and sister clothes from a store like this one, stitched to their size, in whatever colour and print they wanted.

Where the shops ended, the food stalls began. He couldn't help but take a detour and walk past the fruit and vegetable sellers to see if he could catch a glimpse of Fatima. She wasn't there; the stall was closed and Lalloo wasn't sure whether to feel disappointed or relieved. He needed to focus on getting the money, not get distracted by a crush that had lain dormant for years. He found a spot in the shade, far enough from the endless games of cricket being played in the field across the road, and hunched down by a low wall to wait next to Chachoo Chai wallah's stall, thinking desperately about his last conversation with the Alams, trying to find a way through that he hadn't seen yet.

By the time Salman arrived, hopping over the wall and lowering himself next to his friend, Lalloo was wondering if there was even a solution at all.

Lalloo called out, 'Chachoo Jee, take pity on a hard-working man and bring us two cups of tea'.

A young boy of about ten popped his head round the stall. 'Happy to take pity, sahib, just don't take credit, I'm afraid.'

The boy reminded Lalloo of his younger self, fending for himself on the streets of Sadar, and he laughed despite himself. 'I like your new assistant, Chachoo – he'll go far.'

Chachoo, the elderly vendor of the tea stall, smiled at Lalloo from where he sat tucked in the shade. 'He's being trained well.'

Lalloo pulled a lychee out of his pocket and began to peel it, piling the shell into a neat little tower by his feet as a hen wandered by, scratching in the dust, trying to peck at it. He swatted it away with an impatient flick of his hand.

'Kia scene hai?' Salman asked, wanting to know the latest chit-chat, once they'd both been served cups of sweet milky tea.

Lalloo shook his head. 'Yaar, I asked my boss for a loan.'

Salman chuckled. 'Your boss? The great Omer Sahib?' He bowed his head in mock deference. 'That guy's such a tight-ass – why would he ever lend you the money?'

'Well, how else am I going to get it?' Lalloo couldn't help snapping at his friend, the one person he had hoped would sympathise. 'I think I was lucky to escape with my job.' Lalloo spat a lychee seed out into his fist and threw it onto the tower of peel.

Salman slurped his tea, looking thoughtful. 'And what now?'

'At the moment, I'm just hoping they don't fire me.' Lalloo took a gulp of his tea, but it tasted bitter after the lychee.

Salman pursed his lips but changed the subject. 'And how'd it go in the market yesterday?' He nudged Lalloo with his elbow, nearly spilling his drink.

Lalloo put down his cup, angry suddenly. 'Yeah, about that, where did you suddenly disappear off to?'

'Well, you didn't need me hanging around being a kebab mein haddi, did you? How did it go? Did you speak to her?' He wiggled his bushy eyebrows up and down.

Usually, this would've made Lalloo laugh, but today he sighed, trying to be patient. 'Yeah.'

'And?' Salman was still looking at him, eyebrows raised.

'And what?' Lalloo shrugged, but then relented a little, remembering the feeling of talking to Fatima. He spoke softly. 'It was . . . it was great. We chatted. She was . . .' He didn't know what to say. Nothing could explain how he felt around her. When her hand brushed his and fireworks went off inside his chest.

Salman was smiling. 'Did you at least get her number?'

The look on Lalloo's face was enough to make Salman howl with laughter. 'Oh, yaar, you never learn.' He clapped a hand on Lalloo's shoulder in commiseration. 'Looks like you're as much in love with her as you ever were, my friend.'

'No, no. Love? I barely know her.' He shook Salman's hand off his shoulder, hot under the collar of his kameez and desperate to change the subject. He didn't have time for this kind of distraction anyway – he needed to get the money for his parents and nothing else was important at the moment. 'Not everyone has a love life like yours, Salman. A new girlfriend every week.'

Once again, Lalloo was aware he was being harsher than he needed to be, but Salman continued laughing, his eyes bright and full of kindness for his tense friend.

'Oh, you mean Sabeen and Sukhi? Yeah, I can't decide between them, yaar.'

And with that, Salman launched into the latest update on his complicated romantic entanglements. His parents wanted him to settle down with a girl from their village, but he couldn't choose between Sabeen, who was married, lived three streets away from him and was very eager for his attention, or Sukhi, who worked as a sweeper in the house next door and was a little more reticent.

Lalloo had known Salman long enough to appreciate that for his friend it didn't matter which woman he chose, if any. It wasn't even the thrill of the chase. It was the endless pondering over the situation that he loved the most. And, usually, Lalloo was glad of the excuse to stop thinking about his own problems. But today all he could focus on was that Salman was right on two counts – Omer would never have let Lalloo borrow money from the Alams, and Lalloo should've asked for Fatima's number when he'd had the chance.

'Arré, look at you with your idle gossip.' A loud nasal voice called out from across the road, cutting short their conversation. Lalloo didn't have to turn around to know who had interrupted them. It was a voice he was unlikely to forget.

The man swaggering towards them wore ripped jeans and a tight T-shirt, with his chest puffed out like a peacock and his dirty toes poking through his chappal. Taari had worked as one of Heera's men and he'd been there that night at the bhatti, the night with the terrible full moon. Lalloo had been horrified to see him in Sadar last year working at Bulla Chacha's halwai shop. Since then, Lalloo had stopped eating halwa altogether. So far, he'd managed to avoid Taari, apart from a few snide comments on the street that had proved he hadn't changed at all. Lalloo should have known that today, of all days, Taari would sniff him out.

'You're like a couple of old women sitting around a fire.' Taari chuckled as he held a cricket bat in one hand, resting its tip on his shoulder. With his other, he tossed and caught a tennis ball.

Lalloo turned his face away, feeling the tea and lychees swill sickeningly in his belly, hoping Taari would pass them by, but he came and stood in front of them, his head cocked to one side. Lalloo could feel Taari's gaze on him like a cattle brand.

'You're Ashraf's son, aren't you? I knew I'd recognised you. You look so much like your brother.'

Lalloo didn't answer, clenching his hands into slow fists under his armpits. Then Taari swung himself around in slow, deliberate movements and sat down on the wall too close to Lalloo, gripping the bat between his knees. Not wanting to give him the satisfaction of a reaction, Lalloo stayed where he was, fighting to keep every muscle in place.

Salman, knowing the effect Taari had on him, leant across and spoke to Lalloo under his breath. 'Remember, he's just a harmless chootia.'

Taari had brought with him a group of men who crowded around them. Wearing scruffy jeans, chappals and T-shirts, a couple of them held cricket bats. Impatient for the game to start and unable to stand still, they jostled each other, knocking Lalloo's tower of lychee peel into the dust. Lalloo felt their proximity like an electric charge in his veins, but it was Taari's looming presence on the wall to his right that all of his attention was centred on. There was a reason he avoided the halwa shop and it was because, over the years, fear had changed to anger in his body. Every time he saw Taari, it seemed there was a rabid creature in his chest, shaking his ribcage and wanting to get out, and it took all of his strength to keep it under lock and key.

'So, which of you assholes is going to try to beat my batting average?' Taari produced a roll of black electrical tape from his pocket and started wrapping it tightly around the tennis ball. He was so close, Lalloo could smell his aftershave and the ugly hint of body odour underneath. Lalloo's heart beat faster, but still he didn't move.

When Taari had wound the entire roll of tape around the ball, transforming the fluorescent yellow to a dull black, he got up and faced them.

'Challo, we're going to the field across the road and we need more players. Since we've got no one else, you women will have to do.' He winked at the men and they laughed. He peered at Lalloo, tossing and catching the ball with one hand.

'We don't want to play.' Salman stood up and took a protective step towards Lalloo.

'And your friend here? Does he play? Does he even know how to?'

The men sniggered.

Taari pushed his face into Lalloo's. 'Your brother used to play, useless as he was. Now, are you going to come or shall I make you dance?'

Then Taari took his bat in both hands, swung it high behind him and brought it up to Lalloo's back in slow motion. He stopped the bat short of touching Lalloo, making a tocking sound with his tongue, as if he had knocked him for six.

It was like an old film reel started to play in Lalloo's head. Flashes of memory from that night all those years ago. Like an old black-and-white Lollywood movie, where it was dark, the only light coming from the fires. Heera had been there, a smug look on his face, rounding up his men and dogs. They had finished what they'd come for. The women were wailing, keening. A younger Taari had hung back, picking up a cloth that was crumpled on the floor and examining it. It was a dupatta – a woman's honour. Seven-year-old Lalloo recognised his mother's dupatta and watched with empty eyes as Taari bent over and wiped a stain from the top of his shoe with it. He sneered, threw it at Lalloo's feet and walked off.

Taari had the same sneer on his face now.

'Are you going to dance, Lalloo? Like we taught your brother?' Taari swung the bat again, rippling the hairs on Lalloo's scalp.

The bat hadn't touched him, but his entire body was on fire. Little Lalloo hadn't known what to do, hadn't had a choice, but Lalloo would not stand for this. Getting up to face Taari, he couldn't think, couldn't breathe. Taari went to nudge him again with the bat, and, without thinking, Lalloo grabbed it and tore it out of his hand, throwing it onto the floor with a crack. Salman was wrong, Taari wasn't just a harmless asshole, he was vile, compounding the misery and terror he and his men had inflicted on Lalloo and his family years ago. Lalloo was furious to know they could do that and get away with it. Taari didn't get a free pass today. Today he was going to regret his bullying.

Taari was momentarily stunned, his eyes flicking from Lalloo to the cricket bat on the ground, to his watching friends and back again, before drawing himself up to his full height. There was a hush around them, and on the periphery of Lalloo's senses, he felt the bazaar come to a halt. People loved a show. They jostled and crowded nearer until Lalloo and Taari were enclosed in a tight circle – a circus ring with the two of them in the middle.

Lalloo's heart beat faster and faster, the pounding pushing him on. He was fighting his survival instincts. Taari was at least six inches taller, well-built and surrounded by his cronies. And yet the drumming inside wouldn't stop. Lalloo stood up straighter.

Lalloo didn't even see Taari move. A blur of fists, the air forced from his body and a tremendous pain in his abdomen. Lalloo dropped to his knees, his vision blurred, gasping as the lychees fought to come up.

'Get up, you coward!' Taari was raging, red-faced, his eyes bulging.

But Lalloo didn't move. In his head, all he could hear was Abu's voice telling him to be good, to do as he was told. He stayed on the ground, his hands in the dirt, forcing each breath into his lungs as the world spun around him.

Taari gave a barking laugh. 'I knew it. You're pathetic, just like your useless brother.' He bent down and whispered in Lalloo's ear, 'Why did he do it, Lalloo? Why did your brother kill that poor mad boy?'

Lalloo shook his head. From the corner of his eye, he could see Salman staring at him, his eyebrows drawn down in dismay. He could feel the crowd shifting and muttering around them. But what Taari said wasn't true. Jugnu had been kind and generous. He could never have harmed Hasnat. Everything Taari said was poison, all lies.

Lalloo staggered to his feet, shaking his head, but Taari came at him, swinging his heavy fists. A sharp blow to the jaw and Lalloo hit the ground again, this time landing on his back. Everything hurt and whatever pounding it was that had driven Lalloo this far seemed to have fled with his breath, with that last hit and the impact of the earth.

'Forgive him, Taari Bhai.' Salman rushed into the ring. 'There must have been a misunderstanding. He didn't know what he was doing.'

Salman's usual unflappable cheeriness had been replaced with a quiet, submissive tone that Lalloo didn't recognise. And he hated it, hated that his friend was having to apologise on his behalf. His father was right – fighting back didn't do any good. It only spread the misery.

Salman draped Lalloo's arm around his shoulders and dragged him up.

'Take your friend and get his head examined.' Taari tapped the side of his forehead. 'That's what it is – he's gone insane. Just like his brother.'

Salman turned to leave, Lalloo a passive weight on his friend's shoulders, shame and pain holding him hostage, but a group of grinning men stood in their way. Salman sidestepped them, but more circled. Draping arms around each other, they had formed a human wall. The air was muggy with sweat and disappointment; their entertainment in the bazaar had come to a premature end. Everywhere were brown faces and grinning white teeth as the friends were jostled back into the centre. Lalloo, noticing his friend's laboured breath, finally stood straight and managed to push his way through the ring, charging between bodies, hanging on to Salman's arm, dragging him through.

Taari shouted after them. 'You're going to end up like your brother, Lalloo! I know your sort. You just don't know your place in life.'

Lalloo and Salman kept going. Countless pairs of eyes were on them as they rushed down the street. It was then that Lalloo saw a familiar face on the edge of the crowd. Fatima's eyes were wide, too wide to have missed what had just happened, and her hand was held to her mouth, making it impossible to read her expression. Lalloo looked away, wishing for the first time that she hadn't returned to Lahore. He realised his two best friends had both been witness to his shame and his chest hurt in a way that had nothing to do with Taari's punches. He walked faster, pulling Salman along, only slowing once they had turned a corner and were out of sight.

Salman walked in silence with him before tightening his arm around Lalloo gently. 'You OK? Are you hurt?'

'Just my pride,' Lalloo murmured, but he pulled away from Salman before walking on.

'OK,' Salman said, running to catch up. 'But I don't understand. What the hell just happened there? Why pick a fight? Why take on a bully like Taari?'

Lalloo was silent. He knew Salman deserved an explanation, but what could he say that would let Salman understand? Lalloo thought back to those nights in the workshop, crying by himself in the dark, sleeping on his own for the first time in his life, mourning Jugnu, desperately missing Ami and Abu and Shabnam, until Salman had appeared and helped paper over that void. Salman knew Lalloo's parents were in the bhatti, that he worked hard and saved money to one day have enough to get them out, but would he ever be able to achieve that dream? Would he ever be free of the bhatti? Free from Heera and Taari, and everything that had happened there.

'I don't understand, Lalloo,' Salman said quietly, as if he could hear his thoughts. 'What did he mean about your brother?'

Jugnu. How could he even begin to explain what Jugnu had been like? What could he say? That he still missed his brother, with a longing that reverberated from deep within and sometimes paralysed him with grief. That he didn't think that feeling would ever go away. Salman knew that Jugnu had died, but Lalloo had never been able to say how that had happened, or Taari's part in it.

When Taari had spoken those lies about Jugnu, he'd felt crazy with grief and red-hot anger. What would Salman say if he told him about Taari's accusations? Would he believe Lalloo when he said Jugnu couldn't have hurt anyone? Or would he think living at the bhatti did strange things to people, that desperation made people do things they wouldn't have done otherwise? Could Salman ever understand?

Salman caught hold of Lalloo's arm and Lalloo swung around to face him.

'Any time anything to do with cricket comes up, you go crazy. Don't think I haven't noticed. Can you just tell me what's eating you up?'

'Just leave me be,' Lalloo said. 'You don't get it.'

'Of course I don't get it!' Salman was shouting now, throwing his arms in the air in frustration, his hair curled in all directions like he'd been pulling at it. 'You won't tell me anything. Like always.'

Lalloo felt sick, the aches in his body were settling in with a vengeance. 'Go home, Salman. There's nothing you can do. Just go home.'

Seeing the expression on Salman's face made him feel terrible, but Lalloo had to escape. He heard Salman swear under his breath as he walked away, but he kept going, desperate to get away from the bazaar and his friend.

When he was sure there was no one around, Lalloo stumbled over to the side of the road and was sick under a tree. Having heaved up his insides, leaning against the tree trunk, his body trembling, he felt as tired as if he'd put in a full day's work at the bhatti.

Every day at the bhatti had been defined by exhaustion – the ache in his shoulders, his legs cramping from crouching hour after hour, his fingers skinned by the rough clay. He clenched his eyes shut and let the memories he kept buried flood through him, filling him up.

*

It had been a scorching hot day and the clay had felt heavier than usual, the mould harder and harder to lift and turn cleanly to ensure the bricks were perfect. Shabnam squatted beside him as usual, passing him the clay, making sure it didn't dry out, helping him fill the mould. A long line of bricks was laid out beside them, a huge lump of wet clay on the other side, waiting to be moulded. It was a never-ending, back-breaking task.

Lalloo threw down the clay and rubbed his eyes with muddy fingers.

'What is it?' Shabnam asked. 'C'mon, we can't slow down.' She took the mould and started to fill it. 'We've only got two hours before sunset and we haven't even done a hundred bricks. Look.' She indicated towards the line of bricks beside them with her chin so she wouldn't have to stop working with her hands.

But Lalloo was bone-tired and hot – too hot. Before he knew it, there were tears trickling down his face, dark splotches falling on the red earth.

'Arré, what's going on here?' Jugnu, always observant, was coming back from the tube well with a bucket of water.

'He's making a fuss, bhaya, so he doesn't have to do the bricks. Just ignore him.' Even at twelve years old, Shabnam had been bossy.

Lalloo tried wiping his face with the back of his hand, but instead smeared dirt on his cheeks. 'I want a kulfi.' That wasn't what he wanted to say at all.

Jugnu set his bucket down and chuckled. 'Kaale bhoot don't cry, even if they want kulfis, na.' His brother crouched beside him, tilted his chin up and studied him a moment. 'Come on.' Jugnu pulled him up. Lalloo didn't understand the look on Jugnu's face, but his brother had made up his mind about something. 'You're tired. Even bhoots need a break sometimes.'

'But if we don't do them, Heera said . . .' Shabnam was worried, frantically kneading the wet clay with her fists, pushing it into the mould.

Jugnu pulled her away from the clay and took his brother and sister by the hand. 'Don't worry, both of you.' He led them towards their hut. 'The bricks aren't going anywhere. Lahore is built from these bricks, you know. As long as they keep building, they're going to want more.'

Abu was still crouched, working on his own row of bricks, but Ami was by their hut preparing the evening meal, and she looked up as they approached.

'You've finished early today? Right, get out your books. We're doing maths after dinner.'

'But, Ami, I *know* how much the kulfi costs when the baba comes with his cart. I already know my numbers.' Lalloo could feel the tears threatening to overwhelm him again as Ami ladled their food into steel plates.

'If we don't go to school, why do we have to keep doing lessons?' Shabnam joined in as she started to eat her roti.

Jugnu spoke softly to Ami as they were eating. Lalloo watched his mother look over at them, then look back at their brother, press her fingers to her eyes and nod. She sighed. 'All right then, both of you go straight to bed after you've finished.'

Lalloo couldn't believe it. He and Shabnam cleared up their dinner plates and laid out the bedding, throwing themselves down, peeping at each other from beneath their sheet, hardly believing their luck.

But Jugnu had already gone out again. Shabnam started to snore in Lalloo's face, and he turned away from her and towards the open door. Lalloo's legs were heavy, his eyelids even more so, but as they closed, he saw his brother crouched beside the row of bricks they had just abandoned, moulding them one after another, finishing the work he and Shabnam hadn't been able to. He started to say something, but was overtaken by blessed sleep.

Later that evening, Lalloo was awoken by a noise outside and snuck out of bed to look. Taari was kneeling by the bricks, beside Abu and Jugnu. Even from this distance, Lalloo could see the nervousness on Abu's face, the trepidation in his body. Taari stood up and shook his head. Abu said something quietly, but Taari raised his voice and it carried to Lalloo's ears.

'I can't count bricks that aren't there. You should've worked harder, old man.'

Jugnu stood beside Abu, his fists clenched, ready to explode, but Abu placed a hand on his arm and they moved away. Lalloo crept back to his bed and pulled the sheet over his head.

*

Back under the heat of the sun, Lalloo opened his eyes, wiped his face with the back of his hand and staggered on, the taste of the lychees acidic in his mouth. In the distance, he could still hear the cricket being played, the thwack of ball hitting bat. That sound would always take him back to the night of Jugnu's death. The little everyday humiliations at the bhatti had been nothing compared to the terror of that night. What Taari and Heera and the men had done that dreadful moonlit night was the reason he'd been abandoned at Rizwan's workshop, far from his family. It was why he'd had to grow up among strangers, learning to fend for himself. He'd escaped the bhatti, but his parents and sisters were still there, and one day he would find a way to free them. Whatever kind of person Jugnu had been, his brother had loved him and protected him. He owed it to Jugnu.

Chapter Eight

At Rizwan's, Lalloo delivered clothes with Salman for two consecutive Sundays, making the most of what his friend called 'the Eid money run'. It was going to be Lalloo's first Eid at the workshop. At home, Ami had always prepared their best outfits, staying up late at night to make sure they were washed and ironed, and laying them out for the morning. But Ami wasn't here now and Lalloo only owned two shalwar kameezes. One was a cast-off given to him by Mumtaz that used to belong to her nephew and was slightly too small for him. The other was the one he'd come to the workshop in, which only had a few mended tears in it, so it was his best. He would wear one of them, night and day, for a few days, while he washed and dried the other one.

The night before Eid, Lalloo washed his best shalwar kameez in a bucket, vigorously scrubbing to get the oil stains out and hung it up to dry.

When he went to the house for his evening meal, Mumtaz shoved a plate in his direction and was about to close the door, but Lalloo pushed his hand back.

'Can I call my parents? Because it's Eid?'

'Hai, hai, I've taken you in, haven't I? Isn't the roti on your plate from my kitchen? Now you want extra phone calls. You think money grows on trees?' There was no mistaking the slammed door as a definite refusal.

Rizwan didn't like Lalloo turning on the workshop lights in the evening because it wasted electricity, so he returned to the workshop, gulped down his food and lay down in the dark, his eyes clenched tight so the tears wouldn't fall, dreaming of his family. Ami making seviyan, frying the vermicelli in desi ghee, stirring the heavy pot to make sure the milk didn't burn. In his dream, there was never any shortage of either desi ghee or milk. In his dream, Shabnam and Ami wore the finest clothes, with bangles on their wrists and henna on their hands and feet, and Abu came to fetch him on a motorbike. He could almost taste the seviyan on his lips, could almost hear Ami's voice come to wake him on Eid morning.

When he woke up on Eid day, he heard Rizwan and Mumtaz setting off in their car, so he ran outside, raising a hand in greeting, but they drove away without a backward glance or a single spoken word, not even an, '*Eid Mubarak*.'

Desperate to get out, Lalloo dressed quickly and made his way to the bazaar. It was alive with Eid festivities, full of people dressed in their Eid best, buying choorian for their wrists and mehndi for their hands, jalebi and ludoo for their bellies. Families with young children gathered around the Hico ice-cream cart as the children chose their favourite flavours.

Chacha Koola at the mithai stall called out to him as he passed. 'Haan, Lalloo. You didn't go home for Eid, then?'

Lalloo shook his head.

'Come then, come and help an old man out. That kutta, Zeeshan, hasn't showed up to work, today of all days.'

Lalloo joined Chacha, serving the rush of customers shouting and jostling, trying to buy a kilo of gulab jamun or some creamy kheer. He carefully helped weigh and pack the sticky, sweet mithai. It was sweaty, tiresome work, and he was on his feet all day, but it was better than being alone in the workshop.

Five long hours later, the crowd had abated and, as well as a paper packet of mithai, and the day's wages, Chacha slipped something extra into his hand. Lalloo stared at his palm. It was only a few rupees, but Lalloo had never had Eid money gifted to him before.

Chacha saw Lalloo's face. 'Get yourself a treat.'

Lalloo grinned, nodded his thanks and, spotting a familiar figure approaching the mithai stall, sprinted to his friend.

Salman was miserable. 'Oh, yaar, I just couldn't get away. Why we have to go to Kamila Khala's house every year, I don't know. Now the cricket's all finished. Did you get to play?'

Lalloo shook his head. 'Come on, let's go to the khokha. Did you get any Eidi?'

'Yeah, loads. But I can't spend all of it — gotta save up.' Salman wanted to buy a car when he grew up and spent a considerable amount of time discussing which make and model it was going to be.

They pooled their money and bought Frost apple juice cartons, Super Crisp barbecue-flavoured crisps and cola candy from the kiosk. They were kings for the day, weighed down with their loot.

The boys carried their booty to the neighbouring field and sat in the shade of a peepal tree, where they unpacked their sweets. A couple of ravenous stray dogs roamed nearby, their ribcages clearly visible, and Salman picked up a stone, keeping a wary eye out, not wanting them too close.

'You shouldn't throw stones at dogs. It's not nice.' Fatima walked up to them from behind the tree, wearing her Eid finery: a brocaded shalwar kameez in a sky blue with a pink dupatta to match the embroidery on her shirt, pink-and-blue glass bangles on her wrists and pretty white sandals.

Lalloo sensed Salman was going to tell her to push off, so he jumped in quickly. 'We forgot to buy Jack 'n Jill toffees. Have you got any?' He indicated towards their haul of sweets.

She grinned. On her shoulder hung a pretty blue bag, which she now opened to reveal a huge stash. Happy to share, she joined them cross-legged under the tree, the three of them chatting merrily about the various merits of their sweets.

'So, I've been meaning to . . .' Salman had just pierced his straw into the juice carton, when he stopped talking and shot bolt upright, holding his body stiff.

'What is it?' asked Lalloo.

Salman tried to say something, but could barely move his lips. His face was a mask of terror. Lalloo grew scared.

Salman's eyes were huge, his back rigid. 'There's something crawling on my back,' he whispered.

Lalloo saw the end of a tail disappearing under the collar of Salman's kameez.

'A chupkali,' said Fatima in her matter-of-fact voice.

The little green geckos chased one another up and down the tree in the yard outside the workshop all day long. They were everywhere.

'What?' Salman was a boy possessed. He sprang up, stomped his feet, bent over, clawed at his back, trying to shake the creature off him. 'Get it off, get it off!' He was hysterical, running around in circles. He wouldn't stand still long enough for them to help him.

Lalloo and Fatima looked at each other and tried hard not to laugh.

'Stop, will you? I can't help if you won't stand still,' said Lalloo.

'Yeah,' Fatima added. 'If you frighten it too much, it'll drop its tail and run off.'

'What? What? I don't want a chupkali tail on me. Get it off before it runs down my shalwar.'

Fatima took the dupatta off her shoulder, flicking it at Salman's back. Lalloo tugged at his sleeve.

When they finally managed to help Salman off with his kameez, the chupkali was nowhere in sight.

'Where is it? Where's it gone?' Salman was shouting, turning round and round like a dog chasing its tail.

'You sure it hasn't gone down your shalwar?' asked Lalloo, making Salman shout and jump again. Lalloo laughed. 'Calm down, yaar, it's gone.' He picked up Salman's kameez where he'd thrown it to the floor, shook it out and spotted the gecko scuttling away, its tail still attached to its body.

Fatima was giggling. 'It was just a chupkali. It wasn't going to eat you.'

The grin still on his face, Lalloo turned around to point out the escaping lizard to Salman, but his friend was slumped over, bent double on the floor. Salman's face was ashen, his breath coming in such loud rasps it sounded like he had something stuck in his throat, something vicious that squeezed his chest and wouldn't let the air in or out. Lalloo stared. Salman's eyes were bulging, tears started down his cheeks.

Lalloo froze, panic turning his limbs to stone, but Fatima seemed to know what to do. She knelt down beside Salman and studied his face. 'Have you got an inhaler?'

Unable to speak, wheezing loudly, Salman pointed at the kameez Lalloo was holding. Fatima took it from Lalloo, pulling from its pocket a small blue device. Salman put it to his mouth and, with shaking hands, pushed a button, breathing deeply.

For a moment, nothing happened, then gradually Salman's tortured breathing and blotchy skin started to return to normal.

'What is that?' Lalloo asked, looking at the device in Salman's hand, aware that if Fatima hadn't been there, he wouldn't have known what to do.

'An inhaler. It looks like he's having an asthma attack. He needs it to help him breathe.'

Salman's complexion had returned to normal now and he looked sheepish. 'My mother makes me carry it everywhere.'

He tried to make light of it, but Lalloo could see he was shaken, could feel his humiliation and fear. He wiped the tears away hastily with the back of his hand while Lalloo turned away and pretended not to see.

When Lalloo turned back around, Salman was standing over his kameez, groaning. It was filthy where it had been stamped on multiple times. Next to the kameez on the floor, equally trampled on, was a scrap of pink – Fatima's dupatta with a large rip down the middle.

'Dado's going to kill me,' Fatima whispered, wide-eyed.

Lalloo didn't understand. 'Can't you fix it?'

They stared at Lalloo as if he were talking another language. 'Fix it? How?'

He showed his friends the pocket of his own kameez, where he'd stitched up a tear with big, uneven stitches just last week, but they looked at him blankly.

'Challo, follow me then,' he said.

Salman squeezed into his dirty kameez, they gathered up their sweets and Lalloo led them to the workshop. The metal doors clanged open and the bright electric lights blinked on, making them squint, but Rizwan and Mumtaz weren't here to object. Next to his rolled-up razai and sheet was his tin box, which contained his only possessions. He'd put a needle and thread from Mumtaz in there for safekeeping.

Lalloo unrolled his bedding so his friends wouldn't have to sit on the greasy floor and slowly and awkwardly stitched up the tear in Fatima's dupatta. The fabric was delicate and crinkly, difficult to sew. Lalloo glanced across at his friends. Fatima was hugging her knees to her chest, gaping at the empty shells of cars staring down at them. 'So, this is where you sleep?' She was looking at the razai, covered in oil from the dirty floor, and the sheet with holes that made up Lalloo's bed. Realising how this looked through their eyes, he was embarrassed for the first time about his living arrangements. He shrugged and continued stitching.

Salman seemed more interested in the half-fixed-up cars. 'When I grow up, I want to have my own car, maybe a Toyota. Not a measly little motorbike. Girls like boys with nice cars.'

Lalloo looked askance at Salman. For an eight-year-old, Salman seemed to know a lot about what girls did and didn't like. He wondered how he'd found out.

Fatima piped up. 'When I grow up, I want to be a doctor.'

Salman nodded. 'You'd be a good one. You can tell them I was your first patient!' He turned to Lalloo. 'What about you?'

The gritty red clay and choking smoke of the bhatti came to mind. All Lalloo wanted was to get his family out of there. But Heera ... the dogs ... Jugnu. It didn't bear thinking about.

'Hey, I know, we can go into business together,' said Salman. 'We'll set up a massive car showroom with a workshop at the back. I'll buy the cars, you fix them up and I'll sell them to the customers.' Salman, Lalloo knew, could talk himself into and out of any situation. He would make a perfect salesman. 'That way, I can choose whatever car I want for myself. And we'll make lots of money.'

Lalloo smiled. Salman always seemed to have it all worked out.

'There you go.' Lalloo held the dupatta out to Fatima when it was finished.

The stitches down the middle were very visible, but he'd tried his best.

Fatima grinned and jumped to her feet. 'I've got to get back, it's so late . . .'

The boys accompanied her back to the bazaar, but as soon as they reached the mithai shop, they ran into Fatima's dado.

'Where have you been?' She roared at them. 'I've been looking all over for you. Who are these boys? How dare you slip away like that – are you out of your mind?'

Fatima slunk to her dado's side without saying a word.

'And what have you done to your dupatta?' Fatima tried to hide it behind her, but her dado pulled at it from one corner and spread it out in full view. In the fading light of day, the crude white stitches popped on the pink crêpe. Lalloo felt his ears burn red. Fatima looked down at the floor.

'You are never to go near these . . .' She cast a withering look in the boys' direction. 'These street urchins again, do you hear me? They will come to nothing and I will not have my beti go the same way.' She did not try to lower her voice and Fatima hung her head as they both walked off together. Fatima didn't look back at them.

Lalloo was mortified. For getting Fatima into trouble, the things her dado had said about them and the way she had looked at them. He was about to slink away back to the workshop when Salman called out to him.

'Arré, what about my kameez?'

'Take it home and wash it in the sink before your mother sees it. You'll be fine.'

Salman shook his head. 'Oh, no you don't, you're not getting off that lightly. You can come home with me and help me clean it.'

Lalloo looked at him, disbelieving.

'Come on. Ami said I could bring a friend over.'

'She did?'

'Sure, you can stay the night. Besides, we've still got all these sweets to finish off.' He pointed to their plastic bag. Lalloo wasn't sure, but the thought of sleeping in a real bed, or even the chance of a meal cooked by a loving mother was too good to pass up. Salman was part of a large family, he knew. What if they wanted him to sit with them as they ate their sumptuous Eid meal? They could all laugh together at some funny joke Salman had cracked. Lalloo would be a model guest, polite and respectful, and Salman's mother would invite him back time and again.

When they arrived at Salman's house, it was dark. Salman took Lalloo over to the side door. He pressed a finger to his lips, opened the screen door slowly and peered inside to check the kitchen was empty. Then he signalled Lalloo to follow him. The door creaked shut behind them. Somewhere inside, a TV blared and people were talking. They were halfway through the kitchen when a woman's voice called out.

'Is that you, Salman?'

Salman froze, his hand shooting out and stilling Lalloo beside him. 'Yes, Ami.'

'Get yourself ready, Bashir Mamoo and Mumani are coming. We'll eat dinner in half an hour.'

Lalloo was about to creep back out the way he'd come, but Salman dragged him through the kitchen and up the stairs, into his room, closing the door shut behind him.

'You said your mother—'

'Don't worry about it, OK. This is my room; she doesn't come up here. Well, mine and Saif's, but he's away tonight, so it's just us.'

Lalloo nodded, remembering the wrench he'd had to dodge at the workshop last week when Saif had hurled it at him.

'Look, I should go. If someone sees me here . . .'

But now they could hear voices from the kitchen and plates clanging. He wouldn't be able to leave without being seen. His escape route was blocked.

Salman changed his clothes and went downstairs for dinner, and Lalloo was left alone. But this was a wholly different kind of aloneness from the workshop. A hum of conversation filtered through from downstairs and the room was washed in the warm glow of the lamp in the corner. There were two beds covered with real mattresses and clean sheets. He sat down on a bed and tested its springiness. A desk, covered in books and papers, was pushed up against one wall. He opened the wardrobe door and peeked inside. It was full of clothes. So many. How many clothes did two boys need? Laughter floated up from downstairs, and many voices. Salman had a big, warm family. Lalloo listened intently, wondering what they were talking about.

He heard the stairs creaking and ran and crouched behind the bed, but it was just his friend, bringing him a feast of naan and kebab, smuggled under his kameez.

'This is all I could sneak up without anyone noticing, sorry.'

For Lalloo, who'd had nothing to eat all day except some mithai and sweets, and who was used to a diet of daal and often stale roti, the sight couldn't have been more welcome. Salman laid the food on the bed and Lalloo tucked in greedily, the boys giggling and shushing each other. When they eventually turned out the light, they got out their remaining sweets and arranged them in even piles on the quilt, talking in the dark, while they discussed the ideal car to own, and, in Salman's case, the one that would attract the attention of the most girls.

'So are you in on the car showroom idea?' Salman was serious. 'We've got to start making plans.'

Lalloo nodded. He had no other options.

Salman frowned. 'I'm not sure what my mother is going to think of this, though . . .' He paused for a moment. 'What about your parents? Are they dead?'

'No, they live in Chakianwallah, in a bhatti.' Lalloo didn't want to give any details.

Luckily, Salman didn't push for more. 'I can't imagine what that would be like – to do whatever I want, go anywhere, nobody telling me to take my inhaler or not to run too fast. Such freedom, yaar!'

Lalloo considered the last few months and said nothing in reply. If this was freedom, he didn't want it. He could feel the ghost of his mother's hand on his cheek, the caress of his father's lips on his forehead, and he eventually fell asleep with secret, silent tears on his lashes.

They would have got away with it. They nearly got away with it. It would've been the perfect end to an almost-perfect day. But Lalloo's head was once again full of fear and fire as he slept. Alone in the workshop, the skeletal cars didn't mind how much noise he made. But here, in Salman's home in the middle of the night, he sat bolt upright on Saif's bed, bathed in sweat, as Salman's parents ran in startled, his friend looking on alarmed as he screamed.

Chapter Nine

As soon as Lalloo arrived at the Alams' the next morning, Asima told him she needed to be driven to Androon Shahar, the old inner city of Lahore. She seemed preoccupied and fidgety, and Lalloo was relieved because it meant she didn't notice the faint bruise beginning to blossom on the side of his face as a result of his run-in with Taari. It helped that the servants were always half invisible to the bibis and sahibs, only called upon to fulfil a task or listen to instruction.

They weren't far from the house when they were caught in a queue of traffic and Asima started complaining noisily from the back seat. Lalloo knew he had to stay calm today, to be the perfect servant. He'd scared himself with his reaction to Taari's provocation yesterday, but the ache in his jaw and bruises on his chest from Taari's fists were a reminder that he couldn't afford to lose control. As they'd set off, Lalloo had briefly wondered whether he should raise the question of the loan again, now that Omer wasn't here. But as Asima muttered to herself about atrocious Lahori drivers, Lalloo knew she was far too agitated today to risk bringing it up. He had to play it smart, be patient. Rather than dwell on the loan, he watched two young women in matching pink shalwar kameezes cross the road a few cars ahead and let himself think of Fatima.

Fatima had always been the calm one, of the three of them. He hated that she had seen his fight with Taari, that after so many years of her grandmother calling him a street urchin, Fatima might actually think he was one.

Seeing Fatima again, talking to her, even briefly after all these years, had shown him how much he'd missed her. It had surprised him, that feeling, crept up on him when his back was turned and startled him, like the games he'd played with his brother when he was younger. Lalloo was used to people leaving him, but here Fatima was, settling back in, close enough to bump into regularly, to be friends with, and yet somehow that didn't feel enough. He wanted more.

Salman was right – this time he had to do something, even if it was just to explain what had happened with Taari. But how was he going to get her alone to even talk to her? It had been hard enough when they'd been teenagers, before she'd moved away. She was always surrounded by other people, other women. Her mother had died when she was little and she lived with her father and her grandmother, the formidable Chachi Jeera. She was an only child, but there always seemed to be other women around – older cousins or aunts staying over. Certainly, when she was younger, there had been no shortage of chaperones to accompany her. She would slip away when she could and they would meet under the neem tree on the edge of the bazaar. Before she'd moved away, he'd lived at Rizwan's, but now he lived two houses away in the mohalla. There must be a way for them to meet.

'What are you waiting for, na? Drive!' Asima's voice snapped him out of his daydreaming. The traffic had cleared up and cars were honking behind him.

Lalloo drove for another hour in the terrible traffic until they got to Androon Shahar, and he started winding his way through the narrow lanes of the inner city. Asima was driving him crazy. She refused to tell him where they were going and her step-by-step directions were hopeless.

'Second left after the mithai shop,' she said, referring to a scrap of paper in her hand, but there was no mithai shop to turn left at.

Here in the old walled city, everywhere around them, modern life intruded upon the ancient. There were no footpaths, and cars competed for space with pedestrians, motorcycles and donkeys. Ancient brick buildings were encroached by bright-blue tarpaulin awnings; ugly black electricity wires hung limply above. A man had set up a chicken shop in the doorway of a crumbling building hundreds of years old, the elegant wooden balconies above him long bricked up. A cage rammed full of live chickens sat next to him as he used what looked like an antique wooden door laid on its side as his chopping board, plucking and cutting the freshly slaughtered chickens, the waste disposed directly into the open sewer running past.

According to Rizwan, who'd always been ready with a history lesson whenever he'd had Lalloo's ear, this was the city of the great Mughals. Rizwan had had old postcards of all the famous sites to show him. The emperors who had built the Taj Mahal in Agra had loved Lahore and had built the massive Lahore Fort, the famous Shalimar Gardens and the Badshahi Mosque. Rizwan would earnestly instruct Lalloo to visit these places, in denial or oblivious to the fact that, unlike Rizwan, Lalloo had had neither the means nor the wherewithal to do so.

He glanced at his boss in the rear-view mirror. Every few minutes, Asima inspected the watch on her large wrist or patted her brow with the folded tissue in her hand.

The roads became narrower and narrower, but Asima kept waving him on with impatient hands. Eventually, he was forced to stop the huge Range Rover ahead of a road that had clearly only been designed to fit palanquins and donkey carts. 'Bibi, the car can't go any further. It won't fit.' High brick walls rose on either side, hedging them in.

'Well, reverse out then. We'll go another way.' She snapped at him, clearly losing her patience.

A donkey stared at Lalloo in his rear-view mirror. He honked his horn, but it didn't move.

'Get out and do something,' Asima said, her voice shrill.

Before her voice could rise even higher, Lalloo opened his door, careful not to scratch it against the wall, and squeezed out of the car.

An elderly man sat on his haunches on a cart fastened to the donkey, his hands holding a light whip in front of him like a fishing rod.

'Arré, bhai, move out of the way.' Lalloo gestured at him and his donkey, flapping his arms as if shooing them backwards.

The man stared through Lalloo like he hadn't heard him.

Lalloo took a step closer, his voice rising in frustration. 'You've got to move!'

'It's an animal, sir jee – my donkey won't go backwards. The car will have to move forwards.'

The man was as obstinate as his beast, eager to spite the flashy car wallahs.

Lalloo felt a bead of sweat trickle down the back of his neck. This was ridiculous. If he carried on and scratched the car, he would get blamed for any damage, even if it were Asima's fault for getting them into this mess. He tried one more time. 'There's no room, bhai. If you move the cart slightly . . .'

But the man turned his face away as if any suggestion of his moving was a profanity, and then a rickshaw pulled up behind the cart, beeping its horn. The driver leant out, impatient with the hold-up.

Lalloo hesitated, then climbed back into the cool, air-conditioned Range Rover, pulling in the side mirrors.

'Well? Is he going to move?' Asima asked. She looked worried, her hands clutching the damp tissue in her hand.

Lalloo shook his head. 'We'll have to try to fit through.'

A crowd had gathered around them. A young man stood in front of the car waving his hand haphazardly to direct Lalloo forward, providing more hindrance than help. Lalloo did his best to ignore him.

As they inched ahead, Lalloo craned his neck from side to side, moving the car a millimetre to the right or left. But despite his best efforts, he heard the screeching of metal against brick – a sound that lodged itself between his neck and shoulder blade. He gripped the steering wheel tighter and sucked in his breath, willing the car to breathe in too.

It was only when they reached the next square that he could get out and assess the damage. Asima wound down her window to peer at the side of the car. There were a handful of scrapes at least six inches long on the back door, angry and vivid against the shiny metalwork. He wiped his forehead with the back of a shaky hand. Any damage to the car was his responsibility.

'Oh, it doesn't look too bad. You'll have to take it to the mechanic when we get back,' Asima said.

He stared at her, shocked. Once, when a bicycle wallah had come within an inch of the car, she had rolled the window down and unleashed a torrent of abuse at him. Now she spoke as if she just wanted the car washed, but Lalloo noticed she wouldn't meet his eyes. Not for the first time, he wondered what she was up to and where they were going.

'Come on, let's get moving. It must be somewhere close by now.'

'It's no use, bibi, I can't find this place. We'll have to ask someone.'

She sighed as if this were all his fault. 'All right then, call that boy over.'

Lalloo beckoned a young boy selling balloons tied to a long stick. He ran over and thrust a bright-pink balloon into Asima's open window.

'No, no, we don't want any balloons.' Lalloo pulled the boy away from the window. 'We're here for directions.'

Asima spoke as softly as she could, as if she didn't want anyone to overhear. 'We're looking for Pir Wali Ullah. Where can we find him?'

A pir? A holy man who would claim to solve all a person's problems? Lalloo was stunned. He'd never thought someone with so much money would resort to going to a pir. But it explained why she was being so secretive. Omer hated pirs. He thought the spiritual men were all phoneys and fraudsters. He wouldn't be happy if he found out his wife had spent the last hour driving around searching for one.

The boy pointed them towards a brick hut with a corrugated tin roof at the bottom of the street and Asima placed a ten-rupee note into his waiting palm. Lalloo was intrigued. He'd never been to a pir before. As they pulled up outside, a sentry stood guard with a rifle casually slung over his shoulder. A trestle table was laid out, its Formica top stained and chipped, and beside it sat a man on a plastic folding chair, his feet propped up on the table, the gatekeeper who determined whether people were allowed in to see the pir or not.

Lalloo cut the engine and waited, but Asima didn't get out right away.

'This looks like it, bibi.'

'Yes. You wait in the car – don't go anywhere.' She hesitated again and then wrapped her chadar around her like full-body armour before slowly opening the car door.

As Asima approached, the gatekeeper tapped the metal safety-deposit box lying open in front of him with a ballpoint pen. Asima took out her purse and dropped a thousand-rupee note into the box. He tapped the box again, this time a little louder. Asima dropped another note, and another, before she was allowed to push aside the dirty curtain hanging in the door frame and walk in.

Asima spending three thousand rupees so casually wasn't out of the ordinary; she loved throwing her cash about. But this wasn't absent-minded spending on clothes or handbags. Whatever it was that had made her come to a pir, it had to be something important, something she would risk Omer's wrath for. Women went to these saints when other avenues proved futile. Praying for a baby boy, a new job, better health. But Asima had everything, and anything she didn't have she could buy. Lalloo couldn't imagine what she could possibly need from a pir.

While Lalloo waited for Asima in the car, a mosquito found its way inside and buzzed around his ear. He swiped at it in vain. No matter how much he lashed out, it returned to bother him, dogged in its mission. Lalloo waited, tapping the steering wheel, staring at the curtain that doubled as a door to the pir's hut. It'd been over three-quarters of an hour already. She needed to hurry up if there was to be any chance of getting the car fixed today. The mosquito landed on his arm. He froze, waiting for it to settle. Just as it was about to draw blood, he reached out and slapped his forearm. He was too late. His hand came away smeared in dead mosquito and the bright blood the insect had already greedily sucked.

*

Lalloo had discovered what a pir was not long after his family had moved to the bhatti. During the day, while they worked, they would hear strange noises from the hut three doors down. Sometimes a loud bang, other times a wail, often a low keening, as if from an animal in pain. It had been his first real inkling that the bhatti was putrid, festering.

'What is that noise, Ami?' He tried asking his mother, but she told him to mind his own business and keep working.

He discussed it with Jugnu, but his brother was as clueless as he was. Lalloo would often take a circuitous route when he went to fetch water, around the front of the huts to see if he could sneak a glimpse of the wounded animal. But it was always dark inside and he never dared go past at night when a lamp was lit, too afraid to admit to himself he was scared.

One evening as the days were getting hotter, they sat outside on the charpai after work. Jugnu was preparing Abu's hookah for him, stuffing the tobacco inside and lighting it. He glanced over his shoulder and took a few prohibited, exploratory puffs before winking and passing the pipe to Lalloo.

'Wanna try, kaale bhoot?'

Lalloo giggled and inhaled long and deep, just like he'd seen his brother do. He immediately fell into a fit of coughing so bad Jugnu had to thump him on the back, quickly looking towards the hut in case Abu heard them.

They hadn't met many of their neighbours, but they knew Chachi Bushra lived next door. As luck would have it, she came out at that very moment.

'He's a bit young for Abu's hookah, eh?'

Jugnu blushed the colour of jamun and Chachi laughed.

'Don't worry, I won't tell.'

A sudden shriek pierced the air. Dusk had fallen and darkness was rapidly descending. They all stopped still.

'What animal is that, Chachi? We've heard it before – it comes from that hut.' Lalloo pointed out into the murky gloom.

She looked towards the ground and shook her head. 'It's another awful story in this place.'

Jugnu shuffled over on the charpai and offered her the pipe of the hookah. She settled herself down beside them, inhaling deeply before she spoke. 'The Ranas live over there with their son, Hasnat. They moved here when he was a baby and now he's about thirteen.' She grew silent.

The brothers looked at each other, puzzled. Their neighbour gazed up at the sky, blowing out smoke rings. The boys waited patiently.

'What happened to him, Chachi?' Jugnu asked.

'This bhatti, it does strange things to people. It's certainly not for children. He's gone mad, bechara. Completely paagal. It started a few months ago – every time they let him loose, he ran to the bricks and hit his head against them. Last time, he cracked his skull so hard, it split open, blood spilling everywhere, and it took two grown men to restrain him. Now they keep him tied up for his own safety. A thick metal chain like the one they use for the donkey.'

'Why do they have to keep him tied up?' Lalloo asked quietly.

Chachi leant even closer, whispered her next words carefully.

'They say he's been possessed by a jinn.'

Lalloo's eyes were wide, simultaneously wanting to know more and wanting to shut his ears against this new knowledge. Wanting to go back to thinking the noise was just a wounded baby goat. He'd heard stories about jinns. They were very powerful invisible beings that usually shied away from humans. But if one chose to possess a person, any resistance was futile. The thought of having to live next to this mad, possessed child was terrifying.

'What are they going to do about him?'

'They've borrowed more money from the bhatti owner. They're going to have him seen by a pir.'

'Can they cure him with taaweez?' Jugnu asked, pointing to the amulet Chachi was wearing, and Lalloo peered at the silver charm on a thick black string tied around her neck.

Chachi shook her head vehemently. 'Not amulets on their own, but a powerful pir has other means to drive a jinn away. A pir who knows how to control jinn can extract him from a child.'

Lalloo wanted to know how, and why, and what would happen to the mad boy and the jinn, but at that moment Ami marched out of the hut, having clearly overheard the last of their conversation, and frowned at Chachi Bushra sitting on Abu's charpai, smoking his hookah. Chachi had the grace to look embarrassed and immediately stood up, quickly said her salaam and left.

Ami tutted at her retreating back, muttering and shaking her head. 'This absurd talk of jinns and pirs . . . the poor child.' She shooed the boys away, 'No more of this gossiping. Go get the beds ready.'

Lalloo hurried into the hut as the clanging of chains echoed from three doors down, his head full of images of a wild boy with matted, bloody hair tied to the wall with shackles around his neck.

*

When Asima reappeared, she was in a hurry, agitated. She was holding a silver taaweez close to her chest, its black cotton string dangling through her fingers. Lalloo held open the car door for her to climb inside. She looked smaller than usual, with hunched shoulders and hair limp from the heat. He almost pitied her, until he remembered what he could buy for Shabnam for the price of that taaweez alone, and the feeling faded.

The way back to the Alams' house was fraught, with Asima tutting and cursing under her breath. The traffic was heavy and a couple of roads were closed, which meant they were going to be late for Asima's friends' arrival at the house. Asima regularly entertained during the day when Omer was out and the cost of the food alone made Lalloo's eyes water, let alone the decorations – fresh flowers that would wilt within hours, garlands strung across the garden and elaborate displays of sweet treats for guests to pick at, most of it going to waste.

When they eventually swung into the drive, four cars were already parked outside. Asima heaved herself out of the car and waddled into the house before he'd even had a chance to turn off the engine and help her out.

He was about to drive out again to take the car to the workshop when Guddo came rushing into the garden through the outside gate, clutching a brown paper bag, breathing heavily. She saw him and tapped on the front-passenger-seat window with raised eyebrows. Lalloo drew down the window and heard laughter and the chink of teacups drifting from the house. The air was oppressive and still without a hint of a breeze, as if it were expecting something, waiting.

Guddo leant into the car, dropping the paper bag on the passenger seat so she could catch her breath, one hand on her heaving bosom.

'Where've you been?' he asked her in surprise.

'Mrs Khan wasn't expected, but she turned up anyway, and with two of her daughters-in-law, and now I don't have enough chicken patties for everyone.' She waved a hand at the paper bag. 'Samosas. But, more importantly, where've you been? This lot have been waiting ages.' She jerked a thumb towards the house.

Lalloo shrugged. 'Didn't she tell you?' Guddo usually knew everything happening in the house.

'No. She wouldn't tell me where she was going this morning, just that she'd be back well before her friends got here. Although with friends like Mrs Khan, who needs enemies?'

He angled further towards her, whispering, 'She went to see a pir. She got a taaweez.'

Guddo drew back, puzzled but thrilled at the titbit. 'A pir? Are you sure? What does she want with a taaweez?'

'Don't know, but something's definitely going on. You know how much Omer hates them. I think that's why—'

A loud whistling sounded – the call bell for the servants. Guddo was needed in the house.

She sighed. 'That'll be Mrs Khan wanting a throne for her daughter-in-law to sit on.' She turned to go and called over her shoulder, 'We need to discuss, Lalloo. More tomorrow?'

As the door closed behind Guddo, snatches of conversation drifted outside.

'Oh, yes, there's the new place that's opened up on M.M. Alam, around the corner from Bhaya's Kebab.'

'No, really, I mustn't, I have to think about my diabetes, you know...'

'Let me go and get Yasmin to introduce you; she's doing the new advertising campaign for Lux soap, na.'

It had been a long day and Lalloo still had to take the car to be fixed. About to start up the engine again, he saw Guddo had forgotten the paper bag of samosas on the passenger seat in the car. Sighing, he got out. He walked around to the back of the house, slipped in through the back door leading to the kitchen and put the samosas on the kitchen counter. Guddo wasn't in there, but there were voices from the little room next to the kitchen used as a store. That was strange – the store was tiny. Lalloo leant in.

'You've got a taaweez? For Daddy? And what's that going to solve?' It was Yasmin.

'Shh... keep your voice down.' That was definitely Asima.

Then Yasmin said something in a low voice that Lalloo couldn't catch.

'I've told you, I'm trying to fix this,' her mother said in a pleading voice. 'For the family.'

'This is crazy!' Yasmin wasn't even trying to keep quiet. 'You know better than to believe in this mumbo-jumbo. And the other stuff is all in your head. I don't believe you.'

The door burst open and Lalloo leapt back as Yasmin marched into the kitchen past him and out of the room without another word. Asima was left framed in the open doorway of the storeroom, a naked light bulb hanging from the ceiling above, the shelves behind her full of sacks of rice, flour, potatoes and daals, packets of spices and stacks of eggs. She spotted him and sauntered into the kitchen, as if it were entirely normal to be arguing in the storeroom with her daughter.

'Bibi, I'm just going to take the car to the workshop.' He turned to go in a hurry, not wanting to get caught up in whatever mother and daughter were quarrelling about.

She called out, stopping him in his tracks. 'Wait a minute.'

He turned back slowly. She seemed to be thinking.

'I have a job for you.' She paused. 'Tomorrow evening at five o'clock, Omer Sahib will go somewhere. I want you to follow him, but you mustn't be seen, I'm sure you can arrange something. Find out where he goes, and, more importantly, who with.'

He glanced at her briefly, not sure what to say. He often did extra jobs for Asima and Yasmin, but he knew that this was different. Omer would fire Lalloo on the spot if he knew Lalloo was following him.

'If you come back with the information I'm looking for,' she continued, 'I'll give you that money you wanted. As long as you keep this discreet – no one must know. But I will need proof of what Omer is up to, not just your word.'

She spoke defiantly, as if daring him to challenge her on the fact she was going behind her husband's and daughter's backs. But she must've known he would do anything for that money. He didn't care what Asima thought Omer was up to. If it meant he could get the money for his family, he would have to do it.

*

On his way home from work, Lalloo took the car to the workshop in Sadar. Rizwan's workshop, the one he'd grown up in, had shut down when Rizwan died, but this one was run by the friendly Abdul, and the Alams liked to use it for their cars.

Abdul, elbow-deep in the bonnet of a Honda Civic, took one look at the Range Rover and shook his head. 'I've got two of my boys off sick and three cars need fixing before yours. Give us a hand, will you? I can give you the usual rate.' Everyone in Sadar knew Lalloo had worked at Rizwan's for much of his childhood and that he'd take any extra work that came his way.

Lalloo rolled up his sleeves and stepped towards the open bonnet of a nearby Toyota Corolla. He started on oil changes and brake checking of the cars in front of his in the queue and it was like he'd never been away. When he'd first come to Rizwan's as a boy, it had taken him a while to accept Abu wouldn't be coming to fetch him. He was diligent and hard-working, just like Abu had told him to be, and quickly learnt the basic tasks around the workshop. Eventually, he stopped waiting for his father to pick him up and found some comfort in the whir of machinery, the hum of the fans. In the tormenting heat of the Lahori summer, he learnt to ignore the mechanics teasing him. The smell of the engine oil, the cool metal of a spanner in his hands, the reassuring hiss of air in the tyres became his new existence. And after all these years, that feeling had never left him.

As Lalloo inspected a cracked fan belt, he remembered the plan he and Salman had made as children: the workshop they were going to open together, the cars they were going to fix and sell on – their scheme to make lots of money. Salman had wanted to be able to afford any car he liked, but for Lalloo, for as long as he could remember, he'd known he needed to make money to buy his family's freedom. Now, with this new assignment from Asima, he'd finally be able to make a start. With this wedding, he would be getting Shabnam out.

An hour and a half later, Abdul came and slapped him lightly on the back, pulling a few bills from his pocket and putting them in Lalloo's hand.

'Challo, bhai, thanks for your help. I'm going to have to shut up shop now, but I'll come in early and make sure your car's ready for you tomorrow first thing.'

Lalloo nodded his thanks. 'I'll pick it up on my way to work.'

Chapter Ten

That evening, Lalloo returned home tired but hopeful. He had another chance to get the money and this time he would have to make it work. He turned down the narrow galli and into the mohalla. The sun was low in the sky and the tall buildings with flat open rooftops cast long shadows. There were about twenty houses in the mohalla rammed together, jostling for space in a semicircle around the mosque in the central courtyard. As his room came within sight, he couldn't help but look towards Chachi Jeera's house, only two doors down from his, with just a house and a galli separating his home from Fatima's.

There was a lone figure on the roof of her house. He stared up at the yellow shalwar kameez. Was yellow still Fatima's favourite colour? He hardly knew her any more, but, if that was her, what were the chances of finding her alone again? He could explain what had happened at the bazaar with Taari. With a plan for Shabnam's wedding, and after spending the afternoon in Abdul's workshop, fixing broken things, Lalloo was confident Fatima would understand. She had never listened to her grandmother's opinion of him as a child, always preferring to make up her own mind. When he'd laughed with her in the bazaar the other day, it'd felt like the old days, precious moments snatched together under the neem tree. He had to see if they still had that.

Lalloo hurried into his building and ran through the open courtyard to the back, through to the stairs that led up two flights to the flat rooftop.

'Arré, where are you off to? Which shaitan ka bacha is chasing you now?'

Lalloo stopped halfway up the stairs, peering down. He should have known. It was his landlord, Kaka, appearing like a mean-spirited jinn when he was least wanted. He lay stretched out on a charpai in the courtyard, watching Lalloo.

'Nowhere, Kaka Jee. Just getting some fresh air on the roof. The weather is beautiful.'

'Well, don't throw yourself over the top – you've still got this month's rent to pay!' Kaka cackled at his own joke.

Lalloo had to be careful. Kaka was the biggest gossip in the mohalla. If he saw Lalloo talking to Fatima, word would get around quicker than the local stray cat slurping up milk left out to cool and Lalloo wouldn't stand for people saying nasty things about Fatima. He forced himself to walk the rest of the way up. Two long flights of stairs later, he got to the low iron gate separating himself and the roof. Would she still be there? He walked through, stood away from the front of the house so he couldn't be seen from the street below, and looked across.

She was two rooftops away across the alley, but it was her, and she was alone. As if sensing him staring, she turned to look at him. She was so close, he could see the strands of the yellow paranda plaited through her hair, almost feel the grains of daal running through her fingers as she sieved them for stones. And yet, with the alleyway between them, they may as well have been separated by the Indian Ocean.

He didn't think much about what he did next. Of course, the children did it all the time, jumping fast and high, chasing paper kites cut from their string, but he hadn't done anything like this in years. He stepped back a few paces, without letting himself focus on the three-feet-wide alley between the houses, or the three-storey drop down. Without letting himself think that this time if he fell, there wouldn't be any black sludge to catch him. No mother on the other side to smother him with Dettol and love. He took his run-up and kicked off against the top of the wall, propelling himself up in the air. For a couple of seconds, he wasn't sure he'd make it. Then he crashed in an ungraceful heap on the neighbouring roof, still in one piece, his heart banging.

Lalloo still felt like he was flying, unsure of his landing but completely alive. He looked up at Fatima. There were no more alleyways to cross. A waist-high wall was the last thing between them.

'Well, that was incredibly stupid.'

She was halfway across the roof, having stepped towards him, and she was smiling incredulously. Lalloo vaulted over the wall towards her, his heart soaring.

'How else was I supposed to talk to you alone?'

'And *this* was the only way of doing it? Jumping the roof?'

Lalloo laughed. 'Well, I hoped if I got hurt, you could patch me up.'

Fatima raised an eyebrow, no longer smiling. Even with her arms crossed in front of her, her face stern, she was beautiful. 'Is that why you've been picking fights? I'm not a doctor yet, you know.'

'I wish you hadn't seen that.' He looked down at the floor, even now his face burning.

'Are you OK?'

Her voice was suddenly so gentle, he looked up at her in surprise and saw only kindness there. Just as suddenly, he was finding it hard to swallow. Not trusting himself to speak, he nodded at her. People didn't often ask if he was OK.

He finally managed to clear his throat and asked, 'So, are you back for good?'

'Yes, because of Abu's job, but also Dado is getting old. She needs to be in Lahore so she can be close to my aunts and the rest of the family. I worry about her now.'

He wondered what it would be like to have so much family to fall back on. To have someone care for you in times of need.

'How's her ankle?' he asked, remembering the tenderness with which Fatima had examined it. She would make a great doctor.

'It'll get better, if she finds the time to rest it. She may be getting old, but she hasn't lost any of her spark. And I think I know what she'd say if she knew you'd snuck up on the roof to talk to me.'

Fatima's eyes sparkled with that mixture of amusement and mischief which he'd always found captivating.

'But what does her granddaughter think of it?'

She propped one hand up on her hip. 'Oh, I'm very capable of protecting myself from unwanted visitors.'

'How?' Lalloo was intrigued to know what defence mechanism she had in place up here and looked about him.

There was a chair with a table nearby and on it lay a large thali of daal, which she had been sieving for stones by hand – one of the many endless household chores that had always consumed his mother's time. And because it was Fatima, she also had in front of her a large open book. He inched closer and saw complicated pictures of what must be a person's insides, with arrows pointing to each part. It had to be a medical textbook, but Lalloo couldn't tell much more.

After Lalloo's family had moved to the bhatti, school had been non-existent. He could read newspaper headlines and road signs, and messages on his phone, but, despite Ami's efforts, not much more than that. He knew Fatima was clever – she'd always been studious and bookish, and she had been endlessly encouraged by her grandmother and her father – but it suddenly felt more real to see her learning something that he would never be able to understand. He felt unsure of himself again, a lowly driver talking to a soon-to-be doctor. As children, they'd had the bazaar, and games, and helping Bulla Chacha with his goats, and hiding from the many adults in her life, and their differences had felt less important than exploring the city together. But what if it bothered her now?

He was about to comment on the pictures in the book when she dragged an object out from behind the chair and waved it in his face. It was the wooden leg of an old charpai, squat, heavy and two feet long. She had to use both hands to lift it and showed him how she would swing it at a would-be assailant. Lalloo forgot all about the book and burst out laughing.

He held both hands up in mock-surrender, still chuckling. 'Have you ever used that on somebody?'

She smiled, dropping her makeshift weapon. 'No, but I've threatened the stray tomcat with it.'

'You could be Maula Jatt from the old Punjabi movies,' he said, referring to the macho, moustachioed, rifle-wielding hero of old.

Fatima threw her head to one side, posing dramatically. 'I used to love those films.'

'So did I. Salman and I used to sneak into the cinema if we ever had the money.'

'Yeah, I was never allowed to go.'

It didn't surprise him. Any self-respecting family wouldn't have let their daughter go near the corrupting environment of the cinema.

'I know, but cinemas are much better now.' He paused. 'The new Kareena Kapoor movie is out tomorrow. Want to come see it with me?'

Where had that come from? How had he just plucked up the courage to invite Fatima to the cinema? But when he wasn't worrying about it, talking to her felt easy and natural. He held his breath and waited. Her eyes were twinkling fiercely. She tilted her head and looked him up and down for what felt like an age, piercing him with her gaze. Did it matter to her that their lives had grown so far apart?

'OK, then.'

He felt like whooping for joy.

'Fatima, who are you talking to up there?' Her grandmother's voice came too loud and too close from below.

Lalloo flinched and fell into a crouch on his knees so as not to be seen from the floor below, but stumbled slightly and had to catch himself on his hands. Fatima snorted and he grinned back at her unapologetically. If her grandmother saw them together, that would be an end to their plans before they'd even started, and the last thing he wanted was to get Fatima into trouble, even if it meant crawling back off this roof.

'Your ears are ringing, Dado! I'm just sieving the daal.' She flashed a mischievous smile at Lalloo.

'Aren't you finished yet? Are you going to take all day over a handful of daal?'

Fatima made a face. 'Coming, Dado!'

It was only then that Lalloo remembered tomorrow was the day he was going to be following Omer. He could arrange the cinema for another day.

'Oh, about the film . . .' he said in a whisper.

Fatima turned to him and whispered back, 'Yes, you don't even know how lucky you are. Dado is going to my aunt's house tomorrow and my cousin is staying here with me. I should be able to make an excuse and slip away in the evening.'

He didn't want to put her off and the film was always a bit late in the evening. He should be able to do both things: follow Omer and then make his way to the cinema.

Lalloo nodded and pulled out his phone to get her number. He wouldn't make the same mistake again. He tapped at his screen, but it didn't respond. No amount of frantic tapping would awaken it – it was completely dead. Desperate, he ransacked his pockets again. He found a pen but no paper. As she turned to go, he caught Fatima's hand and she swung around in surprise. Still on his knees, he silently lifted his sleeve and offered her the pen. She made him wait while he knelt before her. Then she took it from him and wrote on his arm.

'Fatima? There's plenty of other work to do in the house. You know I can't do anything with this ankle like it is.'

Fatima pulled away quickly, grabbing her thali of daal and her book, and ran down the stairs. He listened to the receding footsteps and the long list of chores Chachi Jeera gave her granddaughter.

A cacophony of green parakeets broke cover, fluorescent against the rapidly darkening sky. Lalloo couldn't believe it. Tomorrow he was going on his first real date with Fatima. Tomorrow he was going to earn the money to get his sister married and then, who knew, maybe one day it could be him? The birds squawked and wheeled about; the entire sky belonged to them.

When all was quiet downstairs, he strode to the edge of the roof.

His ankle hurt but he didn't care. He had Fatima's phone number on his arm and the promise of a date in his heart, and that alone would make him fly.

Chapter Eleven

Lalloo got back to his room still not daring to believe what he'd arranged for tomorrow. He plugged his dead mobile into its charger. So much had happened in just a day; he was tired. About to throw himself down on his charpai, he noticed his screen light up. There were two missed calls from Abu.

He'd bought Abu a phone a few years ago in case of emergencies and even now when Abu called, Lalloo always answered with trepidation, for some reason always expecting bad news.

Hands shaking slightly, he sat down on his creaking charpai and rang Abu back, his stomach churning.

'HELLO!' Abu's voice boomed down the line.

Abu always shouted out his words on the phone. He didn't believe the large distance between Lahore and Chakianwallah could be adequately covered using a soft voice.

Lalloo smiled, holding the mobile out at arm's length. He imagined Abu's hookah gurgling, Ami boiling the water for tea. 'Assalam-u-alaikum, Abu. Is everything OK?'

'Haan, beta.' Abu paused and coughed. 'I got worried when you wouldn't answer.'

Lalloo's smile grew, thinking about what he'd just been up to. Now that he knew Abu wasn't calling for an emergency, he felt only slightly guilty for being distracted by Fatima. 'My phone was out of battery; I just charged it.'

'Well, it's good to hear from you.' Abu coughed again. 'And how is your job going?'

'Very good. And you're not to worry, Abu.' Lalloo spoke quickly, knowing the anxiety that would be preying on his father's mind. 'I've spoken to my boss and tomorrow I'm going to do a special job for her. She's promised me the money for Shabnam's wedding.'

'So they're OK with giving it to you? There's no problem, is there?'

There was another pause while Abu's wracking cough overtook him for several moments. It seemed to be getting worse and worse. The only medical care available at the bhatti was the fake pharmacist who came along once a fortnight on his bicycle with a carrier bag full of expired medicines for sale. Maybe, Lalloo thought, he should buy some cough medicine and take it to the bhatti next time he went.

When Abu spoke again, his voice was raspy. 'I've said I don't want you to risk your job with this. We only have a week left and I can go see Heera tomorrow if needed.'

'No, no, absolutely no need to worry. I'll come by as soon as I have it, then you can start all the preparations.'

'I'm so . . .' Abu's voice broke and he was unable to continue for a moment. Lalloo gripped his phone and swallowed, hard. After a while, Abu cleared his throat. 'I'm so glad, beta. I was worried for a while there. But you've made life much easier for us. Don't think I don't know what sacrifices you are making, even when you don't live at the bhatti.'

Lalloo shook his head, unable to reply. If only he could do more than this, a mere sticking plaster on their life. If only he could actually get them out of that hellish place.

Finally able to speak, he asked after Ami and to speak to his sisters. He could hear voices calling in the background, but they were busy. Consoling himself that he would see them again soon, as soon as he had the money, he said his salaam to Abu and hung up.

He lay back on his charpai, considering the task Asima had given him. He had to follow Omer's car without being seen, so he couldn't take the Range, which was far too easy to spot. A rickshaw or a taxi wouldn't work either, as they might not be able to keep up with Omer's driving. He couldn't chance this – Asima wouldn't give him an opportunity like this again. So, something discreet, fast and nimble. Lalloo knew just what he needed, but given how he'd treated Salman recently, he wasn't sure he'd be able to get it. He knew an apology was in order. Taking a deep breath, he dialled Salman's number, but it went straight to voicemail.

*

The following morning, on his way to work, he stopped at Abdul's workshop to pick up the Range. Salman hadn't called back yet and he decided to go to his friend's shop once he had picked up the car. It might make him a little late for work, but he needed to know he had a plan for this evening.

'Haan, Lalloo, it's ready. Let me get the keys for you.' Abdul went to fetch the keys and Lalloo spotted the Range and walked over to it. True to his word, Abdul had fixed the scratches – you couldn't even tell they'd been there.

While he was waiting, he looked over at the Hiluxes, Altos and Corollas in various states of disrepair in the workshop. In the corner, covered in a sheet, was what looked like a wreck of a car. He'd seen it yesterday and hadn't got round to asking Abdul about it. He was about to do that now when Salman walked in, whistling. 'So, Abdul. What do you think of it?'

Abdul shrugged at Salman and looked towards Lalloo. 'Have you seen what your friend has got up to this time?' He handed the Range Rover keys to Lalloo and walked off, leaving the friends to stare at each other warily.

Salman looked uncomfortable, but he spoke first. 'Yaar, I wanted to say sorry—'

'What are you apologising for?' Lalloo held his hands out. He had never imagined that Salman might think he was the one who had done something wrong. 'I've been lousy. I got into that fight and then you had to clean up after me. I'm sorry, I've got a lot going on at the moment with Shabnam's wedding, but I shouldn't have taken it out on you.'

'I know, yaar, and I should've realised that, instead of laughing at you.'

Lalloo knew that he could have left it there. Salman was relaxed and open again; he'd never been one for holding a grudge.

'Well, to tell you the truth, it's not just that,' he said, instead. 'Taari winds me up about... about what happened at the bhatti... with Jugnu.' He still, after all these years, found it incredibly difficult to talk about, and, as much as he knew Salman deserved an explanation, he wasn't sure he even knew how to say it aloud.

Sensing his friend's discomfort, Salman held both hands up in a peace offering. 'Honestly, you don't have to... it's fine.'

The two friends looked at each other as the early-morning sunlight slanted into the workshop, dust motes dancing between them, and smiled.

'So what's this, then?' Lalloo tilted his head towards the covered car.

'You know the Khawaja family?'

'Who?' The name sounded familiar, but of course Salman knew most of the families who lived in Sadar.

'Live in Thandi Galli. Have a seventeen-year-old son?' Salman continued, seeing Lalloo's blank expression. 'Anyway, they had an old Suzuki Swift and their son managed to crash it into a tree while he was learning to drive. Luckily, he walked away unscathed, but he's now decided he doesn't want it, so they were selling it.' Salman walked across the workshop floor and whipped the cover off with a flourish. 'She's a real beauty.'

Lalloo stared. The body was badly dented all over, but especially at the front. The windscreen was shattered and a door had been sawn off. 'Hate to break it to you, but I wouldn't go so far as to call it a beauty.'

'Arré, yaar, you've got to look at the potential,' said Salman happily, his expression exactly the same as it'd been at seven, or thirteen, or seventeen years old, dreaming up wild schemes that often got them both into trouble. 'This is the start of our showroom business.'

'How much did you pay for this?' The car was in a really bad way.

'Yaar, don't worry. I got it cheap because they were in a hurry to get it off their hands. But look.' Salman was serious. 'If you want to borrow the money, I can sell this and lend it to you.'

Lalloo looked away from the mangled metal and back at his

friend's guileless face. Salman may not know the details about Jugnu's death, or how cold Lalloo's first long nights had been at Rizwan's, or how often he'd cried for his parents, but whenever Lalloo had asked, Salman had always tried to help him. Here he was, again, offering to set back his dream to help Lalloo. After Jugnu, Salman was the closest thing he'd ever had to a brother.

'No,' Lalloo said quietly. 'These are your savings.' Salman had been saving up for a car for as long as Lalloo could remember, and, besides, this wouldn't be nearly enough for Shabnam's wedding. He grinned, wanting to lighten the mood. 'If you want to spend them on a pile of scrap on wheels, who am I to stop you?'

Salman clapped an arm round Lalloo's shoulder, waving the other hand in front of him in an arc. 'You have no vision, yaar. This isn't just my car, this is the start of our future. This is the *first* car in our grand plan. You fix it up, we can drive it for a bit and then I'll sell it on for a profit. Then we'll buy the next one. And the next. Until we can afford to open up our own showroom.'

Lalloo snorted, but Salman continued undeterred. 'Just think about it — you and me driving off, not a care in the world. Like that blue bicycle, but even better. You remember?'

When they were young boys, Salman had dragged across the skeleton of a bicycle he'd salvaged from a ditch. It had no tyres, no chain and even its metal frame was dented. They'd hidden it behind his house, away from his mother, and had worked on it every spare moment. Salman had scoured the streets, bicycle workshops and even rubbish heaps for any spare parts they could use; Lalloo had tried his best to fix it. It'd been worth it, the first time Salman had sat on the seat with Lalloo on the frame behind the handlebars, riding down a hill, the wind whipping through their hair and pulling tears from their eyes.

'You want me to fix this?' Lalloo looked at the battered car again. 'You know you're going to need spare parts. It'll cost you.'

'I've spoken to Abdul; he said he can get me stuff second-hand. It'll be cheaper. Think about it, yaar. If you do this for me, I'll let you drive it whenever you need, even—'

'What am I going to need a car for?'

'What about impressing the lovely Fatima?' Salman wiggled his bushy eyebrows up and down. 'Think about long drives into the sunset.'

He hadn't even had a chance to tell Salman about their rooftop meeting and his date with Fatima tonight. The thought of taking her for a romantic drive in a car was lovely, if a bit far-fetched.

'I don't know, yaar.' It seemed like another one of Salman's crazy plans. 'I only get one day a week off work – it'll take ages to fix.'

'Look, do you remember Kamal Chacha's mangoes?'

Lalloo couldn't quite believe he was hearing this. 'What's that got to do with anything?'

The summer they'd turned nine, Salman had devised an ingenious method of pilfering mangoes from the crates that were delivered to Kamal Chacha's home. When he'd discovered the deliveries had been a regular occurrence, Salman had convinced Mansoor at the shop that he should be the one relied on to transport the fruit. The crates had been heavy, made of rough planks of wood nailed together. En route to Kamal Chacha's, sweating and cursing, the crate hoisted on his shoulder, Salman would loosen a plank, remove a mango or two and nail the wood back. He'd never taken more than a couple from each crate and Chacha had never found out. Every July and August, Salman had enjoyed a regular supply of mangoes, sitting by the stream, licking his fingers to catch the heavenly juices, while Lalloo had looked on, terrified of having anything to do with his friend's thieving.

'You need to make things happen – go out and get what you need. Stand up for yourself.'

'By stealing mangoes?'

Salman ignored this last comment. 'You're always so good. You do what you're told, you don't dare sneak off work five minutes early. You follow the rules and then when things don't go your way, you wonder why.'

Lalloo stared at Salman. It was easy for his friend. They might have roamed the streets together, but Salman had always had a home to go back to at night, parents and siblings to fall back on, a mother who'd pampered him because he'd been a sickly child.

He'd never needed to fend for himself. Lalloo did as he was told; he didn't kick up a fuss. He'd learnt the lesson that Jugnu hadn't.

But Salman was right – maybe things could change. Lalloo knew how much Salman had always wanted a car. He slowly walked around it, running his fingers down the door where the paint had scraped off, holding up a windscreen wiper snapped in two. He breathed in the familiar smell of engine oil and fuel – those smells that had plugged a hole in his childhood.

Salman took a deep breath. 'So will you do it?'

Maybe he would. Maybe he needed to listen to his heart for a change. Lying on his back underneath a car, most issues were fixable. It was a much less complicated way to live one's life. And the profit from selling the car would certainly help with his savings. Like Salman said, maybe it would lead to a showroom of their own one day. It was the only way it would be possible to save up enough money to get his parents out. And, of course, he still needed Salman's help this evening.

He looked at Salman's open, trusting face and nodded. 'All right then, as long as—'

'Yes!' Salman interrupted him, fist-pumping the air, a huge grin on his face. 'I knew you'd do it. Just you wait, Lalloo, our showroom will be open in no time.'

Salman's happiness was infectious and Lalloo held his hands in front of him to slow his friend down. 'As long as you help me with my top-secret assignment.'

That caught Salman's attention, his eyebrows drawing together in curiosity. 'What's that then?'

He told Salman about the mission Asima had given him. 'I reckon the only way to follow Omer without being seen is by bike, so you're going to have to drive me.'

'You sure about this?'

Lalloo shook his head, his face grim. 'No. If Omer catches me, I'm fired. But Abu's getting restless, they've already set a date for the wedding and I don't see any other way of getting this money.'

'Then, of course I'll do this for you.'

Lalloo nodded his thanks. He would make this work – there

was no other way. He drove off to the Alams', remembering what Salman hadn't mentioned about that one time with Kamal Chacha's mangoes.

*

The summer heat had been at its peak. Salman had been en route to Kamal Chacha's house, a heavy wooden crate of mangoes balanced on one shoulder, his face puckered with the effort. Lalloo had been taking no part in his scams as usual, but he'd waited patiently for his friend. It had been after Salman had filched the mangoes and had been on his way back that the problem had begun.

The boys had been walking side by side when a snarling dog had come from nowhere. Nine-year-old Lalloo had immediately frozen. Salman had walked faster, but the big, ugly creature had followed him, past a stock-still Lalloo.

'Lalloo, help!'

Lalloo couldn't do anything. It reminded him of another dog in another time, a large, terrifying beast straining on its chain, snarling in his face. This dog was lean and hungry, sniffing the ripe, fragrant fruit on his friend. Lalloo couldn't move, couldn't help, rooted to the spot. Salman threw a stone at the dog to shoo it away, but it remained undeterred, coming closer and closer until finally his friend broke into a run.

But the mongrel ran even faster.

By the time Lalloo forced himself to put one foot in front of the other, he couldn't see his friend anywhere. He ran up and down the streets, calling out Salman's name, asking the samosa wallah at his stall, even the passing doodh wallah, searching for what felt like hours, and, just as he was about to give up, thinking Salman had probably made it safely home, he came across a figure sprawled face down on the ground near Chandni Chowk. Images of a lifeless Jugnu filled his head. He thought he was going to be sick; it was all he could do not to run away. Panicking, he rushed up to Salman and turned him over. His friend was very pale, wheezing weakly. Lalloo propped him up. Unable to talk, Salman's face was lathered in sweat.

With trembling hands, Lalloo patted down his friend's pockets. 'Where's your inhaler?'

But Salman couldn't answer, just shook his head. Lalloo called to passers-by for assistance, but everyone ignored them, hurrying on, not wanting to intervene. He cradled his friend in his arms, tried to pick him up, but, when he stood, he nearly collapsed, his legs refusing to take the weight. He had to do something.

'Don't worry. I'm going to get help. I'll be right back,' he said to Salman, not sure if his friend could even hear him.

He ran as if the dog were chasing him. Fast as he could to Salman's house and knocked on the door, his chest heaving.

Salman's mother opened it and frowned at him.

'What is it? Who are you?'

'I . . .' He didn't have enough breath to speak, couldn't force the words out quickly enough. He pointed helplessly in the direction he'd come from, leaning his hands on his knees to drag more air into his lungs.

She peered closely at his face. 'Aren't you that boy who sneaked into the house? The one who screamed in the middle of the night? What do you want? Where's Salman?'

Lalloo had got enough of his breath back to splutter out his words: 'He . . . he can't get up. Over near Chandni Chowk.'

The woman let out a shriek and disappeared into the house to get Saif, Salman's older brother. Lalloo led them both to Salman, and as soon as she saw her son lying motionless on the ground, she pushed Lalloo out of the way.

'What have you done to him now? You terrified him last time with your screaming. My poor boy! What has he done?'

Lalloo was speechless, shaking his head.

Saif gently picked up Salman and carried him away, his mother fussing around them.

Saif wasn't at the workshop the next day and Lalloo spent the stretching hours scared, not knowing if his friend was alive or dead. Not knowing if he'd made things worse by freezing up, running too slow, or searching in the wrong places. He looked up at every noise, hoping to see Salman poke his head and his cheeky grin round the door.

When Saif did appear two days later, it was with a sombre

warning: Salman was recovering after being very ill in hospital and Lalloo was to stay away from him from now on. Saif knew Lalloo and Salman were friends and it was spoken as a threat.

But when Salman turned up at the workshop the following Sunday, he looked no different from his usual self.

'Challo, I've only got a few minutes.'

Lalloo followed him in wonder. 'How are you feeling? When did you get out of hospital? Where are we going?'

'You'll see, you'll see,' was all he would say.

He led Lalloo round to Chandni Chowk, where a disused building stood in ruins. He climbed up a half-fallen wall, Lalloo right behind him as always, broken bricks and masonry sliding under their feet.

'I know they're here somewhere . . .' He started lifting the bricks. 'Challo, help me out here.'

Lalloo did the same, worried his fragile friend was pushing himself too hard. 'What are you . . .' He spotted something nestled in between a couple of timber beams. Two plump, orange mangoes.

Salman saw them and grinned at Lalloo. 'Couldn't let the dog get them, could I?'

He plucked up the fruit and they clambered down.

'You rescued me, yaar. You're like Shah Rukh Khan in that movie, running to get help, saving my life. I could have died.' He put a hand over his heart in typical Salman melodrama, wanting to make Lalloo laugh.

But Lalloo didn't feel like laughing, the guilt eating him up. 'I'm sorry I didn't help you, yaar, it was . . . that dog . . .' Salman didn't know about the dogs the night Jugnu died and Lalloo's morbid fear of them ever since.

Salman placed a hand on his arm. 'Here, have this mango – you've earnt it, bhai.'

He planted the massive fruit into Lalloo's palm and the boys sat down right there by the side of the road, tore off the extra-soft peel by hand and dug in with their teeth, the only sound as they ate, their slurping. The fruit was heavy and overripe, and they finished every last morsel.

When he was done, Salman licked his fingers clean and burped. Lalloo giggled and burped in reply. And for no reason whatsoever, the giggles became full-throated laughs, each setting the other off until they were both rolling around on the floor, clutching at their sides.

Lalloo watched his companion; he was so happy, he could hardly speak. How did he get so lucky to have a friend like this?

Eventually, Salman picked himself up, his face rosy with exertion. 'Better go. They won't let me out now; I had to give them the slip. And they *definitely* aren't keen on you. I tried to explain, but you know what mothers are like. Gotta get back.' Before leaving, he looked back at Lalloo. 'But I meant what I said – you saved me, so I've got to be like Shah Rukh Khan's friend and protect you.' Salman pointed his finger at Lalloo and winked, and, just like that, he was gone again.

Were it not for his full belly and a mouth that ached from smiling so much, Lalloo would've thought his friend was too good to be true.

Chapter Twelve

In the driveway, Lalloo put Omer's briefcase into his car and saw him off, grateful he didn't comment on the overnight absence of the Range. Guddo called him into the house and he found Asima in the front lounge, looking out the window as if she, too, had been watching her husband drive away.

'You wanted to see me, bibi?'

She didn't turn around. 'Tonight, sahib is going at six o'clock. Are you ready to do as I asked?'

He swallowed. 'Six o'clock, bibi?' Asima had changed the time and he was meeting Fatima afterwards at the cinema. He couldn't rearrange with Fatima. She was only able to make it because her grandmother was away. He wouldn't get another chance. He should be able to do both. Six wasn't too late; as soon as he'd finished taking the photos, he'd head straight to the cinema.

'Yes,' she snapped at him, impatiently. 'Have you made the arrangements? Can you follow him without being seen?'

'Yes, bibi.'

'Good.'

She didn't ask him what these arrangements were, keeping her attention out of the window, as though she wasn't really talking to him.

'And take some photos. Remember, you're to tell no one about this but me.'

So this was it. One job and the money was his. Asima turned to look at him then, her arms crossed, her look challenging, as if daring him to defy her. He nodded mutely. There was nothing else he could do.

He sent Salman a message with the change of time for that evening and drove Yasmin to a photo shoot in an abandoned factory and then on to lunch with Tania and Tariq. Yasmin barely looked at Lalloo and he couldn't tell if she felt at all guilty or embarrassed about their last conversation, and then he realised she felt neither. For her, it was just business as usual – nothing had changed. She still expected him to keep her secrets and be her friend. For Yasmin, life had always been that way. She got what she wanted and expected.

He waited impatiently outside the restaurant, too jittery to join the other drivers at the khokha having their lunch. He drove Yasmin back home, dropping off Tania on the way, and then took Asima to the shops and back. All day, his thoughts were a tangle of wondering what he'd see when he followed Omer, how he could discreetly take photos, what he wanted to say to Fatima when he saw her.

That evening, Lalloo waited until Omer left in his Land Cruiser before letting himself out of the side gate. Salman was hiding around the corner on his motorbike, helmet in hand.

'Are you ready for this?' his friend asked, kick-starting his bike as soon as he saw Lalloo.

'No.' Everything was happening so fast. His whole body felt like it was tingling, prepped for the challenge ahead. 'But come on.' He swung himself up behind Salman. 'The sooner we do this, the sooner I can get to the cinema . . .'

Salman revved the engine and drove off in the same direction as Omer's Cruiser. 'Cinema? What's this? Who are you going to the cinema with?'

'You were the one saying I should be more confident, so I asked Fatima out.'

'No way! That's amazing! Well, what's actually amazing is that she said yes to you.'

Lalloo couldn't see Salman's face in front of him on the bike, but he could hear the smile in his voice.

'I can't believe you got me to take you on this wild goose chase but didn't tell me you're going on an actual date! And what are you going to see?'

'The new Kareena Kapoor.'

'Kareena Kapoor? You know we always watch Kareena Kapoor together . . .'

Lalloo smiled as Salman prattled on, all the while keeping after Omer's car. The gleaming white Land Cruiser was easy to spot and he kept a watchful distance. They headed out of the cantonment, over the bridge and along the canal, driving past the sprawling tangle of housing societies that Lahore had sprouted in recent years, like mould on the side of half-eaten food. Dusk fell and the sound of the Azaan from multiple mosques, offset against each other, echoed through the air as the sun set. They drove for the best part of an hour until their bodies were stiff and sore.

'Oh, yaar, you're bloody well going to take me to ten Kareena movies and you're going to pay for each one,' Salman muttered at him.

Lalloo ignored his friend. The Land Cruiser had left the main road, driving into the narrow and quiet residential streets of a housing society. Wherever Omer was going, it wasn't to a business meeting. Lalloo made sure Salman kept far enough back to be safe.

By the time the Cruiser came to a stop, night had fallen. Omer had pulled up into the driveway of a house with high gates and equally high walls, much like his own home in the cantonment. Lalloo signalled Salman to keep driving past and Salman parked up one road down. The street lamps were few and far between, and clouds flitted over the moon. The house had two lights on either side of its gate, but otherwise looked dark. Somewhere on the main road, cars were honking and a dog barked in the distance, but otherwise all was quiet. The two of them approached the house on foot, silent as thieves.

'OK, now what?'

Lalloo had to find out what was going on behind those walls.

Staring at the house, he noticed one crucial difference between Omer's home and this one – this had no gatekeeper. No Baba Jee letting people in and out.

'I'm going in,' said Lalloo, with only a slight tremor in his voice.

There were no side alleys; the wall joined onto the neighbours' bricks on either side. The only way in was from the front. Lalloo checked his phone to make sure it was turned to silent and waited until the moon went behind a cloud, leaving them in near total darkness. It was now or never. He took off his rubber chappal and patted Salman on the back.

'Shall I come with you?' his friend asked.

'No, I need you out here. Come on, give me a leg-up.'

Salman gripped his upper arm. 'Wait. What if they have dogs?'

Lalloo nearly froze at that last word, but he had to keep going. He had to get in and out quickly. He shook his head, took a deep breath and stepped on Salman's clasped palms, trying to find a foothold on the smooth concrete wall with his bare feet. The wall didn't give him much grip. Glad he'd taken off his chappal, his bare feet found a little traction against the concrete and he pulled himself up with both arms. He hauled himself over the top of the wall and, hanging on with his fingertips, dropped silently to the ground. It was only as his feet found cool grass that he really thought of the possibility of dogs. His whole body seized up as if his brain had short-circuited and refused to give him any commands at all. He couldn't move or think. Could only imagine a pack of Alsatians racing up to him, teeth bared, throats growling, rushing to tear him to bits.

Moments later, he was still half crouching in the pitch-dark, ears straining for the sound of rushing paws, when the clouds lifted. The moon bared the sweet, empty lawn in front of him and his body slumped in relief, clammy with sweat, his legs shaking. Wiping his brow, his back against the wall, Lalloo cursed himself for his stupidity.

He slid forward step by step, inspecting the front of the house. The façade was dark. Not a single light shone in the windows, but he heard voices and a woman's clear, tinkling laugh. Creeping forward, his heart thumping, he rounded the back of the house and the garden came into view. It took Lalloo a few seconds to comprehend what he saw.

About twelve feet away from him, a feast was laid out on an outdoor table, which was covered with more candles than Lalloo had ever seen together, even in a blackout. Omer sat on a large wicker chair and in his arms was a woman. They were kissing passionately. She faced away from Lalloo, half naked with black hair cut fashionably short. When she turned slightly as they both came up for air, he caught a glimpse of her face and inhaled sharply. *Tania, Yasmin's best friend.*

He blinked, shocked, yet there was no doubting it; Lalloo had spent the last four years ferrying them around and had dropped her back home barely hours ago. He'd never been to this house before, though; Omer must've acquired it especially for this purpose. This was huge and it was going to be terrible. Asima obviously suspected Omer was having an affair, that was what the taaweez must've been about – an amulet to stop her husband from straying – but he'd been tasked with finding out the details and now he would have to tell her it was with their daughter's best friend. He was due to drop Yasmin at Tania's house tomorrow.

Ever so slowly, he reached inside his pocket for his phone. Hands trembling, he made sure the flash was turned off and aimed his camera at them. When he was done, he crept back along the side of the house, retracing his steps, wondering whether the occupants of the garden would hear his heart racing. He got back to the wall and it suddenly seemed much smoother on the inside, with no one to give him a leg-up and no grip for his bare feet. It took him several attempts to finally get over, skinning his ankles as he did so, while his mind darted around like crazy – terrified Omer would come tearing around the side of the house or the imaginary dogs would chase him after all.

'So what was it? Did you see him? Did you get any photos?'

Salman was waiting for him on the other side, whispering in the shadows.

'Yes, come on. Let's get out of here first.' Lalloo grabbed his chappal, stumbling as he put them on and ran back to the bike with Salman on his heels.

He jumped on the bike quickly, urging Salman on and refusing to tell him anything until they were away from there, away from the house, away from the housing colony, back on the main road. Afraid something would happen to break his run of good luck. It was only when they got to the canal with its busy thoroughfare that he let Salman stop the bike. Amid the strings of fairy lights dotted along the water, reflecting on its surface, with traffic rushing past them, Lalloo took out his phone and showed Salman the photos.

Salman stared.

'Who's the woman?'

Lalloo nodded. 'That's the worst bit. That's Tania, Yasmin's best friend. She's the same age as his daughter.'

Salman let out a low whistle. 'The one you drive around everywhere?'

Lalloo could barely believe it himself. 'Poor Yasmin. When she finds out, she'll be devastated.'

'And how's Asima going to take it? I mean, she obviously knew he was up to something. But this . . .'

'Will make her furious.' Lalloo shook his head. 'Well, as long as I get the money . . . and maybe Yasmin doesn't need to find out.'

He looked at his phone, wondering if he really could give these photos to Asima. He didn't like the idea of being the source of such misery, but, of course, he reminded himself, he was just the messenger. Omer was the cause of all this. It didn't make Lalloo feel any better. He knew Yasmin too well to underestimate how devastating this would be. Her father was her hero and Tania was her favourite person, more constant than any boyfriend. They shared everything – clothes, lipsticks, long confidences over the phone, sleepovers at each other's houses. In fact, Lalloo realised that he knew more about Yasmin – what she wore, what she liked, who her friends were, which music she listened to – than he did either of his sisters. In the past four years, he had spent more time with the Alams than with his own family.

Lalloo glanced at the time and hurriedly put his phone away.

'Come on, let's get going. If you go down the canal, you can drop me off at the Shalimar on Bedian Road.'

They had plenty of time to get to the cinema. But as they turned onto the main thoroughfare, traffic was at a standstill. As far as the eye could see, there were red brake lights from the back of cars, trucks, motorbikes and scooters.

'What's going on?' Lalloo asked.

Salman weaved in and out and around some of the traffic as much as he could, but to no avail. Amid much honking, shouting and gesturing, they were stuck.

Lalloo was desperate, but, apart from egging Salman on from behind and making unhelpful comments, there was nothing he could do. He messaged Fatima to let her know and she replied. She was waiting outside the cinema. The movie was about to start. He didn't like the idea of her having to stand outside the cinema alone. It wasn't the nicest part of town and a woman on her own could attract some unwanted attention.

'I'll go down here – maybe we can bypass this bit.' Salman turned down a side lane, trying to take a short cut, but they ended up worse than before.

Half an hour later, Lalloo messaged Fatima again, but this time she didn't reply.

When they finally got to the cinema, it was forty minutes after the movie had started. Salman pulled up just outside and Lalloo jumped off the bike. There were few people hanging outside as the show had already started, but Lalloo ran around looking for Fatima and couldn't see her anywhere. He took out his phone and called her, but only got her voicemail. He messaged her, hoping she was waiting for him around a corner and he just hadn't seen her. While waiting for a reply, he paced outside the cinema, phone in hand.

Ten minutes later, he finally got a reply: she had gone home. He supposed he should be glad that at least she was safe. Dejected, he walked back to where Salman was quietly standing. This had been his big chance with her and he'd completely blown it. Would she trust him again? Without a word, he got back on the bike and Salman drove him home.

Chapter Thirteen

Walking through the gate of the Alams' house the next morning, Lalloo could feel his phone with the incriminating photos burning a hole in his pocket as his anxiety burnt a hole in his belly. He had to fight the urge to continually look over his shoulder, as if there were eyes on him. Last night, he'd risked his job and possibly ruined his chances with Fatima, and it would all come to nothing if he couldn't find a way to show the photos to Asima and make sure she held up her side of the deal. Lalloo wanted to find her right away, to bring all this uncertainty to an end, but he had to be careful. He started unrolling the hose to wash the cars as though it was just another morning.

His routine tasks gave him somewhere to put his excess energy. Baba Jee was complaining about the weather again and Lalloo let the gatekeeper's monotonous drone wash over him as he focused on the soapy suds against his fingers, squeezing the sponge against the bucket, rinsing the dust off the cars, thinking of Shabnam, who would be digging the dirt with her shovel, mixing it with water to make clay, Pinky patting the bricks into moulds.

If Lalloo knew anything about the bibis in this house, they didn't like it when things didn't go their way. What would Asima do when she saw that it was Tania in Omer's arms? And if Yasmin found out . . . he didn't want to think about the devastation that would cause. As he used the hose to rinse the soap from the bonnet, Lalloo reminded himself he was only doing as he'd been asked. He had fixed cars, delivered clothes, run errands, driven around Lahore thousands of times. This was just another job. But Asima had also wanted secrecy and if the servants overheard, word would get out. He had to be especially careful of Guddo's watchful eye. She was so attuned to the family's routine, she would get very suspicious if he acted strangely. So even though it felt almost impossible to wait, Lalloo finished rinsing off the cars and picked up a cloth to begin drying. He would go about his day as normal until he could give the photos to Asima in private, like she had asked. Maybe Yasmin would never need to know.

Lalloo had just finished cleaning the tyres on the Land Cruiser when Omer came storming out of the house and thrust his briefcase at Lalloo without looking at him. Lalloo was glad. He wasn't sure he could meet his boss's eye today.

Barely a few minutes after Omer had driven off, Guddo opened the front door and peered out at him. 'Bibi wants you inside,' she said, jerking her thumb behind her.

He took a deep breath, straightening out his kameez as he stood up, double-checking his phone was still in his pocket, as though it might have fallen out since he last checked five minutes ago. If he could follow and spy on Omer, he told himself, he'd be able to find a way to tell Asima.

'What does she want from you?' Guddo whispered as he passed her to enter the house.

He shrugged as nonchalantly as he could and she followed him inside, dragging her feet.

As he walked into the lounge, Asima was sitting on the sofa. She sat up straight when she saw him, but waited until Guddo had gone into the kitchen before speaking.

'Well, did you follow him?' Asima whispered.

'Yes, bibi, we went all the way to the canal.'

'We?' Her scant eyebrows nearly disappeared into her hairline.

'I was on my friend's bike.' He continued hurriedly, before she could make a fuss, 'So Omer Sahib wouldn't recognise me.'

'So now you've got someone else involved as well?'

'No, no, bibi, my friend is very discreet.'

She opened her mouth to answer but was interrupted by the doorbell ringing, the sound shrill and loud after their hurried whispers, nearly making Lalloo jump.

Asima screwed up her face in irritation and raised her voice. 'Guddo, go see to the door.'

Guddo emerged from the kitchen and went outside to speak to Baba Jee, but was back instantly.

'Bibi, sahib's cousins are here from Sheikhupura.'

Behind her was a middle-aged couple, a large balding man with a short beard and a very thin woman, her hair dyed orange with henna.

Asima's smile was brittle as she greeted her husband's cousins. She turned to Lalloo and he saw in her eyes the same frustration he was feeling. 'I'll speak to you later. Go pick up my pink dupatta from the dyer's shop in Rangwalla Galli; I need it for the wedding tonight.'

There was nothing for it but to go and fetch the dupatta. Lalloo put his hand to his pocket to check his phone again. He'd missed his chance to get Asima alone for now. On the other hand, he thought, the dyer's shop was in Sadar bazaar. He could go past Fatima's grandmother's stall to see if Fatima was there. If he could see her face to face, get a minute alone with her, he could explain to her what had happened. He was sure she would listen and he was so restless, he felt he had to do something or he was going to burst.

The bazaar was busy. Eid was fast approaching, and shops and stalls were doing a brisk trade, the gallis heaving with people. The roads were already lined with parked cars and it took Lalloo a few minutes to find a parking spot. He walked into the narrow, crowded street, dodging the shoppers meandering down the path, gazing at the stalls selling sparkling glass bangles in all sizes and colours. He saw Taari approaching from afar and turned into a side alley, not wanting any more confrontations, aware he was prickling with nervous energy. He turned again into Rangwalla Galli.

'Haan, bhai, Lalloo, what brings you here?' Hamid greeted him outside his shop, where he'd set up a large vat on a concrete stand with a fire burning underneath. He stirred the vat with a long wooden stick, churning the cloth inside to cover it evenly with dark-green dye.

'Asima Bibi sent me,' Lalloo replied.

Seeing the blank look on Hamid's face, he continued.

'She said you have a dupatta for her?'

Hamid slapped his forehead with his palm. 'Baap re, I completely forgot.'

Lalloo's palms felt clammy. Nothing was working out today and Asima didn't need yet another excuse to be angry with him. 'She wants to wear it tonight, yaar. She's not going to be pleased.'

'Look, don't you have any other errands? Come back in half an hour. I'll have it ready.'

Lalloo was hesitant, not sure Hamid would be able to dye and dry the dupatta in half an hour but knowing that he couldn't return to the house without it, when he heard a familiar voice behind him. He peered over his shoulder. Fatima walked past arm in arm with another girl, like the universe had just given him an answer. Lalloo kept his back to them and moved closer, listening in.

'No, no, we'll definitely go to Sunbright Tailors – that other tailor didn't know a thing about making clothes,' Fatima's companion said.

Here she was, without her grandmother as chaperone. It was his chance to try to make amends.

Heart pounding, Lalloo turned back to Hamid, who was riffling through piles of clothes, flustered, looking for the lost dupatta. 'All right, then. I'll come and get it from you in half an hour, but make sure it's done, bhai.'

He knew where Sunbright Tailors was and the now elderly Master Jee remembered him very well from all the errands he used to run. Lalloo also knew the quickest way to get there. He raced down the backstreets as fast as he could, his chappal slapping the soles of his feet as he dodged children playing a game of Pitthu Garam and a mangy stray dog standing in the middle of the road. He rushed over to Master Jee and explained his predicament, the other tailors listening in. Master Jee started to protest at his plan, but Lalloo had already eased himself into the shop and sat down in a corner. By the time Fatima got to Sunbright, Lalloo sat cross-legged behind a sewing machine with a tape measure hung around his neck, as if he were a tailor's son born and raised.

When she saw him, she did a double take.

'What is it?' her sour-faced companion asked.

'Nothing, nothing. I just like this design.' Fatima reached for a kameez hanging on display outside the shop. She was biting her lower lip, trying to suppress a grin, studiously avoiding his gaze. It was all she could do not to laugh and seeing this filled him with relief. Maybe he hadn't completely messed things up with her.

There were four tailors sitting beside Lalloo on jute matting, their sewing machines in front of them, mountains of cloth in all colours and patterns threatening to bury them from sight.

'Master Jee, my cousin and I need new shalwar kameezes,' Fatima's companion said to the head tailor.

Lalloo held his breath. Would Master Jee play along?

Master Jee glanced across at Lalloo and shook his head, but to the women he said, 'Of course, this young man will look after you. Let him show you some designs.'

Lalloo had only just caught his breath back after the run and wished the other tailors would stop grinning like idiots – they were bound to give the game away. Straight-faced, he stood up, but Sour Face chipped in again.

'Is he new? I don't want just any tailor making these clothes. They're special.'

'No, no, bibi, he's one of my best. He was away for his chacha's wedding when you last came.'

'What can I show you? What sort of thing are you looking for?' Lalloo led the two women further into the shop.

Fatima sniffed. 'So how long have you been a tailor?' Her voice was frosty now, her demeanour even more so. He didn't blame her. He had his work cut out. But he already felt calmer, as if her presence was enough to soothe the restlessness he'd been feeling all day.

Fatima waited until her cousin had wandered further in, turning away to admire the clothes on display. Then she grabbed his elbow, one eye on her companion, her voice barely audible. 'This isn't going to work, you know, whatever you're doing. You can't stand me up one minute and then start following me around.'

'I know, I know, I'm so sorry. I've been trying to get hold of you ever since to apologise. I never meant to—'

The cousin turned to come back and Fatima dropped his arm as if her fingers had been burnt by a hot roti.

'Can we see something in the new Gul Ahmed lawn designs?' Sour Face asked.

Lalloo had no idea about Gul Ahmed lawn. 'Yes, all the designs are in the catalogue over there.' He pointed to the stack of magazines, praying she would stay away as she went over to them.

He turned back to Fatima.

'Look, you're right to be angry. I had to run an unusual errand for my boss and it took much longer than I thought,' he finally said in a low voice. 'And then there'd been an accident; the traffic was backed up for miles.'

'Do you realise how many lies I had to tell my cousin yesterday? First about where I was going, then why I was back early? And I had to stand outside the cinema on my own waiting for you.' Fatima's voice was still quiet, nothing her cousin could hear, but there was a force behind it that Lalloo recognised. She wasn't pretending to be angry – he had really hurt her.

'I'm so sorry.' He felt terrible and wished he had better words to prove it to her.

She stared at him, cutting him open with her gaze. Surely she could see right through him, see that he wasn't messing her around, that he was truly desperately sorry. He thought back to yesterday, the task Asima had given him and how little choice he'd had, how important it was he'd got the photos.

'Look, I'll make it up to you, I promise. Give me one more chance, please.'

Her glare softened. 'I did see the traffic jam as I was leaving.' She looked around her at the tailor's shop. 'But what is this? First you're fighting in the bazaar, then you're flying over rooftops and now you're a tailor. Who are you really, some kind of conman?'

He grinned, delighting at the chance to engage with her. 'I'm also a part-time mechanic. We can't all be doctors, you know.'

Fatima permitted him a small smile. 'I've still got a long way to go. I just transferred to the college here. Three years before I even qualify.'

So her grandmother had been right all those years ago. Fatima was destined for much better things than a street urchin like him would ever be. He wasn't much better off and his family were still stuck in the bhatti – no matter how much he worked, how much money he tried to save to one day get them out, unable to dream of any other future until they were free. Ever since that day when her grandmother had led her away from the bazaar, Fatima had never had permission to play with him, had only ever snuck away when she wasn't being watched.

'You know I'm just a driver, right? Once you become Doctor Sahiba, you won't want to know me.' Lalloo tried to sound casual, but knew he hadn't quite managed it.

'Oh, I don't know about that,' Fatima said, her tone equally serious. 'My grandfather used to work as a driver, before he passed.' Her face was still and pensive. Then she perked up again. 'And the only time I tried to drive, I nearly ran someone over. You could be very useful.'

Lalloo smiled and if it was a little bit forced, Fatima pretended not to notice.

'So, Doctor Jee, if I told you my ankle hurts from jumping the roof, would you come look at it?'

She giggled and Lalloo's heart did double backflips in his chest. 'Of course not. You deserve a sore ankle for jumping onto a girl's roof uninvited.'

Sour Face returned once more, catalogue in hand. Fatima still had a mischievous half-smile across her face. Her playfulness, her openness – he'd endure ten Sour Faces for that.

Hundreds of designs later, the cousin had chosen one and then spent a good ten minutes telling him why she didn't like it and all the alterations she would need. Lalloo nodded along, not listening, sneaking glances across at Fatima, delighted he could spend time in her company. After a while, he discreetly checked his watch – he was going to be late back to work. At last, he slipped the tape measure from around his neck.

'Why don't I take some measurements?' He looked towards Fatima, hoping she would follow him to the back of the shop.

But no such luck. The miserable cousin trailed him to where a curtain partially concealed them from view.

Suddenly confronted with a large, heaving bosom, Lalloo panicked. He had no idea how to take measurements. He inched around her, scared to get too close to any part of her body. She looked back at him, on the verge of complaining to Master Jee. He spent barely a minute measuring her height and the length of her arms from behind, careful to stay well away from her chest, before hurriedly returning to the shop floor. Fatima was already halfway out the door.

'Challo, yaar, I'll be late back home. Dado will be waiting!' She winked at Lalloo as she grabbed Sour Face's hand and ran with her down the street.

Lalloo watched them until they were out of sight, unable to look away.

Finally, he turned to old Master Jee, who was looking at him expectantly. 'I, uh, wasn't sure what to measure.'

The other tailors sniggered and Lalloo shrugged. It had been over forty-five minutes since he'd left the dyer's shop. He turned to run.

'How am I going to make this shalwar kameez then?' Master Jee called after him.

'With love, Master Jee, with love!' Lalloo shouted back as the tailors burst out laughing, their laughter and the warm feeling in his chest carrying him all the way back.

*

At the Alams', Lalloo was just parking up when his phone rang. It was Abu. He'd told Abu that Asima had promised him the money, so Abu was expecting him. Any warm feeling left over from his encounter with Fatima disappeared instantly. Lalloo stared at his mobile. He was afraid that if he told Abu he didn't have the money yet, his father would go straight to Heera, but, then, if he didn't answer, Abu might do that anyway.

Lalloo got out of the car. Chota, the gardening help, was watering the lawn. Baba Jee was shutting the gate.

He answered the phone, keeping his voice low, trying to sound confident. 'I just need some more time, Abu. I'll definitely have the money for you in a few days.'

'Lalloo, it's Shabnam.'

Shabnam never called. 'What's wrong?'

'I don't know how to . . . It's Abu. He's collapsed.'

'What happened? Is it the heat?' It was suffocating.

'I think it's more than that.' She sounded scared. 'His cough has been getting worse for months. He keeps getting short of breath and now he can't get up, and he's running a fever.'

For a moment, her words took the breath out of him. He'd had no idea. 'When did this happen?'

She paused. 'Three days ago.'

'Three days? But I spoke to him yesterday. He was coughing a lot, but he didn't mention *this*.'

'He didn't want to worry you.'

Lalloo was furious, but before he could say anything, Shabnam spoke again.

'But listen, na, Heera came over this evening.'

The anger evaporated from Lalloo's body. He couldn't breathe. He leant against the car to steady himself.

'What did he want?' Lalloo could hardly get the words out, his voice weak, barely recognisable even to himself.

'He says we're not meeting our quota.' He could hear the panic in her voice. 'He says we're not going to get paid at the end of the week.'

Lalloo closed his eyes. She didn't need to say that if they didn't get paid, they wouldn't be able to eat.

'I've tried, Lalloo. I worked for so long yesterday, but I can't make enough on my own. Then, after Heera left, Abu struggled to get up, but he collapsed again.' Her voice broke. 'He can't do it and Heera is forcing him to work.'

Lalloo dragged the sweltering air into his lungs, trying to stay calm, trying to think. There was silence on the line.

'Lalloo? Are you there?' Shabnam asked softly.

'Yes.' Lalloo rubbed his temple. 'I'll come over and speak to Heera. Get Abu some time off.'

'I'm not sure that's a good idea. Ami and Abu didn't even want me to call you.'

'I've got to come and see Abu.' He would have to get Abu to a doctor, but doctors cost money. More money from his pitiful little savings. His hands were shaking as he checked the time on his wrist. He hadn't realised how late it was and the journey to his parents was an hour and a half each way. 'I'll come tomorrow, first thing.'

He finished the call and stared at the house. Tomorrow was a working day, but Asima and Omer were going away to this wedding in Gujranwala tonight, so he wouldn't be needed.

Lalloo took a few deep breaths and walked in through the front door. The cool marble floor and shaded windows were soothing, as if tricking him into a sense of tranquillity.

Asima was sitting in the front room, surrounded by guests. He hovered by the door. Guddo came out with a tray piled with empty dishes. 'What are you doing here?' she whispered.

'I have to ask bibi for a day off tomorrow,' he whispered back.

She looked at him incredulously. 'Yes, and I'll head off to the beauty parlour and get my hair done, shall I?'

'I know she's not going to like it, but I haven't got a choice, my—'

'Guddo!' Asima came hurrying out the door, nearly bumped into Lalloo and barked at him, 'Where's my dupatta?'

He'd forgotten all about it. 'In the car, bibi, I'll get it. It's just . . . About tomorrow, since you're going away to Gujranwala, is it possible to have a day off?'

'No, no. Yasmin might need the car.'

She hadn't even given his request a moment's consideration. He knew Yasmin didn't need him; she'd told him so that morning. Asima had already turned away, giving Guddo some orders. When she came back to return to her guests, he stepped in front of the door, blocking her way.

'Bibi, my father is unwell and I need to go see him. Like Major Sahib, he's just collapsed with no warning. But he doesn't have anyone to take him to the doctor.'

Last year, Asima's father had collapsed while she was visiting him. Lalloo had picked up the fifteen-stone man, half carried, half dragged him to the car and driven him and a distraught Asima to hospital. And if the memory of Major Sahib's heart attack didn't persuade her to let him go, nothing would. But still she hesitated.

The phone call from Shabnam had shaken him up. He worried that Abu was worse than she was letting on. She was right – they couldn't afford for anyone to be ill, they needed everyone to be hands-on to make bricks. And Asima wouldn't even let him see his father.

He took a deep breath and lowered his voice. 'I took photos last night of what Omer Sahib was up to. As you asked. Now, I'm not going to show you them right here in front of all these people.' He looked pointedly over his shoulder at her guests, emboldened by his desperation. 'But I need to go see my father tomorrow and when I come back, I'll show them to you in private.'

One of her guests called to Asima from inside the room and she waved her hand distractedly in reply. She shook her head at Lalloo, clearly wanting to get rid of him. 'Yes, yes. All right, then, you can have tomorrow off.'

As she said this, Guddo came out of the kitchen, holding a tray laden with more tea, samosas and chutneys, her eyes bulging at Lalloo being given a day off work, but Lalloo didn't stop to talk. He hurried out before Asima could change her mind, his head full of images of Abu collapsing in the dust, his sister's voice slowly breaking, and Heera bearing down on them, hounding them like they were animals.

What would Jugnu have done?

Chapter Fourteen

As a child, Lalloo had never really understood Jugnu's desire to get out of the bhatti. Lalloo didn't like the work there and he wished they had more time to play cricket, and he'd preferred their previous home by the farm, but he didn't dream of going anywhere else. The bhatti was where his family was – it was his home. But for Jugnu, escaping it became an all-consuming passion.

Once, after everyone had gone to bed, Jugnu woke him up in the middle of the night.

'Shh. Not a word. Come with me.'

Lalloo didn't complain. He didn't even hesitate or stop to think. He'd always wanted to go with Jugnu on his nightly adventures, and this was the first time his brother had let him. He would've followed his big brother anywhere. Jugnu led them out past the rows of bricks, past the dormant chimney. There was nothing frightening about the dark in those days. They were two boys out on a mission with no one to stop them. They walked beyond the bhatti and out into the fields, and kept going until Lalloo began to wonder if there was a point to this trip.

'Jugnu . . .'

'Nearly there. Come on.'

His brother had to half drag him over the last mound of scraggly grass and, as they topped it, Lalloo could at last see what they had come for. A copse of trees and bushes were huddled together. And in among the leaves twinkled hundreds of yellow lights – a celebration of the night. But why would anyone string lights on bushes in the middle of nowhere? As he watched, Lalloo realised they were moving, dancing from bush to bush. Every time he looked at one, it moved away.

'What is it?' he whispered to Jugnu, worried that if he spoke out loud they would disappear.

'Fireflies,' Jugnu whispered back. 'They're *jugnu*. Like me.' He grinned and stepped into the lights. Lalloo ran after him. 'Look.' He cupped his hands over one, capturing it. Lalloo leant forward and as Jugnu moved his palm away, it flew up into the air.

Lalloo was speechless, his mouth hanging open as he stared.

Jugnu tapped him on the chin. 'Shut your mouth or you'll swallow one.' Lalloo immediately clamped his mouth shut and his brother laughed.

They walked right through the fireflies, stopping to exclaim as one landed on a hand or a head. They looked at each other in wonder as their faces were bathed in the warm, blinking light. Lalloo tried to catch them between his palms as Jugnu had done, but they were elusive, flying away or quickly going dark and invisible.

'Hey, Lalloo,' Jugnu called over to him and Lalloo turned round. 'What if we could leave this bhatti? Where would we go?'

'But we can't leave. What about the debt?'

'Yeah, but what if?'

Lalloo was used to this what-if game. Jugnu played it all the time, dreaming up fantastic scenarios.

Lalloo shrugged. 'Back to the old farm.'

'But what if the zamindar won't take us back?'

Lalloo was stumped. He looked at Jugnu blankly.

'If we could go anywhere in the country? Be anything.'

Lalloo stared wide-eyed at his clever older brother, wondering how he could even think such things.

'What if we could leave, Lalloo? Not just us, everybody here, including Hasnat? You know, there's a village I've heard about, a few miles out of the city. Some people who've escaped from bhattis live there together and they arm themselves with rocks and sticks. Every time a bhatti owner sends his men to take one of them back, they gang up on them and fight back. I'm going to get us all out of here.'

Out of the corner of his eye, Lalloo saw a firefly land on his arm. He quickly cupped a hand over it and turned around in delight to show his brother. Jugnu was awash in the soft glow, his face lit up with a huge smile, his slightly too long hair flopping onto his forehead as he reached up to coax it back.

'We're going to get out, Lalloo. We've got to make our own destiny.'

He looked happy.

At that moment, the wind picked up. All the fireflies, their lights twinkling, started taking off into the sky, following each other in droves.

Jugnu and Lalloo watched them go, their faces turned up to the sky. As Jugnu turned to leave, he saw Lalloo standing with cupped hands.

Jugnu crouched down beside him. 'You've got to let it go, kaala bhoot.'

Lalloo shook his head. 'I'll take it with me.'

'You can't. It needs to be with the other fireflies in the sky.'

Tears prickled his eyes as he gradually moved his hand to let the insect out. It didn't respond right away, sat blinking at him on his palm. Then it lifted off, hovering around his head, his hair, for a brief moment, before flying off to join the others.

'Will they be back?'

Jugnu put his arm around Lalloo's shoulder on the way home. 'Sometimes in the dark you can't see them, but they're still there, they just haven't danced their lights on. They'll show up again – they're always around somewhere.'

Chapter Fifteen

Jugnu had always had such big dreams, but he'd paid a price so heavy it weighed on Lalloo's shoulders every day. What if he could do the impossible? What if he could fulfil Jugnu's dream? Ever since he had left the bhatti, he'd carried this hope deep inside him. No one deserved to be in that place, working all hours for so little. He was convinced that was why Abu was ill; working at the bhatti day in and day out, hunched over the bricks in the scorching sun, with no rest and barely any food, had made him sick. But Jugnu hadn't been able to get them out. Was Lalloo mad to think he could do it?

The next morning felt like the air around him had been set on fire. On the minibus, crammed in among scores of other people, sweat dripped down his face and through his clothes. His kameez clung to his back. He was worried about what he'd find when he got to the bhatti. Working there was bad enough without being sick and Abu sounded very unwell.

The chimney welcomed him with blasts of sweltering air, spewing vicious grey smoke into the sky. Shabnam was outside the hut, huddled on the ground next to row upon row of raw, unbaked brick. She didn't rise to greet him, barely pausing in her work.

'How is he?' Lalloo asked.

'Same as yesterday. The fever won't go down and it's like he can't breathe properly.'

She filled the mould with wet clay, tipping it over to make a perfectly formed brick lined up on the ground next to the one before it. Over and over. Her movements were swift and practised.

He'd got out. His parents had made sure of it. He'd hated leaving, but it meant he didn't work at the bhatti now. They were still stuck here. Every day, over and over.

'I'll go see him.'

She nodded.

He didn't usually visit during the day. His parents preferred him to come in the evenings when the work was finished, and Heera and his men were less likely to be around. He could smell the damp clay. Remembered it from fourteen years ago, gritty and red under his fingernails, on his clothes, in his hair, everywhere. Having to work fast enough to make the required number of bricks, while ensuring every single one was perfect. The rows of raw unbaked clay had no beginning and no end – as soon as they were carted away by the donkey, new ones had to take their place.

Lalloo hesitated. 'Do you need a hand?'

Shabnam shook her head. 'If Ami sees you . . .' She looked up and gave him a brief smile. 'Better not.'

The fierce sun glinted off the earth, amplifying its redness.

Pinky was crouched a little behind Shabnam, making her own row of bricks. She worked at half the speed, her ten-year-old hands hurrying to catch up with her big sister. The full mould was heavy and strained her small shoulders as she crouched and lifted, he knew. She glanced at him and his words stuck in his throat – the way she looked up at him reminded him of the way he'd always looked at Jugnu. He squeezed her shoulder as he passed.

Walking into the hut was like stepping into a tandoor oven. The heat was suffocating – too many people feeding on too little air. A fly buzzed, listless and sullen, its drone adding to the denseness. Abu's charpai had been dragged inside, away from the glare of the sun, taking up most of the room. Abu lay with his eyes shut. Ami hovered next to him with a steel tumbler of water.

She saw Lalloo and nearly spilt the whole thing, then she approached him, shaking her head vigorously, and began gently pushing him out of the hut.

'It's OK, it's OK, Ami,' he said. 'I just came to see Abu. Don't worry.' He held both palms up in front of him to stop her, to calm her down.

'Heera . . .' she finally managed to say through compressed lips, her voice terrified.

'He won't, he won't see me. I'll stay out of his way.' He waited until she settled before turning towards the charpai. 'How's Abu?'

Ami could only shake her head. With downcast eyes, she lay a hand on Abu's forehead. Lalloo followed suit. Abu was very hot. Shabnam had said he'd been like this for four days. Lalloo could hear the difficulty with which Abu took every breath.

Abu opened his eyes and saw him. 'Why are you here?'

He tried to sit up, but started coughing, violent wracking coughs that shook his entire body. Even in the darkened hut, his face was ashen. Lalloo sat down on the charpai so Abu could lean on him while sitting up, sipping water. He helped lay his father down again, could feel him burning up under his fingers. He had brought with him some medicine – a cough syrup and some pain relief – which he handed over to Ami, but it was obvious Abu needed proper medical care.

'I'm going to take you to a doctor, Abu.'

'No, no need. I'm fine . . .' Abu paused to catch his breath. 'Don't let this worry you . . . I'll be back . . .' He hesitated again. 'On my feet in a few days.'

The lone fat fly buzzed around the hut as Abu struggled to breathe.

'Go back to your job, beta. I'm fine. Remember, we need to organise the wedding.' Abu's words dissolved into a fit of coughing.

Ami put a wet cloth to Abu's forehead and Lalloo left the hut, not wanting to upset his parents any further.

Abu was much worse than he'd expected. The doctor was at least a half-day's journey away and Abu couldn't walk there. Lalloo had to speak to Heera. It was obvious Abu couldn't work in his condition. If he could get him some time off, he could somehow arrange to take Abu to a doctor and get him well again.

Lalloo headed over to Shabnam. She'd moulded a sizeable

number of bricks in just the time he'd been inside. They lay beside her, stretched out in a long straight row.

'He won't let me take him to a doctor.'

'You know what he's like. And besides, the expense.' She wasn't stopping to wipe the sweat from her forehead. It ran down her nose and cheeks, mingling with the clay.

'I have the money, don't worry. I have some savings. We won't have to take it from the loan for your wedding and I should be getting that soon—'

'Don't worry about the wedding, Lalloo. I keep trying to tell Ami and Abu my marriage is not important. I'd rather stay here and look after them.' She shook her head. 'But how would you even get Abu to a doctor? He's too ill to walk.'

'I'll figure something out, but, in the meantime, he needs to rest. He shouldn't try to work.' Lalloo paused. 'I'm going to speak to Heera.' There was no other way.

The brick Shabnam had moulded broke away in her hands, crumbling at the edges. She threw it into the pile of wet clay and started over again. He could see her hands trembling. 'What are you going to say to him?'

'I'll tell him Abu needs a few days' rest to get back on his feet.'

The next brick broke again and she stopped to look at him. 'Do they know you're going?' She glanced towards the hut.

'No, of course not.' His parents had spent the last fourteen years hiding him away from the foreman of the bhatti. He knew it would be dangerous, but he had no choice.

'Be careful, Lalloo.'

He turned to face Heera's house. He couldn't see it from this distance, but he knew where it was. 'Don't worry about me. What's he going to do?' He tried to sound confident. Nonchalant, even. As if speaking to Heera was no big deal. As if speaking to Heera hadn't put Jugnu's life in danger all those years ago. 'Here. It's not much . . .' He passed Shabnam some folded rupees, all he had left from that month's wages. At least they wouldn't go hungry. She wiped the clay off her hands and took the money, tucking it into the front of her kameez.

Before he'd turned to leave, she was already moulding the next brick. They had to make twelve hundred bricks every day to be fired at the kiln. It didn't matter if you were burning with fever or grieving over a murdered child, twelve hundred bricks were needed every single day.

*

Looking back, Lalloo couldn't remember exactly when Jugnu had started talking about leaving the bhatti. Every week, they were given an allowance to live on and pay for food. The bricks they made were meant to go towards paying off their debt. Heera or one of the other supervisors would come around and tally up the bricks with the wages they'd get and note it all down. They were never told how much debt had been paid off, how much was left or how long it would take to repay. Any questions were actively discouraged.

Jugnu had talked endlessly with Abu and the neighbours about life at the bhatti and the unjustness of their working conditions. Jugnu had been a hard worker and if there was work to be done, you'd always want him on your side. But he'd had a sense of fairness about him. He would never let Lalloo get away with cheating in any of their games – it didn't matter if it was swiping extra cards in rummy or arguing over wide balls in cricket.

A few months after they'd moved to the bhatti, when Taari, who'd been one of the supervisors back then, came to count the bricks at the end of the week, Jugnu started asking questions.

'So how much of our peshgi have we paid off now? What do we still owe?'

But this led to an argument and shouting. Taari left, warning Jugnu not to ask such questions again. But Jugnu went to the city, where he spoke to an organisation that helped people trapped at bhattis, and came back full of anger. It was as he suspected – the debt was just an excuse to keep people in servitude for ever.

He arranged a meeting after a day of brickmaking when Heera and his men weren't around. So many people turned up, they all ended up huddling outside the front of the huts in the dark, daring to light only one of the gas lamps in case they attracted attention.

Most of the bhatti was there as Jugnu stood up in front of everyone. Lalloo listened in awe as his big brother spoke to all the villagers in a low yet commanding voice, the light from the lamp casting a dim, eerie glow.

'If you go into the city not far from here, you will see big, splendid buildings, all of them built with this.' In his hand, Jugnu lifted a single brick. 'This may look like just a brick to the city wallahs, but this is made with our sweat and toil. And we can't leave. Why do I have to build a city I can't even live in? Why do the tears of your children have to water the clay that makes these?'

There was total silence, the villagers hanging on to his every word. Ami and Abu were there too, listening. He spoke about the things they all knew but were too afraid to say. That the bhatti owner charged them so much interest on their debt, it was impossible for them to ever repay it, which was how the debt was passed down to their children; that this was slavery with another name, that this exploitation was illegal as ruled by the highest court in the land. They all sat and listened, as if he were someone important and wise, not a young eighteen-year-old boy. Lalloo held on to every word of his big brother's speech, but he saw people looking over their shoulders, checking their watches, peering into the darkness for signs of danger.

The following day, after work, Jugnu went out somewhere, without telling Lalloo where he was going. After dinner, Chacha Yunis came to see Abu. Ami served them a bowl of roasted chaney while they sat and talked. Chacha Yunis was one of the oldest residents of the bhatti and had so many creases on his face, Lalloo sat trying to count them while he spoke in a low voice. It was only when their guest got up from the charpai that Lalloo noticed how worried his father looked.

When Jugnu came home that night, Abu was waiting outside on his charpai for him, illuminated by the solitary gas lamp, silently smoking his hookah, the bowl of chaney still on his lap. Shabnam was asleep, but Lalloo and Ami listened as Abu confronted him.

'You've got to stop this. If Heera and his men find out . . .' Lalloo could hear the fury in Abu's voice.

'Abu, I've spoken to people. What they're doing is wrong. It's illegal. They can't do this—'

'You don't understand – you're still a child. They can get away with it and that's why they do it. Who cares if it's illegal? The police? The man on the street? No one. They are the police. They're in bed with the politicians.'

'I'm going to speak to Heera—'

'NO!' Abu got to his feet, sending the bowl on his lap flying. The metal clunked on the packed earth and roasted chaney raced across the floor. 'I don't want you anywhere near Heera. And no more talking to the neighbours.'

'But, Abu, if we all get together and—'

'What do you think this is, some kind of game? We all get together and talk our way out of here? They won't let us go until we've repaid our debt. Maybe in a few years we'll have made enough—'

'How many years? Do you even know what interest they're charging us? Maasi Khalida says she came here as a little girl. She must be sixty-five years old now. Chacha Musa was born here, so was his son. What if they never let us go? And what about that boy, Hasnat? He needs a doctor, not to be chained up in a hut.'

Abu shook his head, sitting back down. He looked suddenly old. 'They don't like it if you ask too many questions. You mustn't speak to Heera and I don't want you speaking to these people in the city. I forbid you.'

Jugnu threw his shawl down and stormed off, leaving his father on the charpai.

*

As Lalloo continued towards Heera's house, he thought how he'd never forgotten that expression on Abu's face. He'd been unable to decipher it at the time and it had been many years before he'd realised that his father hadn't been angry that night, he'd been absolutely terrified.

But Lalloo had known, even then, that Jugnu would never give up his dream of leaving.

Heera lived on the other side of the bhatti. Lalloo walked past bricks piled up into a mound with barefooted children clambering over it, the only place they had to play. A girl not much older than Pinky prepared clay with a shovel she could hardly lift. Nobody paid him much attention. A donkey cart trundled by, heavily laden, on the way to the kiln, and a woman stood breaking imperfect slabs with a pickaxe, her toddler at her feet. Over everything hung the haze of dark-red dust and an eerie silence.

This was the first time he'd been back to the bhatti during the working day in years. Nothing had changed, as if the bhatti were stuck in time. All around him, people worked with no relief. Everywhere were the sounds and sights that haunted his memories.

As he drew closer, Lalloo felt his chest being constricted. The last time he'd seen Heera was that awful night fourteen years ago. That smug look, the thinning hair, the condescending voice. Lalloo slowed down and lifted his hand to wipe his face and realised his hand was shaking violently. His legs were just as bad, threatening to topple him.

Jugnu had walked these same steps all those years ago and look what had happened to him. If only Lalloo hadn't stopped Jugnu running, he'd have got away. If Jugnu were here now, he'd know what to do. *Jugnu. Jugnu. Jugnu.* The guilt and the grief were enough to crush him. Lalloo sat on a mound of broken bricks and cradled his head in his hands, his thoughts full of the strange, whimpering noises Jugnu had made the day he'd found him hiding between the huts. The day that had changed everything.

Eventually, the pain in his chest subsided and he looked up. A stray mongrel was sniffing at him. Lalloo jumped and staggered off the mound. Slowly at first, unsure if his legs were steady enough, he walked away, taking deep breaths. He had no choice. He would speak to Heera and then figure out how to get Abu to a doctor.

Heera's house was a brick structure with proper windows and doors. Lalloo had seen it from afar as a child and had never dared go near it. Now he could see it was much smaller than in his head. A small, unpainted bungalow, much bigger than his parents' hut but nothing compared to the Alams' house. It had a verandah in front, with a table and chairs laid out, all empty. The house marked the end of the bhatti.

Lalloo came to a halt. There was no one there and he couldn't quite face up to approaching the front door and knocking on it. The sun glared down at him. It wasn't yet mid-morning, but the heat was already unbearable. He walked around the side of the house and passed an open window. There were lowered voices from inside.

'What do you think we're running here? A charity?'

'Sahib, I've tried my best.'

Lalloo stopped to listen. The window was high up and he couldn't see who was talking, but the voices sounded familiar.

'. . . get production up. Maybe some of them need reminding?'

'Yes, of course, right away. The Ashraf family have been flagging recently.'

'. . . whatever it takes.'

Lalloo's ears pricked up on hearing his father's name. He leant in against the wall as much as he could, his heart banging, but he couldn't make out the rest of the conversation.

A door slammed and footsteps strode away. Lalloo stayed where he was until all was silent. Then he walked quickly to the front of the house.

One of Heera's large cronies appeared, silent and menacing. He stared at Lalloo, but before Lalloo could say anything, turned back in and called for his boss.

It was another ten minutes before Heera came out, holding a drink in one hand. Lalloo was glad to see the passing years had treated Heera badly. His hair – what was left of it – was grey and wispy and combed over from one side to the other in an attempt to cover his bald patch. His kameez was pulled tight over a sizeable paunch.

'Haan, Lalloo Bhai. Good, I'm so glad you're here. It saves me the trouble of having to send for you.'

Lalloo wasn't fooled by the friendly demeanour. He had to fight against the bile rising in his throat as soon as he heard that voice.

'Come. Come sit down.'

Heera sat down on the verandah in the shade and gestured Lalloo towards a chair entirely in the sun. He placed his drink on the table in between them. It was a cloudy pale liquid with ice cubes floating invitingly. He didn't offer Lalloo any. Lalloo guessed it was lemonade and watched the cool glass as it gathered perspiration.

'So, Ashraf is unwell. For the last few days, brick production has been severely down. Something needs to be done.' Heera leant back in his chair and steepled his hands on his belly.

Lalloo cleared his throat. 'Yes, I need to take Abu to a doctor.'

Heera waved a hand in the air as if shooing away a fly. 'Yes, yes, if you want, but what happens to the work?'

'If he can have a few days off, he'll return to work well rested.'

The sun burny overhead and sweat ran freely through his hair and down his back.

Heera shook his head and gave a repulsive, high-pitched snicker. He took a long drink from his lemonade and then looked directly at Lalloo. 'I know you've been away from the bhatti, but maybe you should reacquaint yourself with it. Your family are under contract to produce twelve hundred bricks a day. For the last three days, they haven't done any more than seven hundred.' He paused. His ugly, condescending voice made the hairs on the back of Lalloo's neck stand up. 'Now, I'm a very reasonable man, but I don't own this place. If it were up to me, every time someone sneezed, I would say, "Go! Have a day off work." But this is not my bhatti, Lalloo Sahib, and bricks won't make themselves.'

Lalloo squeezed the arms of his chair until his fingers ached. Five minutes ago, he had heard Heera offer his father's name up to someone – it must have been his boss – like a sacrificial offering. Just hearing Heera's voice was taking him back to the worst night of his life. The man was depraved, delighting in other people's misery. But anger wouldn't help Lalloo now. He leant forward and licked his dry lips. 'It'll just be a few days of him not working and I understand the debt will increase for those days, but then he'll be well and back to work again. Your bricks will get made as usual.'

Heera picked up his chilled lemonade and swirled the glass, making the ice clink. He took a mouthful while Lalloo watched him drink, then slapped the glass back on the table.

'If you ask me, the man's got one foot in his grave as it is. I wouldn't go to the expense of taking him to a doctor; you're just delaying the inevitable. Once the coughing starts – trust me, I've seen plenty like him.' He clapped his hands together as if to gather the attention of an audience, and, despite himself, Lalloo flinched. 'Now, my problem is the work. I need those bricks or it's my job on the line. That mother of yours has gone half-mad, and your sisters . . .' He paused for a moment as if considering. 'I'll have to find out about your sisters.'

The man was as vicious as he'd been fourteen years ago. Lalloo struggled to keep his voice level. 'Don't talk about my sisters like that.'

Heera shrugged. 'If you care so much, give your father a break. Instead of lazing around in the city, come to the bhatti and do some honest work for a change. Your old man shouldn't be doing all this. He can retire and my bricks get made. Everyone's a winner.'

Lalloo was expecting this. This was the whole reason his mother had sent him away as a child. This was why his parents only wanted him to visit the bhatti in darkness. Heera wanted Lalloo at the bhatti to pass the debt on to him, especially now that Abu was unwell.

'Just how long do you expect us to work for you?' Lalloo couldn't help himself. 'How many generations until the debt is repaid?'

Heera's eyes were puny in his big head and he narrowed them further. 'Now, now.' His voice was composed. 'I know you were little and you've been away for a long time, but maybe you're forgetting a few things here.' Heera stroked his own arm and looked Lalloo in the eye. 'Your parents had two sons, didn't they? Perhaps you could remind me, what happened to the other one?'

Lalloo kept his face rigid. It was hard not to slip back into memory, into the terror of the nightmares, but he was no longer a child. Over the years, he'd had to learn to go about normal life with the terror living inside. To be able to damp it down and still buy sabzi from the market, or replace the oil filter in a car. He had lost control with Taari, but he wasn't going to make that mistake here. There was too much at stake. He would not give Heera the satisfaction of a reaction or the excuse to act on it.

Heera leant forward in his chair as if sharing a confidence. 'You thought you got away, didn't you? But you can never escape the bhatti. Your brother learnt that lesson. Don't make me teach you too.'

Lalloo slowly got up from his chair. His legs were shaking.

'Of course, your brother had it coming to him, anyway. You know this. What sort of person drowns a mad child just to stop him making noises at night? Justice was served – nobody can deny it.'

Lalloo didn't think he had anywhere further left to fall inside his head. Coming here had been a mistake. This accusation, he'd heard it on the night Jugnu had died, and then again from Taari. It wasn't new, and it certainly wasn't true. There was nothing he could say that wouldn't make things worse. He turned to leave. But Heera wasn't done.

'So, are you going to come to work here or do I need to elicit some *extra* work from that older sister of yours?'

Lalloo turned to look at him, and Heera sat back and spread his legs wide suggestively, his arms draped around the back of the chair, a sneer on his face.

An icy dread spread through Lalloo's body, starting from his fingers and toes, spreading its way inside him, creeping up his chest, working its way up his body to his mouth, his nose and eyes, threatening to stop his breath. Shabnam had to work at the bhatti every day. Heera had made the threat too easily, too confidently, as though it was something he had already considered. Lalloo couldn't be there to protect her. He had to get her out, get them all out.

'I'll give you a few days to decide, then I expect an answer. But, Lalloo? Don't think you can take your father to the doctor until I have an answer,' Heera said, sounding gentle again. 'We'll watch him for you until then.'

Lalloo clenched his fists and walked away, head down. He didn't trust himself to say or do anything; he had to get out of there.

Chapter Sixteen

After speaking to Heera at the bhatti, Lalloo couldn't face going back to see his family. He hadn't been able to convince Heera to give Abu time off, and, actually, he'd made things worse. He headed straight back to Moti Mohalla full of a rage so intense, he could barely think straight. He had to get the money from Asima right away. If Shabnam got married, at least she could leave the bhatti. She'd be far away from all the evil that existed there and out of Heera's clutches. Then Lalloo could worry about Abu, Ami and Pinky.

He got back to his room and headed for the bathroom. Filling the bucket, he poured water over his body and hair, scrubbing himself with soap, rinsing the red dust off him again and again. Did his family even bother to clean it off any more? Pinky had been born there. She'd never known anything but a single room and thousands of red bricks. She'd never known Jugnu, never had his dreams to fill her head before he died. Lalloo knew that Jugnu hadn't done anything wrong that night, not to Hasnat or to anyone. But Lalloo had – he'd been the one to stop Jugnu from leaving.

All Lalloo had ever wanted was for the family to be together; even after he'd been sent away, he'd wanted to return to the bhatti. But now he understood Jugnu better. Now, the thought of returning to that hut to spend the rest of his life under the punishing sun, supervised by Heera, was impossible. Lalloo had to get his family out of the bhatti at all costs. There was no knowing what Heera would do next.

The first thing to do was get the money he was due from Asima.

It was mid-afternoon and his bosses weren't back from the wedding in Gujranwala until tomorrow. He needed to calm down, to be able to think straight, so he sought solace in the workshop in Sadar. The shop was cool and dark, and provided shelter from the glaring heat. It was also deserted, which meant he could work on Salman's car in peace. It helped him think. Maybe this was a good plan after all. Maybe Salman would be able to sell the car for a profit and they'd go again with another car. Maybe.

He really wanted to speak to Fatima, to hear her calming voice, so he sent her a message. He was working on the suspension, lying on his back underneath the car, when his phone beeped at him. He slid out to check it. She would be in the bazaar, under the neem tree, their old meeting place, in ten minutes if he could make it. He leapt up, cleaned himself up as best he could, and ran. As he neared the neem on the edge of the bazaar, he slowed to a walk, careful not to instigate any gossip, even though there weren't many people around at this time of day.

It was an old tree, with a wide trunk and big spreading branches that gave plenty of shade. Comfortable enough to sit under and wide enough for them not to be seen by anybody walking past the other side. Lalloo walked around and saw Fatima sitting cross-legged at the base of the tree. She wore pale pink today, the colour offsetting her complexion. Her hair hung loose, down past her shoulders, thick and wavy.

She looked up as he approached and greeted him with a smile. 'Well, this brings back memories.'

Many stolen moments had been spent under that tree. Lalloo would tell Rizwan he'd be back in ten, Fatima would give her chaperone the slip on the way home from school, and both of them would run to the neem to exchange the latest chit-chat from the day and snatch a few minutes together.

He sat down next to her, resting his head against the trunk behind him, breathing in her presence, her smile. Her eyes questioned his heaving chest as he tried to catch his breath.

'I ran over from Abdul's workshop,' he said in explanation.

'So, you *are* still working as a mechanic.'

He grinned. 'Just in my spare time. I'm fixing Salman's car for him.'

'And Salman finally got a car.'

They smiled at each other, remembering the many times Salman had bored them silly with stories of the cars he wanted to buy when he grew up.

Then she asked gently, 'Everything OK?'

He gathered his thoughts and spoke softly. 'My father is very unwell. I had a call from my sister yesterday, just after I saw you. I went to visit him this morning . . .' Abu's cough had been so deep, like it had taken root in his chest in order to grow. He had looked so small, so frail. What could Lalloo say about the big man who used to plough the fields and carry Lalloo home on his shoulders, about what he had been reduced to, about why Lalloo wasn't with him? 'My family are the most important thing to me,' he said around the lump in his throat. 'And I just don't know how to help them.'

He fell silent, unsure what else to say, unsure whether he was telling Fatima as an excuse or because he simply needed somebody to know.

She nodded slowly. 'My mother died when I was little. In a car accident. Before that, I used to be such a fussy child that she used to call me a maharani. "Would Maharani Sahiba like some food, maybe some chocolate? Would Maharani Sahiba like to be carried up the stairs?"' She smiled briefly at the memory. 'It used to annoy me no end. But after . . . afterwards, well, I'd do anything to hear her voice teasing me again, to beg her to carry me up the stairs and never climb into that car.'

Lalloo had known Fatima didn't have a mother, but this was the first time she'd spoken of her. He thought back to the long dark nights he'd spent wishing he could turn back time, wishing for Jugnu, for his parents and sister. Nights spent tossing and turning, and screaming out in terror. Had Fatima had nights like those?

'Yes, and you spend your entire energy on existing. Just surviving.'

She nodded. 'I was lucky Dado looked after me. She was my saviour. Who was yours?'

He didn't have to think long about that one. 'Salman, if you'll believe it. I didn't have anyone else apart from the two of you. He used to make up excuses to come see me at the workshop every Sunday, just to check up on me.'

Fatima was hugging her knees, resting her head on her arms as she listened.

'Where are your parents, Lalloo? You would never talk about them when we were younger.'

He hesitated. Even now, only Salman knew. It was not the sort of thing he usually spoke about.

'They work in a bhatti. They're trapped.' His voice was so low, Fatima had to lean in to hear him. 'My parents . . .' He took a deep breath. 'My brother died when I was little and my parents sent me away. It felt like they had abandoned me, like they blamed me for what happened to Jugnu.' He paused. He'd never spoken about this before, even to Salman. It'd always felt like a kind of betrayal to even think about them like this, but with Fatima, maybe because of what she'd just told him about herself, he felt he could speak about it. 'And they've never been the same since. Ami – she . . . she changed. She doesn't speak much any more. I mean . . . it's not that she can't, but she just . . . doesn't. Like there's nothing left to say. Like a world without Jugnu isn't worth talking about.' There was an ache in his throat and he stopped, worried that she'd heard it and would think less of him for it. Instead, she reached out and took his hand in hers. He curled his fingers around hers and they sat in silence together. And eventually the ache subsided.

Maybe it was her hand in his, maybe it was the coolness of her touch. He kept talking, telling her things he'd never spoken about before. 'My . . . my parents are indentured.' He felt his cheeks burning with shame. 'They got a loan from the bhatti owner about fifteen years ago and have been trying to work it off ever since. They get charged such high interest, they're never able to pay it off. I've always felt so . . . ashamed that they're stuck there.'

He faltered and fell silent.

After a while, she squeezed his hand. 'I had a patient once,' she said quietly. 'I was shadowing a doctor, and this man came in. He'd run away from a bhatti. He'd been so badly beaten he was almost dead. But when we stitched him up, when he was able to stand again... Lalloo, he went back. He hadn't even fully healed and he went back.' Fatima's hand was shaking in his. 'It's not your fault, it's not your parents' fault. Those bhatti owners are monsters. They exploit people like your family. It's illegal, even – did you know that?'

Goosebumps ran over Lalloo's arms. Jugnu had sounded just the same. He'd used that same word. 'It's exploitation,' Jugnu had said. 'They can't get away with it.' But Lalloo didn't tell Fatima this, didn't tell her the worst of it. Because they could get away with it, and they had, and Jugnu wasn't here any more to tell him otherwise.

They sat together holding hands and eventually the tightness in his chest began to dissolve. As if he could speak to her about anything. It didn't solve his problems, but it made dealing with them easier. He wasn't quite sure what this relationship was that he had with Fatima, but even he knew what a rare and precious thing it was. He wished he could sit here under the neem tree with her for ever. But the last time he'd had such an intense yearning to hold someone's hand and never let go had been when Abu had come to see him at the workshop, and look how that had turned out.

*

Lalloo had been at Rizwan's workshop for about eighteen months. Lahore had been baking in the June heat, turning the workshop into a metal furnace, and, despite the pedestal fan in the corner and the large doors sprung wide open, sweat had run down Lalloo's face and neck. He'd mopped his forehead with the rag for the tenth time, aware he'd smudged his face in black oil.

'Lalloo, come here, will you?'

Rizwan was shouting from outside. It was Sunday and the workshop was closed, but he was finishing some leftover work from the day before. Lalloo was only eight years old, but he could complete a lot of the tasks on his own and there was always so much to do. He knew what Rizwan wanted. He hadn't got around to working on the Toyota yet and his boss wanted to make sure it was done before Monday morning. He wiped his hands on the rag and headed out.

'I'll get the oil change done tonight. Don't . . .'

His voice trailed away seeing the figure standing next to Rizwan. A little stooped and more ragged, but definitely Abu. Lalloo's only regular contact with his family was the monthly phone call Rizwan's wife let him make from the house. Mumtaz timed him, towering over him and tapping her watch once five minutes were up. After the first call, Lalloo was overcome by nausea so severe he couldn't eat for several days afterwards. It was a physical pain he couldn't rid himself of. The agony grew stronger as the monthly call approached and lessened slightly as the month wore on.

Sometimes in the days leading up to it, he would imagine that Jugnu might answer the phone this time and they would chat about cricket and animals and Jugnu's plans for the future. They would have an hour-long conversation regardless of Mumtaz. Sometimes, despite the screams in his nightmares, he found it difficult to believe that Jugnu was gone, that he wasn't still at the bhatti, fetching water, moulding bricks, taking care of everyone, making them laugh with his antics.

When he called, Lalloo didn't know what to say to his parents. Instead, these phone calls were often filled with silence. Words weren't what he wanted; nothing he could say would convey the physical ache inside. Ami used to stroke his hair when he was tired. Abu would put his hand on his head to shush him when the neighbours were talking. Shabnam . . . Shabnam liked to curl her foot over his knee in her sleep, her hands pressed against his back. And yet, despite dreaming and praying countless times for this very moment, Lalloo didn't know how to cross the space and hug Abu.

They stared at each other, awkward and silent, and Rizwan slipped away. Lalloo approached Abu cautiously. Why didn't his father say anything? Then he came closer and saw Abu's eyes were full, and knew Abu couldn't say anything. He knew what that felt like.

At last, Abu cleared his throat and reached down to hold Lalloo's hand. Lalloo grasped it desperately.

'How are you doing, beta?'

That touch, this presence, was all Lalloo wanted. The weight of

Abu's hand in his was the most reassuring thing in the world. He would've stayed there all day, but the overhead sun was too strong and they couldn't stand in it for long. Lalloo led Abu by the hand out of the workshop through the streets of Sadar, the streets he now knew so well. They wound their way through the alleyways, Lalloo nodding at the stall owners as he passed, not stopping, not letting go of Abu. He brought Abu to the banyan tree at the edge of the bazaar, where they sat, still holding hands. Bicycle tyre tubes hung in the branches above them as they shared the shade with the repair boy, watching rickshaws and motorbikes splutter past.

Now that Abu was here, Lalloo didn't know what to say. He focused on his father's fingers, so big and rough around his own. Finally, Abu spoke.

'Does Rizwan treat you well? Chachi Bushra assured me . . . she said he had dealt with her fairly. He's a good boss?'

Lalloo nodded. Abu had left him with a complete stranger, not knowing how he would be treated or if he would be looked after.

'We saved up for my bus tickets,' Abu said. 'Your mother wanted to come, but . . .' He cleared his throat. 'She sent some food. I don't have long, but do you want to see?'

In his other hand, Abu held a tiffin box. He let go of Lalloo's hand to open up the layers, but let Lalloo grab hold again immediately afterwards. Lalloo was engulfed in the smell of Ami's cooking and a yearning so intense he didn't trust himself to speak. He shook his head, unable to eat.

They sat in silence for a while, watching the traffic pass them by.

'Do you remember the farm? Before the bhatti?' his father eventually asked. 'The home you were born in and all those animals you used to love.'

Lalloo nodded again.

'You used to round up the chickens,' Abu said, smiling a little. 'And Jugnu told you in some countries they herded sheep using dogs. So you got down on all fours and barked and barked, and then your sister joined in. Do you remember?'

Lalloo didn't cry, but he squeezed Abu's hand as tightly as he could, pulling it into his chest.

'And then Ami said, "I thought I'd given birth to children, but they've turned into dogs!" And the rooster jumped on your head and pooped in your hair. I've never seen your mother laugh so hard . . .' Abu's face twisted in a grimace. 'I miss it. It was a mistake, of course, coming to the bhatti. I did what I could for my family, Lalloo, but I know I made the wrong decision. I hope you can forgive me.'

Lalloo knew this, and now his father was finally saying it out loud. Suddenly, the yearning was too great. 'Can I come and see Ami and Shabnam?'

Abu paused and looked down, avoiding Lalloo's gaze. 'Heera hasn't said much about your leaving, Lalloo. But if he sees you . . .'

The very mention of that name was almost enough to make Lalloo never want to go to the bhatti again. Almost. But to hold Ami's hand? To hug Shabnam?

'So when? When can I come back? *What have I done?*' It was all Lalloo could do to stop his voice from wobbling, from winding himself around Abu and never letting go.

'This is not your fault, beta, but you have to stay away. You can be *free*.' Abu made it sound like a good thing.

'But . . . *I can never come home?*' It finally dawned on him. His father was not here to collect him. He was not going to take him back to be with the rest of the family at the bhatti. All the night terrors of the past year came flooding back. He would be alone again. 'Was it because I asked Jugnu to stay? It's my fault the men got him. If I hadn't—' Abu held up a hand to stop the onslaught, but Lalloo continued. 'Is it because Jugnu killed that—'

'That is enough!' Abu said. 'I don't want to hear you saying anything like that about your brother again. Never utter those lies.' Lalloo pressed his face against his father's arm, crying quietly, and Abu softened his tone. 'You can't come back to the bhatti, beta. This is your home now.' Abu glanced around him, squinting anxiously at the sinking sun. 'I've got to get back. I told everyone at the bhatti I was coming to town to help Chacha Haider buy a goat. I have to catch the bus back with him.'

He turned and embraced his son, their clasped hands held

awkwardly between them as Lalloo didn't let go. Lalloo couldn't stop the tears streaming down his cheeks, the sobs strangling his throat. Was this worse than the first time? This time, he knew how much it was going to hurt.

Abu silently broke their embrace and reached down to stroke Lalloo's hair. His hands were shaking, his voice muffled as he said softly, 'It's for the best, beta. I'll come back when I can.' And then he pulled Lalloo's fingers open, one by one, and let go of his hand.

Lalloo wiped his tears and watched Abu walk away. He wanted to shout after him, to kick the tiffin box into the dirt, but he couldn't do that with Ami's precious food. He squatted down, closing up the box to eat the contents later. Around him, the bicycle wallah had three customers queuing up to get their tyres changed. A toddler was crying in his mother's arms as she hurried past, carrying him on one hip and a heavy shopping bag in the other hand, rushing home to make his dinner. Imran Bhai and Naseema Baji from the poori stall walked past and waved at him from across the road.

Lalloo was nearly nine years old. He could fix most of the problems with the cars, could hustle on the side for a bit of extra money when he needed. He was independent, he could survive. But he looked down at his hands now and they were empty again.

Chapter Seventeen

The following morning, Lalloo was scrubbing at a particularly stubborn mark on the Range Rover's back seat when Asima and Omer arrived from Gujranwala in Omer's Land Cruiser. Asima climbed out and Lalloo went to take their bags from the boot. He heard her say to her husband, 'See you in a couple of days, then.' She instructed Lalloo which bags to take in, then Omer turned the car around and immediately sped off. Lalloo wondered where he was going. Yasmin was at Tania's house, so he wasn't meeting up with Tania.

Lalloo followed Asima into the house to drop the bags off. Asima started barking orders to Haleema, the woman who swept the floors, and he could see Guddo with a dusting cloth in the front room. There was no chance for privacy. Lalloo went outside and began to wax the Range Rover, taking his time. It gave him something to do as he waited, otherwise he'd start pacing the lawn.

What felt like hours later, Haleema finished her work and left, and Baba Jee's head lolled against the back of his chair, his nose pointing to the sky as he snoozed in the heat in front of the pedestal fan.

Then Guddo came out of the house. 'She's sending me to buy rice and daal, but we've already got rice and three types of daal. She's going a bit loopy, if you ask me.' She pointed to her head and made small circular movements with her index finger.

When Guddo left by the front gate, Lalloo ignored the thundering in his chest and walked into the house.

Asima was in the lounge sitting on a chair in front of a coffee table, her fingers worrying the gold hoops in her ear, 'Good, they've all gone, so we can talk in private.' She leant forward. 'Now tell me what you saw.'

Lalloo hesitated. 'I followed sahib to a housing society past the canal.' He paused again, unsure how to put what he'd seen into words, anxious at her reaction, no matter what words he used. Showing her the photos would be easier. He walked over, taking his mobile out of his pocket, knowing that once she'd seen these she wouldn't be able to unsee them. This would change things for ever. He cradled his phone and scrolled through the photos one by one, making sure there was plenty of time for her to absorb them.

She saw the first couple and, to Lalloo's amazement, almost chuckled in triumph, her neck wobbling in excitement as she reached for her mobile on the table in front of her. 'I knew it. I knew he was up to . . .' Then Lalloo scrolled to the next photo and she froze.

Tania's face was clearly visible, her black hair cut in a fashionable bob, her striking cherry-red lips inches from Omer's face, her gaze locked onto Asima's husband.

Asima wasn't breathing, her laugh frozen on her face as the colour drained from her cheeks. She clutched desperately at Lalloo's phone, struggling to comprehend. Lalloo kept a firm grip on his phone, but let her swipe frantically to the next photo and the next one, speeding up and then finally stopping on a picture, where she pinched two fingers together and zoomed right in on Omer's self-satisfied expression as he kissed Tania's neck. Lalloo felt sick.

'That is all of them, bibi,' he said gently, turning his screen off and tugging his phone from her grasp.

Asima still hadn't said anything. Her hands had fallen to her lap when he pulled the phone away, but they immediately started fidgeting. She tugged a small sapphire ring off her pinky finger, turning it around and forcing it back on, then pulling it off again, turning it around and pushing it back on. Yasmin had given it as a gift to her mother on her last birthday. But Asima was staring straight ahead, eyes unseeing, as if she didn't realise what she was doing.

'Bibi, I am sorry,' he said. 'I know it is a shock. I didn't expect to see Tania Bibi—'

'Shut up,' Asima said and Lalloo blinked, stunned by the venom in her voice. Her hands didn't stop moving. Her breath was coming too fast. 'Don't you dare utter that name again, do you hear?'

Lalloo stared at her. He'd expected her to be angry, but this was something else.

Her eyes narrowed at him. 'Have you told anyone about these photos?'

'No, bibi, you asked me to—'

'Good. You must delete them right away.' She stared blankly in front of her, seeing something he couldn't, never letting go of that sapphire ring as she twisted it on and off.

'Yes, bibi, but the money.'

She swatted at him with her plump, moisturised hands, like she would a persistent fly. 'Yes, yes, but not now. I've got more important things to do. You can have your money later.'

But Lalloo could hear the panic in Shabnam's voice when she'd told him they weren't meeting the brick quota.

'Bibi, my sister is getting married,' Lalloo said quietly. 'I need this money now.'

Asima's head jerked towards him, her eyes narrowed, but her breath still coming fast. 'I will not hear this nonsense about money from you again,' she said, her voice too loud in the quiet room. 'We already pay you far too much; you're lucky to work here.'

He should've known. His desires weren't of any importance in his boss's life. Promises were small change, to be lost or thrown away. She didn't care about Shabnam's wedding or his desperation, as long as her own needs were met.

An icy rage flooded Lalloo's body. He planted his feet and slid his phone slowly back into his pocket. He remembered how Jugnu had sounded, the exact tone and pitch he had used when something was unfair, when he wouldn't accept something.

'I will not delete those photos, bibi. We had a deal.' He balled up his fists by his side.

She inhaled sharply. 'How dare you disobey me, you—'

He cut her off. 'If you don't give me the money I am owed, I will have no choice but to show these photos to your friends.' He knew he was out of line making threats like these, but Heera's voice was in his head – *the Ashraf family have been flagging recently* – and he had to drown it out. 'Think about what Mrs Khan would say if she saw them.'

She sneered. 'A trumped-up servant, threatening me in my own house? My friends will have no interest in your spiteful lies.' She sounded shrill, although Lalloo was sure he detected a slight wobble in her voice. Her social standing was everything to her, he knew that, but she was fighting back.

'Perhaps not.' Lalloo searched around for something else, free-falling into the muck now – no way but down. 'Perhaps Omer Sahib won't care that you visited a pir, either.' He could feel the blood pulsing in his forehead, he felt reckless, desperate, scrambling for anything that would give him a foothold in the slippery black sludge. Who was the last person Asima would want to know about this? And then he realised his final, triumphant card. 'I will show Yasmin,' he whispered.

Asima went pale and collapsed back into her chair, her hands falling by her side, the façade broken. He almost felt sorry for her.

'You wouldn't.' She gasped out the words, her voice barely above a whisper. 'You can't – it will break her.'

Lalloo knew it would and he didn't want to do that to Yasmin, but Heera's words were still echoing. *I'll have to find out about your sisters.* 'Just give me the money, bibi.'

'I don't have that kind of money just lying around,' she hissed at him.

Lalloo pulled his phone back out of his pocket and tapped at the screen, emboldened now he knew his threats were working. 'It will only take me a few seconds to send the photos to her, bibi. The choice is yours . . .'

A deathly silence hung between them. Then he heard a strange whistling sound as Asima blew the air from her lips.

'Fine,' she said, finally, pushing her chair back and standing up. Her voice was calm again, but her lips were pressed tightly together.

'Come to work tomorrow and I'll sort you out.' She crossed her arms across her chest. 'But remember your place in this household, Lalloo. I've never taken kindly to servants who forget. Now get out of my sight.'

He didn't need telling twice. He left quickly, wanting to get out of there as fast as he could, walking right out of the gate even though he still had a few hours of work left. As he walked away, he pulled his phone out of his pocket and sent the photos to Salman as a back-up. Using these photos for his own benefit, turning against his employer, blackmail? It was all leaving a sour taste in his mouth. But Lalloo already knew that secrets tasted sour, whether you kept them or not. Jugnu had taught him that.

Chapter Eighteen

When Lalloo was seven years old, he had heard a long gurgling wail just as he finished another gruelling day making bricks at the bhatti. Abu had gone to the tube well to wash and Ami and Shabnam had already headed into the family's hut to prepare food for the evening. He couldn't see Jugnu anywhere. Maybe he'd gone to fetch water.

Lalloo listened again and realised that the wailing was coming from the hut where the mad boy lived. He was determined to see for himself. He took a detour around the front of the huts, past the mound of bricks, checking no one was watching him. Hasnat's hut was just like theirs, a mud structure with a corrugated tin sheet for a roof, which baked in the summer sun, and a hole in the wall for a window. He sneaked up to the front, crouching low, and slowly raised himself up to peek through.

Inside was dark and he heard them before he saw them, a snatch of conversation, a familiar voice. Jugnu. What was he doing there? Lalloo's first instinct was to call out to his brother. *Come back, the madness might be catching.* But he stopped and listened. Jugnu was cross-legged on the floor with his back to the window, facing a boy who looked about ten. The boy sat, legs sprawled out in front of him, staring straight ahead. His hair a tangled mess, his face covered in dirt, he had a chain around his neck attached to the wall, and every now and again he reached up and jangled it as if he were ringing a bell. Jugnu was talking in a hushed voice, trying to keep Hasnat's attention. Hasnat wasn't looking at him. What could Jugnu possibly be saying to him? Why did Hasnat look so angry? Then Jugnu whispered something, nudged the boy's elbow, and Hasnat lost the vacant look in his eyes, turned his head to look straight out the window at Lalloo and smiled. A big, wide smile.

Lalloo felt like a thousand jinn had tapped him on the shoulder. With the hairs on the back of his neck standing up and the shaytan on his back, he ran. Not caring whether he was seen or heard, he raced back to the safety of their own family hut, where Ami was cooking roti, and tried to burrow into her embrace.

'What are you doing? What's got into you all of a sudden? You can't do this – you'll get burnt by the fire.'

She pushed him away from her gently so she could continue making the roti, and Lalloo sat back to back with his mother, touching as much of her as he could, taking comfort from her warmth. He couldn't shake the feeling of the boy's eyes locking into his, as if he could see right through into his soul.

The following week, Lalloo noticed Jugnu heading over to Hasnat's place again.

'What are you doing in Hasnat's hut? Why do you keep going to see him?'

He couldn't keep the accusation out of his voice and Jugnu did what he always did when Lalloo got angry – he went infuriatingly calm.

'Arré, kaale bhoot, I'm just talking to him. He doesn't have anyone to speak to. You know he's not that different from you and me.'

Lalloo was incensed. 'What are you talking about? He's mad, completely paagal – you heard what Chachi said.'

Jugnu shook his head and ruffled Lalloo's hair. 'Some people just feel the world more deeply than others. He's one of those souls. Look around you, look at what we do. Which man would say this is sane?'

But Lalloo didn't like it one bit, the boy's wide smile sealed in his nightmares, the jangling of his chains jolting Lalloo awake at night.

Jugnu saw the look on Lalloo's face. 'You don't need to understand, Lalloo, but don't go telling Ami. This is my decision.'

Lalloo knew deep inside that no good would come out of Jugnu hanging around with Hasnat. He didn't know how to explain it, and his brother just thought he was being jealous, but he was right.

*

The next morning, Lalloo stood outside the Alams' main gate for far too long. The eight-feet-high ornate wrought-iron gates stood solid and closed, protecting the family, keeping the rest of the world out. He had a horrible, unsettling feeling in his gut. Fatima had called him a conman and how far was she from the truth now that he was resorting to blackmail? What would she think of him if she knew? But, much like these gates, Lalloo knew the world was closed to people like him. Sometimes you had to find another way. He turned towards the servants' gate, well-worn and familiar, and slipped inside.

His first inkling that something was out of place was seeing Omer's car parked in the driveway. Hadn't Asima said, 'See you in a couple of days,' just yesterday? Lalloo sat down next to Baba Jee in the porch and heard doors slamming inside. Through the window, he saw Haleema running across the hall. Haleema never ran.

'What's happening, Baba Jee?' he asked, still staring at the house.

'I don't know, beta; something's gone wrong.' Baba Jee's lined face was concerned. 'But no one's told me anything yet.'

They didn't have to wait long to find out. Guddo came to the door and before Lalloo could ask, she called out, 'Baba Jee! Lalloo! Bibi wants you inside.'

'What's going on?' Lalloo asked quietly.

She gave him a perturbed look, but didn't reply, just turned on her heel and went inside.

Lalloo and Baba Jee exchanged a glance. Lalloo's gut twisted further.

'Well, bibi gets what bibi wants. We'd better go,' Baba Jee muttered half to himself and rose to go into the house. Lalloo followed.

They walked into the entrance hall and Haleema rushed from the lounge into the drawing room and crouched down on the floor, looking under a sofa. Guddo was already in there, jharoo in one hand, sweeping with the twig broom under the other sofa. Every item of furniture in the drawing room and the entrance hall had been moved away from the wall. Even Chota, the young boy who did the gardening, was joining in the search, moving tables and vases and looking behind them. Asima was nowhere to be seen. The entire household was in disarray. Lalloo glanced towards the lounge and saw Omer quietly standing with his back to everyone, his hands clasped behind his back, looking out of the window. His still figure amid all the chaos in the house sent shivers down Lalloo's spine.

Asima entered the room from the rear door of the house. What was she doing out the back in this heat?

'Everybody line up here in a row.' She barked out the order.

The servants filed into the entrance hall and shuffled into a line, complying silently, trying to make themselves as inconspicuous as possible. Lalloo kept attempting to catch Guddo's eye, but she wouldn't look at him.

Asima came and stood in front of the line-up. 'Now, as some of you know, the reason you're all gathered is because sahib's watch has gone missing. He left it here before he went away and we've searched for it everywhere. Nothing like this has ever happened in this house before and I'm very disappointed it has happened now.' She paused. 'But I'm sure there's a reasonable explanation. I want you all to think back and remember if you might have seen it.'

Lallo's stomach felt like it was full of rats. Big and black with enormous tails, gnawing at his insides. He knew nothing about a watch, but those rats were hungry.

Asima paced in front of the line while she waited for someone to speak up. Silence followed her little speech. No one spoke. Lalloo kept his eyes fixed firmly on the floor.

'I'm going to give you all one chance to let me know the whereabouts of the watch.'

Again, silence. She let it stretch on for a moment, then she looked towards her husband, still standing silently in the lounge, and Lalloo thought he saw Omer give her a nod. She took a deep breath.

'You leave me with no choice. Guddo, go and bring me everyone's bags. They will be searched. So will everyone's pockets.'

There was not a murmur from the line-up. Nobody dared move.

'Guddo, did you hear me? What are you waiting for?' Asima's voice was harsh.

Guddo spent ten minutes going about the house gathering the bags people brought with them to work every day and depositing them at Asima's feet. Lalloo's satchel and Baba Jee's sack were brought in from outside, where they stored them by the front porch. Even though the air conditioning was running full blast, Lalloo could feel trails of sweat racing each other down his back.

He looked down the line. Haleema kept wiping sweat from her forehead, looking around her again and again, as if the missing watch would turn up. Chota looked around wide-eyed, lost. Baba Jee was shaking as he stood next to Lalloo. His frail limbs shuddered; it was a wonder he managed to stay upright. If Baba Jee lost his job here, he didn't have any family to support him and at his age he was unlikely to get any work. He'd end up on the streets.

When Guddo was done gathering, she rejoined the line-up. Asima started at the beginning with Haleema, holding the bag up in front of her with the tips of her fingers as if it was too dirty for her to handle properly and tipping out the contents onto the floor. A change of clothes, a magazine and a pair of flip-flops fell out. The plastic cover on Haleema's lipstick cracked on the unforgiving marble floor. Asima poked at the contents with her foot, finding nothing of interest. She left Haleema's things where they lay and moved on to Guddo, Chota and Baba Jee, taking her time. This was Asima's deliberate, collective humiliation of the servants for the missing watch and it would not be rushed.

Then it was Lalloo's turn. He was the last servant in line, next to Baba Jee. He realised, suddenly, that the phone with the incriminating photos was in his pocket and there was no way to stop Asima from taking it. She could come up with any number of excuses to do so and he could hardly stop her with so many witnesses. But when Asima reached him, instead of tipping out the contents of his bag from a height, she thrust her hand in theatrically and began to remove each item piece by piece. A change of clothes, a bag of nimko, a phone charger. Asima's frown deepened with each item, her hand diving further into the bag, rummaging around, and Lalloo wondered what she would do when she didn't find the phone there. But then, her fist closed triumphantly around something heavy and she pulled it out, dangling it in front of them all – a striking gold Rolex glinting in the daylight.

Haleema gasped. Four pairs of accusing eyes turned to look at Lalloo. Only Guddo turned away. His mind shot into overdrive, thoughts flashing past with every gleam of the watch's face. He didn't understand, couldn't fully grasp what was happening. The phone was still in his pocket.

'Lalloo!' Asima's eyes flashed darkly at him.

Lalloo was shaking his head. 'I didn't take it, bibi,' he whispered. 'You know I didn't.'

And then he heard the unmistakable sound of Omer's hard, leather shoes marching into the entrance hall towards the line of servants. Lalloo's heart was pounding. Omer came closer, dressed in his grey suit and a crisp white shirt, a tight smile crossing his lips as Lalloo looked up desperately. Asima turned and faced her husband, presenting the watch to him.

'We'll be needing another driver. We've caught the thief. He'd hidden the watch in his bag.' Asima's tone was almost perfect, a mixture of disappointed and dismissive, and that was what finally tipped Lalloo off. This was a set-up. She had set him up.

'It wasn't me.' Lalloo licked his dry lips. 'You know it wasn't.' His heart was thundering.

Omer looked too pleased with himself, too in control of the situation. He didn't like surprises, so Asima must have told him something. But how much had she told him?

Lalloo took a step towards the Alams, looking from one to the other, before focusing in on Omer, 'Sahib, please. There is no need for this. I don't want any trouble. It wasn't my idea. Yasmin never needs to—'

Then a blinding crack. Lalloo's head smacked into the wall at the force of Omer's hand across his cheek. A hot, white pain. His jaw felt as if it had been dislocated. Before he could fully gather what was happening, Omer had rummaged in his pocket and grabbed his phone. Lalloo tried to snatch it back, but Omer dropped it to the floor and stamped on it hard, bringing his heel down on it again and again.

'So, this is what it has come to, sahib?' Lalloo let his voice carry across the room. 'I tell Asima Bibi you're having an affair and you both come up with this charade to make me look like a thief?'

One of the servants behind him, Guddo, he thought, dropped something on the floor. No one else moved.

His boss grabbed him by the neck and pinned him up against the wall behind him. The grip so tight Lalloo couldn't breathe, Omer's face inches from his.

'After everything we've done for you.' Omer's voice was a low growl, his breath hot on Lalloo's face. 'You namak-haram, you think you can get away with blackmail?'

Flecks of spit hit Lalloo's nose and cheeks.

Suddenly the pressure on his neck was released and Lalloo fell to the floor. Rubbing his sore neck, his breathing painful, Lalloo slowly got to his feet. He was filled with a now familiar rage at these powerful people who thought they could treat others like the dirt under their shoe, a minor inconvenience. He'd worked for years trying to do things the right way. He'd fulfilled every request the Alams had made of him, kept their secrets, worked himself to the bone, but the Alams just couldn't keep their promises. He had been left with only one card to play, one chance to give his family a new life, and now Asima had pulled the rug out from under his feet again. But he wasn't going to go quietly. It was hard to think now, past the angry pounding in his head, but Asima would have been mad to tell Omer everything, which meant he still had his one card.

'Did Asima Bibi tell you,' Lalloo was almost shouting now, his voice was hoarse, but he forced his words out, '*she* sent me after you to take the photos? Did she tell you that she said she would pay me for them?'

Omer's head snapped towards his wife. Asima's face was ashen, but Lalloo wasn't finished.

'It's too late, anyway,' Lalloo said, gesturing at the broken phone. 'I've already backed up the photos.'

'To hell with them, then. Do you think I care what a bhenchaud servant like you will do with a couple of photos?'

'I think you can think of at least one person who would care,' Lalloo said.

Before Lalloo could say anything else, Omer punched him in the stomach and he fell, winded, to the floor. Still on the ground, a hard thump to his head knocked him sideways. Out of the corner of his eye, he saw Omer had taken off his shoe and was holding it in his hand. He curled into a ball to protect himself as the blows with the shoe kept coming.

'Daddy! What are you doing?' A terrified voice interrupted the violence and a stillness followed.

Lalloo squinted through one eye that was already swelling. Nobody had noticed Yasmin opening the front door. She stood there with a horrified expression on her face. Lalloo was once again the spectacle in the ring. The entire household had been watching his humiliation, unable and unwilling to intervene.

'No! Yasmin. Stay out of this. This is no concern of yours.' Asima tried to block her daughter's path, but Yasmin ignored her and walked across the hallway to her father.

Omer was breathing heavily. 'It's all right, I'm done here anyway.'

He dropped the shoe to the floor and the leather hit the marble with a crack.

Yasmin wouldn't be deterred. 'What is going on?'

Lalloo got to his feet, swaying a little, his feet crunching on pieces of his smashed phone.

'I'll tell you.' Lalloo's voice came out as a croak. The rage inside him was red-hot. Omer twitched towards him. 'Your father is having an affair, Yasmin,' he said, looking her straight in the eye.

'That is ENOUGH!' Omer roared and lunged for him again, but this time Yasmin put her arm out to stop him and he pulled up immediately. Omer pointed a menacing finger at Lalloo. 'Enough of your lies. You will never set foot in this house again.'

Lalloo wasn't going to stop now – he had nothing to lose any more. He was done with making himself small. 'Your father is beating me because I have the evidence.'

Asima stepped forward. Her voice was shriller than usual and her face still colourless, as if she herself had received the blows. 'Silence! You should beg forgiveness from sahib,' she said, pulling her chin up.

'Beg forgiveness?' Lalloo wiped his lip with his sleeve and it came away smeared with blood. 'From a man who beats up his servant and cheats on his wife with his daughter's . . .?' He glanced at Yasmin. 'Why don't you ask your father who he was with?'

Omer charged at him again, but this time Lalloo was ready and pushed him back.

'Tania.' He spat out her name, furious. Wanting to hurt as much as he'd been hurt, lashing out with no regard for the consequences.

Yasmin's head whipped back, her eyes wide and unblinking. She stared at him uncomprehending and then turned to look at her father. Omer was already storming from the room. Asima glared at Lalloo, but her hands were held before her as if to ward off another blow.

Lalloo looked around him, at the other servants still standing with their eyes to the ground, wincing as he stooped to pick up his bag and his things that had been spilt on the floor.

'Good luck with your pir,' he called to Asima as he left the house. He marched out of the tall gates for what he knew was the last time, shutting him out of the world of power and wealth he'd been allowed to catch a glimpse of. But what did these rich people know about family? What it was to truly love and to risk losing that love. Money didn't teach you how to do that.

The sky outside had turned brick red. The heat of the summer had brought with it a great dust storm making the air thick and heavy. Lalloo's face was smeared in blood, his kameez torn and his feet burning on the hot ground. The wind blew droves of red dust into his eyes and mouth.

He couldn't believe what he'd just done. He'd felt powerful, almost indestructible, standing up to Omer like that. His brother had always stood up for himself, never prepared to silently suffer an injustice. But Lalloo could feel the rage simmering, slowly settling in his bones with chinking sounds like hot metal left to cool. Jugnu had paid the heaviest price for taking a stand. Lalloo battled through the dust storm, keeping his head down and his eyes half-closed. He couldn't see where he was going, could only see the men that night with their dogs, hear their voices as they called Jugnu's name. The dust made his eyes weep and stung his cut lip, like salt rubbed on a wound.

Chapter Nineteen

The pounding on his door was deafening. Lalloo lay as still and silent as a corpse on his charpai. He was bathed in sweat from the roots of his hair to his ankles. He'd come back to his room to rinse the blood off his face and the dust off his body, and try to figure out what to do next, and hadn't realised that his rent had been due yesterday.

'I know you're in there – open up!'

Lalloo dared not move in case the charpai creaked. Kaka couldn't know if he was actually inside or not. He hadn't even turned on the ceiling fan in case his landlord had heard it whirring. When Lalloo walked out of the Alams' that morning, he'd also walked out on three and a half weeks of wages. Lalloo had started saving to get his family out of the bhatti after his first month working with the Alams, and he knew exactly how much money he had hidden in a plastic bag under the bedding of his charpai, each note smoothed into careful piles and held in bunches with elastic bands. He held his breath.

'How long do you think you can hide from me? Huh?' Kaka called.

The room reverberated with every thump. The noise stopped momentarily and Lalloo pictured Kaka wiping his brow, not used to all this exertion, before starting again.

Lalloo had only ever taken money from that bag for the family. Once, to pay for Shabnam to get stitches when she'd cut her foot on broken glass; once, to have one of Ami's teeth pulled; once, to get the family new blankets during an especially hard winter. And yet the bag was still pitifully small. He couldn't bring himself to open it now, to pay Kaka, when that money was the only small safety net his family had for emergencies. He should just about have enough money in there to take Abu to a doctor and buy him medicines. He also needed to get himself a new phone so he could contact his family and give them his new number.

For an old man, Kaka had amazing strength. The rusty bolt groaned and the ancient wooden door – Lalloo's only escape route – shuddered under the onslaught. There was only one window high up, which showed a few inches of white-hot sky. The paint on the walls was bubbled – blistered and peeling from years of humidity and heat. The sweltering air and the persistent thumping were making the room shrink. The air was being squeezed out of it. All Lalloo could do was lie still and hope Kaka didn't actually break the door down.

Lalloo couldn't afford to be out of a job, not even for a day, but what would a job even solve right now? Lalloo's hands started to shake, his eyes burnt and his heart felt like it might explode in his chest. He had no income and no plan. He remembered the look on Heera's face as he'd threatened Shabnam, the way Yasmin had flinched when Lalloo had shouted at her, the sound of Abu's coughs as they'd echoed down the phone. If he could get a new job, maybe he could ask for a smaller loan from his new boss; maybe he could bribe Heera to let Abu have a few days off and get Abu to a doctor. Maybe he could convince Abu to delay Shabnam's wedding to give Lalloo time to come up with a new plan. But he had no job. He saw Heera's face again and his threatening sneer. He thought of how he had messed this all up and his heart beat faster until it was louder than the thumping on the door.

'You think you can get away with this? I'm not leaving until you open this door,' Kaka continued.

The only time his landlord was ever off his charpai was when he asked for the rent. Lalloo could picture him now, standing outside the door, alternately banging on it, pressing his ear against it to check for any sound, and verbally abusing it.

'Arré, what's all this din, Kaka Jee? Is your house on fire?' A woman's voice, but Lalloo couldn't make out who. As long as it wasn't Chachi Jeera.

'Have you seen that beghairat, Lalloo? He's avoiding me.'

'He's your tenant, Kaka Jee, you should keep track of him. Let us have our siestas in peace.'

Kaka kept muttering as Lalloo heard the woman stomp away.

There was a final smack on the door. 'Listen up, you chootia.' Lalloo could hear the snarl in his voice. 'If you haven't paid by the end of the week, I'm getting Taari Bhai to come break this lock. Then you'll find your belongings in the gutter.'

This is what hell must feel like, Lalloo thought. Fiery hot, with Kaka thumping on his skull all hours of the day, demanding rent he couldn't afford to pay. He would have to wait until Kaka drank himself to sleep before he could sneak out. He wished more than anything for Jugnu's guidance. Jugnu had always had a plan. But it was a familiar feeling in his life – wishing for Jugnu and being confronted by the slap in the face that was Jugnu's absence.

*

Ever since they'd moved to the bhatti, Jugnu had been a night-time wanderer. Lalloo would wake in the night and instantly know Jugnu had gone. He wouldn't be alarmed – it happened often enough.

He'd close his eyes and wait. Whenever Jugnu returned, Lalloo would pester him: where had he gone this time? What had he seen? And, usually, Jugnu would have some story to tell, of the neighbour's goat who'd grown to five feet tall and carried him away to a magical land, of a clay monster that had climbed out of the bricks and kept him prisoner in an underground dungeon, or fighting for a firefly queen who'd ruled the lake, battling a serpent king with three heads.

Except this night had been different. Jugnu hadn't returned for so long that Lalloo had eventually fallen back asleep. When he'd woken again, the spot next to him had still been cold where his brother should've been. He hadn't known the time, but surely soon they would have to get up. What would happen if Abu woke and

Jugnu wasn't there? What had been so important that he couldn't get back before morning? Just then, Jugnu had appeared.

'Bhaya?'

Lalloo sat up, wanting to reprimand his brother, but stopped. There was something strange going on. Jugnu was silent as usual, but as soon as he slipped in through the doorway, Lalloo could sense it, smell it. His brother was soaking wet from head to toe. His slightly too-long floppy hair was plastered to his scalp, his kameez sticking to his torso, his shalwar sucked in on his legs, making him look painfully thin. Even his chappal made a squelching noise as he walked.

'What happened to you?' Lalloo whispered.

He was expecting his brother to shush him like he always did, afraid of waking their parents, but Jugnu came and sat down heavily beside him, water dripping everywhere.

'Bhaya? The bedding's getting soaked.'

'He's gone, Lalloo. It's all my fault.' Jugnu dropped his head into his hands as he mumbled. Blood dripped down his wrist from a cut deep in his hand. He was shaking so hard that Lalloo was suddenly afraid.

Beside them, Shabnam stirred in her sleep.

This seemed to galvanise Jugnu. Standing up, he stripped out of his soaking clothes and dressed in a fresh shalwar kameez from the tiny almaree that stored their things.

'Where did you go? Who's gone?' Lalloo pleaded with his brother, but Jugnu's eyes were blank and he didn't respond.

The family were stirring. Lalloo leant over to put his hand on Jugnu, but his brother stepped away. Jugnu scooped up his wet clothes and left the hut without looking back, leaving Lalloo with no stories this time to lull him back to sleep. No comforting tales of heroes and adventure. Just a brother who seemed to have gone far, far away, and he didn't know how to get him back.

Chapter Twenty

It was hours later that Lalloo heard Kaka's loud rhythmic snores through the walls of his room and snuck out, glad to finally be free. The first thing he did was swing by Salman's shop to get a new phone and luckily Salman was able to sell him a cheap one. His friend's shop was busy though, so there wasn't much opportunity to talk. Dusk had fallen and with nowhere else to go at that time of day, Lalloo decided to finish off the car at the workshop. Abdul had given him a key, so he let himself in.

Lalloo quickly got started on the car and lost himself in the work. As always, working on a car – overhauling an entire engine, fixing a suspension or plugging a flat tyre – calmed him like nothing else did. The worries of the world fell away while he was trying to find the source of an oil leak. It was his refuge. He wanted to finish up on Salman's car and he spent the rest of the night immersed. He was beneath the car, fingers tracing along the freshly fitted oil pan gasket, when he heard cocks crowing and birdsong outside. He tightened the last header bolts, made sure the exhaust was sealed and then topped up every fluid one last time – radiator, transmission and brake. He clambered out from underneath, tiredness making his eyes ache. The car was done. He couldn't wait to see Salman's face when he saw it finished and sent his friend a message.

Half an hour later as he was checking the spark plugs, a sound at the garage door made Lalloo step back, wiping his grimy hands on a cloth.

'Come and see this, yaar . . .' The words died in his throat as he turned.

'Thought I'd find you here.'

Fatima stood in front of him, immaculate in a pale-blue shalwar kameez, her hair clipped at the back of her head, everything around her dimming in comparison. He became acutely aware of his filthy hands and dirty fingernails, his clothes stained and dishevelled, no better than the street urchin he used to be all those years ago.

It was Sunday today so she wasn't at college. He hadn't spoken to her since Omer had broken his phone yesterday, but she had come looking for him. His heart was dancing a bhangra in his chest. His ears and the back of his neck were hot. Whenever he saw her, she was so vivid, more real than anything else in his life.

'You haven't replied to my messages or returned my calls. What's going on? Are you OK?'

'I'm so glad you're here. I broke my phone and had to get a new one.' He fished his phone out of his pocket to show her. 'I was afraid I'd have to go jumping over the rooftops again to get your number.' He grinned at her, but Fatima wasn't smiling. 'What is it? Is something wrong?'

He indicated the bench by the side of the car and cleared it of a box of spanners and wrenches. They sat on it side by side.

She spoke hesitantly. 'An old school friend of Dado's came round yesterday.'

He waited.

'I was in the kitchen making tea, so I didn't hear all their conversation, but it was about forging a stronger friendship by turning it into a family bond.'

'Huh?'

She sighed. 'Her grandson's a doctor. She wants to get him married. To me.'

Lalloo swallowed. 'To you?' Marriage wasn't something he'd even thought about. But the idea of Fatima with someone else . . . He looked at his hands, still grimy with engine oil, and unclenched his fists.

'She said two doctors getting married makes for a strong relationship.'

'And . . . do you want to marry him?' he asked cautiously.

'Last time I saw him, we were nine years old and he kept picking his nose and licking his fingers.'

Lalloo laughed weakly. 'I'm relieved you paint such a sordid picture of my competition.'

'Are you though? Competition?' She sounded earnest. 'Because Dado will ask me and I'm running out of excuses to give her.'

Had there been other proposals too? From other families? Probably. She was beautiful and smart, and the age where parents worried about their daughters.

'Tell her his nose is too big.' He stood up and walked towards Salman's car again.

'Lalloo . . .'

'I . . . Fatima.' He paused and turned around. 'I lost my job yesterday and it's not been easy.'

'You'll get a new job, though?'

He nodded. 'Yes, but . . . my circumstances. My family.'

It was no surprise she was getting proposals from educated men with money, doctors and the like. Her family would expect any man she married to be able to support her financially, to be able to provide for her. Maybe this was the time to accept they were too different to ever be together? He couldn't even provide for himself, couldn't keep his family safe. Lalloo's throat was beginning to burn and suddenly he wanted Fatima to leave, wanted to slide back under Salman's car and take it apart to put it back together again.

Fatima caught his arm as he walked past, turned him towards her.

'Do you think that's what I worry about? How much money you have? Where your family comes from?'

'If you marry this doctor, you'll have a comfortable life. You'll be well-off, both have jobs you enjoy. It sounds perfect.'

She let go of his arm and leant back. 'You know, Lalloo, when you asked me to the cinema, I couldn't believe it. You never asked me anywhere before.'

'What?'

Fatima ignored him, gathering steam. 'On that last day before

I left Lahore, I almost thought you might say something. You had that look on your face, the one you used to get whenever we walked past the chips or the chaat stall and had no money. Like you wanted something, but didn't think you'd get it. But you said nothing that day and I thought I was imagining it.'

Lalloo stayed absolutely still, not daring to move, or even breathe. What was she saying?

Fatima searched his face. 'Are you trying to put me off? I haven't waited for you for years just so you can fob me off this easily. You'll have to tell me properly. Do you want me to go?'

He stared at her. 'You've waited for me?' He'd thought he was the only one who'd tried but failed to keep her out of his mind all these years.

'For the boy who sewed up my ripped dupatta so I wouldn't get in trouble? The friend who ran slower whenever we ran with Salman, so Salman wouldn't feel like he was unable to keep up? The man who helped my grandmother, even when she called him names? Yes, Lalloo. I've waited for you.'

Lalloo couldn't believe that the world was still turning. He could hear voices of people walking outside, a goat bleating, a vendor selling boiled eggs. People going about the start of their days in the normal way, but inside the workshop, time had stopped. He sat down beside her again, his legs weak. He tried to find words that made sense, to tell her he had waited too, that he couldn't do without her soothing voice, her sparkling eyes, but the words had all deserted him.

She was still watching his face with a hint of a smile on hers. 'I don't care how successful or not you are.' She reached out her hand and placed it on top of his. 'And Dado will come round. But I need to know that you want this too.'

After everything that'd happened the day before, and having been up all night working on the car, Lalloo should have been exhausted, but he wanted this moment to last for ever. A cool morning breeze was blowing through the workshop door, Salman's car stood ready before him, Fatima was holding his hand and she'd waited for him. In this moment, nothing much else mattered. He nodded and turned his hand over so that their fingers were entwined, hoping she would understand.

She squeezed his hand and smiled.

'Right, good,' she said in her practical voice. The voice you would trust to make things better if you were ever sick. 'I should probably get back. Dado will be waiting for me. I told her I was going to buy eggs, so I'll have to get some on the way home.'

He felt guilty about causing her to lie to her grandmother. No respectable family would be OK with their daughter sneaking out to see a man who had made no commitment to marry her – that was why she had to lie, to sneak about. But if he could somehow make it official, if he could get a job, sort his parents out, then maybe he could send his parents over with a marriage proposal. Maybe her family would accept him then.

He smiled and nodded towards the car. 'I could take you in the car – it'll be quicker.'

She laughed and her nose wrinkled in that way he always thought adorable. 'No, someone will see us. But have you fixed it, then?'

He stood up and pulled her along with him, refusing to let go of her hand as he walked her around it. He'd sweated over it, cursed it, coaxed it, and it was just about ready.

'It needs a paint job, but that's pure aesthetics. You should've seen it a week ago. Every dent and scratch has been hammered out of it and the engine practically hums. Salman's going to love it.'

She smiled at his enthusiasm and sat in the passenger seat so he could rev the engine.

He ducked his head, blushing. 'Sorry, I'm going on and on about this car.'

'No, don't be sorry. It's quite an achievement. You should be proud of it.'

Then she leant across and kissed him on the cheek. Time slowed right down. In a haze, he turned his head to look around at her and stared into those stunning eyes. He'd been watching Fatima for so much of his childhood, he'd forgotten she might be watching him too. Without thinking, he moved closer to her and, before he knew it, he was kissing her. His hands were shaking as he lifted them to cradle her face and bury them in her hair. She tasted of stolen mangoes and the first rays of sunlight after a storm. As they broke apart, she smiled shyly back at him. He felt as if he might burst with happiness.

After Fatima left, Lalloo snuck back to his room to shower and change, and, this time, caught a bus to Ichhra, a less affluent part of town. The houses here were smaller than the Alams' and crammed together, the streets more crowded.

He spent the day going from door to door, the sky white-hot, the sun relentless as he walked through the streets. At every house he approached, he was turned away by the servants. When he managed to speak to the sahib of the house, the conversations were all the same. *How much experience have you got? Where did you work before this? Yes, I know Omer Alam. Why did you leave?*

Lalloo left his phone number with them, but didn't expect a call back. Omer would make it impossible for him to find a new job.

By the evening, he headed back to a house where a servant that morning had asked him to return to speak to the boss as they might have an opening for a driver. It was the only hope he had. The cars parked outside were a grey Corolla and a white Suzuki. This family obviously weren't as rich as the Alams, but wealthy enough to afford a driver. It wasn't much, but there was hope.

He rang the doorbell and a woman answered wearing a pristine shalwar kameez with a dupatta on her shoulder so heavily starched it could've stood up on its own.

She took one look at him and made to close the door. 'We don't need anything.'

He took a step forward, aware that he looked worse for wear, having been traipsing the streets all day. 'No, no, bibi, I'm here for the job. As a driver? Your cleaner asked me to come back to speak to you.'

'I don't need a driver, I hired one yesterday.'

Lalloo had spent all day going from door to door, begging for a job. He hadn't slept last night, his feet ached and he hadn't eaten all day. He was bone-weary.

'But, bibi, she asked me to come back this morning. I have lots of experience, I—'

'I said I don't need a driver.'

She went to close the door again and Lalloo reached across to stop her.

'Bibi, I—'

'What are you doing?' Her voice rose to a shriek. 'How dare you? Let go of the door. Bobby. Bobby!'

Lalloo shrank back in horror as a large man in a dirty shalwar kameez came hurrying around the side of the house.

'Get this man out of here and lock the gate behind him.'

There was no time to say anything. Lalloo ran out before Bobby could lay his hands on him, but as he exited the gate, the huge guard managed to aim a kick at his backside that sent Lalloo sprawling in the dirt. The gate shut with a clang as Bobby bolted it tight.

The dirt from the side of the road stuck to his sweaty face and hands. He brushed himself off as best he could and started on the long journey back home. There wasn't a hint of cloud in the sky, no solace in even the promise of rain. He had no money, no job and no way to pay the rent on his room. And that awful feeling in the pit of his stomach kept reminding him just how dangerous Heera could be.

With no other options, tonight Lalloo just wanted to get back to his room and wash the day's dirt and sweat off him. He got off the bus and walked towards the mohalla, wondering whether it was late enough to risk it. Would Kaka be asleep by now? A car was honking its horn incessantly somewhere behind him.

The horn grew louder. 'Arré, chootia, the whole world will hear me before you do.'

He turned at the familiar voice. Salman was in the car Lalloo had fixed, hanging out of the window to swear at him. Lalloo hadn't painted it yet, so it was a very distinctive non-colour. Some of it was bare metal, reddish-brown rust showed through and there were traces of blue from its previous incarnation.

'Yaar, this still needs a paint job. What are you even doing here?' Lalloo asked.

'Driving around Sadar like a headless chicken looking for you. You weren't answering your phone.' Salman leant across and opened the passenger door. 'Get in.'

Something about his friend's face made Lalloo jump in without asking any questions. Salman sped off before he'd even had a chance to shut the door. Lalloo looked at his phone – he'd missed four calls from Salman while he'd been out job-hunting.

'So are you going to tell me what's going on or am I being kidnapped?'

Salman didn't say anything and Lalloo slumped back in the seat, spent. As long as he got dropped back home afterwards and didn't need to walk anywhere, it was fine by him. They drove in silence. Ten minutes later, Salman parked outside an abandoned building in a dark street and turned to face him. In the dim borrowed light of the neighbouring building, his friend's face was mostly in shadow, giving him a sinister look.

A tightness started up in Lalloo's neck. 'What is this?'

Salman paused. 'You know my taya's son has just joined the local police station?'

'How would I know? Should I care?' Lalloo was tired and not in the mood for guessing games about the whereabouts of Salman's cousin.

'Yeah, you should. Because he recognised your name. Your old boss is charging you with robbery and assault. He's filed a police report and everything.'

Lalloo's stomach churned. He stared at Salman. 'Omer's told the police I assaulted him?'

'He's told them where you live. They'll throw you in the lock-up and break your legs.'

Salman wasn't wrong. How many times had he heard stories of that kind of police brutality? If you were poor, had no influential connections and ended up in jail, you'd be lucky if you only got a few broken bones, especially if a wealthy man wanted to keep you there.

'Saala, beats me up and then reports *me* to the police?'

The shadows crept around them in the gloomy darkness. Salman was silent.

'It's hard enough trying to find work. Now he wants to destroy me completely.' Lalloo held his head in his hands, drained.

'You blackmailed his wife. It's like spitting in his face. He's not going to let a servant get away with that.'

Salman was right. He'd been so naïve to think that he could just walk out of Omer's house and not need to watch his back. This was a rich man's world.

'You can't go back to your place. You never know when the police will come and take you away. They might even be waiting for you now.'

Lalloo paused until he was sure his voice would sound steady and then shook his head. 'I don't have anywhere else to go, yaar.'

Salman put a hand on his shoulder. 'You can stay at the shop.'

'I can't . . .' Lalloo shook his head.

'Only until you've found yourself a new place.' Salman dangled a key on a short chain in front of him. 'But no one must see you.'

Lalloo didn't have a choice; he couldn't go back to his room. He wasn't even sure he could handle Kaka, let alone the police on the end of Omer's leash.

Salman started up the car again and Lalloo sagged back in the seat. He should've been used to it by now – this sudden displacement, being made homeless with little warning. It had happened enough times in his life already. They set off through the narrow streets and it felt like the world was drawing in on him again, things happening that he had little control over, just like when he was a child.

The last time Lalloo had been made homeless, he was seventeen. He'd been running the workshop almost single-handedly for years by then. Rizwan would sit outside on his chair, read poetry all day long, occasionally greet a customer. Other mechanics had come and gone, but Lalloo had been there the longest, so even though he'd been the unpaid apprentice, he'd made sure the cars had been serviced and ready on time, the clients had paid and the other boys had done their work.

Over the years, Rizwan had come to rely on him. Lalloo had grown used to the giant man who'd taken up position every morning under the tree outside and had philosophised about the state of the country, world affairs and religion. He would bark out poetry or monologue about an obscure period of history, whether Lalloo had been interested or not, and his ramblings had become the background noise to Lalloo's work. So it had been a shock when he'd died of a sudden heart attack and his widow, Mumtaz, had announced she would sell the workshop, and with it Lalloo's livelihood and his home.

He had begged Mumtaz to change her mind, even offering to run the workshop for her, to let her keep the profits and take a small salary for himself, but she'd been true to her word. Within weeks, it had been sold and he'd had to move out. He'd tidied up and swept the shop floor for the last time. He'd left his razai and sheet behind and had put his meagre possessions into a plastic bag. Mumtaz had given him a reference to find work elsewhere and some money to tide him over for a week or so – ten years he'd worked for her and her husband, and that had been the only money he'd ever got from them. He'd staggered out of the workshop that day with no idea where to go, leaving his childhood firmly behind him.

Salman drove Lalloo into Sadar bazaar through the quiet backstreets, neither of them talking. As they turned into the road near Salman's shop, something caught Lalloo's eye and he glanced up. A new billboard had just gone up. Yasmin's huge face stared down at him beside an image of Lux soap. She had a huge smile, her teeth sparkled and her skin glowed. How easy had it been for her, with her daddy's connections, to walk into her dream job? How easy for her to smile when people paid her so much money to do it? Lalloo's jaw still ached from Omer's fist. Even now, Lalloo could see Omer's face contorted, his chest heaving as he finally dropped his shoe to the ground, Yasmin walking in, new designer handbag on her shoulder. All he wanted was a decent job for himself and a good life for his family. All he'd asked for was a chance to earn it, and now he was jobless and hungry, and everybody he loved was in danger if he couldn't find an answer.

The fury Lalloo had felt yesterday morning at the Alams roared back to life in his chest. Yasmin had promised to help and then changed her mind. Asima had hired him for a job and then refused to pay him, and Omer had beaten him for telling the truth and now was setting the police after him. Lalloo's chest felt like it was smouldering, full of a rage so hot, something had to give or he was going to burst.

Salman parked outside his shop and his friend unlocked and pulled up the shutter as quietly as possible, just enough to let Lalloo creep in.

Salman held out his hand. 'Give me your keys, I'll fetch your stuff from your room.'

Lalloo fished them out. 'As long as you go in when Kaka's asleep, you'll be OK. He won't wake up. But if you see police hanging around, just leave it.' Lalloo paused. Whatever was coming, Salman didn't need to get caught up in this. 'And be careful.'

After Salman had left, Lalloo sat down on the floor in the dark, leaning against the shelves full of mobile phones and their accessories. His parents were still relying on him to get the money and here he was, huddled on a concrete floor, hiding from the outside world. If Fatima saw him now, what would she think of him? No job, no money, no place to live.

It was time to take matters into his own hands. There was no point grovelling in the dirt, trying to get a job that wouldn't materialise, and which wouldn't pay him enough anyway. The Alams had more riches than they knew what to do with. This was the sort of money they wouldn't miss in their lives. He realised he'd been thinking about the problem the wrong way round. He'd already earnt the money – he'd done the work and now he was owed for that work. The real issue was finding the right place, the exact time to be paid.

Going over and over the idea, looking at it from every angle, he examined every detail until he had it all figured out. He was actually going to do it. That decision helped calm the rage inside him, until it was a steady glow. The plan was risky, but if he could pull it off, it would solve all his problems. And even better, he could do it first thing tomorrow.

A stray dog barked outside, starting all the neighbourhood dogs howling, but Lalloo didn't flinch. He heard Salman's car pull up outside, footsteps approaching and the shutter being raised quietly again.

Salman had stolen into his room at the mohalla and dumped his meagre belongings into three plastic bags. He'd also rolled up Lalloo's bedding so he wouldn't have to sleep on the hard floor.

'You didn't run into anyone?' Lalloo asked. The rage was still simmering, but it was under control.

Salman shook his head. Lalloo rummaged through the bags until his fingers closed around his cricket ball. Of all his possessions, this was the only thing that was irreplaceable.

'Is that everything?'

Lalloo nodded, stopping Salman as he was leaving.

'I can't . . .' His voice croaked, the angry fumes in his head clearing for a minute as he looked at his friend, for whom hiding a fugitive and sneaking past the police was not too much to ask. He cleared his throat. 'Thanks for everything.'

Salman took his hand and placed his car key in it. 'Take the car to go job-hunting further away tomorrow. The Alams don't know the whole city and the police are lazy. I'm sure this will die down after a month or so.' His friend patted his shoulder. 'It's gonna be OK.'

Lalloo nodded at Salman, but didn't disillusion him. He wasn't going to look for a job, but the car would come in handy.

Alone once more, Lalloo rolled out his bedding on the dusty floor behind the counter and took out his cricket ball. His last semblance of stability, that tiny room he'd called home, was now gone, but he still had this ball. The one Jugnu had given him the last time they'd played cricket. The ball Lalloo had had in his pocket when Abu had taken him away from the bhatti that very night and left him with Rizwan, the night Jugnu had wanted to run away and hide. But now Lalloo was the fugitive, the one who needed to hide. Was this his punishment for begging Jugnu to stay?

Lalloo didn't have any photos of Jugnu. The only reminder of his brother, of his family, was this ball. And he did now what he hadn't done since he was a child. He lay down and clutched the ball tightly to his chest, inhaling its musty leather odour, until, eventually, sleep came for him.

Chapter Twenty-One

'This Sunday, bhaya, you promised.' Lalloo was being petulant because he was tired – tired of all this clay, these bricks, this constant, back-breaking work. He missed Makhan, missed running in the fields around their old house with the great blue sky overhead, but most of all he missed the hours and hours spent playing cricket with his brother, every spare moment, every day after school, practising bowling, scoring runs, taking wickets.

Sunday was their only day off at the bhatti, the only day they could play cricket, and now Jugnu was trying to wriggle out of that too.

'OK, all right, this Sunday we'll play. Oh, and I've got a surprise for you.'

But, despite Lalloo's insistence, Jugnu wouldn't let on what it was. He kept Lalloo guessing, and Lalloo's guesses became more and more extravagant as the week wore on.

'You haven't got something boring like clothes, have you? Shoes, because these ones are broken. A new house so we can move away from the bhatti?'

At the last one, Jugnu looked up at him, studying his face closely. 'Not yet, my kaale bhoot, but I'm working on it.'

And then to make Jugnu laugh, because Lalloo disliked that pensive expression, he said, 'It's a goat. You got me a goat so we can feed it the leftover roti and then we'll slaughter it and have it for dinner on Eid!'

Jugnu only smiled.

But, for the rest of that week, Jugnu was out of the house most nights, and during the day he made his bricks in straight-faced silence, no longer singing silly made-up songs for Shabnam or sneaking his bricks into Ami's pile so that she could finish earlier. There were no practical jokes, no outlandish schemes. Lalloo didn't know what to do, how to reach out and bring his brother back.

That Saturday night, he came home dripping wet. The following day, the promised day for cricket, Jugnu came home at first light, dripping wet, and rushed out with his wet clothes in his hand, leaving Lalloo to pretend everything was fine when Ami, Abu and Shabnam headed to the market to buy food. It was far, and he knew they'd be gone most of the day. Alone, Lalloo tried exploring the fields around the bhatti like he used to at home, but it didn't feel the same. It was only when he came back, after a long day of finding nothing, not even a mouse, that he heard the noise.

Instinctively, he knew there was nothing to be frightened of. He expected to find a small animal, trapped and afraid, but he found something else. Jugnu sat hiding between the huts, hugging himself, unable to stop shaking. His face was smudged with dirt as if he'd been crying. Lalloo sat silently beside him on the ground. He was mumbling something to himself and Lalloo leant in to hear.

'It wasn't my fault . . . I didn't know this was going to happen . . .'

Lalloo put a hand on his arm until the shaking subsided.

'What is it, bhaya?' Lalloo whispered, almost too afraid to ask.

Jugnu shook his head and wiped his face with his hands. 'Nothing. It's nothing.'

Lalloo cast around for something to say to distract his brother. 'Did you hear, the Ranas have moved to another bhatti?'

Jugnu's head whipped round so fast, it took Lalloo by surprise. 'What? How do you know?'

'Ami told me. Their hut is empty – they left this morning and no one got to speak to them before they went. At least we don't have to be kept awake by the mad wailing of that crazy boy any more!'

'You don't know what you're talking about!' Jugnu snapped at him, pushing his little brother away.

Lalloo sat dumbfounded. What on earth had got into him?

Jugnu cleared his throat and stood up. 'Come on. You said you wanted to play cricket, so let's play.'

He marched out of his hiding place, with Lalloo cautiously trailing a couple of steps behind, back into their hut, where Jugnu fished the surprise out of his bag and showed him. A hard cricket ball. Not a tape ball, this was the real thing, red and shiny. Lalloo was speechless at first, holding it, savouring its weight, its leathery smell.

'Don't get ahead of yourself – it's not new,' said Jugnu, seeing the look on Lalloo's face.

Lalloo couldn't believe his luck. He was running head first out the door before he stopped and turned, looking at the dirt streaks down Jugnu's cheeks. 'But . . . are you OK?'

'Come on, I thought you wanted to play. Are you going to stand around all day talking?'

There was a bat to go with the hard ball, Jugnu skilfully showing him the difference in playing with it. Some boys from the bhatti joined them, a pile of stacked bricks their wicket. Lalloo hit shot after shot, the smoothness a revelation, but the best part was the bowling. Nothing was better than when he got to caress the ball, when he could spin it and it carved through the air and found its mark.

But Lalloo had never bowled with a hard ball before. It was too heavy, too slow, and it wouldn't spin the way he wanted it to. However much he tried, he couldn't get Jugnu out. Frustrated, he kept at it. Every time he bowled, Jugnu hit the ball far over his head.

'Hey, I thought you could play cricket?' Jugnu had a smirk on his face.

Jugnu had never indulged Lalloo when they played, but today he was aggressive, playing as if his life depended upon it. Every shot went for a boundary, goading Lalloo, daring him to get him out. His eyes were wild, angry. Lalloo took it as a challenge. He knew he could do it, he just needed the right spin. He just needed it to leave his hands in the exact way he'd been practising.

'My fault, yaar, you're too young to play with a hard ball. Shall I fetch the tape ball for you?' Jugnu said.

Lalloo took his run-up, the light was starting to fade, the day departing, and this time as soon as the ball left his fingers, he knew it was perfect. It was the most beautiful delivery of the day. It sliced through the air, bounced and, at the last moment, spun. It took Jugnu by surprise, hit the wicket so hard the bricks cascaded to the ground. Lalloo yelled and ran across the pitch, his forefinger raised to the sky. He'd done it. The perfect spin. This was the doosra – 'the other', the ball that spun in the opposite direction to what was expected. Not many bowlers could carry that off.

He would never forget the look on Jugnu's face at that moment. Shock, embarrassment, and deep brotherly pride.

After Lalloo had finished his victory lap of the pitch, Jugnu lifted him in a bear hug and they walked back to the hut together, Jugnu's arm affectionately over his shoulder, a huge sheepish grin on his brother's face.

But afterwards, as Lalloo was proudly pocketing his new ball, he saw Jugnu hunched over in the bushes, violently throwing up before wiping his face with the back of his hand.

It was the last time Lalloo ever played cricket. Later that day, he walked into the hut and found his brother packing an old school rucksack. Jugnu was stuffing it with clothes and stale roti, and Lalloo hovered at the door, confused, until he saw Jugnu lifting the gadha on the charpai where Ami kept the small pile of family money. Even at seven years old, Lalloo knew what that meant.

'You're leaving?'

Jugnu spun around, and, for a moment, he looked like a stranger, his face drawn and angry, but then he took a breath and he looked like Jugnu again. He smiled uneasily and tilted his head, like a child caught stealing all the sweets. 'No, of course not. Where would I go without you?'

Lalloo stared at him, defiant. Jugnu was holding half of Ami and Abu's money.

'I'm not stupid,' Lalloo said. 'You're running away! You're leaving us here!'

'Lalloo, you don't understand,' Jugnu said. 'I have to go tonight before they come.'

Without thinking, Lalloo snatched the bag from one hand and the money from the other. Jugnu came towards him, pleading with him to listen, but Lalloo backed away, the bag held out of reach behind him. He had trusted his brother when he'd claimed he'd make things right, would get them out of there, but all Jugnu cared about was himself.

'I'll make sure I get you all out too, but I've got to go now. Please, kaale bhoot, you've got to listen to me.'

He made a lunge for his things, but Lalloo dodged out of the way, keeping the bag out of reach.

Suddenly, they heard a sobbing from the door, Ami and Abu returning with a crying Shabnam, who'd tripped and scraped her knee. His parents didn't notice the tense stand-off between the boys. They were late for dinner and Ami rushed to prepare the daal and roti.

'Jugnu, I need fresh water from the tube well. Lalloo, lay the dastarkhawan on the floor, and what have you been doing all day? I asked you to wash these dishes.'

In the noise and scramble, Lalloo made sure Jugnu's bag was close to him. He kept a wary eye on his brother that evening, Jugnu gesturing at him to stay quiet as they moved silently around each other.

When they went to bed that night, the moonlight glowing through the curtain, Lalloo turned away from Jugnu but kept his eyes open, trying not to sleep, worrying Jugnu would slip away before morning and leave them all in this place without him there to make it seem bearable.

Chapter Twenty-Two

In the sobering light of day, after being forced out of the mohalla, with no money for breakfast and all of his belongings in plastic bags, Lalloo's plan from yesterday seemed more attractive, not less. He was crouched by the bus stop with a good view of the main road, dressed in an old pair of black jeans, a plain black T-shirt, a cotton shawl and some old trainers. It was the perfect location, set back and slightly elevated so he could easily look into the cars that stopped at the petrol pump. Salman's car was parked in a back road hidden from sight.

He'd spent most of the night awake, tossing and turning on the hard concrete floor of the shop, barely cushioned by his bedding, letting every bruise and ache from Omer's beating remind him why he had to do this. He could lay down for ever, thinking about whether it was the right or wrong thing to do, but that wasn't going to feed his hungry belly, and it definitely wasn't going to get his family out of Heera's grasp before it was too late.

Taking up his hiding place in the shade, Lalloo felt he was sweating the river Ravi down his back. The months of dry heat had turned oppressive. Buildings, people, cars – everything choked under thick layers of dust. The leaves on the trees were coated so heavily, they looked grey. Puffs of smoke-like dust floated in the hazy air. Lalloo's jeans were too tight, his clothes too black. He longed for his loose cotton shalwar kameez.

'Bhai Sahib, would you like a balloon?' A young boy, not more than five years old, was trying to sell him a red heart-shaped inflatable. Lalloo shooed him away.

A group of men playing cards, squatting in the shade of a nursery wall, invited him to join them. Not wanting to be distracted, he turned away and pulled out the newspaper he'd brought with him, but his hands were shaking so much he had to lay it out in front of him while, at the same time, never taking his eyes off the road. He watched the cars pulling up, the attendants who were on hand to fill up the tanks, and the drivers as they waited. He kept an eye on the card players, who eventually trickled away, and the balloon sellers and vendors desperate for any rupees they could get.

He'd been sitting for a while, long enough to be ignored by the other people on the street, when he saw the white Land Cruiser approach exactly on time. Every Monday morning at 10 a.m. There was no mistaking it. He'd spent hours of his life washing and polishing that car – he would recognise it anywhere. This was it. If he did this now, there was no going back.

Heart pounding, Lalloo held his newspaper up like a shield, his hands suddenly steady. His entire chest felt constricted, but his breaths were coming smooth and unwavering. Confronted with the sight of the looming Cruiser, he wondered if he should change his mind while he still could. If he were caught, they'd lock him up and throw away the key. He'd never see his family or Fatima again. And that was if the police caught him before Omer did. If his old boss got hold of him, the beating he'd received at the house would be nothing in comparison. But thinking of the beating was helpful. He had bruises all over his body. Being strangled against the wall, crouching down into a ball and being beaten by a shoe – the pain and humiliation were still with him. Nobody deserved that.

The car drew nearer. He could see Omer and the empty passenger seat next to him – Lalloo wouldn't get this chance again. Standing up, he held the paper in front of his face and walked towards the Cruiser, wrapping his shawl around his head as if walking into a sandstorm.

Omer stopped the car at the pump and wound down his window. There was an attendant to fill the tanks, so he didn't need to get out. He spoke briefly to the man at the pump, who started to fill the tank, bored and indifferent to what was happening around him. The fuel tank and the driver's seat were both on the same side of the car, leaving the passenger side unattended. Lalloo strolled up from behind the Cruiser. Once he was level with the back windows, he was shielded by the car and out of sight of the attendant, and he pulled the shawl over his mouth so only his eyes showed. There was no time to think now.

He could see Omer sitting in the driver's seat, through the back window. Omer picked up his phone. Lalloo crouched down, moved to the front passenger door and opened it. The briefcase was exactly where it should be, in the footwell on the front passenger side. He grabbed it and ran.

Out of the corner of his eye, Lalloo saw Omer turn to look at him from the driver's seat, but he didn't hesitate, pelting away at full speed.

Omer bellowed behind him. 'Oi, chor! Get him! Stop that thief!'

Other shouts joined Omer's. Lalloo raced off the forecourt, his getaway planned through narrow alleyways so Omer couldn't follow in the car. But as he shuffled through the shrubbery, his shawl caught on a dry bush, pulling him back. The more he struggled, the more the shawl wrapped itself in thorns. The voices behind him were getting louder. A desperate wrench, the unmistakable sound of ripping fabric, and he was free.

Fleeing down a side road, Lalloo ran and ran until he was away from the pump, away from the shouts and panic. A quick glance behind him confirmed he was alone, so he pulled the shawl off his face and gulped in some air, his body sodden with sweat. Not ready to stop running yet, he kept going until his lungs were screaming.

Finally, he came to a stop in an alleyway. He pulled a plastic bag from his pocket and put the briefcase inside, then sagged against the wall, waiting for his breathing to return to normal. This was nothing like running with Salman, stealing Kamal Chacha's mangoes, or making deliveries. Those felt like happy, carefree times. This was terrifying. Every rustle of a leaf made him jump, every far-off car was coming to chase him, every gust of wind was after him. The consequences now were far more severe.

When he got some breath back, he strode to the road where he'd parked Salman's car, avoiding the busy streets. His heart was still thundering. He clutched the briefcase in the bag to his chest as if to reassure his poor heart, let it know that it'd all been worth it. The briefcase felt too light. Omer used to fill it with cash almost every single day. It would be just his luck to pick it up empty.

When he pulled up outside the shop, Salman was inside, perched behind the counter on his phone.

Lalloo glanced around before getting out of the car. The shop was empty, the bazaar quiet, most people having lunch or their midday siesta.

'Back already? How was the job-hunting?' Salman jerked a thumb at the food stall next door. 'Wanna get something to eat?'

Lalloo didn't answer. He turned and threw down the shutters as Salman stared at him, puzzled. Both of them took a moment to adjust to the dim light inside and then Lalloo took the briefcase out of the bag.

'What have you done?' Salman spoke slowly.

Lalloo took a deep breath. 'I didn't have a choice. This was the only way, yaar.' He gently laid the briefcase in front of him on the floor and crouched down beside it, a delicate and precious thing.

Salman shook his head. 'Is this . . .?'

Lalloo nodded. 'He keeps his cash in here. I've seen him do it loads of times. I was the one who put the briefcase in the car every morning. Now all I need is a bit of luck.'

He clicked the clasps of the briefcase, but they were locked shut. Heart thumping, he rummaged behind the counter, found a pair of large scissors and stabbed at the leather case with frantic, desperate jabs. Salman looked on as he finally managed to flip open the mutilated lid. Lalloo froze as he gazed at the tightly packed rows of bundles of cash staring back at him.

Chapter Twenty-Three

Both Lalloo and Salman were stunned into silence. The shop was hot and airless.

'Tell me I'm hallucinating and you haven't actually robbed your old boss.'

Lalloo leapt up, clasping a hand over Salman's mouth, and glanced over at the shutter. He wasn't taking any chances. He spoke quietly, his mouth close to Salman's ear. 'Shut up, OK? These walls have ears.' He slowly removed his hand.

'So I'm right? That is Omer's?' Salman shook his head, but his voice was quieter this time. 'Have you gone mad?'

Lalloo shrugged. 'He's filed the case with the police, na? He's already made me a thief. I might as well live up to the name.'

Salman stared at Lalloo as if he didn't recognise him. 'I thought I'd hidden an innocent friend in my shop, but you really are a thief.'

Lalloo took a deep breath and crouched back down by the briefcase. 'Look, I appreciate everything you've done, but I've decided . . .'

Salman came out from behind the counter and leant in over him, still keeping his voice down. 'You decided to dress up in black and play robbers? This man is not to be messed with, Lalloo. You don't go stealing from one of the most powerful men in Lahore.'

Lalloo stood up, pushing Salman away. His legs were trembling. The fleeting high at seeing the bundles of cash was gone, replaced by pure fear.

'My father is ill, Salman. He can barely stand up, but he drags himself to work every day. Heera wants me to come to the bhatti to be his slave for ever. Omer has fired me and wants to throw me in a cell and break my legs. What do you suggest I do, huh?'

He started pacing the tiny space, too jittery to stand still. What little light made it in through the closed shutter was throwing eerie shadows into every corner. From the shop next door, a jaunty Bollywood tune crept in.

Salman stared at the briefcase. 'How much is there?' His voice was more measured now.

Lalloo hummed to the tinny, cheery tune as he paced, intensifying the stifling atmosphere in the room.

'More than I thought there would be. More than I need for my sister's wedding and Abu's treatment.'

'What about the police?'

'Don't worry, I'll leave this place. They can't come looking for me here.'

He did a lap of the shop again, the tune masking his dread.

'And what if they come after you?'

'I'm going to get my parents out of there.' There, he'd said it out loud. This was his chance. He'd never be able to do this again. 'There's enough money here to buy them out of debt. I'm going to get them out of that bhatti.' He was going to do what Jugnu hadn't been able to.

'Isn't that dangerous, Lalloo? Your brother? Is it even possible?'

Lalloo had never told Salman the details of what had happened to Jugnu, but Salman knew enough to piece it together. He knew the terror in Lalloo's past took the form of Jugnu's death.

Salman put his hand on Lalloo's shoulder, concern etched on his face. 'And you've got to be careful about Omer. He won't take this lying down – he'll have people out looking for whoever's taken the money. You know he has eyes and ears everywhere.'

Lalloo nodded at his friend to reassure him. He turned to the open briefcase, picked up a bundle of cash and, tearing the paper strap that bound the money together, fanned the rupees through his fingers.

'I'll go to the bhatti this afternoon.'

Chapter Twenty-Four

Lalloo changed out of his black clothes and snuck out of the shop into the bazaar, which was still quiet in the midday heat. The shops and their wares spilt out into the street. He passed a row of fluorescent-pink inflatable rocket ships hanging under the awning of the toy shop, dozens of glass bangles lined up in shoeboxes, glittering in the sunlight, and garlands of plastic flowers in pinks, reds and yellows. He stopped below a massive sign announcing *Raja Bag House*, where satchels, holdalls and children's school bags in all shapes and colours hung in the windows and doorway. He saw the rucksack he wanted immediately. It was black, cheap and nondescript.

He got back to the shop, the shutter still down, where Salman was trying unsuccessfully to doze in his chair behind the counter, and transferred the bundles of money into the rucksack. This way he could keep the money with him always. It was the safest thing to do.

As he emptied the last of the cash and reached the bottom of the briefcase, he noticed some papers and was about to take a look when a loud thundering made him jump. Salman leapt up and the friends looked at each other in alarm. Somebody was thumping on the closed shutter from outside. Lalloo took the briefcase and shoved it into a drawer behind the counter, zipped up the rucksack and crouched behind the counter.

'Kaun hai, bhai?' Salman called out without opening the shutter, while Lalloo's heart hammered in his chest.

But it turned out to only be a disgruntled customer wanting a new mobile. Salman turned him away and Lalloo's breathing returned to normal.

Lalloo borrowed Salman's car again. It would make getting to the bhatti so much quicker. On the side of the road, a teenage boy had parked a wooden three-wheeled cart with two tall, white, metal cones pointed upwards, selling ice-cold kulfis on a stick for thirty and forty rupees. Lalloo would have loved to buy one to cool himself down, but this was not the time. As he drove away, rivulets of sweat ran down his temples and under his arms. The days of driving the Alams' air-conditioned Range Rover were long gone. The air shimmered and danced on the road ahead, too hot to lie still.

On the long drive to the bhatti, he stowed the rucksack of cash safely under the passenger seat, out of sight. He was going to get his family out. It should be as simple as that — he'd pay off the outstanding debt and they would be free. He ignored the rolling feeling in his stomach, the fact that Heera would want to know where he'd got his hands on that kind of money, and that they didn't like people leaving the bhatti, no matter what. He was going to make it happen.

Lalloo had never done this journey in a car before. Everything looked different. He remembered his first return to the bhatti. Over the years, he'd spoken with his family on the phone, first on Mumtaz's phone and then on an old mobile phone that Salman had managed to scrounge for him, and Abu had visited him once or twice. When Mumtaz had sold the workshop after Rizwan's death, Lalloo couldn't stand to be alone another minute. He had used some of the little money Mumtaz had given him to pay for the buses and had set out to go home, ten years after Abu had cycled him away.

Now, Lalloo left the main road, driving along the broken path on the last leg of the journey, the windows wound up to keep the swirling dust from getting in. The car was a sweltering furnace as the silent dust storm raged outside. He drove at walking pace, barely able to see, and by the time he parked at the end of the road, the car was shrouded in red.

He stepped out onto the scorched earth, his kameez sticking to his back. A couple of women walked past, stacks of bricks piled up on their heads. A man rode a heavily laden cart pulled by a donkey. Nobody paid him any attention. Nobody had paid him any attention on his first return, either, only Shabnam had stepped forward, suddenly a beautiful young woman who'd grabbed his hand and pulled him into the hut, welcoming him with her familiar smile. The rest of his family had stared at him as if he'd been a stranger, or a jinn come to haunt them.

Pinky came running up. 'Bhaya, bhaya, where did you get the car?'

She ran around it, trailing a hand over the rusted exterior, leaving prints in the dust. That the mere sight of a beat-up car could get her so excited embarrassed him.

Lalloo ran his hand over Pinky's hair and she grinned at him. She was still so young. She didn't have the wonderful memories of Jugnu that he had, but thankfully that also meant she didn't have the memories of losing him, either. When she was finally away from here, how long would it take Pinky to make up for the childhood she had lost? When he'd first seen her all those years ago, she had been a six-year-old child sat wearing filthy and torn clothes, playing with a lump of clay. She had gazed up at him, unrecognising, and his heart had broken. Her face had been Jugnu's face.

Masses of clouds were gathering in the sky, but they hadn't toned down the heat. Ami and Shabnam were working outside. When they saw him arrive, they followed him into the hut. Abu lay on the hard floor on top of a slight quilt, his hacking cough no better, still running a fever.

'I have some good news. I have the money. Ma, you can start arrangements for the wedding. Abu, I am going to take you to a doctor. I've borrowed a car so you won't have to walk.' He spoke quickly, hoping they wouldn't ask too many questions.

Ami clutched his shoulders and kissed the top of his head as he bent down. On the first day he'd returned, Abu, his forehead more creased, his frame more bowed, had risen to greet him, engulfing him in a bear hug, tears streaming down his cheeks. But Ami had just sat there, motionless, without any acknowledgement of his presence. Shabnam had explained Ami's muteness and Lalloo had recognised it hadn't been a physical illness his mother had suffered from. He had approached her softly, sat beside her. Eventually, she'd turned to him, petted his cheek, took his hand and held it to her heart. She had looked at him in wonder, like a wasted woman in a desert would gape at an oasis, thinking it a mirage.

Abu raised an arm. Lalloo knelt down on the floor beside him and only then realised how laboured his father's breathing was. A fine film of sweat coated his face. He struggled to speak. Lalloo caught his hand and clasped it to his own chest.

'No need to say anything. I will arrange it and let you know. I'll come and pick you up.' Abu was much worse than before. As soon as Lalloo had spoken to Heera, got permission to take Abu to a doctor, he'd arrange an appointment, at a proper clinic.

Lalloo stood up, giving Ami some cash he'd brought from the briefcase, glancing down at Abu shrivelled up on the floor, a shadow of his former self.

'Come on, we should get back to work,' Shabnam said. A lone bulbul outside chirruped out its desolate song.

Abu tried to get up, but Shabnam stopped him.

'You're to rest now, Abu. You can work again tomorrow.' She turned to Lalloo. 'If he overdoes it, the fever comes back.'

Abu was still working every day; he didn't have a choice. Heera had insisted.

Lalloo followed the women out, still looking back at his father.

Ami and Pinky sat next to the row of bricks they'd each left earlier, but Shabnam moved to one side to prepare more clay and she pulled Lalloo along with her, out of earshot of the others.

'How did you get the money?' She attacked the earth with her shovel.

He watched Pinky struggle with the heavy brick mould. He had the money now and the sooner they were out of here, the better. He would need to speak to Heera, but he had to be very careful about how he approached the subject.

'Enough money for the wedding and the doctors?' Shabnam

mixed the dug-up earth with water, churning it with her shovel, turning to stare at him.

He took a deep breath. 'Look, I've sorted it out. This is what Jugnu would've wanted.'

Her face hardened. She stopped digging and placed a hand on her hip. 'Jugnu got himself killed, Lalloo. I don't care what Jugnu would've wanted. I don't want any stupid schemes. I want to know what you're up to.'

He was startled by the ferocity in her voice, shocked to hear her speak like that about Jugnu.

After an entire childhood yearning to return to his parents, all Lalloo had wanted when he'd first come back had been to get away from this desperate place. His brother's absence had been everywhere. In the way Pinky smiled at him with Jugnu's smile. The way Abu had shrunk, hunched over with the weight of the years on his shoulders. The sadness that erupted on Shabnam's face when she thought he wasn't looking.

And Jugnu's absence was still everywhere today. He suspected it always would be. Lalloo knew he couldn't risk telling Shabnam about the money until they were all safe and far away. It was too dangerous to talk about leaving the bhatti – he of all people knew that only too well. He stepped closer to her, placing a hand on each shoulder. 'There are no schemes, OK. I have the money now. For us. I'm going to speak to Heera and take Abu to the doctor.'

She shrugged her shoulders away from him, wiped her forehead with the back of her hand and started up the shovelling again, attacking the earth with more violence. 'I will not bury another brother, Lalloo. Just stay away. Talking to Heera is what got Jugnu into trouble. We may not be free, but we're together. I don't need to get married. I'll stay here and look after Ami and Abu. We'll be fine.'

Of course they weren't fine. Anyone could see that, but he knew why she was saying it. He knew she was desperate for everything to be OK. It wasn't the right moment to tell her what he was planning. He'd speak to Heera now, make all the arrangements and then let them know. If Jugnu were here, he'd have done the same. He'd have done everything he could to make his family safe. Lalloo was sure of it.

*

A wake of black kites circled on the currents as Lalloo walked to Heera's house, their soaring wings silhouetted against the white-hot sky. Gliding, they rose higher and higher, their shrill calls echoing in the still air, searching for carrion, rats or roadkill. He knew Jugnu had spoken to Heera and even the 'big boss' – the owner of the bhatti – about leaving, and that had caused all the trouble, but what he was doing was different. This was a business transaction. He had the money, he wanted to buy his parents out of their debt. And Heera wasn't stupid – he wouldn't refuse all this cold, hard cash. Would he? Lalloo kept putting one foot in front of the other, kept walking and tried to slow his frantic breathing.

And what about when he managed to get them out? When they were finally free, where would they go after all these years? He couldn't see them living in the hustle of the big city. They needed somewhere peaceful and calm where his parents could retire. Maybe in a village, where he could learn to till the land, be a farmer. Shabnam could look after Ami and Abu. Pinky could walk to school. They could keep chickens. It would be a big change for them all. But he couldn't ignore the part of his brain that kept clamouring for attention. What about his life back in Sadar? Everything he was familiar with – his friends, Salman? What about Fatima? Would she be content to come live with him in the countryside?

This time, there was no one at Heera's house. Lalloo asked one of the children working nearby and was pointed in the direction of the chimney. Taking the long way round so he wouldn't pass his parents' hut, he spotted Heera on the big mound the chimney sat on. Lalloo clambered up the red clay towards him, the chimney spouting thick grey smoke. The air was even hotter and heavier here – the summer heat compounded by the fire raging underneath. He could feel it beneath his feet, hot through his chappal.

Raw bricks were buried in the earth in a circle, where they baked in the underground fire. There was an opening where new bricks were stacked at one end and the fired bricks were unearthed at the other. The cycle went on, never-ending, new and old orbiting the chimney, the fire fed constantly.

From up here, Lalloo could see most of the bhatti. In another one of his poetic moods, Rizwan had told him about the architecture of the Mughal emperors who'd built the Badshahi Mosque and the Taj Mahal. Their buildings were beautiful and cool, even in the summer heat, and the walls were inscribed with the words of the famous poet, Amir Khusrau.

If there be a Paradise on Earth, it is this, it is this, it is this.

But if there were hell on earth, it was definitely this. As far as the eye could see, the sun bore down on bare red ground and piles of red bricks. The earth had been stripped naked and scrubbed until it bled.

Heera held a long metal stick with a hook on one end. He stood next to two rows of metal caps embedded into the ground.

'Haan, Lalloo Sahib, so you're here again. I take it you've thought about my offer?'

Just the sound of his voice with its condescending lilt made Lalloo nauseous. Heera lifted a metal cap with the stick. Hot smoke came billowing out of the hole underneath and he peered inside. Lalloo caught sight of flames burning underground.

'Yes, but I have a different proposal for you.' Sweat was already gathering on Lalloo's forehead and under his kameez.

Heera replaced the cap. 'Proposal? I see.' He turned away from Lalloo and shouted at a half-naked boy preparing a run-up over a pile of bricks, 'Oi! What are you up to? You think you're here to play?' The child scampered off.

'I want to know the amount of the debt on my parents.'

Lalloo scrutinised Heera's face, but Heera was impassive. He picked up the adjacent metal cap, checking the temperature of the fire burning beneath their feet. Lalloo had to step out of the way of the hot smoke. The heat of the sun above and the smouldering fire below was making him feel dizzy. Heera was quiet for so long, Lalloo wasn't sure he'd heard him.

Lalloo cleared his throat. 'I said—'

'I heard you,' Heera said softly. 'And why would you want to know that?' He replaced the cap and only then looked up at Lalloo.

A sparrow fluttered past and landed just in front of Heera so that as he walked up to the next cap, he nearly kicked it. The sparrow flew up out of reach, but then just as quickly came back, perching nearby again.

Shoo. Fly. Lalloo wanted to shout at it. *Get away, while you can.*

'I had a great-uncle who's died and left me some money, and with Abu's health so bad, I thought it might be time he retires.' Lalloo paused. 'Of course, I know you can't be out of pocket and your debt must be repaid.'

'You realise the debt will run into many lakhs? You'll have to pay in cash?' Heera watched Lalloo's face closely. Lalloo kept his expression as neutral as he could and nodded, barely trusting himself to say anything.

They walked on, Heera lifting and replacing the caps as he went. 'I didn't know you had an uncle?'

'My grandfather's younger brother. He lived in Sialkot.'

Heera nodded. 'I will need to speak to my boss. Come back here day after tomorrow and I'll let you know.'

Lalloo walked away. He could feel Heera's eyes on his back; it was all he could do not to break into a run. He got in the car and, as he made to leave, saw Heera's henchmen watching him, the red dust swirling around them as he drove out of hell, Shabnam's words in his ears.

I will not bury another brother.

Chapter Twenty-Five

It was late afternoon and Lalloo and Salman were sitting in Salman's shop. Lalloo had bought them bottles of Shezan and Pepsi. He had money. For the first time in his life, he didn't have to worry about it. Money had always been a constant anxiety in his life. He still had to be careful, he didn't know how much Heera would claim was needed to pay off the debt and interest. But, for now, he could spend a little without feeling guilty.

Lalloo had filled Salman in on the conversation with Heera the day before.

'So now I need to find a place where they can move in, even just for a couple of weeks, after they move out of the bhatti.'

After the life-changing events of the day before, Lalloo was actually letting himself get excited about the prospect of a future, for his parents, his sisters, and for himself.

'Do you think it's finally happening, then? They're gonna get out?'

It was more than he could possibly have dreamt of only a couple of weeks ago.

'It's got to. What else am I going to do with all this money?'

Salman gave him a couple of addresses for houses for rent for Lalloo to check out later.

Lalloo's phone pinged at him. He glanced at it and immediately got up.

'What is it?' his friend asked.

'Yaar, you know when I was fixing up your car and you mentioned I could borrow it whenever I wanted?'

'Yeah . . .'

'Well, Fatima finishes college in a few minutes, so I said I'd take her out in the car.'

There were so many things to do, so much to arrange. And yet all he felt like doing was talking to Fatima, hearing her voice, just to be near her, to feel the touch of her hand. He knew no matter what happened, she would be part of his life. He couldn't think of a future without her.

By the time Lalloo got to her college, the bell had rung and students were walking out, bags on their backs, chattering incessantly. He couldn't see her. Had he missed her? And then there she was, a lone figure walking out the gates, a heavy bag on one shoulder, a pile of books clasped in her arms in front of her. She spotted him and walked towards the car, looking around her to check no one was watching before getting in.

She sat beside him on the passenger seat, grinning. 'What's this?'

'I thought I'd take you for a drive.'

'Dado mentioned something the other day, about Kaka making a fuss?'

'Yes, I couldn't afford the rent, so I had to move out of the mohalla. But I'm looking for a new place now.'

He didn't tell her he'd spent the last two nights sleeping on Salman's shop floor. He had money now, he'd find somewhere soon enough.

Instead, he asked her about her day at college. It had been so long since he'd set foot in a school and he was genuinely interested to hear about her life, her friends. She chattered on and he loved hearing her talk, the excitement in her voice as she relayed the details of her friend nearly setting fire to the laboratory table with a Bunsen burner. The conversation came easily and, with it, the laughter. He glanced at her on the passenger seat, the afternoon sun streaming in, lighting up the strands of hair that had escaped the bun and lay in a beautiful messy tangle around her face, her mouth wreathed in smiles. The casual way she gesticulated with her hand as she told her story, the way her eyes twinkled. And he knew he'd made up his mind – he knew he wanted this to last for ever.

He drove the long way round to the new golgappay stall on the outskirts of Sadar. This one was not as popular as the other one, and, according to Salman, the food was not as nice, but there was less chance someone would recognise them here. They sat in the car and ordered two plates of the house special.

'So should I be buying these, then? How's the search for the new job going?' she asked, as a boy who worked at the stall brought them two plates of golgappay, bulbous wheat rounds filled with chickpeas, onions, potatoes and yogurt, served with sour imlee ka pani. He knew they were her favourite snack, but he'd never dared to take her when they were younger, in case they were seen by someone. They took the plates from the boy and Lalloo made sure to give the child a fifty-rupee tip. The boy beamed and went off skipping, and Lalloo couldn't help smiling.

'It has actually come up with some surprising results,' he said.

'Oh?'

How much of what had happened yesterday should he tell her? What would she think of him if she knew what he'd really done? Would she understand the choices he'd had to make? His reasons?

'I may be able to get my parents out of the bhatti.'

She reached across and touched his arm. 'Lalloo, that's fantastic news!'

He was moved by her enthusiasm; she knew how important this was for him.

'Shall we start eating?' He indicated towards the plates in their laps. 'They'll get soggy otherwise.' Golgappay had to be eaten right away, otherwise the crisp shells would soak in the yogurt and get soggy.

They each picked up one of the balls, dipped them into the bowl of imlee ka pani on the plate and crunched them whole. The golgappa exploded with flavour in Lalloo's mouth. The sweet yogurt and sour imlee ka pani created an irresistible combination the chickpeas and potatoes were satisfyingly filling. He looked towards Fatima, who had a beatific expression on her face.

'It's not been finalised yet, but hopefully I'll be sorting it all out soon,' Lalloo said after a while. Heera had asked him to go back to the bhatti tomorrow and he was counting down the hours. 'But, it's got me thinking . . . what did you say to your dado about that marriage proposal?'

She scrunched her nose up as she finished the golgappa she was eating. 'I've fobbed her off for now. I've told both her and Abu that I want to fully qualify before I consider marrying anyone.'

His heart was pattering in his chest so fast, he had to put down the golgappa in his hand. 'You know you were talking about waiting . . . for me?' She tilted her head to one side and looked at him with those big, sparkling eyes, and his heart missed several beats. 'I'm going to get my parents out and they'll need to find a home somewhere. But after they're settled, and that might take a while . . . well, will you wait for me a little longer?'

'Bhai Sahib, how are they? Would you like another plateful?' The young boy was back at the car window, probably after another tip. Lalloo shooed him away and looked back at Fatima.

Her face broke into a slow smile that spread across her entire face, but she paused awhile, just looking at him, before she said, 'I thought you'd never ask.'

Lalloo didn't want much more. If he could have, he'd have made that moment last for ever. Sitting in the car, Fatima by his side, both of them laughing as they each crunched delicious golgappay in their mouths.

After dropping Fatima off near her house, Lalloo drove to the posher part of town. The building he was searching for was three stories high, with a glass front that gleamed in the surrounding dust and heat. The parking spaces around it were full of Mercedes and Hondas, and his little beat-up, unpainted Suzuki took the last available spot, completely out of place. The sky was overtaken by voluminous black clouds blocking out the light. It wouldn't be long now – something would have to break.

As he entered through the glass double doors, the sudden chill of the air-conditioned room made him shiver. The lady at the reception desk looked him up and down, and Lalloo was suddenly very aware he hadn't had a proper wash in a couple of days. His chappal was covered in dust and his kameez stuck to his back after the long drive.

'Drivers for pick-up must wait outside,' the receptionist said.

'No, no. I've come to make an appointment. For my father.' He had brought Rizwan here once for medical treatment.

The receptionist shook her head and placed a laminated sheet of paper in front of him.

'These are the doctor's charges. He takes cash only. If you can't pay up front, he won't see you.'

Lalloo glanced at the paper and brushed it aside. The clinic was expensive, but he was expecting that. 'That's fine. When can I get him seen? It's urgent—'

'No, you don't understand. I can't book you in.' She picked up the sheet and showed it to him again, pointing to the figures with her ballpoint pen. 'These are the charges.'

He should've known. Even though he was no longer a driver, he still looked like one. Lalloo took out a bundle of cash he'd stashed into the zipped pocket of his shalwar and thumped it on the desk. 'It's important my father sees a doctor.'

She stared at the money, sniffed and peered down at the appointment book on her table. 'Acha, the earliest is Thursday next week, at two o'clock.'

Thursday next week? But try as he might, she insisted the doctor couldn't see Abu any earlier. Resigned, he finally agreed.

'And bring the money with you.' She didn't look up at him as she entered his name on a computer, and he left the building before she came up with another excuse as to why he couldn't be seen.

He was about to get back in the car when a large drop fell on the dusty ground ahead of him. He searched the dark sky, so overcast it could've been evening, and held out his hand for more. There was nothing. But the next moment, the drops were everywhere, fat and heavy. As he got into the driver's seat, they gathered into a deluge and he wound his window down, stuck his arm out and let the water splash over him. Finally, after having kept everyone waiting for weeks, the monsoon had arrived. Lalloo inhaled the scent of the musty earth as it greeted the shower. The rain was being thrown from above, drumming hard on the roof of the car like dhol wallahs at a rich man's wedding – gearing up to beat their drums all night long. The windscreen wipers worked frantically to keep up. Little gullies of rainwater ran off along the side of the road, the ground refusing to absorb the moisture it had yearned for. He turned onto the main road, driving slowly, his visibility limited.

The roads and footpaths were already beginning to gleam. Layers of dust accumulated over months washed away, so everything could now breathe. Leaves peeped out bright green from the trees, where a moment ago they had been a dull grey. His arm and shoulder soaked through, Lalloo wound the window up.

A couple of half-naked children ran in the rain, holding their skinny arms aloft, their faces lifted heavenward. Shalwars drenched, they jumped up and down and ran around each other. He grinned. After the heat of the last few weeks, he felt like joining them. Shop owners were throwing down the shutters. Customers wouldn't venture out in this weather, and everybody headed home before it got worse.

Up ahead, water had gathered on the ground. The entire road was flooded. He slowed down, praying the rain hadn't had time to damage the surface underneath. The last thing he needed was to break down. He blindly drove in second gear through the flood without stopping. It was deep already, about half a tyre's width, and the car sent a tidal wave either side of the road.

The next road was flooded and impassable, so he was diverted along M.M. Alam Road, the main thoroughfare lined on both sides with expensive shops, boutiques and popular restaurants. The road was jammed with a combination of too much traffic and a half-flooded street. As the car crawled along, he let his mind drift, reliving the conversation he'd had with Fatima earlier. Thinking of how his parents would take the news of being freed from the bhatti, how much of a shock it would be to Pinky, who'd never known any other life. He was pulled back into the present by a chorus of horns being honked. People were yelling and calling out. Maybe a car was stuck. It was as he passed Zazzu's, Yasmin's favourite restaurant, that he realised what the obstruction was.

Paparazzi on two motorcycles drove very slowly beside each other, the traffic swerving around them to pass. There was a woman walking along the road. With no footpath, the rain had turned the dirt path into mud. The deluge had soaked through her clothes, making them translucent, and the driver in front of him leant out of his window and stuck two fingers in his mouth, letting out a loud wolf-whistle. Other drivers around him honked encouragingly. One by one, the cars and trucks were overtaking the motorcycles, but it was slow-going. No one was in a hurry to move away from the spectacle. The lorry overtook the motorcycles, honking its horn appreciatively as it went, and Lalloo became level with the young woman.

She was desperately trying to wrap her wet dupatta around her, something to offer protection from prying eyes, but it kept sticking to her body. Then one of the motorcyclists drove his bike straight at her, snapping photos as he went. She let out a cry and slipped in the mud.

Lalloo caught a glimpse of her face, but the rain was so heavy, he couldn't be sure what he'd seen. He sped up, overtook a rickshaw and the motorcycles and parked up a few yards in front of them. He got out and was instantly soaked to the skin.

He ran towards the shivering woman and as he got closer, he knew he'd been right. He called out.

'Yasmin! Yasmin Bibi!'

Chapter Twenty-Six

'Yasmin,' Lalloo tried again, but through the roar of the rain and the braying of the horns, his voice was drowned out. He ran closer, but she must have thought he was another tormentor. She swerved to avoid him, head down, trudging through the mud. He rushed after her, weighed down by the deluge, called again, and this time she heard her name. She looked up. It still took her a few moments to recognise him through the downpour, but he saw in her face that she had. Thank goodness.

He pointed at Salman's car and they both ran towards it. The motorcyclist drove straight at Yasmin to block her getaway. Lalloo stepped out in front of the bike and the mud made it too unwieldy for the motorcyclist to manoeuvre around him. The man shouted, angry, but Lalloo ignored him and peered over his shoulder – Yasmin had reached the car. Before the motorcyclist could react, Lalloo turned and ran himself. He lost one of his flip-flops in the sticky mud, but there was no time to retrieve it. Stumbling to his car, his clothes heavy, his entire body wet through, he drove off as fast as he could, before the crowd morphed into a mob. The cars and vans behind him honked their horns in protest as he drove away, robbing them of their entertainment.

He kept driving until he was clear of the traffic, making sure neither of the motorcycles was following him. The roads were almost deserted now, people forced inside by the weather. He stopped in a side street, wiped the water running down his face and hair, and checked his rucksack was still safely stowed under the seat out of sight. Then he glanced in the rear-view mirror. Yasmin looked like a half-drowned cat. Her usually perfect, movie-star hair clung limply to her face and black make-up ran down from her eyes onto her cheeks. She was hugging her arms to herself, trembling.

The water dripped off Lalloo's hair and ran down the nape of his neck and he resisted the urge to shake his head like a dog.

'Bibi, what were you doing all alone in the rain?'

Maybe Omer hadn't got another driver yet, but there was no way Yasmin should have been walking on her own.

She spoke in a low, measured voice full of spite. 'I was trying to sort things out with Tania. I thought I could speak to her and make some sense of things, but turns out I can't even stand to be in the same room as her. I had to get out of there as soon as possible. And that stupid new driver was nowhere to be seen . . .' Then she looked straight at him in the mirror with fury in her voice. 'You knew it was Tania. Why didn't you come straight to me and tell me?'

She still had her new red handbag on her shoulder. The last time he'd seen her, he'd been crouching on the floor with her father raining blows on his head, and this was what she thought to say to him?

He kept his voice calm. 'Shall I drop you home?'

She had the grace to look slightly embarrassed then and looked around. 'Whose car is this?'

'I borrowed it from a friend.'

It was a very different car to the Range Rover she usually sat in and maybe that reminded her of when she'd refused to help him. She looked disconcerted.

'I'm sorry for the way Daddy treated you. That was wrong. You have always been good to me.'

He was surprised by this and nodded back at her in acknowledgement. He hadn't expected her to apologise for Omer's actions. In a way, he felt sorry for her, for how her friend had betrayed her. All the money in the world couldn't buy you friendship. He was lucky to have Salman.

'Would you like me to take you home?' he asked, more gently this time. But it was only as he said these words that the full realisation of what he'd done hit him. What was he thinking? Picking up Omer's daughter in the rain – *and then offering to drive her home?* Omer would hand Lalloo straight over to the police if he came within a mile of him. The fact that he'd just saved Yasmin would be beside the point.

Luckily, she was shaking her head vigorously. 'I'd rather not be at home at the moment. After your revelation the other day, Mummy and Daddy won't stop fighting, and to top it off Daddy's briefcase got stolen yesterday. He's very angry. Can you take me to Sofia's instead?'

He couldn't help glancing at the seat beside him, glad he'd hidden his rucksack full of cash underneath it. 'Your friend Sofia who lives in Balashah?'

Balashah was a good hour's drive away. The return trip would be at least two hours. He looked at his petrol gauge, knowing the tank wouldn't last, unwilling to waste his precious cash on fuel.

She must have seen him looking and, with more insight than he would have given her credit for, she said, 'I can give you money for petrol. Please take me.'

That was something at least. Inwardly sighing, he started the engine.

'Bibi . . . don't tell Omer Sahib I picked you up today.'

She met his eyes in the mirror and nodded.

'Don't worry, I won't be telling Daddy anything. I have no desire to share anything with that man.'

He was wary as he approached the next petrol pump, scanning the forecourt before pulling in. There was no reason to be cautious. They weren't in the cantonment where he'd robbed Omer and he was sure Omer hadn't even seen him drive away, but he had a feeling of distinct unease. But in this weather, there were no other cars – even the attendants had forfeited their posts. He got out, wringing water from his still-dripping kameez, and started to fill up the tank.

A black koel landed on the pump, ruffling its feathers, taking refuge from the downpour. Every time Lalloo moved, the bird shifted its neck, watching him. He was on edge the whole time, willing the pump faster, watchful of everything around him. When he finally pulled out of the petrol station, a black Range Rover came out from behind. It definitely wasn't Omer's car. He had to stop being so paranoid.

The rainstorm had slowed from its earlier frantic fervour into a determined downpour. It came down steadily, beating its rhythm on the roof. It wasn't evening yet, but the sky was so overcast, the day had turned dark. He switched on his headlights.

The extreme weather had emptied the streets of people. The Alams always told the cook to fry pakoras when it rained. Sometimes Guddo would sneak some out to Lalloo and Baba Jee as well. They would sit under the porch, watching and listening to the pattering, inhaling the aroma of the rain, while the spicy pakoras warmed their bellies. Lalloo's stomach rumbled as he drove on.

It had grown even darker by the time he got to the final stretch of his journey, a deserted expanse of road about a mile long, with no street lights and only room for a single lane of traffic. The road was elevated, surrounded on both sides with fields that were a newly washed bright green. A solitary brown horse grazed in the rain.

Lalloo was halfway down the road when he noticed the car in his rear-view mirror. It had its headlights on full beam and suddenly sped up – a big, black Range Rover. It drove right up behind, headlights glaring and honking its horn. Lalloo gripped the steering wheel tighter and sat up in his seat. He moved over to the side of the road, the car behind repeatedly honking.

Yasmin's bored voice was saying something to him, but the drumming on the roof and the honking from behind were too loud. Was this the same black Range Rover from the petrol station? The headlights in the mirror blinded him. Palms sweaty on the wheel, he tried to stay calm. This was just an impatient Lahori driver.

Lalloo moved over again and slowed down to let the Range overtake. He was relieved when it drew up alongside him, expecting it to pass. But it didn't overtake, it slowed, and the two cars drove beside each other neck and neck. At that moment, the sky was split open with a flash so bright, it turned the night into day. In the burst of lightning, he saw the passenger-seat window nearest him roll down. The man inside turned to face him, wearing a black balaclava. As Lalloo stared, the man raised a gloved hand to point a gun directly at his head.

Yasmin saw it at the same time as Lalloo did and screamed. Instinctively, he slammed on the brakes. The Suzuki skidded a little on the wet road, but screeched to a halt. The big Range Rover beside them shot forward. A bundle of nerves and instincts, Lalloo didn't think. There was no time. He rammed the gearstick into reverse and wrenched the steering wheel round as far as it would go. The wet tyres skidded in protest as he spun around to head in the opposite direction, pursued by the rumbling of thunder. He floored the accelerator, but it made no difference – the Range Rover was on his back again seconds later. Lightning lit up the sky once more, this time right overhead. The deluge was thicker now, the windscreen wipers frantic, visibility reduced to a couple of feet. Lalloo's palms were slick with sweat. He had to clutch the steering wheel so tightly to stop his hands from slipping that his knuckles were white. Yasmin was shouting something from the back, but he needed to concentrate on what he was doing with every ounce of his being.

The thunder rumbled into a crescendo with a vicious crack, but even that couldn't drown out the shot from the gun. The front window exploded into droplets of glass around his arm and face. Yasmin screamed. Was she hurt? Then there was another shot, and another – he felt a tyre burst underneath him and the car left the road. Was that blood on his kameez? He twisted the steering wheel, but it didn't change their trajectory. The car was still moving but underneath was simply air. They were airborne, like in Salman's favourite Bond movie, except this wasn't a slow-motion stunt. This was real life. They were heading for the fields, but it took an age to fall.

As they plunged through the air, Lalloo caught a glimpse of the moon peeping from behind the clouds. He wondered if the horse had run away. He wondered whether his parents would see his mangled body. He was thrown forward and braced himself. The crunching of metal resonated through him. Through his arms, in between his shoulder blades, down his chest and into his stomach. He felt a stabbing as he fell into the steering wheel just as the moon came out fully from behind the clouds and lit up the sky, the car and the rain.

The moon had been there when the men had come for Jugnu, a witness to everything that'd happened that night. Lalloo hadn't been able to do anything to protect his brother then, and he wasn't able to do anything for himself now.

Chapter Twenty-Seven

A large yellow moon hung too low in the sky the night the men came with dogs and guns and cricket bats, fourteen years ago. Lalloo held his new cricket ball in his hand, feeling its weight, rubbing his fingers over the stitches, smelling its heavy leathery smell as he relived the glory of bowling Jugnu out with his spin ball a few hours earlier. He lay on the floor, with Shabnam on one side and Jugnu on the other. Everyone was asleep. Jugnu twitched, dreaming. Every time his brother stirred, Lalloo held his breath, worried he'd wake up and want to leave, but Jugnu slept on. Lalloo passed the ball from one hand to the other, holding it close. He had hidden Jugnu's bag where his brother couldn't find it, just in case.

He wasn't sure how long he lay there, but it must have been past midnight when he heard the dogs and the unmistakable sound of many heavy boots grinding the dirt underfoot. He sat upright, his heart beating loud and fast. Through the light curtain that covered the doorway, he could see a circle of blazing, fiery torches approaching the hut. Then there was a deathly, heavy silence.

He stretched out his hand towards his father, his fingers shaking, as a blood-curdling roar ripped through the air and the men burst into the hut. His father sprang upright, as did his brother. Ami screamed and pulled Lalloo and his sister towards her, her arms circling them both. The men pushed them out of the way, shouting. Amid the chaos, a foot lashed out and kicked Lalloo in the ribs, winding him. Shabnam started to cry. Why were they here? And then he realised. *Jugnu*. One of the men punched his brother in the stomach, the air rasping from Jugnu's throat, and then they dragged him from the hut, their faces gruesome and jinn-like in the flickering torchlight.

Abu roared and surged forwards after his son, stumbling out of the hut. Ami followed, a small desperate plea escaping her lips. 'No.' Lalloo scrambled out behind his parents, with Shabnam following.

Outside, Jugnu was being forced down on his knees, one man brutally fastening his hands behind his back. Two big men stood either side of him, wearing balaclavas, carrying cricket bats. Others were standing around, some carrying torch fires, others holding metal chains that restrained the dogs. They were waiting for something.

Jugnu was struggling against the ties on his hands. 'What are you doing? *Let me go!*'

The man beside him struck him with the back of his hand so hard Jugnu fell face-first to the ground. The other grabbed him by the hair and forced him back up. A trickle of blood dribbled down his chin. Abu rushed to Jugnu, but the dogs barked at him, straining at their chains. The men pushed Abu away and he stumbled backwards. Ami reached to catch him and pull him back, Shabnam clinging to her legs. The men tied a gag around Jugnu's mouth so he couldn't speak. Jugnu was shivering now, his kameez ripped.

Then Lalloo realised what they were waiting for. A silhouette strode towards them in the golden moonlight. Heera. Ami whimpered beside him and Lalloo's heart felt as cold and desperate as a litter of newborn kittens, weighted with rocks, thrown into the river to drown.

'Wake up the whole bhatti.' Heera barked out the command. 'Everyone needs to see what happens to a filthy rat who goes sneaking around, thinking we won't notice. Wake them up. Now!'

The men went round all the huts. Lalloo spotted Taari among them, banging on the walls, shouting into windows, until the entire bhatti had woken. They trickled over, family by family, shivering and wide-eyed, bunched up in shawls against the cold, sensing evil.

'Over here, over here, hurry up!' Heera shouted at them and they gathered around him, forming a silent circle, Jugnu and the two men in the middle, the chimney looming over them all.

Heera waited until he was sure he had everyone's attention. Fear had dried up even Shabnam's tears.

'You're all wondering why you've been woken in the middle of the night. You have this young man to blame. This . . . rat,' Heera spat out the last word, 'has been sneaking around, interfering with things that don't concern him.'

Jugnu's eyes were large, and he was shaking his head from side to side. Heera ignored him.

Lalloo's heart was beating so loudly, he was surprised Heera didn't hear it.

'As you know, the Ashraf family moved to the bhatti about a year ago. This piece of scum here has had a few ideas recently. He thinks I am running some kind of charity. He wants a house to live in, food in his belly and to be paid for the privilege. An honest day's work is beyond him. He thinks it's unfair. He'd rather play cricket all day. And not only does he want to leave, he wants others to leave too. I want you all to understand something. This man is a murderer. He killed the Ranas' poor mad boy last night by drowning him in a stream. An innocent child. And I'm sure you'll agree, evil should be stamped out wherever it is found.'

There were gasps from some of the villagers. People were frantically whispering. Lalloo looked towards his parents. Was Heera talking about Hasnat? Hasnat was dead? Abu was looking at Heera, shaking his head desperately. And then a thought made Lalloo's blood run cold, something that no one else in the family knew – Jugnu had come back dripping wet last night. But he wouldn't have done that to Hasnat. Surely Heera was lying.

'Now I would like to show you what happens to people who interfere, who think they can leave here before their debt has been repaid,' Heera continued.

Abu shuffled into the middle of the ring. He had his hands clasped in front of him, palms together.

'Heera Sahib.' Abu's voice trembled.

Up until now, Lalloo had been scared. But when he heard the tremble in Abu's voice, terror hollowed him out.

'Sahib, I would like to beg forgiveness. My son is young and impetuous. He didn't know any better. You may be mistaken, but whatever he has done, I will take responsibility. I am willing to work for you for the rest of my life, Sir Jee. Let him go tonight and I will make sure he never says a word about leaving again. He's just a young boy.'

Heera let Abu finish and then put one hand on his hip. 'Forgiveness doesn't come this easy, old man.'

'Please, I will do anything.' Abu walked slowly up to Heera, got down stiffly on all fours and, lowering his head, kissed Heera's shoe.

Lalloo could barely breathe, petrified at what Heera would do next.

Heera sneered, waved a hand dismissively at Abu. 'Get back, old man. We can't have insects like these spreading their diseased ideas to the whole bhatti.'

One of the men pushed Abu back to the perimeter of the circle and while his back was still turned, Heera nodded to the two men standing either side of Jugnu. They raised their bats. The first blow that hit Jugnu caught him behind the head and he fell heavily to the ground. Ami screamed and ran to him, but one of the men blocked her and held her back. Another two held on to either side of Abu as he kicked and thrashed. The men beside Jugnu used their cricket bats like pickaxes, steady and rhythmic, as if they were breaking up tarmac on the road. Lalloo shouted and ran towards Jugnu full pelt. He was scooped up by one of the men and planted on the ground again, arms held behind his back. The blows came thick and fast, on every part of Jugnu's body. Heera walked round them, inspecting their handiwork, calm, methodical.

The dogs could smell blood and barked in frenzy. Lalloo wanted to run to Jugnu again, to pull him away, but Taari held a dog on a chain inches away from him and Shabnam. Lalloo stood in front of her, a human shield, while she clung to him sobbing great big tears of fear. He was so close to the dog, he could see saliva dripping from its jaw as it fought against its chain. It barked in his face. Taari loosened the chain enough to let the dog jump closer to Lalloo. Shabnam screamed and Lalloo flinched. Taari laughed.

Lalloo could hear the wails and shouts from the villagers, the dogs growling and barking, but from Jugnu, nothing. No screams or cries of pain. Just the thud, thud, thud of the cricket bats as they found flesh and broke bone. Ami was on her knees screaming. She was making all the noise her eldest son wasn't.

At some point, Heera called to the men and they stopped. Both their bats were stained with blood and they were panting as if they'd put in a hard day's labour. Jugnu lay on his front, motionless. There was complete silence. One of the men prodded Jugnu's shoulder with his foot. Nothing.

Heera called out to the villagers, 'OK, I think we've done enough tonight. This cockroach has been taken care of, but, if there's any more, don't think I won't come after them. Let's hope we've stamped out this disease.' He clapped his hands. 'All right, back to your beds. Nothing more to see here.'

The villagers slunk away into the shadows in silence. Soon, there was only Lalloo and his family left. The men moved away, their cricket bats resting on their shoulders. They'd had a good innings. As the torches and dogs receded, Ami and Abu rushed to Jugnu. Lalloo watched from where he was, waiting for Jugnu to turn around and sit up.

'What's the matter, kaala bhoot?' Lalloo knew he would grin and say. 'You thought I was a goner, didn't you? I was just playing along with them. You fell for it!'

But Jugnu didn't move.

'Did you see those dogs? Huge teeth,' he would say. If only he would sit up. 'I wasn't scared.' If only his leg wasn't bent at an impossible angle.

Ami sat beside Jugnu on the ground and turned him around to cradle him in her arms. She held his bloodied head to her bosom and clasped his upper body to her, howling. Abu was next to her on his knees, crying softly. Lalloo saw Jugnu's face just before Ami hugged his brother to her. Lalloo didn't need to see anything else.

He turned and saw the men departing, piling into the back of the pickup trucks. He saw Taari wipe his shoe with Ami's dupatta and throw it down. Then he saw something he'd missed up until now. A man in a long black car was parked by the edge of the huts. He was far enough away that he wasn't involved, but he'd clearly been watching everything that had happened from afar. Masked behind dark sunglasses, he gave Heera a nod as the foreman approached, rolled up his window and drove off. The men were gone within minutes and the family were left in the desolate light of the full moon.

Slowly, in twos and threes, the villagers crept out of their huts. To wrap their arms around Ami's shoulders, to cry with Abu, to console the children.

'No, no, he's still warm. He's still my Jugnu!' Ami screamed as they tried to prise her away from Jugnu's body.

One of the women hugged Shabnam. Somebody untied Jugnu's hands and laid a sheet over him. Lalloo watched, his tears all spent, unable to move. *Wake up, Jugnu. Let's go catch fireflies.*

After some time, Chacha Yunis spoke through the tears that were flowing into his short white beard.

'We need to bury him tonight.'

Abu shook his head, unable to say anything.

'They will come back in the morning and take his body away. If you bury him tonight, at least you will have a grave for your son.'

Chacha Haider picked Jugnu up, still covered in his sheet, as if he were picking up a sleeping child. He placed him gently onto a charpai. The men, women and children sat around the charpai, some openly weeping, some silently crying, some stunned into silence. Someone pushed Lalloo to the front and he approached Jugnu. He lifted the sheet from Jugnu's battered face, smudged red with dirt and blood. He touched Jugnu's forehead, brushing his slightly too-long hair back one last time. Ami was right; he was still warm.

Four men hauled the corners of the charpai onto their shoulders and the others gathered around. Lalloo turned to see Ami behind him. The dupatta that usually covered her head was gone. She grabbed a handful of her hair and tore it out in her fist as the men walked past the smouldering chimney on the long, slow trek to the cemetery.

Chapter Twenty-Eight

A searing pain burnt across Lalloo's head. Blinking, he struggled to open his eyes. He saw a large dark mark on a pale wall – blood? And a crack where the wall met the floor. Three tentative insect legs emerged. A cockroach scuttled into view, waving its antennae high in the air. It crossed the floor, weaving its way past, drunk in its freedom. Lalloo kept his body absolutely still and looked around him. He was alive.

A voice groaned from somewhere he couldn't see, somewhere far away. Lalloo remembered the dark and the screams. He tried to sit up, but pain skewered him in the chest. A sheet covered him, and his chest and left leg were swathed in bandages. The slightest movement hurt. A large room full of people, some in beds, some lying on mattresses, others on the bare ground. A hospital. The light in the room was pale, a solitary tube flickering at one end. There were no windows, no telling if it was night or day. No one walking around, a few grunts and some shuffling, but mostly people sleeping. Night, then? But how late?

In his head, all he could see were the shots and the storm. He frantically tried to recall details. He could remember the screaming from the back of the car, the relentless rain in the looming dark, and looking down the barrel of a gun. How was he alive?

He looked about him to calm himself down, trying to breathe. There were probably fifty people crammed into the room. Two ceiling fans swirled sluggishly overhead. The air was clammy, thick with the smell of unwashed bodies. There were no men with guns here.

And then, panic slapped his face like the ferocious heat of a Lahori summer. His rucksack. It had all the money in it and it'd been under his seat. He craned his neck, wincing in pain at the movement, but it wasn't lying anywhere near the bed. His entire future was in that bag and it had disappeared. He checked his pockets. His mobile was gone and so was the bundle of cash he'd kept there.

His mouth was parched, but there wasn't a nurse he could call. He heard a high-pitched screaming in his head – *Yasmin*. She was nowhere in sight. But this was the men's ward, so of course she wouldn't be here – and her father would have whisked her away to a private hospital as soon as he'd heard she'd been in an accident.

Her father. The thought of Omer made Lalloo shudder. What had he been thinking picking Yasmin up? He should have left her there and driven off. If Omer was angry before, he would be livid now his precious daughter was . . . was she injured? Was she even alive? Why had they been shot at? Did someone want to kill him? Or Yasmin? Who would want him dead? Maybe he was meant to be killed so they could kidnap Yasmin? But how would anyone expect her to be in Salman's car?

Exhausted, his head pounding, he shut his eyes to suppress the questions and saw the window being rolled down, a gun pointed at his head. Ignoring the pain in his chest and the immobility of his leg, he hauled himself up into a half-sitting position, propped himself against his pillow, determined not to relive the crash. But he couldn't shake it, couldn't switch off the noise and the images in his head. He sank into a fitful sleep, woken by the sound of gunshots time and time again.

*

When Lalloo fully awoke, it was to an aroma that wrung his stomach out. The man in the bed next to him was so wrinkled and old, he must have been in his nineties. He had thick, myopic glasses and a crusty hearing aid and sat on his bed with an open tiffin box in front of him, dipping his roti into daal, making sure it was soaked through and soft before fishing it out with his fingers and chewing it with toothless gums. Around them, the room bustled with relatives arriving with breakfast for the patients. The smells hung heavy in the air and Lalloo's stomach protested.

Lalloo couldn't help himself. 'Chacha Jee, why are you torturing me with that delicious smell?'

The old man dragged his tiffin box closer to him, as if he feared Lalloo would pounce on it. He chewed ferociously and then swallowed. 'Don't you have any family to bring you food?'

Lalloo swallowed. He wondered what his parents were doing. Would Abu be trying to make bricks today? He'd given his parents some money from the rucksack when he'd visited. Would they have started preparing for the wedding, not knowing Lalloo was in hospital?

Lalloo shook his head, looking away. 'They don't even know I'm here.'

A younger man sat next to his neighbour on the bed. He smiled at Lalloo.

'Don't mind my chacha – he enjoys his meals a bit too much in his old age.'

He tore half a roti and picked up one section of the tiffin box. The old man grumbled and tried to grab it off him, but his nephew held it just out of reach.

'You shouldn't be having so much, Chacha, not when your kidneys have failed.'

The man handed the food to Lalloo, who hauled himself up despite the pain in his chest. The tiffin box contained only a tiny bit of achaar and he wolfed it down with the roti. But half a roti and a mouthful of achaar didn't go far.

The nephew chuckled. 'Alhamdulillah, you certainly needed that. What happened to you, brother?'

Lalloo shuffled, uneasy. 'A car accident. I was going too fast in the rain and I must have lost control. I can't remember too much . . .' He didn't even know what day it was, how long he'd been unconscious.

The man took out his phone and pointed it at Lalloo.

'Here, call your parents and let them know where you are. They must be concerned.'

Lalloo took the mobile and checked the date on it. He'd lost a day. The night he crashed was a Tuesday and today was Thursday morning. He'd been brought in, patched up and had only just woken up. Trying to get his head around this, he dialled while the man looked on.

Thankfully, Salman picked up right away.

'Salman? I've been in a car crash.'

'What? Where are you? What happened?'

'It's a long story. I'll tell you when I see you.'

'Are you OK?'

'I'm . . . Well, I'm alive, which is a miracle in itself.' He realised his voice was shaking. It really was a surprise to be alive after the events of Tuesday night.

'OK, I'll come right away, where are you? Where did this happen? Were you driving the Suzuki?'

Lalloo held his head in his hand. He'd forgotten all about Salman's car. He didn't know what condition it was in, but it couldn't be good. 'Yeah, sorry, yaar, I don't know what's happened to it.'

'Don't worry about that, now—'

'No, actually, it's important.' He glanced up, conscious his neighbour was listening in on his conversation. 'My rucksack with all my, uh . . . important things was in the car, under the seat.'

Salman paused. 'Do you mean the money?'

Lalloo nodded. 'Yeah. You've got to get it for me, yaar. My whole future is depending on that bag.'

He told Salman the name of the hospital the man had given him and where he'd been when the car had crashed.

Salman thought for a moment. 'They may have towed the car by now. Let me find out where they've taken it. I'll come as soon as I can.'

Lalloo hung up and returned the mobile to its owner. There was nothing left to do but wait. All his money was in that bag. Without it, he had nothing. No future, no hope. He'd given his parents some money to tide them over, but he couldn't get them out of the bhatti. He was drained and in pain and had nothing to distract him except the thoughts and worries that kept whirling around in his head. He would've loved to speak to Fatima. Talking to her always calmed him down and put things into perspective, but he had no phone, no way of contacting her.

He was still worrying about his bag when he heard a loud stream of foul words so coarse that even Kaka would have been shocked. Lalloo turned his head to see a big woman entering the ward dressed in a uniform that once must have been white. She had a generous head of curly black hair with shocking white streaks running through the front, tied back at the nape of the neck in a bushy ponytail. Her low heels in sensible shoes clack-clacked on the floor and she was glaring at her phone, mumbling to herself. Lalloo looked around him uncertainly. Was she a nurse? The other patients didn't seem to think it was anything unusual.

She turned her head and caught his eye. 'Well, well, look what the sun's dragged out.'

Was she talking to him?

She strode up to his bed. 'Yes, you. You've caused me enough tension already and my belly is full of stress at the moment.'

'You mean, you don't always swear like a . . .' He tried to think of a polite way of putting it, but she wasn't listening.

'My supervisor,' she said, pointing to her phone. 'He thinks I've been stealing!'

Lalloo felt very disoriented. 'Well . . . have you?'

'I don't steal from just anyone – my heart's not made of ice. Just my supervisor leaves money in the top drawer in his office and I take some for my chai pani every week or so. The way I see it, it's justified. Nobody can survive on a pittance. I'm just taking opportunity where I find it. If he doesn't want me to have it, he shouldn't put it in the same place every week. Anyway, I think he might have found out.'

The whole situation, the conversation, the setting, this woman – it all felt surreal. The patients in the neighbouring beds weren't even turning their heads.

'So, yesterday, I go in and take some extra because it was my birthday and everyone needs a little treat every now and again, and today he's summoned me into a disciplinary meeting. He didn't even bother calling me, just sent me a message. Who does he think he is?' She waved her phone at him.

'Do you think he's going to fire you?' Lalloo thought he may as well go along with the conversation and see if he could find out something useful.

'Fire me? Huh! Saala thinks he's better than me. I'll show him.' She spat a mouthful of paan juice and it went flying from her lips, the bright-red betel juice narrowly missing his neighbour's bed and staining the wall behind it.

'Was it worth it, at least? Did you have a good birthday?'

She gave him a huge grin. 'Did I have a good birthday? As if that's a question worth asking.'

She picked up the chart at the end of his bed and looked at it briefly.

He blinked and swallowed. 'Uh, can you tell me what's going on?' He looked down at his chest swathed in bandages, his leg in a cast. 'What happened?'

'They found your car in a ditch. You have a broken leg and some cracked ribs. And a bullet just scratched you. You'll live,' she said, matter-of-factly.

'Did they bring in my rucksack? My phone? I had some money in my pocket—'

'That's enough questions from you, sunshine. I'm Billo, the head nurse. That's Sister Billo to you and I'm in charge around here. Now, don't play games with me. I'll not have any disrespect from you. What was that girl doing in your car when you don't even work for the family any more? Where were you going? Why were people shooting at you?'

'How do you . . .?'

'How do I know? I've had her father here kicking up a huge fuss.' She held her hands on her hips and glared at him, as if he were to blame for the hassle she'd been receiving.

'Here? Why is he here?' Lalloo broke into a cold sweat thinking about Omer in the same hospital. He could be beside him any second.

'Only because his daughter is too ill to be moved. He's been trying everything to get her taken to a private hospital, but she has to stay here until she's stable.'

Yasmin. 'Is she badly hurt?'

'Bullet in her spine. It doesn't look good. He's been asking about you. You'd better get your story straight – you're going to have some explaining to do.'

Had the gunmen been after Yasmin? Who would want to shoot her? It didn't make sense. If someone was after her father's money, surely they'd want to take her hostage or something. Who'd want her dead? Either way, Lalloo knew, her father would blame him.

He looked about him wildly. It wouldn't take Omer long to find him. 'I need to get up. I can't stay lying in this bed.'

'Hmm . . . don't want to be found, eh?' She cackled, showing a mouth full of red-stained teeth and gums from a lifetime habit of chewing paan. 'Don't worry, I haven't told him about you. You can rely on Billo to keep your secrets. He was a bit too arrogant for my liking. Can't stand arrogant rich men – unless they're paying me, of course.'

'Can you get me some crutches or something?'

She stared at him as if he were speaking a foreign language and then laughed. 'And would Your Highness like a motorised wheelchair as well? Or maybe a private room with your personal doctors to see to you twenty-four hours a day?' She started to walk away. 'I'm already running around after the family, might as well extend the treatment to their ex-servants!'

'It'll be one less bedpan for you to empty!' Lalloo shouted after her. 'And what about my rucksack?'

But she was already gone.

*

Lalloo's body was done in and, despite himself, he dozed off. When he awoke drenched in sweat, he lay on his bed hoping that staying as still as possible would keep him cool. It wasn't working. The heat hadn't lessened in ferocity, but it had changed from a dry, intense burning to a cloying humidity, where the sweat never evaporated and clung to your body until you were drowning in it. The ceiling fans did nothing but swirl recycled hot air around and around.

Lalloo propped himself up against the headboard and saw a pair of crutches leaning beside his bed. He didn't know where they had come from, but he was grateful. If the bullets had been meant for him, would the attackers know he was in this hospital? Would they try again? Lying prone in the hospital bed, he felt like a sitting duck. The sooner he could get mobile with these crutches, the sooner he could get out of the hospital, away from any would-be attackers and away from Omer.

Reaching for the crutches, he gasped at the shooting pain in his ribs and had to slow down. He shuffled his bottom to the edge of the bed and eased his bandaged leg over the side. What felt like an electric current shot up his leg and through his torso, but he didn't let it stop him for long. He manoeuvred his way off the bed, transferring his weight onto the crutches bit by bit. Standing up, he shifted his weight onto his good side to take a step. The movement jerked his body and pain stunned him for several minutes. Slowly, he took a couple of steps and then a few more.

After an age, he reached the door from where he could see into the ward opposite. Billo was there, leaning over a bed, but instead of tending to the patient, some kind of negotiation was going on. He stepped into the shadows by the open doorway to watch. After a protracted conversation, the patient on the bed discreetly passed over some cash and Billo handed him a box of pills. So that was how things were done around here.

Before Billo had finished with her transaction, Lalloo turned around to hobble back. He'd only taken a few steps when she flounced in on her clacking heels.

She gave him a cursory glance and glanced down at the crutches. 'I see you're up and about. Just don't advertise you got those from me.'

'Thank you for them, but why not?'

'It'd be bad for business. I told you, I'm not running a charity here.'

There were more urgent things to discuss. He looked around him to check no one was nearby.

'Where is Yasmin? The bibi in my car?'

She scrutinised him through narrowed eyes. 'Why do you want to know?'

'I need to make sure I keep my distance from her father.'

'You've made some powerful enemies, haven't you?'

'How is she?'

Billo shook her head, her unruly hair threatening to break free from its ponytail. 'It's not looking good, but it's too early to tell. She's in the Liaquat ward. You won't bump into him here.'

Billo pointed out that the Liaquat ward was on the opposite side of the hospital, so he was far away from Omer at least.

He hobbled back past the other patients, some too poorly to move, others regaling their neighbours with loud stories of how they'd ended up here.

He'd only just made it back to bed when Salman appeared. Despite the intense pain all over Lalloo's body, the fact that he'd been shot at, that he could've died, he looked at Salman's familiar face and broke into a grin. There was no one he'd rather see right now.

'Sorry, yaar, I came as fast as I could.' Salman was wheezing, barely able to get the words out. He handed Lalloo a paper bag of samosas. 'This is all I could get in a hurry. You must be hungry?' He took his inhaler from his pocket and squeezed a puff into his mouth, waiting until his breathing got back to normal. 'What on earth happened?'

The walk to the doorway and back had tired Lalloo out, but, before his friend could say another word, Lalloo gathered up his crutches again, indicating to Salman to follow. Billo was still on the ward and there were too many inquisitive ears here. He couldn't risk being overheard. Salman raised his eyebrows, but followed him out.

Lalloo hobbled out of the ward to the front of the hospital. It was late in the afternoon and, outside the glass doors, rain splashed down hard on the concrete floor. The entire world had turned grey and damp. A welcome gust of fresh air blew in with every bleeding patient or crying toddler who entered. In the lobby, there was a waiting area with rows of empty plastic chairs. Lalloo lowered himself down in one, exhausted. Salman sat next to him and

Lalloo quickly told his friend all he could remember of the crash and the details Billo had filled in earlier. Salman took another puff of his inhaler and breathed out slowly.

'Who wants you dead? Or was it Omer's daughter they wanted? Rich man like that must have plenty of enemies.'

Lalloo recalled the gun pointed straight at his head through the open window of the black Range Rover.

He shook his head. 'No, I think it was me they were after.'

'So someone tried to kill you, but ended up shooting Yasmin instead? But who wants you dead?'

'I don't know.' He shook his head. 'I've got Omer hanging around the hospital. He's already got the police case registered against me and now he can point them my way. But did you find the car? Was it in a bad way?'

'There's hardly anything left of it.' Salman had a mournful look on his face.

Lalloo closed his eyes. He'd wrecked Salman's car, his childhood dream. 'I'm so sorry, yaar.' He was just glad Salman hadn't been driving it. 'As soon as I can, I'll make it up to you. I'll fix you up a better car.'

'Don't worry about it. It was too good to be true anyway, me owning a car. It was totally crushed as well – it's a miracle you're alive. Anyway, the thing is, there's no money.'

'*What?*'

'No rucksack, no money. I checked under the seat, everywhere. Then I searched the place where you crashed, just in case it had fallen out. There're tyre tracks on the road where the car went into the ditch, but still no rucksack.' He put his hand on Lalloo's shoulder. 'I found your phone, though, on the floor. Whoever took the rucksack missed this because it got wedged under the seat.' Salman handed Lalloo his mobile with a broken screen.

It was his worst fears realised. Without the money, he had nothing. Lalloo stared up at the ceiling, speechless. He felt like the blood had drained from his body. They both sat in silence, the relentless thrumming of the rain crashing into his thoughts. He had come so close. Talking to Heera, getting Abu an appointment, talking to Fatima. All his hopes and plans had just crumbled.

'How's Yasmin?' Salman asked at last.

'Apparently she's worse off than they first thought.'

'What I don't understand is why Omer hasn't handed you over to the police already.' He looked at Lalloo. 'He must know you're here.'

Lalloo nodded slowly. 'Yeah, and he must be raging.'

'Unless . . .'

'He's planning something much worse than just giving me over to the police.'

'We need to get you out of here, Lalloo.'

'And where would I go? I haven't got anywhere and I've no money either.'

'We'll come up with a plan. I'll think of something. And then, as soon as your leg is healed, you can get another job.'

The friends studied each other for a moment before Lalloo said, 'You're right. I've got to get out of here. Billo hasn't told him where I am yet, but it won't take him long. I can't go back to the shop – we'll have to find somewhere else for me to hide out.'

'I'll get on it.'

Salman left then, promising to come back having found somewhere for Lalloo to go. Lalloo stayed where he was, slumped in his chair. As desperate as he was to get away, he couldn't see any path ahead.

A far-off ambulance siren grew louder and louder until it was shrieking right outside. Dusk had fallen. A rush of cold air as the doors opened and a throng of people hurried past, a man with an arm in a sling, shouting at a doctor. A stray cat wandering in behind him. He heard and saw everything from a distance, numb, in shock.

Then he felt a hand on his shoulder from behind. Lalloo spun around, despite the pain. Behind him stood Billo. How long had she been here? Had she overheard them?

'You look like you're troubled. Is there anything I can help you with?' She nodded. 'Let Sister Billo look after you.'

'I'm . . . I'm fine.' Lalloo picked up his crutches.

'I see the crutches are coming in handy.'

Lalloo hauled himself up out of the seat.

'They weren't free, you know. You owe me for those. I saw you and thought to myself, now there's a resourceful man – he'll find a way to pay me.'

Lalloo started limping away.

'Everything has a price,' she called out behind him.

He looked back over his shoulder. Billo stood with a fixed smile on her face, nodding knowingly, like a vulture circling, honing in on her next victim.

Back in the ward, Lalloo didn't sleep much that night. After the temporary relief of the rain, the heat and humidity had returned in full force. The ward was hot, the air unbearably close. He kept thinking back to the bhatti. His family crammed together in the tiny mud hut, with no relief from the clamminess or the mosquitos. Abu up all night, coughing and feverish. Lalloo had his phone back and he could call them now, but what would he say to them? He was all out of ideas; they were stuck there for the rest of their lives. He had failed them. And in Moti Mohalla, what was Fatima doing? Would she be thinking of him? What would he tell her now?

Chapter Twenty-Nine

Salman wasn't returning until the afternoon, so, to give himself something to do, Lalloo spent the morning staggering up and down the hospital corridors with his crutches, trying to ignore the hunger in his stomach and the pain in his chest and leg. The last thing he'd eaten was the samosas yesterday and he had no money to buy food. The rucksack had disappeared from the car. Whoever had taken it must've known it was there. Was that why he was shot at? A robbery gone wrong? But who would know he'd had that kind of money? Did Omer suspect? He had no answers, just gnawing pangs in the pit of his stomach.

He really wanted to talk to Fatima, to hear her voice. But he couldn't tell her he was here; she'd want to visit him. She couldn't see him like this. He felt like he needed to protect her from all these bad things that were happening in his life. Without the money, he couldn't provide for her. Her father and grandmother would never accept him. He had nothing to his name, he certainly couldn't give her the life they would want for her. He needed to get out of here, sort himself out before he spoke to her again, made her any more promises.

By the time Salman arrived with some daal roti, Lalloo was tired and ravenous. He was so hungry he didn't realise Salman was uncharacteristically quiet.

'What is it, yaar?' It was only when he finished the food that he noticed Salman had placed a holdall by his feet. 'What's in the bag?'

Salman was reluctant. 'I, uh . . . I had to clear your stuff from the shop.'

Salman was wheezing loudly again. Lalloo glanced into the holdall. Salman had taken the carrier bags from his room in the mohalla and emptied them into the holdall. Everything seemed to be there.

'Thanks, yaar, there's so much you've had to do for me . . .'

'It's fine. Don't worry about it.' Salman looked around them nervously. 'If you've finished eating, shall we go for a walk?'

Lalloo licked his fingers clean and, despite his weariness, grabbed hold of his crutches. Salman brought the holdall with him. They came out of the ward, into the hall, and this time kept walking until they found a long empty corridor. The concrete floor was barely clean, the tube lighting overhead harsh and unforgiving. It hadn't rained today and the air was heavy as the humidity built up, ready to burst.

'Well?'

'It's just . . . when I was clearing your stuff, I found the briefcase.' Salman paused and took his inhaler from his pocket, taking a puff. 'You know, the one the money was in.'

Lalloo had been meaning to get rid of it. So much had happened so quickly, he'd hidden the mutilated case in a drawer under the counter, thinking he'd dump it later.

'I threw it away, but it had some papers in it . . .'

Lalloo had only glanced at the papers in the bottom of the briefcase and they had seemed important, but he'd been distracted by other things at the time. But now, something about the way Salman was talking made Lalloo wary.

'And?'

His friend's gaze darted behind him and he started talking nonsense about the new Bond movie just released. An orderly was making his way down the corridor, rattling a trolley in front of him. Lalloo waited impatiently until the old man was out of sight.

'The thing is,' Salman said, 'they were ownership papers. With Omer's name on them.' Salman stopped again, looked at Lalloo and then looked down before continuing. 'Lots of land, factories . . . and bhattis.'

Lalloo felt hollow inside, his breath fast and shallow. 'Bhattis?'

He'd known Omer owned various land and businesses, but hadn't known he owned any bhattis.

'Yeah. It made me think – what bhatti do your parents live in?'

'Three-One-Six. In Chakianwallah.'

Salman bent down and retrieved a stack of papers from the hold-all, crouching on the floor as he leafed through them. 'He owns about five bhattis...'

He took so long that Lalloo's leg began to ache. After a minute, Salman slapped the paper he was holding with the back of his hand.

'This is definitely it. Bhatti Three-One-Six, Chakianwallah.' He looked up at Lalloo. 'Omer owns it, Lalloo.'

Lalloo's head spun. His hands holding the crutches suddenly ice-cold, he staggered against the wall.

'How can...? But...' If Omer owned the bhatti, he owned all the people who worked there, including Lalloo's parents. 'Show me.'

They pored over the document together. Salman had always been the better reader, but Lalloo could still make out bits. The paper said it in black and white. *Omer owned the bhatti in Chakianwallah.* He felt sick.

'Has it got a date on it, Salman? Did he just buy it?'

'No, this is dated twenty years ago.'

'Could the date be wrong?'

Salman shook his head. 'It's a legal document.' Then he voiced Lalloo's thoughts. 'Everything that happened with your brother would've happened while Omer owned it.'

Lalloo didn't know what to say. He asked Salman to read the document to him again from start to finish, memorising it.

By the time Salman finally put the papers back in the bag, Lalloo was shaking with a mixture of fatigue, pain and shock.

'I'll leave these with you. I've got to go, I've got to close the shop.' He walked Lalloo back to his bed and placed a hand on his shoulder, concern etched on his face. 'I think I've found a place for you to hide, but it's not ready yet. Are you going to be OK here?'

Lalloo nodded. With shaking limbs, and hands alternating

between ice-cold and sweating hot, he tried to make sense of it all. He'd thought he had escaped the bhatti, but all these years he'd been working for the same man who owned it.

On that night, when the men had stopped and the dogs had been called off, the fires receding, little Lalloo, standing on the outskirts of all this terror, had seen a man watching from inside his long black car. The boss had been the last to arrive and the first to leave. He'd nodded, rolled up his window and driven away. Omer had not wanted anybody causing disruption to his well-organised business. He couldn't have Jugnu leading a revolt among the bhatti workers. He'd had to make sure the problem had been nipped in the bud, so he'd given the orders and had been there to see them carried out.

*

Lalloo spent a long time lying on his bed, lost deep in his thoughts, trying to come to terms with what he'd just discovered about his old boss. That evening, he hobbled up and down the hospital corridors looking for Sister Billo. She was a resourceful woman, didn't always play by the rules and she'd offered to help him. And that was exactly the kind of assistance he needed. He had an idea that could get him out of here and simultaneously get him some money, but it was quite unusual, and he knew she responded to money. He just wasn't sure whether he could trust her. He found her hunched over a small TV in the waiting area, watching a new Bollywood movie.

'I was just coming to find you,' she said, abrupt as ever. 'Your plasters need to be changed tomorrow and then you can go home.'

He leant in. 'I've got a proposition for you, Billo.'

'A proposition? At my age? I'm flattered.'

'Don't be, it's strictly business.'

She looked at him closely to judge how serious he was. 'We'd better go in here if you're going to talk like that.'

She indicated a door in the corridor behind him that he hadn't ever noticed before, then removed a large bunch of keys from her waist like a prison warden. It led into a tiny room lined floor to ceiling with shelves full of bandages, sheets, boxes of syringes, gloves and all manner of pills, capsules and tablets. No wonder she kept this locked; it was a treasure trove. It was so small and so packed that once he had folded himself and his crutches inside and Billo's vast bulk had joined him, there was no room left. They were almost touching each other.

Lalloo cleared his throat. His palms were sweaty and he dropped one of his crutches. It was too painful to bend down to get it, so she had to do it for him, manoeuvring her way carefully around him.

'So, do you really have something to say or are you just getting cheap thrills being in here with me?' She gave a belly laugh.

'How would you like to celebrate your next birthday in true style?'

She eyed him speculatively. 'I'm listening.'

'You know you were telling me how you help yourself to pocket money from your supervisor's drawer?'

She folded her arms across her hefty bosom and cocked her head to one side, staring hard at him.

He tried again, licking his dry lips. 'You don't want to work in this hospital for ever. Have you thought about your retirement plans? I mean, I'm not saying you're old or anything, but . . .' He realised he was rambling.

Billo sighed. 'Come on, spit it out. Let's hear what you're trying to say.'

Lalloo took a deep breath. He didn't know if he could trust her, but at this point he didn't have a choice. 'OK, I know these things happen in hospitals. And you told me yourself, if someone pays enough, anything can be done.'

Billo kept staring at him, so he continued.

'It's a bit like the hero in *Dil Kehta Hai*, when he's in trouble and he comes up with the plan to help his family. I need to die. I need to get my parents out of the bhatti. And I need your help.'

He'd thought about this a long while. This was the only way to make sure his family would be safe.

She kept her arms crossed over her chest. 'You're calling yourself a Bollywood hero?' He opened his mouth to protest, but she continued. 'And why would I want to help you?'

'You'd be handsomely rewarded.'

She snorted. 'You haven't got two paisas to buy a pot to piss in.'

'Wait until you hear me out.' He told her what he was proposing and watched her face closely.

But the smirk on her face was gone. 'Paagal ho gai ho?' She was tapping the side of her forehead with her forefinger like he was mad.

It wasn't the reaction he'd been hoping for. The tiny storeroom was stifling. Sweat was dripping from every part of his body, his hands clammy, his breathing suffocated, but he had to try to convince her. He couldn't get away without her. This was the only chance his parents were ever going to have.

'You can have a quarter of the money. You would have enough to quit work altogether.' He paused. 'No more changing bedpans. Ever. Bollywood movies on repeat.'

He knew he sounded desperate, but he held his breath, could tell she was starting to consider it.

'You're asking me to risk my position at the hospital and make some very powerful enemies, just so your family can get away?'

'I'm sure you've arranged something like this before. And it'll make you a rich lady.'

She shook her head. 'I have a comfortable life here and, besides, I don't do deals with madmen.' She reached across and opened the door, shooing him out.

Lalloo returned to his bed, feeling both physically and mentally broken. He was running out of ideas and time, and the consequences would be dire.

*

That night, the aches and groans of his fellow patients were all around him, swollen in the humidity that sat over the room like a heavy blanket, refusing to let misery disperse. What he wouldn't give for a cool breeze on his face and a carefree trip on the back of Salman's motorbike to eat golgappay.

Still in pain and hungry again, Lalloo was exhausted but couldn't sleep. He'd had a missed call from Fatima, but he couldn't talk to her. He scrolled through all the messages he had ever exchanged with her, lying there playing and replaying them, hearing her voice, remembering her face, her hair, the way her nose wrinkled when she laughed, her lips when he kissed them.

And then an unmistakable retching sound, the acrid stench of undigested food and the shouts of his fellow patients, the calls for a nurse who wouldn't come. He made the mistake of looking around him and saw the sick man in the corner. The foul smell in that airless room was too much, making him want to retch himself. His crutches were by his elbow, within easy reach. Hauling himself up, Lalloo stumbled out of the room, holding his breath as he passed the frail, trembling man.

He shuffled through the dark corridors, now all too familiar, past the large, bare rooms overflowing with patients crying out. He must stay in the shadows. A couple of white-coated nurses walked past, a man pushing a gurney, but no one took any notice of him. The wards creaked and groaned as the hospital settled itself to sleep. As he hobbled past patients lying on bare mattresses in the corridor, a bony hand stuck out and caught his good leg, nearly toppling him.

The man was a skeleton covered in flesh, his eyes staring at Lalloo unseeing. 'Just some medicine, Doctor. I can't stand the pain any longer.'

'I . . .' Lalloo hesitated, scared. 'OK, OK, I'm sure the doctor will come soon.'

'Please?' The man's grip on Lalloo's leg was strong enough to hold death at bay. Lalloo bent over, gritting his teeth against the pain in his chest, his crutches in hand, and prised the man's fingers off his leg.

He hobbled away, steering clear of patient after patient packed in tightly together. Through the labyrinth of corridors, around the back of the hospital, there was an open courtyard where large metal bins of medical waste were stored. Lalloo had stumbled upon it that morning, but apart from the stray cats, no one seemed to use it. He made his way outside and slowly lowered himself down to the ground in between two large metal drums, his back against a brick wall. A stray cat, dislodged from its home, mewed at him furiously as it scrambled out of the way. The stink of the medical waste decaying in the heat was overwhelming, but it was better than being in that stifling ward. The afternoon's rain had cleared the sky and the clouds hadn't yet gathered for their next downpour. The sky was full of stars twinkling at him, like tiny blinking fireflies, teasing him with their infinite freedom.

'What the hell do you think you're playing at?'

The voice came as a shock and Lalloo flinched. He hit his head hard on the wall behind him, only just stopping himself from crying out in pain. He knew that voice only too well. But it wasn't shouting at *him*, it was coming from near the hospital door. He sat still despite the frantic scrambling of his heart, listening.

'You think you could get away with this? Do you have any idea who you're speaking to?'

Slowly, shifting forward to see past the bin, Lalloo dared a look in the direction of the voice. It was pitch-black, but the glow from the mobile illuminated Omer's face, contorted in fury as he spoke into it.

'You've really fucked this one up. He's the one who's robbed me – and my *daughter* ends up lying in a hospital bed unconscious. How the hell did that happen?'

Heart thumping, hands shaking, Lalloo leant back. So Omer knew he had robbed him. He tried to stay as still as possible, barely daring to breathe, but his leg was beginning to cramp. He desperately needed to stretch it out.

'You're damned right, you'd better. But not here. He leaves the hospital in a few days, then you can finish the job.'

The wooden screen door creaked as it was pulled open and Omer moved to go back inside, but before it slammed shut behind him, Lalloo's leg went into a spasm, knocking the crutch lying beside it, which banged into the metal bin. The clang was amplified in the small courtyard and in the silence of the darkness around them. Lalloo froze. Clinging to his leg, he held his breath. He heard footsteps as Omer walked back outside, and then silence. A bright glare flicked on. Omer had turned on the light from his phone. Lalloo was seconds away from being found – a cripple, crammed in between two metal dustbins. What would Omer do if he found Lalloo eavesdropping in the dark? His life meant nothing to this man.

There was a mew and a scampering as the stray cat Lalloo had shooed away earlier jumped onto the bin, a glorious racket. The light shone directly onto the animal, and it hissed and spat. The glare went out and Omer's footsteps retreated into the hospital. Vowing to feed strays for the rest of his life, Lalloo slumped against the wall, feeling like he could breathe again. But only until he recalled the conversation he'd just overheard. Omer had tried to have him killed and his men were coming to *finish the job*.

He dared not go back to his bed that night, spending it sitting up hiding behind the bins after overhearing Omer's conversation. At dawn, the first light crept into the sky and he awoke, cold and covered in dew, his body aching. Reaching down to grab his crutches, his hand touched a warm ball of fur cuddled up next to his leg. The stray had taken a liking to him after all, or maybe she just wanted her home back. She was the creamy hue of a freshly cooked burfi. He stroked her fur with fingers that were cold and stiff.

'You saved my life yesterday, little Burfi.'

She mewed at him.

He was limping back to the ward when Billo cornered him and corralled him back to the storeroom. She eyed him up and down, making him wait. 'The doctors have done some tests on Yasmin. They don't think she's going to walk again. Omer keeps asking which ward you're in and I can't stall him much longer. You need to sort something out . . . before he realises his daughter will live the rest of her life as a cripple.' She paused. 'So I've decided to help you die.'

Lalloo was stunned. 'What made you change your mind?'

'Don't worry, this isn't out of concern for your family, I'm thinking about my future. I've got to take opportunity where I find it, but if you want it done quickly, I want half the money.'

Before he could protest, she started counting out a list on her fingers of all the tasks she needed to arrange. She raised an eyebrow and rubbed her forefinger and thumb together slowly. He was entirely at her mercy and she knew it.

He nodded. 'How soon can you organise it?'

'We'll have to move tonight. I will tell Omer you need an operation on your leg because it hasn't set the way it should. What I won't tell him is that you won't make it off the operating table alive.'

'Will you be able to prepare everything on time?'

'Leave it with me. I already know the doctor who'll do it.'

She'd obviously thought this through.

He swallowed, his throat suddenly dry. 'Is he reliable?' Now that Billo was in and the plan was a reality, Lalloo was terrified.

'Oh, he'll play ball. He'll get his cut and he'll do as he's told.'

Lalloo grimaced. It was all very daunting, but it would be worth it to get his parents free. Another thought occurred to him. 'What if Omer demands to see the body afterwards? You know, proof that I'm dead.'

'It'll already have been dealt with. Standard hospital procedure for poor patients. We can't have dead bodies clogging up morgues when no one's going to claim them. You'll be one of those.'

They spent a long time huddled together in the storeroom, heads almost touching, planning every detail. She put a price on everything as if he were picking and choosing from a menu – cobbling together a life for his family.

'A car for the journey will be very expensive . . . Train tickets? Well, it depends on where they want to go . . .'

Chapter Thirty

Lalloo had just got back to the ward that morning, having planned everything with Billo, when Salman walked in. As soon as he saw him, Lalloo felt a heaviness in his heart that he'd never felt around his friend before. He couldn't tell Salman about the plan because his friend would just try to talk him out of it. But Lalloo knew it was his family's only option.

He hobbled slowly over to the bed and lowered himself down. He'd have to watch what he said.

Salman was gasping for breath once again.

'You OK?' Lalloo asked, concerned for his friend.

'Yeah, yeah, just the asthma flaring up slightly.'

Salman took a puff of his inhaler while Lalloo told him about the encounter with Omer in the night.

'How did Omer find out it was you?' Salman asked once he'd got his breath back.

'It must've been the car. I drove your car to the bhatti and I drove away in it when I took the briefcase. Somebody must've seen me. It's not exactly discreet.' He'd never got around to painting the Suzuki, with its bare metal body and patches of old blue paint peeping through. Lalloo massaged his aching leg. 'Then Heera tells him Ashraf's son has come into some money and they put two and two together.'

Salman's eyebrows wrestled each other in concentration.

'So he knows you stole his money and then you tried to buy the debt back with it.' Salman paused and gave a low whistle. 'No wonder he's mad at you.'

'Yeah, the only thing he didn't reckon with was my giving Yasmin a lift.'

'We've got to get you out of here. I've found—'

'No. I'm not hiding again.'

'But you heard him – the men he hired are going to come back and finish the job. As soon as you're out of the hospital—'

'I just need some time to think. Then I'll decide what to do.' He'd already decided, of course, but he couldn't let Salman in on the plan. Ever since they were children, Lalloo had always shared everything with Salman, but he couldn't drag his friend into this. The fewer people who knew about it, the better. He'd already put Salman in danger by driving his car around. He had to be very careful now. The look on Salman's face broke his heart. What his friend didn't know was that this was the last time they'd ever see each other again. Before Salman left, Lalloo hoisted himself out of bed and hugged him fiercely.

Lalloo went through the holdall his friend had brought him. He would have to move quickly. Taking out everything except a couple of changes of clothes and Jugnu's cricket ball, he limped out to the courtyard, carrying the things he didn't need any more, and threw them into one of the large bins.

Then he found an empty corridor and called Shabnam, his throat dry, his heart thumping.

'Tomorrow is your day off.'

'Yes?'

'When you go to the market in the morning, I want you to take everybody with you – Ami, Abu and Pinky.'

'Why? It's a long journey. Abu can't walk very much and Ami needs her rest.'

'You won't be going to the market. Get on the usual minibus, but get off a stop earlier. You know, the truck stop with the food stalls?'

'What's going on, Lalloo?'

'If anyone asks at the bhatti, say you're taking Abu to the dispensary for some medicine, or you're shopping for your dowry. Don't take any of your things; it'll just cause suspicion.'

'So where will we be going, then?'

He could hear the pure fear in her voice, and with good reason. If they were caught, their lives were at risk. He tried to keep his voice from trembling, to sound confident. She had to trust him.

'At the truck stop, behind the petrol pump, there's an abandoned goat shed. You can see it from the road. Sit inside, out of sight. Ami and Abu can rest there. Don't attract attention to yourselves and don't leave the place. I'll let you know what to do.'

'So the wedding . . .'

'This is more important, Shab.'

'You mean . . .'

'Yes.'

'NO.' He could hear her breathing fast and shallow, her voice panicked. 'Heera's men have been watching us ever since you spoke to him.'

'It's just a regular trip to the market. They won't know anything different.' His entire plan hinged on his family agreeing to it. Without that, it was pointless.

'No, it's too dangerous. I said no heroics.' Shabnam's voice became shriller. 'I won't have you be like Jugnu—'

'Jugnu only died because I stopped him leaving that night,' Lalloo said before he could stop himself.

'He put himself in danger. He shouldn't have been so reckless—'

'Don't speak about him like that!' Lalloo was almost shouting. He had tears in his eyes, his fist clenched.

There was silence on the line.

Then Shabnam spoke softly. 'I know how much you loved him. He was always your hero. But you don't have to be him.'

Lalloo swallowed the tears in his throat and gathered himself, taking deep gulps of air, glad no one was there to overhear him. It had been Jugnu's dream, and then it had been his, for as long as he could remember, to one day get his family far away from that infernal place. Jugnu had died trying. And for the first time in Lalloo's life, it might be possible now. Until it happened, he knew he couldn't think of anything else. Couldn't plan for anything, couldn't get on with his life. Every other thing in his life would be on hold until he could set his family free. Despite the risks, they had to give it a try.

He kept his voice as calm as possible. 'You've got to trust me on this, OK? I've got it all worked out. We won't get another chance and I don't know how long Abu can last in the bhatti the way he is.'

There was a long pause.

'How . . .?' She sounded close to tears.

'Don't tell the others until the very last minute. I don't want them panicking.'

'What if they won't come?'

'You can persuade them. You know you can.'

'And Heera? When he comes looking for us?'

'You won't be expected back until the day after. So you'll have a day's head start before you're missed.'

'And when they do catch up with us? You know they always come after people. They have guns and dogs and—'

'I need you to trust me, Shabnam. You'll be long gone before they even start looking.'

'What about you?'

He was silent for a while.

'Don't worry, I've got it all worked out.' He rested his head against the wall, wishing he believed his own words, wishing he wasn't putting them all in such grave danger.

Lalloo knew where the Liaquat ward was. Billo had told him when he'd first arrived at the hospital so he could avoid it. Now that he had arranged everything with Billo, he had to go see Yasmin – he felt he owed it to her. After what he'd overheard, he knew the car crash was Omer's fault, but, despite her father being behind this, she was an innocent. If he hadn't picked her up in his car, she wouldn't be here today. He'd been the intended victim and he felt slightly guilty that she was the one who'd ended up badly injured in hospital.

On the other side of the building, through long corridors and up a flight of stairs, he inched his way forward, having to pause frequently, frustrated at his pace. He had to be careful. The last thing he wanted to do was bump into Omer. The hallways here were cleaner and no patients lined the floor on mattresses. There weren't fifty people to a ward; the rich people each got a room to themselves. But it was still engulfed by the overwhelming half-metallic, half-disinfectant smell that permeated the entire hospital.

Lalloo approached the room that Billo had told him was Yasmin's and hesitated at the open door, listening for any sounds from within, but there were no voices, only the beeping of machines. He sneaked in and closed the door behind him. There was a small, frail figure on the bed, an oxygen mask concealing most of her heavily bruised face. Though she was covered with a sheet, every part of her body seemed to have tubes attached to it. There were half a dozen machines by her side, beeping at regular intervals. He could barely recognise her, but somewhere in among the wires, Yasmin lay asleep.

She was in a bad way. He should have expected this, but seeing her made it real. She was a broken kite – its wings shattered, its eyes hooded, its spirit tethered to the ground. It wouldn't even attempt to fly. He remembered her up on that billboard. What kind of future awaited her now?

He looked around the room, at the machines, the wires, the mask. He touched the hand resting on top of her sheets. Her fingers were warm and her eyelids flickered open, her eyes gradually focusing on his face.

He leant towards her. 'I just wanted to say, I'm so sorry for everything that happened.'

Her expression became animated and she grabbed at his hand, lifting her mask with the other.

'It's not your fault, Lalloo. He's after you.' Her voice was hesitant and raspy, and he could just about make out what she was saying. 'I'll do everything I can to stop him, but you need to get out of here.'

He stared at her, stunned.

'I should've helped you sooner, but I didn't know what he was really like. I've heard some things over the last day or two . . . But go. Get far away.'

So she'd finally woken up to the monster her father really was. But did she know about the car crash, about the lives extinguished at bhattis? There was no time to explain. She was pushing his hand away.

'Thank you, bibi.'

He squeezed her frail fingers and hobbled out of the room as fast as he could, looking over his shoulder as he went. She may not have been able to help him with the money, but if she could stop Omer from coming after him now that would be the biggest favour she could do him.

Back at his ward, Lalloo knew he had to face the task he'd been dreading the most and had put off till the last moment. Salman wasn't the only one who'd be left behind. When he died, he'd leave Fatima behind too and he didn't want her pining for him. He needed her to get on with her life. He couldn't avoid the phone call any longer.

She answered immediately. 'I've been trying to call you. Where've you been?'

'I . . . Things have been difficult.'

'What do you mean? What's wrong?' She picked up on the hesitation in his voice.

He took a long, deep breath to steady his quavering voice, then closed his eyes and spoke softly. 'Fatima, the reason I'm calling is because I can't do this any more.'

There was silence on the other end. 'What's this?'

The words caught in his throat, not wanting to be spoken. He swallowed. 'I'm caught up in a few things and I don't think this is going to work out. We don't have a future together and—'

'I've told you I don't care about money. What is it – are you in trouble?'

He loved that voice, he could listen to it all day long. It was the memory of sitting under the neem tree, swapping Jack 'n Jill toffees; feeding the newborn baby goat outside Bulla Chacha's house; jumping rooftops just to talk to her again.

This was a once-in-a-lifetime connection and he was throwing it away.

'It's not that.' He paused, unable to keep the sadness from his voice. 'I've been thinking a lot about us . . . and I don't think we can make this work.'

He couldn't tell her the truth. It was too risky. She had to believe the lie. He was no longer interested in her – he'd changed his mind.

'Hold on a minute, you can't promise me one minute and then go back on your word the next. I've told you I don't care that you're a driver and I'm a med student. I don't understand, you said—'

'I know what I said, but I have to go away. I'm not coming back and I can't take you with me. It's best we end this.' Would this be the last time he heard her voice? Her face, those startling eyes – they would possess him for ever. There was no other way. He'd debated this with himself over and over, but he had to do this for his family's sake, and for hers – if he let her go now, she could be with someone else. He fought to keep his voice under control. 'I don't think . . . We're just not meant to be. And you deserve better than this.'

She gasped and then . . . silence. And somehow that was worse than if she'd shouted and raged at him. He wanted her to say something, but, of course, there was nothing left to say. They both stayed on the line, not talking. He could hear her shaking breaths. Until, finally, gently, without saying anything else, he ended the call.

He lay on his bed, his fists clenched, his throat tight. Most people didn't get the chance to say goodbye before they died and at least he'd been able to do that. He'd spent countless moments going over every scenario in his head. Thinking through possibilities and consequences. He could no longer be with Fatima, but this gave his family the best he could provide for them. This was the only way. Now he just had to make sure it worked. He'd done the right thing; he was sure of it. He'd known it would be difficult, but the amount of pain in her voice had been unbearable. He closed his eyes, trying to shut out her beautiful voice and the sound of her tears falling as he'd put the phone down for the very last time.

Lalloo stayed awake, counting down the hours until midnight. His teeth were set in grim determination; he would carry out his plan no matter what. There was no other choice. He either ended his life this way or Omer's men were going to hunt him down and kill him. This way, he could make sure his family got to safety. The trouble was, he was putting all his trust in Billo and he wasn't sure he could rely on her. There was nothing stopping her from taking all the money and going back on her word. But there was no changing his mind now. Shabnam's worst fear might indeed come true – she might have to bury another brother. But it could also be the start of something new. A new life for his family, free from fear and bondage. Now that he'd made the decision, tomorrow couldn't come soon enough. He couldn't wait to die.

It was gone midnight when Lalloo hobbled down to the basement. The stairwell was almost pitch-black, every sound he made magnified, every second he slowed a danger to his plans. At the bottom, he limped along a corridor towards an obscure shadow at the end. A person-shaped shadow. He dared not call out. He shuffled closer and let out a huge breath when he saw Billo.

'Well, finally! For a minute, I thought you weren't going to show,' she said.

He shrugged at her, too nervous to speak.

She pushed open the door behind her and he was blinded by the sudden light. When he finished blinking, he made out a bed, some metal implements. Here, in the dead of night, deep in the bowels of the hospital, the usual paraphernalia of a sickbay. A doctor stood by, ready in a gown, cap and gloves. He saw Lalloo and nodded at him.

Lalloo felt frozen under the bright lights.

'Don't worry, he knows what he's doing.' Billo ushered him towards the bed, trying to reassure him.

He knew people had to make awful choices just to survive. His own parents had abandoned him in the hope he would have a better life. Jugnu had somehow been involved in Hasnat's death. And here he was having to make another impossible decision to get his parents to safety.

He didn't have a choice – this was the only hope his family had left. It had to work.

WHEN THE FIREFLIES DANCE

He'd barely lain down when Billo stepped up, mask in hand, looming over him. She put the mask to his mouth and after a couple of breaths, his eyelids began to feel heavy and everything fell into a groggy darkness.

Chapter Thirty-One

Lalloo opened his eyes and lay stunned in silence. The doctor, the lights, the hospital – it had all gone. There were no groans of shuffling patients, no clacking of Billo's heels on the floor. Complete stillness. The sour metallic smell of the hospital had also gone, replaced by something equally unpleasant, a rotting, musty odour.

Still groggy, he could make out a dingy room with a few rays of light leaking in through the shutter slats of a window. His body was drowning in agony. Not sure he'd be able to move, he inspected his abdomen with his fingers. It was covered in so many new bandages he was like a living corpse from a terrible horror movie. Sitting up slowly, he gritted his teeth. The room shifted with every movement. He swivelled bit by bit until his bare feet touched dirty concrete floor. By the bed, on the floor, was a box of pills and a parcel, sitting beside his bag and crutches. He reached for the box and that action alone set his entire body on fire. Slowing down, he rammed a couple of pills into his mouth, swallowing them without water. He wanted to sleep for a week, but that was a luxury he couldn't afford.

He looked through the parcel – papers, tickets, clothes and keys, all arranged by Billo, all part of the plan. She seemed to have kept her word so far. Naked apart from his bandages and a hospital gown, he was wet with sweat. The room looked derelict. There was a large metal hook on the ceiling directly above the bed, but no fan hung from it. The walls bore the remains of plaster long peeled away and the floor was potholed concrete. The shutter on the window was broken, half hanging off its hinges. He could smell mould and rot, and something else. As he hesitantly moved to stand up, something scuttled by at the edge of his vision and he turned his head in time to see the long fat tail of a well-fed rat.

He bent over to take his phone out of the bag, very slowly to minimise the pain, and went to check the time, but was distracted by a voice note from Salman. He hesitated, then listened anyway. It was clear something was wrong. Salman's breathing was ragged and his voice slow. His friend had to stop every few words and take a breath that sounded like it was being dragged over a serrated knife. Lalloo had heard Salman like this before, but never as bad. His battered lungs sounded like they were giving up on him.

'It's not too bad, just . . . my mother and Saif making a big fuss over nothing. I'm going into hospital . . . to have it checked out. So . . . I won't be able to make it in to see you. But if I'm . . . here for long, I'll . . . send Saif with some food for you.'

Lalloo immediately went to record a message in reply and then stopped. What was he thinking? The whole point of this was that the world believed he was dead and Salman had to believe that as well. He shouldn't even have listened to the message. It was the old Lalloo who'd had Salman as his childhood friend. The friend who was across the city from him right now, maybe even dying, but there was absolutely nothing Lalloo could do. That had been the pact he'd made by leaving his old life behind. He held the phone close to his chest, head bowed, and leant against the bed.

The old Lalloo was dead. The one who'd been threatened by his boss, who couldn't make ends meet, helpless in the face of cruelties towards his family. He'd put all that behind him. It was time to start afresh.

After a while, he lifted his head and looked at the time on his phone. He swore – it was hours later than he would have liked.

Then he saw the oblong bundle wrapped in a plastic bag on the floor, partially hidden by his bag. He opened it, tearing the parcel in his haste. He counted the cash and swore again. Then he counted it once more to double-check.

Billo had removed his kidney and given him only half the money he'd been promised. Either she'd not been able to get a good price for it, or he'd been conned.

Chapter Thirty-Two

Now he'd woken up, minus a kidney and the world thought him dead. It was time to find himself a home with his family.

Still groggy, and dizzy every time he moved, Lalloo pulled out a shalwar kameez from his bag and dressed slowly. He was frustrated at his pace, but dressing himself was painful and he had to keep stopping to rest. His bag carried nothing but the barest of essentials: his phone, a change of clothes, spare bandages and Jugnu's cricket ball. He placed the two packages from Billo into the bag and took up his crutches.

Lalloo was going back for the very last time and he was going to get his family out of the bhatti for good. Despite only having half of the money from Billo, he was still going to make this work. The urgent thing at the moment was to get his family and leave Lahore, before a search party could be sent for them.

He staggered to the door, eased it off the latch and peered outside. The door opened out onto an empty street and the burning sunlight made him blink. He leant against the open frame, and breathed in gulps of hot, humid air. He should've been angry – he only had half the money, his entire body was throbbing with pain and he still needed to rescue his parents. He wasn't out of trouble yet, but he was breathing. He was half surprised he'd even made it this far.

There was an old Honda Civic parked directly outside that looked like it'd seen better days. He limped up to it, fished out a black key and fitted it inside the lock. Billo had kept that part of the bargain at least. He lowered himself gently into the car seat, wincing in pain as his stomach bent in on itself, and started up the engine. His head still floundering, he gave Shabnam a call. Now that he was dead, he'd have to get rid of the phone too, but for now he needed it to contact his family.

'Lalloo, where are you?'

He could hear the naked terror in her voice and her horror fed his. 'I'm on my way.' His voice was hoarse, rusty from not talking in hours. He cleared his throat. 'Where are you?' Worried something had gone wrong in the short window they had to escape.

'We're waiting in this goat shed, like you said. At the truck stop. We've been here all morning; you haven't been answering your phone. Ami is sick with worry . . . you can't do this to her . . .'

Relief flooded through him more powerful than any painkillers. 'Stay where you are. I'm coming.'

The truck stop had a petrol station, some food stalls and a few shops. There were people around, but it was never very busy. Once when he'd been coming back from the market with Jugnu, they'd got off at that stop to buy samosas as a treat but had been caught out by the rain. They'd run and taken shelter in the goat shed. It had had a musty, abandoned smell even then. The brothers had sat on a couple of hay bales, eating their warm samosas, Jugnu with his arm around Lalloo's shoulders, until the downpour had stopped.

But Lalloo had been longer than expected while his family had been waiting, wondering when he would turn up, what had happened to delay him, or even if he would turn up before the men who would drag them back to the bhatti. He knew that terror in Shabnam's voice.

He drove up to the shed with caution, checking there wasn't anyone around to see them. He was about to stagger out of the car, when the door opened. They must have been watching the road through a crack in the wall. The burden on his shoulders lightened as his family filed out, one by one, and climbed into the car. Abu came first with Shabnam, one arm around her shoulder, leaning heavily on her. Pinky came next, in a hurry to get out of the dark room, pulling Ami along by the hand. Ami looked scared, vulnerable. This was a lot to ask of her, of all of them. Shabnam helped

Abu into the back before sitting in the front passenger seat and they drove off in silence.

'Beta, you shouldn't have done this. This is very dangerous.' Abu was breathing noisily. He peered over the driver's seat. 'What's this? What happened to your leg?'

Abu grabbed Lalloo's shoulder from behind, jolting his chest backwards. His clothes covered his other bandages, but the cast on his leg was visible. In all the commotion, Lalloo had forgotten they didn't even know he'd broken his leg. The pain was so intense, Lalloo bit his tongue to keep from crying out. He swallowed, barely able to speak.

'It's nothing, Abu. I'll tell you later. I need to concentrate on driving now.'

Abu sank back, pacified for now, or too scared of the answers to ask any more questions.

'Bhaya, where are we going?' Pinky was excited, jumping up and down in her seat, eager for the adventure.

'Far away from the bhatti. We're going to make a new home.' Lalloo tried to smile through his pain.

'They'll come after us!' Ami was loud. He hadn't heard her speak a few words louder than a whisper in years and her voice filled the car. Her eyes were wide, staring at something the others couldn't see. 'They'll come! They have torches and dogs and cricket bats.' She grabbed Pinky's arm, squeezing it tight, her voice rising into hysteria. 'They have—'

'Ami.' Shabnam reached over into the back seat to her mother and held Ami's hand, trying to get her attention, to bring her back. 'Ma, we're going far away. Nobody is going to find us. We'll be safe. Won't we, Lalloo?' She turned to Lalloo for support. Ami continued to gaze into the distance, while Pinky shrank back.

'Nobody needs to worry. I have a plan. We're going to disappear.' Lalloo injected as much confidence into his voice as he could muster, smiling at Pinky in the rear-view mirror.

He checked all around the car as he drove. They had joined a main road by now and the traffic was busy. A black Range Rover was directly behind them. It was nothing, just another car like so many others on a busy road. But he was sweating, his palms slippery on the steering wheel. The Range Rover pulled up alongside him and it was all he could do to not cry out in terror. But just as quickly, it overtook him and was gone. He wiped his shaking hands on his kameez, wondering if Shabnam had noticed anything.

'Did anyone see you leave?' he asked Shabnam quietly once he'd recovered.

She shook her head. 'No, we left early.'

'They'll come. You wait and see.' Ami was even louder, her eyes wide, sitting bolt upright in the seat. Pinky reached out and stroked her hair with slight fingers – the child mothering the mother.

Lalloo and Shabnam exchanged a glance.

'This is going to work, Shabnam. I promise,' he said under his breath.

She nodded and smiled briefly. 'I know it is.' Then she reached across and pressed his shoulder in reassurance.

Chapter Thirty-Three

Lalloo drove like a jinn was chasing him. Using every shortcut he could remember from his years of driving around the city, overtaking every vehicle, driving as fast as he could. Getting out of Lahore quickly was essential. Extra vigilant, he checked all his mirrors, peered around him as much as he could. Every vehicle passed, every junction crossed, even any bystanders turning to watch him drive by, his paranoid brain considered as threats.

His family were in the car, he had put them in this extremely dangerous position and he was responsible for what happened next. They'd placed their trust in him and he wasn't going to let them down. Any elation at getting this far in his plan had passed, with raw, primal fear creeping its way back into his body where it belonged. If they were caught now, it'd be certain death for all of them.

Driving was uncomfortable, even in the automatic Billo had got him, but considering the journey ahead of them, it was sheer luxury. As far as he was aware, they hadn't been seen as they'd left, but it was far too risky to drive all the way. Besides, he had to return the car as arranged – he still needed Billo as an ally.

His family were stunned into silence. They didn't ask any more questions, wouldn't tempt fate by getting excited at their newfound freedom. Pinky had picked up on the sombre mood and now sat quietly staring out of the window, never in her life having had the chance to travel this far from home. When they got near the railway station, he found the agreed street and parked the car. It was a quiet back alley with barely any traffic.

'We're here.' He kept his tone as light as possible. There was no point in panicking anyone. 'We're going to catch a train.'

'I've never been on a train before!' Pinky brightened up.

Shabnam scrutinised Lalloo as he gathered his crutches and hauled himself out of the car inch by inch. He was glad she couldn't see the full extent of his bandages, he didn't want to have to explain himself just yet.

Billo had arranged disguises for them and he quickly handed them out. There were burkas for Ami, Shabnam and Lalloo, thick black shrouds to make them invisible. Three women and a child travelling with an elderly gentleman would not be what Omer's men would be searching for. His crutches were a bit of a giveaway, but there was nothing he could do about them.

Lalloo tried to pull the burka on over his head, but the pain was too much. Shabnam helped him, gently lowering it over his body before anyone else noticed his compressed lips, his drained face. Pinky giggled when she saw Lalloo in a burka, a laugh so loud he momentarily forgot his pain.

She was a child caught in the middle of life-changing events she couldn't possibly fully understand, much like he had been. He was worried she might say an innocent word to a stranger that would give them away. Worried about the effect all of this would have on her if – once – they made it to safety. Hopefully she was young enough that these memories of the bhatti would eventually fade.

'Now, remember, Pinky, we're disguised. Call me baji, not bhaya. Shabnam, you're going to have to do most of the talking.' Since he was wearing a burka, under the veil he was Pinky's sister, not her brother, but his voice would give the game away.

It was hot and airless under the black shroud, and it smelt of mothballs. There was only a narrow slit for the eyes and Lalloo struggled to see where he was going, grappling with his crutches, ignoring the pain that threatened to rip his body apart. Their strange group half walked and half hobbled their way to the station, with Lalloo lagging behind them.

The painkillers had worn off already. His body felt like it

had been abandoned by the roadside, a wake of vultures pecking away at it, eating him from the inside – devouring his liver, nipping at his remaining kidney, gobbling down his entrails. He had to ignore the vultures, otherwise he'd never survive the journey.

There were lots of people around them now. Shabnam and Pinky were charging ahead, the station platform full. *What if they walked straight into the waiting arms of Omer's men?* He tried to hurry after them, but somebody knocked his crutch and he lurched forward, bit his lip to stop himself crying out and tasted the metallic sweetness of his blood. Stopping his sisters in the shade of the ticket office, he waited for Ami and Abu to catch up. There were too many people. He longed for the solitude and darkness of the derelict, rat-infested room he'd woken up in. His family were even more cowed by the sudden noise and bustle, used to their daily seclusion. They stood huddled together while he scanned the platform.

A few porters lingered, pretending to look busy. Most people were sitting on the floor with their baggage. A young man perched on a suitcase in a corner, a brown chicken tucked firmly under his arm, feeding it grains of corn from his outstretched palm. A family sat on a bamboo mat, eating stuffed, rolled-up parathas. His stomach flipped. He couldn't believe the vultures would leave any room for hunger in his body. The pain threatened to crawl into his eyes and blind him. He leant his head against the wall and spoke into Shabnam's ear, barely able to talk. She hurried away, weaving expertly between bodies, and came back with the information they needed. The next train to Karachi had been delayed, but was due any minute now. They could get on as soon as it arrived. But platform two was on the other side of the tracks, up, over and down long flights of steps. Lalloo refused to look up as he climbed, taking one hobbling step at a time, willing himself forward.

It was as he climbed down the last stair that Lalloo saw a young man wearing dark jeans and a black leather jacket, bizarre in this heat, leaning against the wall, smoking a cigarette. Lalloo looked on in horror as the man's gaze drifted lazily across everyone on the platform in turn. Could this be one of Omer's spies? Would Omer have a lookout at the station? His parents wouldn't be missed at the bhatti until tomorrow. And surely Omer wouldn't look for a dead man at Lahore station?

Lalloo pushed closer to his family as they stood in a quiet huddle under ineffectively swirling ceiling fans, not daring to talk to each other until finally the green-and-yellow train pulled up at the station. The wait was probably only a few minutes, but it felt like hours.

There was a massive surge forward. Was the man getting on too? Lalloo didn't want to be knocked again but couldn't risk being left behind – they didn't know how long the train would stop. The platform was so full of people, it was difficult to move. Shabnam helped Abu as they negotiated the porters, the fruit sellers and the beggars.

It was as busy inside the train as the platform had been outside. Most carriages were already taken, people spilling out of the windows. By the time they found a place where they could all sit together, Lalloo was shaking. Pinky sat down nearest the window, staring wide-eyed around her, Abu in between her and Shabnam. Opposite them, Ami and Lalloo had to squeeze in beside a large man with his sleeves rolled up to his elbows and his belly threatening to burst out of his shirt. He had his trousers hitched up with the help of braces and large sweat patches under his arms. It was a few minutes before Lalloo got his strength back and the shaking subsided. He asked Shabnam to take his pills out of his bag and swallowed a double dose quickly.

'Bhaya, bhaya, look! Can I have some?' Pinky pointed out the window at a vendor carrying a tray of sliced coconut.

Before Lalloo could say anything, Shabnam leant over and squeezed Pinky's arm. 'Not bhaya, remember? Baji.'

Lalloo took some change out and ushered the vendor over, hoping the people around them hadn't noticed. The big man sitting beside Lalloo didn't look up, too busy mopping his brow with a handkerchief and reciting something under his breath.

Lalloo checked the time, wishing the train would depart. He

peered out of the window, trying to catch sight of the man in the leather jacket, but he was nowhere to be seen. Pinky was happily munching her coconut. Ami and Shabnam, their faces hidden behind the burkas, were looking out of the window. He wanted to reach out and take Ami's hand to reassure her, but even the slightest movement caused him spiralling ripples of pain. He sat still in his seat and closed his eyes.

Suddenly, fear drove at him like a four-tonne decorated truck on a single-lane highway. Its headlights blazed at him, its horn boomed its jarring refrain and he couldn't jump out of its way. His family had left their home and belongings at his say-so with barely a moment's notice and had placed their trust in him completely. If they were caught, the consequences were too horrific to think about. But they hadn't questioned his actions at all. And this bloody train still wouldn't move. A deep booming horn sounded. Lalloo flinched.

Doors slammed, people shouted and finally, *finally*, the huge train started to roll forward. The horn was the signal for them to get going. The train slowly gathered momentum, but it wasn't until it pulled out of the station that Lalloo allowed himself, ever so slightly, to relax in his seat. Pinky licked her fingers; Abu leant back in the seat with his eyes closed. And Shabnam. Shabnam was looking at him.

When they came to a stop in Khanewal hours later, Pinky stood up, restless.

'Bha . . .' She stopped herself. 'Baji, can I get off the train?'

Lalloo and Shabnam exchanged a glance through their veils.

Shabnam got up and spoke to a woman sitting in the next compartment before returning. 'We stop here for ten minutes. I'll take her.' She nodded at Pinky. 'We'll go find the toilets.'

'Don't do anything to attract attention to yourselves. And don't take too long.' Lalloo kept his voice low, struggling to keep his anxiety in check.

The platform was lined with food stalls selling chaats, shami kebab, biryani, chai and cold drinks. Vendors were passing their window carrying thalis of food. He ushered one over and bought some samosas and bottles of Coke. When Pinky returned with Shabnam and saw the food, her grin said it all. They sat in silence, devouring the samosas.

While they ate, he scrutinised the platform for anyone familiar, just in case, and as a porter moved out of the way carrying a water cooler on his shoulder, he thought he recognised a face. Surely it was too soon for anyone to be looking for them? He craned his neck to look again, but the person was turned the other way. Then he heard footsteps running through the carriage, coming towards him. He looked towards the exit, cursing himself for not sitting closer to the door.

'Are you all right?' Shabnam had noticed.

The train boomed its horn to signal it was about to depart, and a couple with five children ran thundering past their seats. He nodded at Shabnam in relief. The horn blew again, the vendor collected the empty bottles and doors were slammed shut.

The country rushing past them sent happiness racing through his body. Green fields with straggly trees, electricity pylons towering above and the minarets of a mosque receding into the distance. The train was carrying them away. Away from the bhatti. Away from Omer and his men. Pinky stood up and wrestled the window open. Hot air and dust blasted into the compartment, billowing over the shroud that covered him. He inhaled through the burka – even through the musty covering, he could smell the first daring scents of freedom.

As night fell, they began to drop off, their heads lolling back on the seats or on each other's shoulders. Pinky lay her head in Abu's lap. But Lalloo couldn't sleep. His eyes were so tired they hurt, but he couldn't bring himself to close them. He watched them all now, terrified at how vulnerable they looked, and thought of Jugnu. What would his brother think?

He had one more task to do. He took his phone out of his pocket and turned it on. There were eleven missed calls from Salman's brother, Saif, but no clue as to whether Salman was OK. Lalloo kept telling himself there was nothing he could do for Salman, to put his friend's voice out of his mind, but a desperate sadness lodged deep in his chest. Was Salman, even now, lying in a hospital bed worrying about Lalloo? Would he be hassling his older brother to leave his side and bring Lalloo some food? Was he even alive? And what kind of a friend did that make Lalloo, absconding, without even a comforting word to the person who was the closest thing he had to a brother? Would Salman ever learn the truth or would he think Lalloo was dead? Would he ever forgive him if he did?

There was also a message from Fatima. Reluctantly, he played it. At first, she sounded angry.

'I thought what you did was so unfair. No explanation, nothing.'

There was a long pause and then her voice became softer.

'I want to hear from you again, Lalloo. Call me if you can.'

He had to take deep, slow breaths to calm himself down. He wanted to take her anger and hold it deep inside himself, carry it with him everywhere – it was what he deserved. He replayed the message again and again, committing every syllable, every inflection to heart. Finally, he scrolled through all the contact numbers on his phone, deleting them one by one, until there were only two left. Salman and Fatima. He wanted to play Salman's message again, to listen to his voice one last time, but he didn't think he could stand to hear him in so much pain. His thumb hovered over the names. Then he deleted them both. If only it were this easy to erase people at the touch of a button.

Before he could stop himself, he turned the phone off, took out the SIM card and hoisted himself up from his seat, using his crutch to brace himself against the trundling of the train. Moving slowly so as not to disturb his sleeping family, he shuffled towards the window and pulled it open as quietly as possible. The dank night air clamoured into the carriage. Out in the dark, the train was stealing him away from Lahore for ever. Away from golgappay and midnight motorbike rides, from laughter and secret late-night phone calls. He took a deep breath, threw the phone and the SIM card out into the night and shut the window as regret slammed into his chest. Returning to his seat, he held his head in his hands and finally let himself cry, huge hot tears that soaked the veil of his burka and wracked his entire body.

Chapter Thirty-Four

A shout startled Lalloo awake. Blinded, he lurched forward in his seat, scrabbling at his face, remembering just in time it was only the veil that had been knocked askew in the night. He rearranged it so he could see, heart thundering, and sat back gripping his midriff in agony. The cry had come from the man sitting next to him. The noise had woken everyone. The sky outside the carriage was clear and bright. He checked the time – it was very early.

'Are you all right, bhai?' Abu asked the man.

But the stranger was lost in his own world. He didn't answer, didn't even acknowledge the question. He muttered loudly to himself, staring into his lap.

Lalloo was dog-tired. Most of the night had been spent worrying, the rest of it trying to sleep sitting upright. By their faces, his family felt the same, though no one complained. They all knew what the alternative could have been. They all knew their future could yet turn out much worse. Ami and Shabnam stood up in an attempt to relieve their cramped limbs. Lalloo could feel a dampness spreading across his midriff. His bandages must be leaking. Luckily, everything was covered by the black burka. His whole body was drenched in pain. He didn't dare stand up in case he collapsed with dizziness. He took some pills and waited for the agony to subside. Outside, the country was rushing by. They still had half a day before they reached Karachi.

Three quarters of an hour later, they came to Hyderabad station. The morning sun cast a hazy pink glow over the world, softening the ugliness of the concrete buildings and pillars. It was a big terminal, but it was early and quiet. A cleaner was sweeping the floor with a jharoo, a stall owner was just opening up, displaying yellow and red packets of Lay's crisps and brightly coloured bottles of fizzy drinks. An armed policeman stood on the platform, beret on his head, rifle casually slung on his shoulder. Lalloo stiffened when he saw him, but the policeman was idly watching the train come in, hands in his pockets. A few passengers waited to board, some with children, most with luggage.

Today was the day the family would be missed at the bhatti. And Omer at the hospital would find out soon enough, if he didn't know already, that Lalloo hadn't survived his operation. Surely he would suspect foul play. The more he considered it, the more and more uneasy Lalloo became at the thought of getting off at Karachi, the plan he'd originally talked through with Billo. It was a major hub and if Omer suspected they had caught a train out of Lahore, it would be an obvious place to look. He could barely walk. If Omer and his men were waiting for them at the station, they'd be captured as easily as a bevy of quails driven towards their hunters. But getting off before the main station would mean a longer journey into the city, with him barely mobile. Which one was riskier? He wanted so badly to turn to Salman, to call his friend and seek his counsel, to talk through the pros and cons of his plan. But he couldn't. He was on his own.

He leant forward, waited until he had his family's attention, then spoke in a low voice. 'Before we get to Karachi, there is a little depot called Drigh Road. We'll get off there. I'll tell you when it's here.'

'I thought we were going into the city?' Shabnam asked.

'We will, but Drigh Road is smaller. It'll be safer.'

He hoped he was right.

Dark clouds had gathered and blotted out the sky as the train pulled up at Drigh Road, a sleepy little station. It was nearly deserted.

'It'll only stop for a few minutes; we'll have to be quick.'

Lalloo took a deep breath before struggling up from his seat, bracing himself against the waves of pain and nausea that threatened to overwhelm him.

Just before the train stopped, the large, sweaty man beside them grabbed Lalloo by the wrist. Lalloo pulled back, terrified, before the man spoke quietly. 'Be careful, bhai, there are eyes everywhere. If you need to go discreetly, take the alleyway behind the station.' Lalloo was too surprised to stop and say thank you. There was goodness everywhere.

They clambered off, their limbs tired and stiff. And as they did, the clouds broke and the rain hammered down. Lalloo stepped out and was drenched within seconds. The vultures inside him had woken up and they were hungry – pulling and tugging and pecking away at his innards. Ami, Pinky and Shabnam hurried on ahead, with Abu struggling behind them. It was difficult enough limping through the vulture attack, but now this stupid wet burka impeded his every move as the sheets of rain pummelled him. Every pore of his body was screaming. The painkillers didn't seem to be working. His head ached, his vision was blurred. He felt hot even in the pouring rain, sweating and feverish. All he could think of was the next step ahead of him. As long as he could make it to the safe house without falling down, he'd be fine. But for the first time he began to wonder whether he would make it.

Once outside the station and through the alley as the man had said, his family took scant shelter under a peepal tree and waited for him.

'Where are we going, bhaya?' Pinky asked pleadingly when he finally limped over.

'We'll catch a rickshaw. Come on, there'll be one around here.' There were barely any vehicles in sight. He set his jaw and hobbled as confidently as he could along the street in the downpour.

When they finally hailed one down and squeezed in, dripping wet, Lalloo passed the address to the driver. The route to the place Billo had arranged for them would now take longer than if they'd stuck to the original plan, but this had felt like a safer way to get off the train. What he hadn't expected was the torment of the journey itself. As the rickshaw rattled along, he felt every pothole, every bump in the road deep inside his bones. He gritted his teeth and gripped the metal handrail, once again thankful the burka hid his face from view. His kameez kept clinging to him, but it wasn't because of the rain. He felt weak all over, barely able to sit upright.

They stopped outside a shabby, deserted building. The plaster had peeled off in patches, exposing the brickwork underneath. One window was bricked up and the other had a wooden shutter fastened across it. His entire body was shaking as he unfolded himself from the rickshaw. Shabnam took money out of his bag to pay the rickshaw wallah, grabbed the key and unlocked the rusty padlock on the large wooden door to let them in.

'Lock it again on the inside,' he told her, trying not to collapse as soon as he walked in. Ami and Shabnam threw off their wet burkas, but Lalloo kept his on. He couldn't let them see the state of his clothes. The shack was completely empty, except for two bare charpais in each of the two rooms and a ceiling fan hanging from a large hook. It was basic, but it was clean and dry and certainly a big improvement on the rat-infested room he'd woken up in.

'Ami, Abu, Pinky – you get some rest.' He pointed to one of the rooms. 'Shabnam, come and give me a hand.' Or that was what he thought he said, mumbling something barely intelligible at them.

He tottered into the other room, with Shabnam behind him.

'Close the door and help me take this infernal thing off,' he said, struggling with the sodden burka.

When she finally peeled it off, she gasped. 'What have you done?'

He glanced down. His kameez was almost entirely dyed a deep crimson.

'The bandages need changing, that's all.' He tried a smile, but it was more of a grimace. 'There're spare ones in the bag. And my medicine.'

She stood frozen, staring at him horror-struck, and he realised it must remind her of Jugnu. Jugnu and his broken body after the men were done with him; Jugnu before they covered him in a sheet and buried him in the ground. The images of that night were seared into *his* brain; she must remember it too. How could she not?

She would not bury a brother. He had promised her that. But had he been speaking about Jugnu, or himself? His head was pounding and spinning. He had to get a grip on himself or he'd never be able to lead his family out of this situation he'd got them in, but at the moment he could barely manage a coherent thought. Maybe he wouldn't make it. Maybe it all ended here in this dilapidated shack. At least his family were out of the bhatti. He should tell Shabnam that there was money they could use if he didn't make it. He tried pointing to his bag and saying *money*, but the words weren't coming out right. He saw Shabnam look at him in alarm.

He was going to call out to her again, to reassure her, but the walls were no longer standing still. Nor was Shabnam, or was it Fatima? She had turned on the ceiling fan but the room had started spinning all on its own. *Turn it off*, he wanted to say. *Stop the room*. And maybe he did say it out loud, because he saw her flinch.

And then he was falling and falling, and it seemed to go on for ever, ending in a deep, sweet blackness.

Chapter Thirty-Five

Lalloo woke up with a start and clutched his abdomen. It was dark, but he could make out Shabnam sleeping in the charpai next to his. His bandages had been changed. They were clean and dry, and he was wearing the spare shalwar kameez from his bag. He wasn't sure what time it was, but it was a miracle he was still alive. All was quiet, save for the pounding in his head and his body. He didn't try to move, he didn't think he could.

Lalloo closed his eyes and saw Heera on his early-morning walk around the bhatti, breathing in the cool air before the humid heat of the day. He saw Heera approaching the hut, concerned that the Ashraf family weren't out moulding the bricks. Saw him enter and his face change from concern to anger.

There was a village Jugnu had mentioned once, a few miles out of Lahore, where the few people who had been lucky enough to have escaped from bhattis had set up home, banded together, in constant fear that the bhatti owners would come after them. In the search for their family, Heera might send his men there first.

But Lalloo could also picture, very clearly, Omer's face when he took the phone call from Heera with the news. The Ashraf family had disappeared. He saw Omer storming through the hospital corridors. Omer in the supervisor's office with Billo and the unlucky doctor who had operated on Lalloo, demanding to know what had happened to his ex-driver, demanding to see the body. Would Billo be able to withstand the pressure? Maybe. Would the unwitting doctor? Maybe not. And Billo had more than her share of the money. There was nothing stopping her from revealing Lalloo's whereabouts. Would she take money from *Omer*? He wouldn't put that past her.

Though he was grateful for a roof over his head tonight, Lalloo knew they would have to move quickly. Just in case.

What he wasn't sure of was how much more his body could take.

When he woke in the morning, Shabnam had opened the shutters on the barred window, letting in the crisp light, and was leaning over his charpai.

'I'm going to get us some food.'

'No. It's too dangerous. I'll go.' He moved to get up and winced.

'You'll be more noticeable in the bazaar.' She laid a gentle hand on his shoulder. 'If they're looking for you, they'll be looking for someone on crutches.'

She was right, of course. He sagged. 'Take some money.' He pointed to his bag.

She looked around at the bare, ugly walls. Dusty cobwebs hung in the corners and a lone chupkali clung to the ceiling, looking down at them both. 'Whose place is this anyway? Is it safe here?'

'For now. But we need to move when we can. As soon as I've rested a bit, I'll find us somewhere. I promise.'

She nodded and made to leave.

'Remember to keep your burka on and don't talk to anyone.'

Lying in bed, trying not to worry about how long she'd been gone, Lalloo could hear the low murmur of his parents' conversation drifting in from the room next door. The gecko on the ceiling had moved so it was directly above him. If it fell . . . What would Salman have done? He smiled – he certainly didn't have the energy for Salman's reaction. If Guddo were here, she would bring her long-handled jharoo and chase it away with minimal fuss. She'd done it enough times in Yasmin's room.

It was strange thinking he would never see those people again, never know how things would turn out for them. They'd been part of his life for so long. Had Guddo missed him? He would miss her and the long counselling chats they'd had together. Would Baba Jee keep his job until retirement? And Yasmin? She was a determined young lady. Even if she never walked again, he had a feeling she'd get what she wanted from her life. He remembered the look on her face as she told him she would try to protect him from her father. If she could do that, he'd always be grateful. Yasmin would be fine, and Asima too. As for Salman . . . Lalloo felt like an arm or a leg had been chopped off. He could still function, but life was different, would take time to adjust to. He didn't want to even think about Fatima at the moment. It was too overwhelming.

When the key turned in the lock, his body tensed instinctively, but it was his sister, wafting delicious smells into the house with her.

'Did you find any food? What did you bring?' Pinky rushed to her.

They must all be starving.

'Fresh tandoori roti and hot daal. Here, take this and start eating. I'll see to bhaya.'

She brought him his share of food and helped prop him up. He ate it straight out of the plastic bag, scalding hot so it burnt his tongue. It was the best thing he'd ever tasted.

When he was done, he wiped his mouth with the back of his hand. 'How's Abu feeling?'

'He's better for having rested last night. And he's in better shape than you.' She paused. 'How much did you get for your kidney?'

He hadn't needed to tell her. She'd taken one look at his wound and seen the cash in his bag.

'Enough to get us here and to settle in for the first few weeks. After that I'll find a job.'

She crouched in front of him, her voice fierce.

'You should never have done that, Lalloo. It was a stupid, reckless thing to do.' Tears threatened to spill from her eyes, and her tone softened. 'But it is incredible. It means we can finally leave. You've sacrificed so much for us.'

He couldn't bear to see her sadness. 'It was the only way.' He reached for her hand. 'You've got to make your own destiny. Jugnu used to say that.'

She smiled. 'He'd be so proud of you.' She squeezed his hand. 'I will work too, you know, to support us.' She stood up, grinning. 'And the good news is, I've found us a place to stay.'

He was stunned. 'What do you mean?'

'I overheard a woman speaking to her sister about her tenant moving out without notice, so I struck up a conversation with her at the vegetable stall.'

'Vegetable stall? I thought I said not to speak to anyone, Shab.'

'I was only pretending to buy the aaloo. I told her I have elderly parents and two sisters. So you'll have to wear your burka in case you're seen.'

Who knew Shabnam could be so enterprising? He wanted to be cross with her, but couldn't. It was exactly what they needed, a quick and temporary move, and it meant they didn't have to rely on Billo's silence. The relief must have shown on his face.

She grinned again. 'She said the rooms were ready right away, so we can go as soon as you feel strong enough.'

Lalloo looked out of the barred window at the traffic rushing by. It felt so strange, after all these years, being with his family again, being taken care of by Shabnam. The sky was a bright blue. Pinky was giggling in the room next door as she filled her belly with hot food.

Salman was going to be fine, he just knew it – this was just another asthma attack he'd recover from. And Fatima would become a top surgeon. She would marry, have children. The thought made him choke up, but it was all he could wish for, for them, that his friends would be happy and successful. And then, somehow, some day, he would figure out how he was going to spend the rest of his life without them. How he was going to fill this massive hole in his life that had been left by his friends' absence.

Chapter Thirty-Six

Three months later

After Lalloo had recovered and was sufficiently mobile, one of his first tasks was to get Abu to a doctor. He wouldn't go to the local clinic – the doctor there was more likely to be an unqualified fraud. Despite the risk, Lalloo waited until he was steadier on his feet to travel to the big hospital.

Abu was reluctant. 'I don't need a doctor. I'm much better already.'

But Lalloo insisted. The journey was a long one; they had to change two minibuses to get there and as soon as he walked into the building, that all-too-familiar hospital smell bombarded him again. He pushed down his anxiety before it overwhelmed him.

They waited on uncomfortable plastic chairs for a long time until they were finally ushered in to see someone, a small man with a shiny bald head and a harried expression.

'What do you do for a living?' the doctor asked, pressing a stethoscope to Abu's chest.

Abu stared in front of him as if he wanted to neither see nor hear the doctor.

'He used to work in a bhatti, making bricks,' Lalloo answered for his father.

The doctor frowned and immediately sent Lalloo and Abu to the X-ray department to take a picture of his lungs.

Lalloo knew the hospital would be expensive, but he was astounded when the clerk told him how much the X-ray alone would cost. What money he had wouldn't last very long if they spent it like this, but Abu's treatment was important. If he could just get him well again, it would have all been worth it. Up and down flights of stairs and through long narrow corridors, they finally made it back with a large brown envelope. The doctor held the black film up to the light and shook his head.

'I'm afraid the dust from the bricks has damaged the lungs.'

Would the fallout from working at the bhatti follow them around for the rest of their lives?

'Is that what's causing the cough?'

The doctor nodded. 'And the breathlessness.'

'What about the fever? He hasn't got it now, but it keeps coming back.'

'When the body has to work too hard, it can cause a fever too.'

Abu sat silently watching a row of ants weaving its way up the wall, every one greeting each other as it passed. He hadn't reacted to the doctor's diagnosis at all.

'How much will the medicine cost to fix this, Doctor Sahib? I want my father well again.'

The doctor was silent, holding up the X-ray film again and scanning it, as if looking for something. Lalloo began to think something was wrong. Then he finally put the image down, sighed and turned to look at them.

'I'm afraid there's no cure for this.'

'What do you mean?' Surely he'd misheard. He was willing to pay whatever it took. For the first time in his life, he had the money.

The doctor took off his glasses and rubbed them with a handkerchief. He looked tired as he put them back on his nose. 'How long has he worked at the bhatti?'

Lalloo paused. 'About fifteen years.'

'That's a long time for the dust to irritate the lungs.' The doctor shook his head and paused. 'I'm afraid it's caused irreversible damage.'

'Irreversible?' Lalloo looked from the doctor to Abu.

Abu was still staring in front of him, as if this conversation had nothing to do with him.

The doctor saw the look on Lalloo's face. 'I can give him medicine to relieve his symptoms. That way, things won't get any worse.

But retirement may be a good option for him. We don't want to aggravate his condition any further.'

Lalloo nodded dully. He'd never thought there'd be no cure. All those horrific years and now this.

As they left the hospital, Shabnam called. 'What did the doctor say?'

He wanted to shout. *No cure. Irreversible.* He wanted to throw his phone at the wall. He swallowed and put his arm around Abu's shoulder. 'He's given us some medicine. To make him more comfortable.'

At least he could pay for Abu's retirement.

Chapter Thirty-Seven

They lived in a small house next to a rubbish heap. Every day, municipal trucks piled their rubbish onto the dump and every morning swarms of women and children came, some of them not even wearing flip-flops on their feet, to sift through and collect plastic, paper, metal, anything that could be sold on and reused, like scavengers picking a carcass clean. Because of the dump, the house was cheap. At the moment, it was bearable, but Lalloo didn't want to think of them here during the summer heat, or the monsoon. Still, with two bedrooms, a kitchen, lounge and toilet, it was more space than any of them had been used to.

They had moved three times since that temporary house Billo had arranged for them, and this felt like a place they could finally put down roots. Since they'd come to live here, Ami had begun talking a little more each day, Pinky now had the time to play like a child should. He knew the scars inside would take a long time to heal, but it was a start. And Abu had started smiling. A little rest had given him his breath back. He spent his days sitting on a charpai outside the front of the house, soaking in the winter sun. Lalloo would often join him while his own body healed. Father and son taking turns to peel kinoo for each other, regaining a familiarity that had been severed for too long.

One day, as they sat in companiable silence side by side on the charpai, Lalloo heard a slight sound and turned to see tears running down Abu's face. His mind immediately jumped to worrying, Was Abu in pain? Was he not comfortable here? Would he like to live somewhere else? Did they need to move again?

He reached across and gently touched his father's arm. 'Abu?'

Abu reached up to wipe the tears from his cheeks and shook his head. 'I was just thinking about your brother. The sacrifice he gave to try to get us out of that place. And the sacrifice you've had to make. It's a guilt that eats me up every day.'

Lalloo remembered Fatima's words. 'It's not something you need to be ashamed of, Abu. We were all being exploited.' He thought for a moment, then plucked up the courage to ask something that had been worrying him for so long. He wasn't sure if he wanted to hear the truth, but finally knowing would be better than not knowing.

He took a deep breath. 'Abu, why did Heera say Jugnu killed that boy, Hasnat?'

He half expected a rebuke from Abu; his father had never wanted to speak about this before. Abu looked away, his face clouding over, the question clearly bringing back unwelcome memories. He was silent for so long, Lalloo almost regretted asking.

Then, finally, Abu cleared his throat. 'Jugnu came to me devastated the morning after it happened. He had befriended the boy and was practically mad with grief. The Ranas were determined to get out of the bhatti for their son's sake. They'd borrowed more money from Heera to take him to a pir, but it hadn't helped. They wanted to take him to a proper doctor. Jugnu said he tried to dissuade them, told them the stories of what happens when people try to escape, but they'd already heard the stories – they'd been there longer. They were desperate. They wanted to get him far away from that infernal place, get him medical attention before he died in that putrid hut, tethered to the wall, screaming into the dark.

'They thought if they went in the dead of night they might make it. Hasnat's father said he had a brother who'd agreed to take them in for a few days and lend them money until they found their feet. Jugnu just had to show them the way past the guards, then they were on their own.' Abu sighed and passed a hand over his eyes. 'So, in the end, Jugnu agreed to show them the way. He'd taken to wandering about at night. I knew about this and had warned him against it, but he always said it helped calm him after a day of brick-making, to gently stretch his body, and he never went far.

'So, that night . . .' Abu paused. 'Jugnu told me, that night he snuck out after we were asleep and crept the few doors down to Hasnat's hut. They were waiting for him, wide awake in the dark, not daring to light a lantern in case it attracted attention. Hasnat's mother had tied their belongings together in a ragged bundle that sat at her feet. His father kept rubbing the backs of his hands, as if he wanted to rid them of any of the clay from the brick-making. Hasnat sat cross-legged on the floor. He still had a collar around his neck, but they'd removed the heavy metal chain and replaced it with string because it was quieter. Apart from this, they had nothing. Jugnu said Hasnat turned to him and smiled. The poor kid didn't know what was going on.

'They left quietly. Hasnat's mother held his hand and, once they were away from the huts, talked softly to him. So softly that Jugnu couldn't hear what she said. His father held the bundle of their belongings and kept hold of the string that was attached to the collar around his neck.

'They had reached the outskirts of the village and Jugnu had said his goodbyes and had turned around to head back to the bhatti when he heard the sound they'd all been dreading. Luckily, he managed to slip into a copse of trees out of sight. They came in big pickup trucks with the men piled in at the back. They had guns and torches. He saw Heera first of all, standing up at the back, like a bad omen. But they were all there – Taari and Shaani and Jeeda.'

Abu paused again, his ever-present cough overtaking him. Lalloo felt his blood running cold. Around them, the doodh wallah was going door to door on his motorbike, milk canisters tied to the side of his bike, pouring milk into the container their neighbour brought to her front door. A child with a water cooler strapped to his back was walking down the street calling out, 'Aandey, garam aandey!' advertising hard-boiled eggs for sale. Abu's quiet monotone and the ordinary world around them was in stark contrast to the story he was telling. There was a muted dread in Lalloo's gut.

He knew a version of what came next, almost didn't want Abu to carry on.

'The Ranas didn't even try to run. Except for Hasnat. As the cars drove up behind them, engines revving, he broke free from his father holding the string attached to his collar and his mother clinging to his hand, and took flight. Jugnu wasn't sure whether he knew where he was running to or what he ran from, but he made a beeline for the canal, to the horrified shouts of his mother behind him.

'By this time, the men had disembarked and surrounded his parents, and a few of them gave chase to the boy. He didn't look back, didn't respond to any shouts, he waded straight in, the water coming up to his knees. It must have been icy cold, but he didn't hesitate, he kept pushing in further and further. The adults gathered at the water's edge and shouted at him, calling, but he showed no sign of stopping. It was up to his chest now, but he walked calmly on. He looked back just once. Turned to his mother and waved. Jugnu said . . .' Abu faltered, tears in his eyes. 'Jugnu said he looked happy. Then his head was under and there was no more sign of him. His mother was screaming, her voice carrying crystal clear on the night sky. Shouting over and over that he couldn't swim. His father tried to run in after the boy, but Heera hit him with the butt of his rifle and he bent over double to the ground.

'The men waited around for a bit, not daring to go in themselves. The water was dark and uninviting. Hasnat's parents couldn't take their eyes off it, hoping their son would reappear, his head bobbing up, smiling all the way to the other side of the canal. Everyone else knew he wasn't coming back. The men shrugged their shoulders and left, dragging his distraught parents away, forcing them into the pickup trucks at gunpoint.

'Jugnu knew he should get back to the bhatti before the men did, but he stayed rooted to the spot, and after the men had gone, he went in. He said it was so cold he felt like his heart would stop beating from utter shock, but he couldn't leave Hasnat there. He searched the area where he'd last been seen, went deep down to the bed of the canal, swam further upstream, and then back to where he'd first got in. He combed every inch of that water, but he couldn't find him. Finally, he gave up and walked back to the bhatti, shivering with cold.

'Jugnu kept saying over and over how he saw Hasnat's wide, toothy grin, how he could still hear his mother's screams in his head. Hasnat's parents would still have to work at the bhatti for the rest of their lives, and now their only son was gone. They would come back every day to an empty hut and Jugnu felt it was all his fault.'

Lalloo sat stunned. That night, Jugnu had walked back dripping wet to the silent and dark huts. He had crept into his home and found Lalloo wide awake to greet him. He saw his open trusting face, just a few years younger than Hasnat, and this time he had no answers, no tales to tell, just sopping wet clothes, an uncontrollable shaking and a screaming in his head that wouldn't go away.

'They moved Hasnat's parents to work at another bhatti, probably so they wouldn't be able to tell us what really happened. The men were keeping an eye on Jugnu because he'd been making a fuss about wanting to leave. When the boy drowned, your brother was just a convenient scapegoat. What happened wasn't his fault, I told him that.'

Jugnu had felt responsible for Hasnat's death, Lalloo knew that. *I lost him, Lalloo, I lost him.*

Lalloo shook his head. 'Bechara Hasnat, he must've been really mad to do something like that, walk into freezing-cold water without stopping.'

'Sometimes I think he was the only sane one of us all. He knew they had come to take him back to the bhatti, so he chose the water instead.'

Jugnu wasn't a murderer. Heera and Taari had been lying, blaming him for something that wasn't his fault. His brother had only ever helped people; he'd wanted to get them all out of the bhatti. Heera had used Hasnat's death as an excuse to beat him. Lalloo felt tears slide down his cheeks as the weight that had been sitting across his shoulders ever since he was a child turned into a balloon and started floating away.

'But, Abu, you know Jugnu tried to leave that night? And the only reason he didn't get to safety was because I stopped him.' That day, Lalloo couldn't imagine anything worse than Jugnu leaving them behind. Now, of course, he knew there were many worse things, horrors he couldn't even have dreamt up, nightmares that had started that very night. How he wished he could take that backpack and that money and push them into Jugnu's hands and say run, run fast, and don't ever look back. 'I was too selfish to let him go, but if I had—'

Abu interrupted him with a tender hand on his shoulder. 'Beta, you were a child. A child who adored his older brother. None of it was your fault. I've spent half my life blaming myself for doing this to all of you, but you mustn't think like that. That way, only madness lies.'

Lalloo sat still and closed his eyes, feeling the anchor of Abu's hand on his shoulder, his gentle touch.

'And now look, you've managed to give us a second chance. We get to enjoy this.' Abu indicated the charpai they sat on, the razai wrapped around them against the chill and the weak winter sun on their backs.

A cyclist trundled past with a cage full of sparrows wobbling on the back of his bike. The enclosure was tiny, crammed full of the little brown birds, some perched on the metal bars chirping loudly, others sitting on the floor of their prison. Lalloo flagged him down.

'How much?' he asked.

'Two hundred rupees for five, sahib.'

Lalloo took the money out of his pocket.

The man opened a small door in the cage, reaching into it as the chirruping reached a crescendo. When he withdrew his hand, it grasped a little brown sparrow. He looked towards Lalloo and Lalloo nodded. The man threw his arm up in the air releasing the bird and it took flight mid-air, soaring away. Then he did it again.

And again. The birds chirruped and rose, swirled and circled back, celebrating their freedom, the noise rising to a clamour as more and more sparrows joined them.

The next morning, the air nippy with the coming of winter, Lalloo lay in bed, selfishly enjoying not having to get up. His leg was healed, but it still ached in the cold and he snuggled under his quilt. His bed was in the lounge, next to the room the girls shared. He could hear Shabnam rushing to get ready for work, Pinky singing to herself as she dressed for school. The early-morning traffic had started up, and trucks and motorbikes were whizzing past the house. Just as he was being lulled back into sleep, he heard shouting, then a clattering of steel plates striking the ground.

He stumbled out of bed to find Pinky shaking, Ami and Shabnam crowding around her.

'Abu won't wake up!' Pinky was saying over and over again. She was dressed in her freshly pressed school uniform. Abu was the one who walked her to school every morning.

Lalloo rushed into Abu's room and parted the curtain to let in the light. As soon as the sun fell on his father's face, he knew. He slowly lowered himself to sit beside him on the bed. He didn't have to touch him or try to shake him awake. Abu was still. Gone in the night. Ami came and sat on the other side of him and lifted his cold fingers to her eyes.

So much sadness washed over him, Lalloo wasn't sure if he'd ever be able to stand up again. He hung his head, his chin touching his chest. All the pain and heartache, all the sacrifice, what was it for? He still hadn't been able to save his father.

After a while, he felt a heavy hand on his shoulder and looked up to see Shabnam's eyes bright with tears. The front of his kameez was wet. He hadn't realised he'd been crying.

'You did it, Lalloo, you gave him these last months in peace.'

He looked across at Abu. Apart from Pinky's sobs, all else was silent. It looked like he was resting. Still, and at peace.

AISHA HASSAN

They clung to each other, brother and sister, like they'd done at their brother's death many years ago, and cried big, hot, shameless tears.

Chapter Thirty-Eight

Lalloo would get used to Karachi eventually. It was a city of relentless concrete and noise. Everything was grey. Straggly bushes suffocated among the endless monolithic apartment blocks, while thick grey fumes hung above traffic crawling along grey roads. The only relief Lalloo could find was the sea. He would sit for hours watching the crashing waves, the persistent motion, the unforgiving tides.

It was so different from Lahore. Here, the trees were tall, wavy palms, the birds were greedy gulls, and even the air was different, salty and clinging. But Karachi was also a city of immigrants. Over the decades, it had absorbed, changed and been changed by hundreds of thousands of people. People who could take refuge in its hustle and bustle, who could revel in the anonymity that living with two hundred lakhs of people could provide. He would get used to it. He would learn to love the salty stench, the clammy air that plastered his face. At least here, the summers weren't scorching, the sea countering the heat. At least here, no bhatti chimney loomed over his shoulder.

Lalloo sat on a giant boulder, looking at the waves. The sky was overcast and grey. Before he had left, Billo had promised him a letter and he'd been taking the journey across town to that first address every week to check for it, desperate for news from back home. It had arrived that morning. He took it out of his pocket and reread it slowly.

I promised you news and I thought this was important for you to know.

Omer came charging in a day after the operation, barged up to my desk, shouting. A hastily convened meeting was held in the office with my supervisor, the doctor and myself. Through it all, he was shouting as if he wanted to wake the dead, which, of course, is exactly what he wanted. But despite all the ranting and raging, I didn't give him anything and I made sure the doctor didn't either. My supervisor didn't suspect a thing. It was just another rich man kicking up a fuss because he wasn't getting his own way. He asked to see the body, like you said. I was prepared, of course. I had found a druggie in the galli behind the hospital. It's not hard to do – everyone knows they shoot up there. He was definitely gone, but not yet cold, so he was despatched to the local mosque for a quick namaaz janaza and a burial in a pauper's grave. So that's where you lie, and Omer was told you'd already been buried. Forgive me for not attending the funeral!

A day later, I was there when the doctors told him that his daughter will live but she'll never walk again. She's paralysed from the waist down. And his reaction? Not what you'd expect. The selfish bastard gave up. Just like that, he went from a fighting tiger to a dead man walking. It was all in his face. After that, I saw him every day as that dead man. Chootia, couldn't even be bothered to get dressed! He ditched his pristine foreign suits and only wore crumpled shalwar kameezes, his hair uncombed, his face unshaven. He was indistinguishable from one of the hospital orderlies. He barely spoke. He went from charging around the hospital as if he owned the place to shuffling along beside his wife, propped against her, as if he was the one who couldn't walk.

It's terrible for the daughter, of course, but I think this is good news for you. If he stays like this, I don't think you have anything to worry about. He won't be chasing after you. I didn't see him on the phone once.

I made a point about becoming friendly with the wife. When she first came in, she was a terrified mouse who could barely speak up. Then she became the one who told him what to do and where to sit. They were stuck in that room with their daughter for days. Him silent, her chatting away. Once, I heard her trying to persuade him to sell up his business interests. To retire. She was talking of selling factories or something. Soon after, Yasmin was stable enough to be moved to a private hospital so that got them out of my hair.

Your friend came to see you though, Salman. And he brought a girl with him. You never told me you had a girlfriend! Pretty little thing. Beautiful eyes. I had to break the news of your death to them gently. I was very convincing, I swear I should win an acting award – I hear Bollywood calling. Akshay Kumar, here I come! Poor things, it came as such a shock. They were very upset. I almost shed a tear myself! Sounds like you'll be sorely missed.

Briefly, the sun peeped out from behind the clouds, sickly and weak, but enough to light up the water before him. The waves glinted like the artificial jewellery of a poor man's bride. Lalloo folded the letter and put it back in his pocket.

He hoped Fatima would forgive him for the hurt he'd caused her. All he'd wanted ever since they were children was for them to be married, and to spend the rest of their lives together. Small moments of shared pleasures, laughter and understanding. But it was not to be. She was strong and determined, and he knew she would get through this. She would get her medical degree, she would be successful. He hoped she would be happy with whatever path she chose in her life. He was the one who felt he'd been permanently hobbled, a physical loss, as if it were more than a kidney that'd been torn from him when he'd left Lahore.

He blinked back his tears. He would've loved to speak to both Fatima and Salman, but that was foolishness. Despite everything Billo said, he couldn't be sure Omer would stop looking for him. Let them think he was dead. Instead, he composed words to Salman in his head.

Dear Salman,

I know what I've done is unforgivable. You've given me a lifetime of laughter and friendship, and I've repaid you with duplicity and dishonesty. I hope you understand my reason for it, though – it's the only way I could get my family to safety.

I can't tell you how happy it makes me to hear that you made it through and you're alive. Hopefully the Lahori smog won't be too severe this winter. I know it always makes your asthma worse. I miss not knowing what will come next for you and not being there with you as it plays out – which scheme you'll hatch next, which woman will catch your eye. I'm sorry I couldn't help fulfil your dream of creating a car showroom. I hope you know your friendship saved my life. Without you, I don't think I'd have been able to survive in Sadar.

Maybe in a few years, when enough time has passed and it feels safe, one day I'll come looking for you. Maybe you'll be able to forgive me this deception. I'll find you, a successful businessman with a whole chain of shops, and we'll catch a movie like we used to and go for golgappay afterwards, and you can regale me with your adventures in the bazaar.

I hope you can find it in you to forgive me.

Yours for ever,
Lalloo

He whispered the last few words and let them fall into the sea, carried to him on the water. One day, if fate allowed, if enough time passed, he hoped he'd be able to tell him in person. He still owed Salman a car – he'd promised to rebuild one for him one day.

The sun had gone and the day had turned chilly. An ugly grey gull squawked overhead, quickly joined by the rest of its flock. They screeched and shrieked, circling high above him, unwilling to leave him in peace. The spray rose up and slapped his cheek, mingling with tears that streamed down, and the sea air clung to his fragile body. He breathed in great gulps of it, feeling it relieve the pain, slowly healing him from the inside out.

As he approached the house today, Pinky came running out, still dressed in her school uniform.

'Ami's been waiting. She's made the halwa.' She grabbed Lalloo's hand. 'Come on.'

He nodded and let her pull him forward. He didn't need the crutches any more, but whenever it was bitterly cold, he could feel the stiffness in his leg. His abdomen had been left with an ugly, vivid scar that ran halfway across his hip. Maybe the scar would fade with time, but his body would never be the same again. It would always bear witness to his past life, a reminder of what they'd gone through.

He entered the house and Ami put a steaming bowl of gajar halwa on the table. They were running low on their stash of money, but Lalloo made sure they had enough to afford the little luxuries like this.

'Shabnam not back yet?' he asked.

Ami looked out of the window and shook her head. 'She should be any minute now.'

Pinky sat down at the table, staring at the bowl, impatient.

The front door opened and Shabnam rushed in. 'Am I late? Sorry, I had to help close the shop.' She hurried to Ami, who greeted her with a smile and a gentle hand to brush the top of her head.

Shabnam took off her coat. That was another luxury. They all had weather-appropriate clothes now, though even buying them from the second-hand mundi was expensive.

They sat around the table in mismatched chairs and held up their hands in front of them as Lalloo offered a short prayer. Tears rolled down Ami's face. Lalloo went over and put an arm around her shoulder.

'We can't even grieve by his grave any more,' Ami whispered.

Lalloo thought back to this time last year. The hour-long trek to the cemetery, the rose petals, the darkness.

But it means you don't have to live where he was killed, either, Lalloo wanted to say. If he never saw that chimney again, it would be too soon.

Ami looked up into his face. 'Who will visit his grave now?' she said pleadingly.

He saw the grief in his mother's eyes and, in a strange way, Lalloo was glad. For the longest time, he'd only ever seen emptiness there. She'd spent hours today preparing Jugnu's favourite dish. Choosing the best carrots from the market, peeling and grating them with extra care, cooking them in desi ghee.

'This halwa smells delicious, Ma,' said Shabnam, trying to

distract her as they sat at the table and she served it to everyone in the good china bowls.

'Jugnu always said gajar halwa was his favourite, but I prefer badaam. What do you think, Shab?' Lalloo slung his arm around her shoulders.

'I think you're talking nonsense as usual.' She smiled, shrugging him off. 'Jugnu was right.'

The gajar halwa was warm and just the right amount of sweet. There should have been six around that table, eating that delicious halwa, but Lalloo looked around at his beautiful, worn mother and spirited sisters, swallowed his sadness and smiled.

Shabnam checked her watch. 'I'd better go. Lessons start in twenty minutes.'

She went to a night school, run by a charity that educated women. Lalloo followed her out to the front door as she shrugged on her coat again and grabbed her bag.

'Do you think you've taken on too much, college and work?'

She grinned. 'I love it! English is my best subject, but even Pinky picks it up faster than I can.'

'You'll get there. Who knows, you could be manager of my garage once I've set up.'

'Yeah, but I'll have to get to grips with the maths first.'

She had one foot out the door, ready to head off, when he leant towards her and lowered his voice. 'I had a letter from the nurse at the hospital who helped me escape.'

Shabnam stopped and looked at him warily. Lalloo stepped out of the house with her and gently pulled the door shut behind them.

'She thinks Omer is a broken man. That he won't be coming after us any more.'

She breathed out a huge sigh, but then her lovely brow puckered once more. 'What do you think?'

'Honestly? I don't know, Shab.'

She nodded towards the house. 'It's lovely to see Pinky doing so well.'

'Yes, and Ami.'

She put her hand on his arm. 'You've done well, Lalloo.'

He nodded. So far, so good. Nobody from his previous life knew they were here, not even Billo. The keys had been sent back to her, and, after the letter, there would be no further communication. As long as they could stay in hiding, they were safe.

Watching his thoughtful expression, she asked, 'When do you get your keys?'

She knew that would bring a smile to his face; he couldn't help himself. He'd proudly put down a deposit for a mechanic's workshop not far from the house. 'Soon, Shab, very soon.'

As Shabnam hurried away to college, Ami came to the door. 'We still have to get her married, beta.'

He looked at Shabnam's retreating figure. These days, she was formidable, hell-bent on getting the education she'd missed out on as a child. He didn't fancy being the one to tell her she would have to give it all up to cook rotis for her husband.

'No rush, Ma. She'll get married when she's ready.'

Ami was distracted. 'Pinky, that's enough!'

She hurried inside. Pinky, after a third helping of halwa, was running away with the whole bowl. Ami chased her around the table. He could hear laughter, and then Ami's clear, bright voice. 'All right, all right, you can have some more. For your brother's sake.' He had missed this mother. She wasn't the same, but he hoped time away from the bhatti would help heal.

He stood at the door, watching a barefooted child with a heavy backpack walk home from school. In the empty plot of land opposite their house, a tipper truck was dumping a load of bricks onto the ground. Jugnu's voice filled his head, *The whole city is built with these bricks and we made them. We built this city, Lalloo.* The boy who'd helped build the city had never got to live in it.

He closed his eyes and could almost pretend he was standing outside his room in Moti Mohalla, watching Fatima walk by with her grandmother, waiting for Salman so they could go for golgappay. Salman with his rattly chest and a heart so big, so full, he'd adopted Lalloo as soon as he'd seen him.

Dusk was beginning to fall and as he was about to go back into the house, he caught a flash from the corner of his eye. He stopped in his tracks and turned to face it. But there was nothing there. Then another, not in the same place but almost where he'd seen the first one. Just a blink of light – there and gone again. And then he saw them as if they'd been there all along, he just hadn't spotted them. Hundreds of fireflies in the bushes next to the house, blinking on and off, their light barely visible in the hazy dusk.

Pinky came running out, saw what he was looking at and squealed with delight. Ami came up behind them and leant in the door frame, smiling.

'What is it, bhaya?'

Lalloo gazed at them awhile, entranced, just like the first time he'd seen them.

'*Jugnu*, Pinky. They are *jugnu*.'

He knew his brother was watching over them, happy for them. Proud of him.

His sister had brought her cricket bat. 'Come on, bhaya, today's the day. You promised you'd teach me.' She grabbed his hand and started pulling him towards the field behind the house.

Lalloo let himself be dragged behind his beautiful sister who looked so much like Jugnu, it hurt. 'You're right, Pinks, I did. Come on, then.' He took Jugnu's cricket ball out of his pocket and went with her, looking over his shoulder at the jugnu dancing into the night.

Author Note

The outskirts of many major cities in Pakistan are dotted with brickyards, noticeable by their tall, red chimneys. Here, millions of people live their lives in virtual slavery, making bricks. Bonded to work until their 'peshgi' – loan – is repaid, entire families of men, women and children end up working for generations at the kilns, while their loans keep accruing phenomenal rates of interest. An estimated 4.5 million people, including one million children, work in slave-like conditions at around 20,000 brick kilns across the country.

Families indebted and working at the brickyards are often desperate, poor and illiterate, and have no idea how to calculate their loan amounts or how much of the loan is being paid off. They earn below the minimum weekly wage and are forced to borrow more for life's eventualities. Many children are born into bondage and remain so for the rest of their lives, with little opportunity to either gain an education or their freedom.

The practice of bonded labour has been illegal in Pakistan since 1992; regardless, millions of people live their lives in sheer misery under intolerable conditions and there is no economic incentive or political will to solve the problem.

Photo Credit: Aisha Hassan

Acknowledgements

This book has been many, many years in the making and I have had countless challenges and so much love and support along the way. There are many people to whom I give my heartfelt thanks, a few of whom I mention here. So, thank you:

To Hellie, you saw great things in this story right from the start and believed in it even when I faltered. This book wouldn't exist without you. Thank you for your dedication and incessant belief. To Ma'suma and the teams at both Jankow & Nesbit and WME Books, I've been lucky to have support from both.

To Charlotte, from that first breathless moment when you read this book to the endless tireless edits. Thank you for your commitment and passion. To Rachael Lancaster for the fabulous cover and Suzanne Clarke for copy edits. To Snigdha, Lucy, Elizabeth, Sarah and Harry for all the hard work in getting the book out there.

To the many writing pals I've had over the years who've provided support, encouragement and constructive feedback and helped transform the first few words of this story into the novel it is today.

To the many girlfriends who've been with me throughout. A more supportive bunch would be hard to find. My various covens of witches, who've cheered me along when the going is good, and picked me up off the floor when I needed it. Here's to much more dancing around fires (metaphorical or otherwise) and warm cackles of endless laughter.

To my children, yes it's here, I've finally finished it. No, I'm no longer working on the *same* book. Thank you for being the annoying, delightful, wonderful people you are.

And as ever to my parents and siblings, my eternal gratitude.

And now, on to the next one . . .

Credits

Aisha Hassan and Orion Fiction would like to thank everyone at Orion who worked on the publication of *When the Fireflies Dance* in the UK.

Editorial
Charlotte Mursell
Snigdha Koirala

Copyeditor
Suzanne Clarke

Proofreader
Jane Eastgate

Audio
Paul Stark
Louise Richardson

Contracts
Rachel Monte
Ellie Bowker

Design
Charlotte Abrams-Simpson

Editorial Management
Anshuman Yadav
Charlie Panayiotou
Jane Hughes
Bartley Shaw

Finance
Jasdip Nandra
Nick Gibson
Sue Baker

Production
Ruth Sharvell

Marketing
Lucy Cameron

Publicity
Elizabeth Allen
Harry Taylor

Sales
David Murphy
Esther Waters
Victoria Laws
Rachael Hum
Ellie Kyrke-Smith
Frances Doyle
Georgina Cutler

Rights
Rebecca Folland
Tara Hiatt
Ben Fowler
Alice Cottrell
Ruth Blakemore
Marie Henckel

Operations
Group Sales Operations team